Reviewers on *Nicholas, The Lords of Satyr*:

RAINE:
THE LORDS OF SATYR

ELIZABETH AMBER

APHRODISIA

KENSINGTON PUBLISHING CORP.

http://www.kensingtonbooks.com

PROLOGUE

Satyr Estate, Tuscany, Italy
September 1823

Some months ago, a parchment letter laced with a disturbing hint of ElseWorld magic arrived at the Satyr Estate in EarthWorld. Penned by King Feydon, it read . . .

> *Lords of Satyr, Sons of Bacchus,*
> *Be it known that I lie dying and naught may be done. As my time draws near, the weight of past indiscretions haunts me. I must tell of them.*
> *Nineteen summers ago, I fathered daughters upon three highborn Human females of EarthWorld. I sowed my childseed whilst these females slumbered, leaving each unaware of my nocturnal visit.*
> *My three grown daughters are now vulnerable and must be shielded from Forces that would harm them. 'Tis my dying wish you will find it your duty to husband them*

and bring them under your protection. You may search them out among the society of Rome, Venice, and Paris. Thus is my Will.

The imminent demise of King Feydon and the news that his three half-Human, half-Faerie daughters are in danger sends the three handsome Satyr lords in search of FaerieBlend brides. Forces that protect the gate between EarthWorld and Else-World are at a low ebb when one of the brothers is away from the estate, so they must go singly. Eldest brother Nick has already found and wed Jane, the first of the sisters.

Now it's second brother Raine's turn. But he's been wed before, disastrously so. Though he's willing to see his duty through by marrying again, he's reluctant to share his heart . . .

1

Venice, Italy
September 1823

Jordan shifted on the wooden chair upon which she'd been carefully posed, causing the drape over it to slip sideways and slither into a heap on the floor.

The artist's charcoal paused.

"Sia tranquillo!" he snapped. "Be still, can't you?"

"Simple enough for you to say," Jordan grumbled, retrieving the drape and attempting to pat it back into some semblance of its former placement. "I've been sitting in this position for so long I'm stiff as a sailor's cock."

The artist flexed his charcoal-smeared fingers. "Taci! Silenzio, you vulgar creature! No one's forcing you to come here and display yourself in such a manner."

His charcoal resumed its scratching upon the sheet of vellum perched on an easel before him.

"No. Of course not," Jordan murmured solemnly. "I do so thoroughly enjoy having my portrait sketched."

The artist shot her a probing glance that sought to permeate her disguise, as though it had suddenly occurred to him she might actually possess feelings. Then he waved a hand as though to flick any concern for her away.

"And well you should," he huffed. "I lower myself in doing this sort of work. Why, I've created portraits of the finest families in Venice! I've sketched the daughters of the Patricelli family. The sons of the Tuchero. Even descendants of the Medici!"

"Impressive."

The artist nodded, then sighed and set about his task again. "But I'll not be signing the revered name of Vito Mondroli to this day's work, I can assure you of that."

"One can hardly blame you," Jordan agreed. The trace of levity in her voice went unnoticed. An artist at work was rarely a good conversationalist. She yawned and peered wearily from the eyeholes of her gilded bauta mask. She was exhausted.

Last night she'd had the dream again. As always, it had come to her in three parts. Not as connected acts in a theatrical play, but as three isolated and unrelated incidents.

First had come the long-eared brown rabbit.

Second, the droplets of blood splashed upon her thigh.

Then third and last, the ribbons had appeared. There were seven of them, in all the colors of the rainbow. They'd reached to her from a storm, beckoning like wild, elongated fingers. They'd come close to tease and caress her cheeks with their slippery, satiny smoothness. If she could only grab what they offered, they promised to pull her from the storm toward safety. Toward happiness.

The same dream had persisted every night for the past week, leaving her hollow-eyed today. She'd soon know what it all meant. Ever since she'd turned thirteen, such dreams—always in three parts—had come to her nightly, foretelling hints of the future.

It was late afternoon now, and Jordan wanted nothing more

than to return home and seek her bed. But she had many hours yet to go here.

A dozen or so dramatic strokes of charcoal later, Vito Mondroli whipped the rectangle of vellum from his easel. With a twist of his fingers he flipped it toward her.

"There, what do you think?" He actually sounded like her opinion mattered.

Jordan angled her head, studying it. "I think my mama will most likely hang this one above the mantle in the grand salon facing the campo."

Mondroli looked scandalized.

"I'm joking," she assured him, rolling her shoulders and stretching her back. Really, the man had no sense of humor.

He pivoted his work back toward himself and scrutinized it. His eyes darted up to snag hers.

"You don't fool me," he said, scratching a finger along the bridge of his nose and leaving a trailing black smudge behind. "You may pretend you're not ashamed to be cursed with such a body, but under that mask I'll wager your cheeks are bright red."

He was right. Jordan *was* ashamed. But not of her body. Only of the fact that it was on display in this way.

At least Mondroli wouldn't have the satisfaction of seeing his barb had struck home, she consoled herself. He wouldn't dare attempt to see her expression below the mask.

Before Signore Salerno had left them alone in the theater together, he'd made it crystal clear to the artist that he wasn't to attempt to learn her identity or to take any liberties whatsoever with her person. Fear of losing a commission always kept the artists in line, were they tempted to touch.

Jordan rubbed her bottom and forced a jocular tone. "Only my rear cheeks are blushing I assure you, Signore Mondroli. But I imagine they're only numb from that last sitting."

This time the artist snorted in a manner that was almost a

giggle, appearing as surprised to hear himself emit such a sound as she was. In the throes of amusement, his face contorted into unbecoming angles and his horse teeth were grotesquely exposed. It was most unattractive, and she vowed to herself not to make another jest in his presence.

Jordan surveyed the sheets he'd placed helter-skelter against the walls, standing them on edge along the oak plank floor of the stage as he'd finished. Each portrait captured a different angle of her.

Yet not one of them showed her shiny raven hair, which was cropped just above her shoulders, or her stubborn pointed chin, or the intelligent dark eyes that gazed from her mask.

"They're good," she told him honestly, for they were. "Considerably better than the artist Salerno engaged last year."

Like the progeny of many other wealthy Venetian families, Jordan had sat for more than one portrait. In fact, every year of her life on the fifteenth of September, a series of sketches had been made of her.

However, unlike the portraits of other wealthy young Venetians, Jordan's would never be hung in her family home. Or in a museum. Nor would it be sold in the Venetian piazettas where artists hawked their wares.

Her mother would never view the drawings she'd insisted Jordan sit for today. She wouldn't even allow Jordan to speak of the events of this day. Though her mother might choose to ignore what happened here in this theater, Jordan didn't have that luxury.

If her mother had asked, she could have told her that each year Salerno commissioned an artist to create her likeness, so the smallest changes in her body would be recorded. In the forthcoming months, he would take these portraits of her on tour to other lecture halls in other cities. The success of his business interests all rested on his exclusive access to the notorious creature he exhibited to the public every September—herself.

For as long as she could remember, her mother had told her in no uncertain terms that her birthday belonged to Salerno. It had been promised to him on the very day Jordan had entered the world as a babe, in exchange for his ongoing silence on an indelicate family matter only she, her mother, and he were privy to. Were this secret to get out, it would destroy all three of their carefully constructed lives in an instant.

"Bah, the creator of those other sketches was an incompetent," said the artist, breaking into her thoughts. She turned to find him admiring his own work. "I apprenticed under a master before the French came. I enjoyed the patronage of the finest families in Venice and beyond."

"So you said," Jordan noted.

He clucked morosely and shook his head. "But Venice is poor these days. Patrician families are selling art, not commissioning it. I take such work as I can find. When Signore Salerno offered to hire me—"

His words drifted off as the sound of distant voices reached them. Both their heads swiveled toward the curtain, trying to hear beyond it to the seating area of the small theater.

The voices and accompanying footsteps grew louder.

Jordan's eyes dilated. "They're coming," she whispered.

"Fretta! Affrettarsi! Up on the table," Mondroli urged, fluttering both hands in distress. "I have one last sketch to complete."

Ignoring him for the moment, Jordan went to the velvet curtains that separated the small stage where she and the artist were hidden from the rest of the dimly lit theater. She stroked a finger down the central slit where the two drapes met when closed as they were now. One of her dark eyes peered out.

As she watched, Salerno strode into the theater, looking important and successful in his white surgeon's coat. It was an affectation. There would be no surgery today, only discussion. "A medical investigation" was the wording he had used on the notices he had distributed in order to advertise today's event to barber-surgeons, hospitals, and other such establishments. The leaflets were effective, drawing learned men of science and medicine to see her, like flies to a carcass.

His coattails fluttered as he strutted down the corridor dividing the theater seats. His hair had thinned since she'd seen him last year. The dark shank of it that remained was slicked back from his head like oily feathers.

A V-shaped flock of medical men followed in his wake as if they were a formation of geese that had begun migrating now that September had come.

Salerno's sharp gaze cut to the curtain as though sensing she watched. His small eyes were cold black pits, void of empathy.

Jordan's head snapped back like a turtle's and she twitched the drape shut.

"Per favore—on the table!" the artist urged.

Carefully, she folded the edges of the curtains one atop the other as though to seal Salerno out of her life. If only it were that easy.

With a sigh, she turned back to Mondroli. "How do you want me this time?"

"On your back! On the table, please!" He spread the square of satin he'd taken from the chair over the top of an elongated table. "Signore Salerno requested a series in all the same positions as in these other portraits of you. The only one I have not yet completed is . . . "

He thumbed through a stack of likenesses done of her last year, plucked one out, and set it upon another easel nearby. "This one."

The portrait was only a partial view, she saw. Good. That meant it wouldn't matter if she put her shirt back on. She looked around for it and then remembered Salerno had removed her clothing when he'd left her with Mondroli earlier that morning.

A cloak hanging on the peg in the corner caught her eye. Detouring on her way to the table, she snatched it up and draped it over her shoulders. It was rich and fine. No holes or other defects marred its velvet or its satin lining. It was Salerno's.

Jordan turned her back to the table and sat, pulling herself up on it. Swiveling lengthwise, she lay on her back and snuggled the cloak around her shoulders and breasts. They wouldn't be depicted in this particular sketch.

The legs of the artist's chair scraped as he moved closer. She bent her knees high and wide, exactly as she'd been posed in the portrait from last year. Mondroli positioned himself like a midwife, his sketchpad resting on the table just between her ankles.

"Si, that's it." He flicked a glance at the other portrait. "And spread your, um—"

"Labia majora and minora," Jordan supplied, reaching between her legs. Over the years, she'd learned all the medical terms for her body parts from Salerno and those he brought to examine her.

Mondroli was already sketching her outline. Once he filled it in, his final drawing would be a close-up of her genitalia. He'd cropped her body so the resulting shape of her belly, nether regions, and lifted thighs formed a sort of M on his page.

Forking two fingers, she unfurled the ruffles of her labia. They were plump and full. Unusually full. In fact, whenever she stood, they hung low on either side of her slit. Turning her head to the side, she glanced at the portrait from last year. It was an accurate, detailed depiction, and showed her labia had been far thinner and more feminine then. What had caused this strange thickening? It was worrisome.

Mondroli cleared his throat. Flicking two fingers up and down, he gestured toward her crotch. "Your, uh, thing. It's in the way."

With her hand, Jordan reached to adjust that part of her that had so complicated her life—the shaft of masculine flesh that had grown from her body where a clitoris would have been on any other woman. She lifted it to lie on her abdomen, pointing its tip toward her navel as it had been in the other portrait. Far too large an appendage for a woman, yet rather small for a man, the presence of this rod forever doomed her to hover in limbo somewhere between the sexes. Not quite a man; not quite a woman.

Yet at her birth, a choice in gender had been made for her. It had been decided by her mother and Salerno that this appendage would be deemed a phallus. And that she would live her life as a male. Of late she had begun to fear they had been more accurate in their choice than they knew.

Ever since her labia had first thickened some ten months ago, her phallus had begun troubling her. It sometimes awakened, thickened, pulsed, yearned in the pitch of night. When the dreams came to haunt her.

"Esteemed colleagues!" Beyond the curtains, Salerno's voice boomed throughout the theater.

Jordan and the artist flinched simultaneously. She snatched her hand away from arranging her privates as though she'd been caught doing something naughty.

"Today you will witness a true marvel," Salerno proclaimed. "One you'll surely deem worthy of your travels here for this medical debate. For behind this very curtain, I have obtained for the purposes of medical study, a"—he paused here for dramatic effect—"*person*—of a nature you've likely not seen before, nor ever will again. Some may call such creatures monstrosities . . ."

He droned on, but Jordan tuned him out. She'd heard it all before. "If only he could locate conjoined twins and a goatboy as well, I do believe he'd have the makings of his own carnival exhibition," she muttered.

The artist ignored her, intent on finishing his work. His fingers moved furiously, his strokes more hurried now that he knew his time at his task was drawing to an end.

Jordan watched him work between her legs, wishing he would slow his pace. She dreaded the examination that would certainly follow this portrait session. However, at the same time, she longed for an explanation for the changes that had taken place in her body over the past year. And Salerno and his medical cohorts could undoubtedly supply one.

Salerno's voice rose, catching her attention and signaling the imminent unveiling.

She let the cloak drop away, revealing her nakedness. Pushing up on her elbows, she awaited what was to come.

"Gentlemen! I bid you behold—"

The curtain swayed as her tormentor tugged on its tasseled pull cord. The heavy velvet parted and swept back with a flourish. And Salerno's gloating voice introduced her as . . .

"—the hermaphrodite!"

2

Achoo! Achoo! Achoo!

Lord Raine Satyr—the secondborn of the three wealthy and sought-after Satyr lords—sneezed in triplicate. Pigeons scattered as he stalked across the expansive Piazza San Marco toward the streets that would lead him to the theater where the lecture he planned to attend was to take place.

Behind him, a pair of bronze figures clanged their hammers on the great bell in the clock at the top of the Campanile.

Five o'clock. It couldn't be. He pulled out his watch. It was.

By the seven devils, he was late! The afternoon lecture regarding the grapevine-destroying pest known as phylloxera would be well underway by the time he arrived. He disliked not being punctual. He disliked this cold. And he thoroughly disliked Venice at the moment.

Unsure as to how long his business might keep him here and not wishing to spend any more time in the city than necessary, he had taken rooms just southeast of Venice on the island of Lido. The palazzo hotel he'd chosen had once housed a wealthy family, but times were hard and they'd been forced to vacate when they could no longer pay their hefty tax bill. One of the Austrian interlopers, who'd come in the wake of the departing French, had bought the place and now rented its rooms to visitors who could afford such luxurious housing.

He'd left Lido an hour or so earlier and crossed the lagoon toward Venice in a private gondola. However traffic in the Grand Canal, the main artery of transportation through the city, had been congested because of some sort of accident farther ahead. So he'd chosen to disembark at San Marco and was now making his way on foot to his destination along the Riva del Vin on the far side of the Rialto Bridge. After the completion of his business, the gondola would await him at a prearranged location on the southeast bank of the canal near the terminus of the bridge.

Though he determinedly kept his eyes from straying as he walked, familiar sounds assailed him. Like vipers waiting to strike, memories lurked everywhere in this city. Crowding him. Reminding him of what he'd prefer to forget.

He'd been born in Venice and raised here in the bosom of a well-off shipping family. Heir to the Altore fortune, he'd been schooled and expected to one day succeed his father at the helm of Altore Shipping.

However, at the tender age of thirteen, his life had taken a dramatic turn in a single afternoon. On that day his mother had admitted a long-held secret. That in fact he was not the son of the man he'd called father for thirteen years. Rather, he was the bastard son of the infamous Lord Marcus Satyr, whose randy exploits had been a source of titillating gossip throughout Italy while he'd lived.

Within hours, Raine had been banished to live out the rest of his years on the Satyr Estate in Tuscany. There he'd been raised under the guidance of his true father and had learned what it meant to be of Satyr blood.

In typical forthright fashion, Lord Satyr had bluntly informed him soon after his arrival that he was not entirely Human, but rather was a half-breed with the blood of both EarthWorld and ElseWorld coursing through his veins. He'd discovered that he had two half-brothers—Nicholas being older than he and Lyon being younger. The three of them were heirs to a dynasty that was far more affluent and far more indispensable to the survival of both worlds than he could have ever previously imagined.

He hadn't set eyes on Venice, or on any member of the Altore family, since that horrible day fourteen years ago. His steps quickened to outpace memories he'd rather not retrace, and he started down another alley that was barely wide enough for two men to pass.

Achoo! Damn this disorganized, verminous city. Since Napoleon had been driven out, it had fallen into a calamitous state of disrepair and poverty through no fault of its current Austrian leadership. The poor were everywhere, sneezing and coughing. Yesterday he'd caught some of what they were spreading when he'd purchased a small gift for his sister-in-law Jane from a young ragazzo in the piazza. Within the pocket of his coat, he fingered the tangle of ribbons he'd bought from the ragtag boy who'd been peddling them dockside outside his hotel.

King Feydon's deathbed plea had brought him here. He hadn't wanted to come and begrudged this duty that had been foisted upon him to locate and wed one of the dying king's FaerieBlend daughters. The harvest was underway on the Satyr Estate in Tuscany and there was much to do. But according to Feydon—who was not to be trusted—his three FairieBlend daughters were each in some sort of danger and time was of the essence. His older brother, Nick, had found the first of the daughters, Jane, on the outskirts of Rome in mere weeks. The threat to her had indeed proven to be real, but she was now safe on the estate and happily wed to his brother.

That left Raine with the task of locating the second of Feydon's daughters. Twice he'd gone to Paris on wild goose chases. He'd wound up concluding he might not have been meant to find the daughter in Paris after all. That left the one here in Venice. It was just like Feydon to play such a cruel prank as to send him to this city, which held so many painful associations.

He turned a corner and his jacket flapped in the breeze that came off the canal. At last! He started across the Rialto Bridge, passing the shops that lined it without pause. Ahead on the far side, a barge was unloading its cargo of wine along the Riva del Vin.

The smells of sea and of silk, wood, candle wax, perfume, and bread from the shops were indiscernible to him. Without the use of his olfactory senses, he felt strangely cut off from the world around him.

"Are you here for the lecture, too, signore?" a nasal voice inquired from behind him.

Twelve hells! Raine whipped around to confront the man who'd spoken. Having someone sneak up on him was extremely disconcerting. Normally, his impressive beak of a nose scented the approach of everything and everyone within sight and beyond. Double damn this cold.

"You do not remember me?" the man who'd accosted him asked.

Now that he examined his assailant, Raine realized he was familiar—a clerical man of some sort if his robes were any indication. He wore the bishop's violet-colored zucchetto—the skullcap. And the alb—a robe tied at the waist of his potato-shaped body with a corded cincture. Though built as oafishly as the roughest dockworker, he had a simpering girlish quality that sat strangely on shoulders so broad.

The man introduced himself as a bishop, pressing all ten of his well-manicured fingertips to his chest to emphasize his importance as he did so. A pair of close-set brown eyes peered from his doughy, unhealthy complexion, but they failed to smile along with his mouth, lending his face an expression of falseness.

"I'm stationed at the Church of Santa Maria Del Gorla," he announced loftily, "not fifty miles from your estate. We met at last autumn's festa della vendemmia—the festival of the grape harvest."

Raine sneezed. Considering that an adequate reply, he then turned and continued on his way. The man two-stepped alongside him, his words and feet attempting to keep pace.

"As you may know, I attend the vines at the church. I expect to bring my vintage to the harvest festival as always next month. You'll remember my efforts from previous years perhaps? But of course mine is a modest attempt, ever to be humbled by the lofty wines produced by you and your brothers at Satyr Vineyards. Ah! Such ambrosia!"

Raine never knew how to respond to social blather, so he simply didn't respond at all. He normally left such niceties as social discourse to Nick and Lyon. Without his brothers to run interference, he was at the mercy of this man and anyone who wished to pass idle conversation with him.

Fortunately, or perhaps unfortunately, the bishop seemed able to carry on a conversation for the two of them. "I assume you are here for the lecture? Naturally. Why else? I'll accompany you, for I, too, am here for the exact same purpose. Not that the phylloxera had assaulted my vines. No, no, nothing of the sort. I assure you my grapes grow healthy and plump and bursting with readiness for the harvest."

He drew the quickest of breaths, then continued on. "Imagine the coincidence of two men from the same region of Tuscany arriving for the same lecture in Venice on the same afternoon. We might have shared a conveyance and conversation on the journey northward had I known. Perhaps on the return?"

Raine shuddered at the very thought of traveling with this man's constant chatter. Plus the bishop had an annoying way of eyeing him up and down as though he were famished and Raine were a delectable crostoli cake.

Quickening his stride, he left the bridge behind him, forcing his companion to hike his robes and break into a trot. Impervious to any subtle rebuffs, the bishop buzzed along at his side like some sort of annoying insect.

To his great relief, Raine saw the carved front doors of the lecture hall a short distance ahead.

"The lecture?" he inquired of the first attendant he came upon inside the building.

"Si, signore. You'll find it upstairs in the theater on the right," the elderly man told him, pointing upward. "Or is it the left? We have several lectures in session here today. I'll summon an escort."

"No need. I'll find it," said Raine.

"Si! Si! Signore Satyr and I will find our way," the bishop assured the man, nudging him aside.

Raine's long stride took the upward-curving stairs two at a time. The bishop followed in a mincing prance. "You'll be returning to Tuscany soon I trust? To prepare your submission for the vendemmia festival?"

"I sincerely hope so," Raine replied truthfully. His home at Castello di Greystone on the Satyr Estate was precisely where he should be now, assisting with the harvest of the family grapevines and attending to the racking and blending of fermented grapes already harvested and crushed in prior years. His work was his life, and he felt out of sorts when not attending to it.

But it was a lucky stroke that he'd happened to come to Venice in search of Feydon's daughter just in time for this lecture. The phylloxera was of great concern to him and his brothers. Every possible cure for it must be studied and exhausted. In the end he feared that its origins might prove to be not of this world.

Deep in the heart of the Satyr Estate stood a secret that had long been guarded by his family—an aperture that was the only joining point between EarthWorld and another world unknown to Humans. Called ElseWorld, it was home to creatures spawned by gods of a bygone era. Shrouded in mist and foliage, the portal's rocky entrance lay hidden just through an outer gateway formed by three gnarled trees—the oak, ash, and hawthorn of Faerie lore.

If the phylloxera's origins were unEarthly, it meant the more malignant creatures of ElseWorld had already somehow infiltrated this world. If he didn't discover the means by which they'd done so, the pox was certain to eventually reach Satyr lands. The consequences of that could prove devastating.

For it was written that if the vines of the Satyr were ever felled, the gate would fall as well. And if that happened, ElseWorld creatures would spill into EarthWorld, wreaking havoc.

By the time Raine reached the landing, the huffing, puffing bishop lagged half a staircase behind him. Raine tried the first door he came to and stepped inside with the bishop hard on his heels. Both came to an abrupt halt at the sight that met their eyes.

Across the dimly lit theater, a man outfitted in white surgeon's garb stood before a velvet stage curtain. An air of expectation permeated the well-packed audience that appeared to be largely male. With the man's brisk tug on a cord, the curtains swung open to reveal two figures on the stage beyond him. He waved an arm in their general direction, announcing in a grandiose voice:

"Gentleman! I bid you behold—the hermaphrodite!"

3

When the curtains opened, all eyes fell on Jordan. She faced the audience for this initial inspection, assuming the semireclining pose Salerno had taught her years ago. Both arms were braced straight behind her, with elbows locked and her hands flat on the table, fingers outward. Her back was arched so the surrounding light caught her chest. Her knees were high and widespread. Salerno wanted the features of her body that were so at odds—breasts and phallus—to be prominently on display.

As always, there were gasps and murmurs.

"Aberration. Monstrosity. La Maschera," they whispered.

La Maschera—The Mask. It was what Salerno had dubbed her in view of the bauta she wore as a disguise. He felt it lent an air of mystery and intrigue to the novelty of her, his prized exhibit.

Those in the back rows stood for a better look. Goosenecks craned. Avid eyes were eager for a glimpse of her—the human freak show Salerno had promised them all today.

Typically, most of the attendees were medical men, here only in the interest of scientific study. But there were also those who came hoping to be titillated or to gather an amusing anecdote with which to amuse other acquaintances in the days to come.

Inspired by her strangeness, some gawkers in the farthest rows would eventually turn silent and slump in their seats. Their hands, hidden under hats or coats on their laps, would begin busily working at their cocks.

In fact, the show today was exactly the sort of event that would appeal to some of her wilder male friends here in Venice. She dreaded that one day she might gaze into the audience at one of these annual spectacles and find Paulo or Gani in attendance.

Her greatest admirers had come early enough to garner prime seating in the front row as always. They were the ones Jordan privately dubbed the Worshippers, though they referred to their group as LAMAS, an acronym for the La Maschera Admiration Society. Comprised of a half-dozen men and women, they'd come every September for the past five years. They saw her as some sort of mythical goddess and occasionally wrote odes in her honor, which a disinterested Salerno passed on to her. They were an odd but harmless bunch.

After the initial wave of speculation and consternation waned, Salerno extended a hand in Jordan's general direction. "Learned colleagues and interested spectators—I offer for your enlightenment a living specimen of ambiguous sex! One willing to be examined for the purposes of advancing science."

Jordan lifted a hand and wiggled the tips of her fingers at the audience. A nervous rustling wafted across them. In general, medical men were more accustomed to attending lectures involving the study of cadavers that were far less animated than she. Only the members of LAMAS waved enthusiastically to her, tossing posies and small tokens onto the stage.

The artist stood suddenly, dragged his chair away, and shuffled through his drawings for a few moments. His footsteps were loud in the momentary quiet as he made to withdraw from the stage.

Jordan turned her head and watched him go. She saw that he'd finished the last sketch and left it positioned on the easel. He'd portrayed her genitals three times actual size. They'd been faithfully rendered. He really was quite good.

"Bear witness to this spectacle. This miracle of science," Salerno went on. Like a conductor, his hands moved in staccato gestures to punctuate his words and lend them added importance.

Jordan looked beyond him, scanning the sea of faces blurred by darkness. Because of her, Salerno's reputation had spread far and wide. Today the theater had filled to capacity. Several hundred were in attendance. Candles lit the stage, so they could easily see her. But beyond the candles, the crowd of onlookers appeared to her as shrouds with shadowed features.

"Hermaphroditism has never been as pronounced in any other subject, now living or dead," Salerno was saying. "This is a rare opportunity, I assure you. The subject is nineteen years of age. Such cases rarely endure so long. Early death due to venereal disease or suicide are typically the fate of these creatures."

Jordan rolled her eyes. "No, really. Don't bother trying to spare my feelings," she muttered sotto voce.

It wasn't that Salerno was being intentionally cruel to her. He didn't care enough about her as a person to bother with cruelty. To him, she was merely a medical curiosity. A stepping stone to fame and glory in his chosen field. That she might also be a human being with feelings was immaterial. His lack of empathy made him all the more dangerous.

In time, Salerno grew weary of his own voice and called for the interrogation to commence.

"Why the mask?" a voice inquired from the crowd.

"It is a requirement the subject's family insists upon," Salerno replied. "Hence the moniker, La Maschera."

"But why specifically the bauta when any mask would have done?" another called.

"I've always worn the bauta of Carnivale," Jordan returned. "Even before the Austrians."

Salerno shot her an annoyed look. She might have to obey him in most things, but she refused to play the silent victim he would prefer her to be. He should be accustomed to that by now.

Onlookers always questioned the mask, but it had taken on added significance this year. Because some Venetians who still rebelled against Austrian rule had chosen to disguise themselves behind Carnivale masks to make mischief, such masks had recently been outlawed. The festival that had for centuries been so integral to the city was now forbidden.

"Let me direct your attention to matters below the subject's neck," Salerno said, indicating her bosom. His hand was cold as he took the weight of one of her breasts between his thumb and two fingers, lifting. "Paired with what is displayed between the subject's legs, such objects often draw *titters* from the crowd."

Jordan cringed at the pun, having heard it before from him on every birthday since her breasts had developed. She'd had to bind them every morning thereafter to perpetuate the fiction that she was entirely male.

"They're not much proof of sexual ambiguity," a voice complained. "I've seen men with tits as big."

"But only fat men, I'll warrant," Salerno quibbled. "And this subject is hardly fat." He let her breast flop free.

"Let's hear the subject speak further so that we may judge the quality and timbre of the voice," someone called.

Jordan tilted her jaw to a challenging angle. "What would you have me say? That you're a toad? A prick? An ass?"

The questioner blushed. Appearing quite sorry he'd dared

ask, he meekly added, "The voice is too low to be strictly female, yet too high to be male," before quickly reseating himself.

Another man stood. "Has the, uh, subject been clean shaven? Does, he, she, uh—" His words trailed off as he searched for the appropriate pronoun to apply to her.

Nouns always sprang with ease to the audience's lips when they beheld her—freak, specimen, subject, monstrosity. At the Paris school of medicine where she'd been taken for observation as a child, she'd been labeled *le malade*, the ill one. But no one ever knew what pronoun to apply to her. Sometimes they labeled her "her," sometimes "him," and worst of all, in imitation of Salerno, "it."

"You may to refer to the subject as 'La Maschera' or 'it,' " Salerno informed him.

"Very well then," the man continued. "Does it have a beard?"

"Of course, just look between its legs," joked another voice from somewhere in the audience.

The group guffawed. Jordan affected a bored expression. She'd heard the jest before from other doctors in other theaters.

"I only wondered if its jaw might have been clean shaven before this event in order to throw us off a proper diagnosis," the man protested.

Salerno's hand cupped her jaw, massaging. "Soft as an infant's behind, I assure you. Come. I invite you to feel for yourself."

Jordan steeled herself for what was to come. This invitation would be the first of many.

The questioner strode forward. His fingers stroked Jordan's cheeks, neck, and throat. He tilted her jaw one way and then the other. She purposely caught his gaze, hoping to startle him with her unusual obsidian eyes.

Under her unwavering stare, he quickly dropped his hand. Wiping it on his pants leg, he stepped away.

"Beardless," he pronounced to the audience, before striding back to his seat.

More questions came, thick and fast. None were new to her. But she lay in wait for the one question to which her answer would be new. It would almost be pleasant to see the shock on Salerno's face.

"Is the vaginal canal blind?" someone asked.

"No, there is a small perforation at its climax," Salerno assured him.

"How small?" asked yet another.

"Discover it for yourselves." Salerno beckoned the two questioners toward the stage.

Jordan lay back, folding her hands across her midriff. This was proceeding as all the other events had in prior years. In some ways, it was boring. In others, painful. But first and foremost the exploitation engendered a deep, private humiliation in her.

Salerno produced a pot of ointment. It was passed between the two men. The first of them scooped a dollop onto two of his fingers.

Salerno sought a glass of water to soothe his vocal chords as he waited.

A cold, lubricated finger slid along her slit, finding her opening. It poked inside her. Anger filled her as steadily as the finger, but she focused on breathing evenly, waiting for it to be over.

"No virginal barrier," announced the first poker, suspicion coloring his tone.

"It once existed, I assure you," said Salerno. "It was breeched years ago by other investigations."

Yes. Jordan remembered.

The finger probed deeper, searching, until even the knuckles of the hand had folded into her. Eventually the finger prodded the end of her canal, exploring the perforation it found.

"Ah! Yes, I feel it."

Jordan gritted her teeth against the cramping in her abdomen.

He pulled out.

The lubricated finger of another replaced his in her vaginal channel, probing again. The man found the opening, nodded in agreement, and then withdrew.

Fury swelled in her, but she tried to tamp it down. Whatever was done to her on this day, she must allow, she reminded herself. Her mother's as well as her own continued comfort depended on her obedience.

Obedience. How she detested the word. Every year she balked when Salerno came for her at dawn, but her mother always wept and pleaded. Was one day too much to ask of a child so that her only parent might live in luxury for the other 364 days of the year? she wheedled.

Jordan's father's wealth—a considerable fortune—had hung in the balance that morning when she was born nineteen years ago to this day. He had been struck dead in a hunting accident only a week prior. If Jordan had been pronounced female upon her birth, a distant male cousin would have inherited it all. She and her mother would have lost the lovely house and its sumptuous furnishings, the investments, the jewels, the social standing, and the esteem of every patrician family in Venice.

But were Jordan to be pronounced a male—ah! That was entirely different.

Salerno, a young surgeon at the time, had attended her mother at the difficult birth. When Jordan had been born a case of ambiguous sex—one body possessing both male and female parts—he'd been crafty enough to see the potential for his future. A bargain had been struck between him and her mother. He had pronounced Jordan male. And her mother had inherited the entire Cietta family fortune.

For all of her nineteen years, Jordan had faced the world as a man. She wore trousers, was addressed as signore, and was given the respect due a wealthy young man of family name and status.

But this was not what she wanted. And as each day passed, she chafed under her masculine mantle and grew ever more desperate to make a change.

"If a creature has a phallus, it is male. It's as simple as that," a man in the audience postulated.

"You call that puny little cannoli a phallus?" scoffed another, waving a hand in the general direction of Jordan's genitals.

"I hear that's what the ladies say to you in the privacy of their bedchambers," Jordan quipped.

Laughter exploded.

"Yes, I call it a phallus," Salerno interjected, raising his voice in an attempt to restore order. "What would you have it called?"

"A hypertrophied clitoris," the man replied, loudly so as to be heard over the din.

Salerno sliced the air with his hand. "Absolutely not. There's no such organ to be found here. I contend the phallus has displaced it."

"May I put a question directly to the subject?" another man called out.

"Yes," Jordan shouted back, before Salerno could. "But I don't guarantee an answer."

"Quiet, please!" Salerno commanded moving to the forefront of the stage. "Only then will we continue."

When order was finally regained, the man tossed his query at her. "Do you bleed?"

"No," she replied with a shrug. It was an easy question.

The questioner snapped his fingers. "That's settles it then. There is no uterus. No womb."

"Whether or not a uterus exists is a matter undetermined as yet," said Salerno. "I'm sure you realize that some women who possess female organs do not bleed, yet they are still female."

"Overall, do you have a sense of maleness?" another voice asked her. "Or femaleness?"

Her eyes found Salerno's. "Femaleness," she said defiantly.

"Never of maleness?" the questioner pressed.

She hesitated. "That's difficult to say. For instance, I enjoy needlework and female fripperies. But at the same time, I enjoy male pursuits—riding a good mount or having a stiff drink and a good laugh with friends. Of course, I don't mean to imply I ride and do needlework literally at the same time."

A few uncertain snorts and giggles came and were quickly snuffed. Her interlocutors preferred to think of her as a specimen under a microscope. When she revealed humor, they were uncomfortable and never quite certain what to make of her.

"Are you now living in society under the guise of female?" someone shouted.

Salerno held up a hand, rebuffing the question. "The subject's family forbids that question and all others that might lend clues as to its identity."

Grumbles rippled over the audience.

"I object to the term *it,* which seems inappropriate and demeaning," an Englishman wearing spectacles protested.

"What would you have me called?" Jordan snapped.

"An abomination!" someone shouted from the back of the theater.

Heads swiveled backward, peering toward the far end of the center aisle. Two men had entered unnoticed at some point and now stood there.

Jordan sat forward and shaded her eyes, trying to better see them. The one who'd spoken was rounded with too much flesh, but the other was broad shouldered, narrow hipped, and extremely tall. She felt the tall one's eyes travel over her. Weighing her. Did he think her an abomination, too?

She squinted, trying to make out his features, but found it impossible to decipher them clearly through the dimness. His bearing was straight, almost rigid, giving the impression he was well over six feet.

Her cock perked to attention under his lengthy inspection and she hunched, hugging her arms around her knees to hide it.

The tall one's gaze darted up to lock with hers. Sparks of silver caught the candlelight. He'd seen her desire, his eyes told her, and he wanted her as well. But somehow she sensed he didn't like it.

"You're a monster. A creature of the devil," the squat man beside him stated with unshakable authority.

The taller one remained silent, ignoring his companion. So he would not defend her. But then why should he? No one ever had. She would defend herself.

Her eyes shifted from him to the other one. He wore the robes of a bishop. It mattered not what he thought, she told herself, but she could not let his slanderous comments pass unchallenged.

"Why should my external genitalia define me as a monster?" she argued. "For all you know I could be a saint in my heart."

"Blasphemous creature!" the bishop snarled, shaking a finger at her. "It's obvious you're no saint."

At that moment, a thin, anxious man stepped up to the pair of interlopers at the back of the theater.

Salerno moved toward the center of the stage, obscuring her view of them. Raising and lowering his arms in a flapping manner, he attempted to regain the attention of his audience.

"Gentlemen, please. Let us continue with our debate . . ."

Jordan pushed herself higher, trying to peer beyond him. But the two men in the aisle were gone now. Disappointment shot through her.

"You will note the presence of labia minora and labia majora as can be found in any female," Salerno droned on, moving to her side.

Reluctantly, she released her grip on her knees and splayed them. With one hand, Salerno reached between her thighs.

"The labia majora is not fused—" He broke off, abruptly leaning closer to peer between her legs. "What the devil?" He grasped her phallus between his thumb and two fingers. Gently he squeezed.

His excited eyes came up to meet hers. "I'll be damned. I do believe you have the makings of a hard-on."

4

Once the velvet curtain had swished open, Raine's silver gaze had been drawn as iron to a magnet to the figure that half-reclined upon a table ringed in candles. She was splendid.

In spite of her contradictory body parts, it didn't occur to him to question for a moment that she was inherently female. He simply knew it in the marrow of his bones.

"Pardone, signore," a voice intruded from somewhere nearby. Distantly, he noted the bishop engaging the annoying babbler in a discussion. But Raine continued to stare at the stage, transfixed.

His gaze made a slow sweep of the figure on the table. She was petite but held herself regally, exuding a presence that had captivated the interest of an entire audience. How many men or women could recline naked in a public auditorium and still retain an air of proud disdain toward the onlookers, he wondered.

The dull sheen of her golden complexion caught the candlelight. Her eyes and hair were dark and lustrous. Her breasts were high, plump, and well shaped, but modest—each of a size that would neatly fill his hand. Her waist and hips were slender but curved. And below, in the nest at the crook of her thighs, lay a shy, delicate cock.

A hermaphrodite.

But why was she here, allowing herself to be publicly displayed like the main course on a platter at a formal meal?

And why did he want to climb onstage, crawl onto that table, and make a feast of her? At the sight of her, his own cock had hardened into a thick, strangled bulge within the crotch of his trousers. A powerful lust had risen within him, almost as though it were already Moonful.

But the moon would not reach its ripest fullness for another week. He'd never experienced a Calling time away from the Satyr Estate, at least not since he'd become an adult. However, it seemed unlikely he could finish his business here in Venice and be home before then. He would have to plan carefully to satisfy his cravings, yet avoid discovery.

When the harvest moon rose in the sky in seven days, his body would alter, becoming more powerfully potent. It would change physically in a way that had once terrified his former wife. During the Calling his mind would be overtaken with the need to rut from dusk to dawn.

Much like it had been the moment he'd laid eyes on the seductive creature onstage.

"Eh, signore?" The apologetic voice nagged at his attention again like a buzzing gnat.

Raine tore his fascinated gaze from the woman at the opposite end of the theater and looked down to see an obsequious man standing before him and the bishop. He was speaking, repeatedly punctuating his words with nervous little half bows. How long had he been standing there?

"Pardone, pardone, biglietti—"

Achoo! Raine sneezed, silently cursed, and then asked, "What did you say?"

"Si, signore. Pardone, pardone. As I was explaining to your companion, tickets are required to attend Signore Salerno's medical lecture this evening," the man told him, obviously relieved to have finally snagged his attention.

"I assure you we have no interest in remaining here to witness such a disgusting display," the bishop butted in.

Raine's eyes went back to the stage, but the lecturer had moved in front of the woman now. Several in the audience were standing, hurling questions toward them, and their height further obscured her from his view. She hadn't been struggling, and her eyes hadn't been drugged. For whatever reason, he assumed she was here of her own free will. And he had pressing business elsewhere.

Without another word, he pivoted on his heel and exited the theater.

Upon Raine's abrupt departure, the bishop ended his conversation with the ticket taker in midsentence.

He'd seen the bulge that tented the crotch of Satyr's trousers. His moody companion might pretend indifference to anything sexual, but that horrendous creature on the stage had piqued his interest.

And since the bishop's interest had been piqued by Satyr since he'd first seen him at the harvest festival nearly a year ago, he wasn't particularly pleased to note the fact. He'd come all this way for the lecture on the off chance that this elusive Satyr son might attend. More reclusive than his two brothers, he rarely left their Tuscany estate. Despite the bishop's best efforts, he'd only managed to spot him a half-dozen times last year, and then only from afar. Yet his infatuation had flourished all the more for being denied.

He scurried into the hallway, watching Raine head for the other lecture hall. His eyes devoured the splendid shape of him. Of his broad shoulders, narrow waist, and muscled thighs.

Many times he'd imagined those very thighs braced as he himself rutted between them. Imagined the cries of ecstasy he might rend from that man's lips. Imagined him hard and begging.

A sudden idea came to him. Perhaps he could procure the abomination on display in the theater for a private party of three later tonight. If Satyr were stimulated by the charms of La Maschera, perhaps he might not be averse to a certain suggestion the bishop hoped to put to him. Once sufficient wine had flowed between them all, perhaps other more personal fluids might be exchanged between them as well.

He would speak to the surgeon onstage about hiring his creature for the evening or perhaps longer. But if he departed this theater, the white-coated lecturer might escape before he could deliver his request. Yet he couldn't let Satyr get away without learning where he was lodging in Venice. What to do?

As Raine's steps quickly ate up the carpet ahead, the bishop made a decision. He turned back to the attendant who had trailed him into the hall. "I've decided not to attend the lecture on phylloxera tonight after all. I will take part in this lecture instead."

"But signore," the man whined, preparing to launch into his rehearsed speech again.

"Si, si. You needn't hound me with your complaints again. What is the price of a ticket to this lecture?" he inquired, gesturing toward the door.

At the attendant's reply, the bishop handed him the money and a little something extra.

"I will pay you again to return here to this theater later tonight and inform me when the gentleman who just went down that hall departs the other lecture for the streets," he said.

Pocketing his offer, the attendant nodded eagerly and started to move in the direction Raine had gone.

The bishop grabbed his arm, staying him momentarily. "Do not let him know you're watching him."

"No, no. Of course not. Rest assured I will be discreet."
Once he had bowed several more times, he was on his way.

The bishop stared down the hall after him, hoping he could
be trusted. Then he turned and re-entered the theater

Several medical fools from the audience were onstage now
with the abomination, still questing for answers. The hermaphrodite offended his eyes and its speech, his ears. But seeing it
being poked and prodded raised his cock. He rearranged the
skirts of his alb to conceal the fact and quickly found a seat in
the back row.

His hand slipped under folds of fabric, found his stiff prick,
and began pumping. On occasions such as this when stealth
was required, his bishop's robes proved extremely useful garments.

The clerical profession was not his first choice, but the family fortune had been lost some two decades ago and he'd been
forced to make his way in life somehow. If he succeeded in
snaring a protector such as Satyr, it would greatly enhance his
standard of living.

His hand pumped on, taking his mind far from the subject
of phylloxera or the church. His hopes were in full blossom regarding the possibilities the night held and his lips were still and
silent for once as he mentally rehearsed the persuasive words he
would ply when he and Satyr were alone at last.

5

More than an hour later, the crowd in the medical theater had finally exhausted their questions and departed. This left only a select group of five men, each of whom had paid Salerno a premium for a more private examination of her. Once they'd gathered onstage, Salerno swished the curtains closed, cutting off Jordan's view of the now-empty seating area and creating a more intimate setting for the remaining group.

Outside she heard the clock bell in the piazza strike seven. She wouldn't be officially free to return home until midnight. Five hours to go.

But no one here was in a hurry to end the evening except her. Wine and a tray of stemmed glasses were brought out, and the men prepared to idle the evening away in her company.

Two of the guests were Venetian aristocracy, she quickly deduced. With nothing better to do and more money than they knew how to spend, they'd lingered here to relieve their boredom at her expense.

A third one was more serious, an Englishman who nudged

his glasses up and down his nose every so often. It was likely he at least had stayed for the purposes of true medical study.

The fourth was a large, bearded Sicilian whose deep-set eyes studied every inch of her as thoroughly as the artist had. A back-row type, his interest was obviously selfish and prurient.

The fifth man was a late arrival, one she'd seen before. It seemed the bishop who'd decried her earlier was back for another look. Unfortunately his tall friend was nowhere to be seen.

"There's nothing here to interest a man of the church," Salerno said suspiciously, when the bishop tried to make his way backstage to join the others.

"On the contrary," the bishop returned. His eyes searched the interior of the stage beyond Salerno, lighting on Jordan. "I assure you that my purpose here is not on the church's behalf. I come asking a favor. One that will benefit your purse." He whispered something to Salerno that Jordan couldn't hear.

"La Maschera is not for hire," Salerno told him, shaking his head.

The bishop's face mottled, his displeasure at being refused apparent. His tone turned louder and wheedling. "I will pay whatever you deem fair."

But Salerno still held him off. "La Maschera is mine for this day only. At midnight, it must be returned to its domicile. Now be off." He tried to swish the curtain closed on the stout man.

"Wait!" the bishop insisted, grabbing the edge of the velvet drape before it could shut him out. "Though the church is my calling, I assure you that I take a strong interest in numerous scientific matters."

"And in abominations as well?" Jordan asked, pitching her voice so he would hear.

The bishop's eyes impaled her, stopping the very breath in her throat.

He pulled out some currency and made a show of stuffing it

in Salerno's hand. "When I accidentally bumbled into your theater earlier, I was told tickets were required for this event. You'll take this I trust in lieu of the usual purchase price?"

Salerno peered inside the bag of coins, jiggling it to test its weight. Grudgingly, he moved aside so the bishop could enter. "Very well. I'll not argue further. In view of unforeseen developments, I'm anxious to get on with tonight's examination."

The clink of crystal told Jordan some of the others had begun filling their glasses. Leaving his guests to their own devices, Salerno came to her side holding a toolcase, a pen, and a small notebook.

"These are new, eh?" he asked her, rubbing a finger along her plumped labia.

She shrugged. Three of the guests gathered around them—the bishop, the Englishman, and the Sicilian—watching as Salerno again palpitated the twin lumps in her labia. Mentally distancing herself from what was happening, she stared at the ceiling, noting a rather large water stain that had been caused by a leak at some earlier time. It resembled a brown rabbit with unusually long ears. She tensed, realizing where she'd seen just such a rabbit before.

In her dreams.

Transfixed, she felt herself fall helplessly into the pit of her nightmare.

"Hello? Hello?" Salerno's loud voice jarred her. "When did you first notice evidence of testes forming in your labia?"

Her eyes jerked toward him. He was looking at her strangely as though he'd been trying to garner her attention for some time. She swallowed, finding her throat dry. The pull of the dreams was growing stronger, reaching her even during waking hours.

"Testes?" Jordan repeated. "But are you certain that's what they are? They're so small."

He waved her question away. "Don't quibble with my medical expertise. I know what I see! When?"

"About ten months ago," she replied.

His cold, veined hands lifted her phallus—limp now—and twisted and turned it, examining. Calipers were brought out of his toolcase to measure its length and girth at rest.

By now, she was inured to such examinations. Or so she told herself. Disassociating herself from what was happening, she continued to locate animal shapes among the ceiling's water spots.

"From this angle the creature could be male or female," a tipsy voice said from somewhere behind her. The two Venetians were apparently well on their way to becoming drunk. And from the sound of things, they were busily viewing the portraits the artist had made of her.

Jordan knew which particular drawing they were studying. It was the only one that could be described in that way. It was a rear view. She'd posed for it on her knees, her head bent low to rest on her folded forearms. In that position, the puckered ring between the cheeks of her buttocks gapped slightly. But they were right. It was one view in which she appeared normal, yet it was impossible to tell her gender.

"And who would know the difference in the dark?" came the first man's slurred rejoinder.

"Not a buggerer like yourself I presume . . ." Jordan quipped, twisting to fling the words toward them.

The man's companion slapped the fellow on the back, guffawing. "I do believe you've been insulted, il mio amico."

Too soused to take affront, his friend only raised his glass in a sloshy toast. "A bung is a bung is a bung is amongus," he singsonged.

Jordan was immediately angry with herself for reacting. Her eyes sought the ceiling again, but the water stains failed to recapture her attention.

"No change in size from last year," Salerno announced. Having measured her flaccid shaft in all dimensions, he scribbled a notation in his book. Then he asked the question she'd known would eventually come. "On what date did your penis first engorge?" His pen hovered over the page, waiting.

When the dreams had begun to plague her in earnest. When they'd become so frequent and compelling that it had become difficult to discern the difference between wakefulness and slumber. On the night dark masculine voices had begun to whisper carnal suggestions to her, causing her to writhe and gasp. Causing her shaft to harden and lift and to spill its ecstasy, despoiling her bedsheets. But she would tell him none of that.

"Well?" he prodded, scrutinizing her. "Is the question so difficult?"

"Ten months ago, the same as when the lumps formed in my labia," she answered truthfully.

"I'd like to measure it at full attention," Salerno told her. "Stroke it into tumescence for me."

She glared at him, appalled, but he took no notice.

"Shall I do it?" he inquired helpfully when she didn't obey. "Or one of the others here? Or would you prefer that I bring in a female to provoke it? There are doubtless plenty of whores prowling the streets, even on a night like this."

Salerno would do exactly that, she knew. He was oblivious as to how revolting his suggestions would seem to her. Even if she explained, there would be no way to make him understand. He was as ever incapable of empathy with another human being.

"Whores?" one of the drunkards echoed, his interest perking. "Where?"

He and his tipsy companion roused themselves to gather with the others around her, intrigued by the prospect of new entertainment.

"I'll do it. But I require privacy," said Jordan.

Salerno tsked and blustered, shaking his head. "This is no

time for false modesty. I want to observe the process to see if it proceeds normally. Where's that tub of ointment?"

The bishop located the pot and extended it toward her.

She frowned at it.

"Do you require assistance after all?" the bishop asked.

"Not from the likes of you." Jordan snatched the cream, swirled two fingers in it, and then curled her torso into the most concealing hunch she could manage. Closing her eyes, she blocked out her observers.

At ease, her phallus was only slightly longer than her palm. She worried at it for a few moments, searching her mind for inspiration. A vision of the shadowy, taller man who'd earlier come into the theater with the bishop sprang to mind. Her shaft invigorated. Six silent men watched her stroke herself to hardness.

"Ah, to be young and have a cock that rises so eagerly," said one of the drunkards, toasting her.

Two droplets of red wine splashed on her thigh. She stared at them. The splotches looked like—blood. This, too, was just as she'd seen it in her dream.

Her gaze darted around the room, searching warily. Where was the third part of the dream? Where were the ribbons? When would they come to her? And from which direction?

Salerno shoved her hand aside and took the measurements he required. "Five point one inches." He scribbled in his notebook, and then replaced his silver tool in its velvet-lined case.

The two drunkards watched as the bishop's hand took over her movements on her shaft, squeezing toward its tip. She put a hand over his to stop him, but his fist tightened on her cap, forcing the slit at her tip to separate like a tiny mouth.

"An excretory canal for urine," supplied Salerno, leaning over to observe.

"And sperm?" The bishop gazed directly into her eyes. She felt a brief flash of recognition. But she was certain she'd never met him. Surely he only resembled someone else she knew.

With a mighty shove at his chest, Jordan pushed him away. "Don't touch me."

"Answer him," said Salerno, his pen poised once again to note her reply.

Though her blood boiled, she made a show of studying her nails, affecting boredom. "Yes," she replied.

The Sicilian stroked his beard. "Then do you suppose the subject could actually father a child?"

Salerno eyed her speculatively. "Difficult to say. I suppose a whore could be brought in to test the theory in actual practice."

"I'll not impregnate any whores for you," Jordan protested, pulling herself into a tighter ball and wrapping her arms and the cloak around her knees. "Even if I'm able to. Which I'm not."

"You deny that you possess testes? A phallus? You deny all evidence of your God-given maleness?" asked the bishop.

"No! In a physical sense I'm not completely male or female. And I accept that. I simply wish in my heart to live as a woman in this world." How good it felt to say it aloud.

"Are you sexually aroused by men?" asked the Sicilian.

"Yes." She glanced at the overabundance of sweaty black hair that swelled from his collar and between the strained fastenings of his shirt. "Well, not all men."

"Disposed toward men," Salerno noted in his black book.

"So you wish to engage in sodomy?" the bishop inquired.

"Thank you kindly for the offer," said Jordan, "but—"

The bishop hissed between his teeth, raising a hand as though to strike her before catching himself. "Blasphemous creature! If you must wear the Carnivale mask, it should be the moretta. Lips as foul as yours should remain forcibly buttoned."

The moretta he referred to was a mask that covered the entire face but had no string attached to tie it fast. Instead, it was held in position by its wearer biting a button on the inside of the lips. This necessitated that its wearer remain mute or lose the mask!

"Have you ever been sexually aroused by a woman?" one of the drunkards inquired, drawing her gaze.

She shrugged, a little embarrassed. "Yes, but likely no more often than any of you have been aroused by a man. Whether its owner is male or female, a beautiful body, face, and spirit combined in one package tends to draw every eye. Do you not agree?"

The men shifted uncomfortably, unwilling to admit the truth of what she said.

"But if you were forced to choose one and only one gender as a sexual partner for the rest of your life on this earth, which would it be?" prodded the bishop.

It was a question that dogged her. Did the circumstances of her body dictate that she could never be satisfactorily partnered for life with only one gender? If so, how could she ever hope to find love—unless she found another hermaphrodite who happened to suit her disposition! And what were the chances of that?

"Must it be one or the other?" she asked. "Can your God not find it in His heart to allow the possibility that there might be a sliding scale in such matters? Can a body such as mine not seek its pleasure with both genders?"

The bishop's doughy complexion turned an apoplectic hue. "Again you blaspheme!"

"But earlier tonight, you said you do not bleed," the Englishman insisted, ignoring the outburst. "Aside from your breasts and vaginal canal, what is the source of this belief that you're female?"

Tapping her head, then her chest, she said, "It's something my mind and heart direct me toward."

He nodded, seeming to understand.

Salerno gestured toward her testes and wilting cock. "I must agree with the good bishop. With these new developments, your claim to womanhood seems to be hanging by a fragile thread."

He leaned low to her ear. "Perhaps my lie to your family was not so large after all."

She turned her head, whispering, "Then your hold on my family lessens."

His eyes slitted. She'd spoken unwisely.

When she averted her gaze from him, it fell on the bishop. He'd overheard their conversation, and she saw the flash of curiosity in his eyes. She patted her mask making certain it was still in place.

"What if you were to mate the subject with a man?" the Sicilian inquired suddenly. "If a child resulted, would that not prove it to be a female?"

The six men studied her speculatively.

Salerno tapped his chin with a long finger. "Or what if the subject were to mate with both a man and a woman, all under the strict surveillance of a theater full of medical men? And what if, in the course of such an experiment, La Maschera were to become both father and mother, all in the course of a single night?"

The Sicilian's eyes lit. "Now that would be something to draw crowds!"

"I'll never agree to such a thing," said Jordan. "You know I wouldn't. I'm no animal in heat to be caged and mated. And I would never indiscriminately bring children into this world. If I were ever so fortunate as to bear offspring, I would want to parent them for all the years afterward. If I were a wife—"

"What man would take you as a wife if it turns out that you cannot bear his children?" one of the Venetians countered.

"A man that loves me," she replied heatedly, though even she didn't believe her own claim.

Salerno raised his hands up and down as though patting out a fire. "Calm down. It's not possible to experiment tonight anyway. To ensure accurate results, any woman you mated would have to be quarantined for nine months prior to copulation. And for as many months afterward, it would be someone's task to ensure she remained celibate. That's the only way to validate that any offspring she bore had resulted from your seed."

"But what of my suggestion? The subject could still be given the ultimate test of femininity—one that would determine if it's capable of motherhood," the Sicilian insisted. From the bulge in his trousers, Jordan garnered the distinct impression he was willing to take on the job.

"My family wouldn't be pleased by such a result," she said, eyeing Salerno pointedly.

She sensed the bishop paying close attention. "Is there no medical inspection that could satisfactorily determine gender?" he inquired. "Some evaluation of femaleness other than the ability to bear children?"

Salerno shrugged. "A woman is what she is because of the uterus. This dictum has been relied upon by the medical establishment since first decreed by Jan Baptist van Helmont, the Flemish physician in the seventeenth century. However, the factual presence of such an organ can only be determined by an invasive physical search."

"One that could be performed tonight?" the bishop prodded.

The spectacled Englishman spoke up, shaking his head. "Gentlemen! You're not contemplating—? No! It's too dangerous."

"What would you have to do exactly?" Jordan asked, feeling reckless with the desire to strengthen her claim to femininity.

"Don't agree to this," the Englishman warned her.

"Bah!" Salerno said, waving away the other man's plea for caution. "The subject is here to be explored of its own free will.

What I suggest is a routine procedure I've done several times before. A well-informed hand such as mine, lubricated and inserted into its rectum, would quickly detect the shape, size, and location of a uterus if one exists. Any discomfort would be minimal."

"Minimal!" scoffed the spectacled man.

Paling at the description of what was involved, Jordan beckoned Salerno closer.

"A private moment, gentlemen!" he told the others. They grudgingly turned away as he leaned in to listen to her.

"If you dare perform such a search," Jordan whispered, "regardless of what you find, I swear to you I will put an end to these annual demonstrations."

"What will your mother have to say on that?" he asked mildly, unconcerned at her threat. She'd made it many times before.

"I don't care," said Jordan firmly. But they both knew she was lying. Her mother was beautiful, sought after, and self-centered. Jewels, society, and gaiety were the substance of her life. Sudden poverty would not agree with her. If Jordan were exposed not to be a verifiable male, her cousin would inherit. She wouldn't see her own mother cast into the streets, and Salerno knew it.

His beady bird eyes bored into hers. "Don't make threats on which you cannot follow through. I believe I'll perform the search tonight, with or without your agreement. However, I'll offer to strike a different bargain with you in exchange for your cooperation: one birthday."

"What do you mean?"

"If you make this easy, I'll not come for you next year on your birthday."

Her heart skipped a beat. He was offering two years of freedom. It was almost worth it. Almost, but—

Without giving her a chance to decide either way, Salerno straightened and craftily rubbed his hands together.

"The search is on! First, I'll need my clyster apparatus to cleanse the creature's rectum. Where's my medical bag?" He rummaged around, found the bag, and pulled a metal syringe from it. As long as her forearm, it had a thick needle on one end and a pump handle on the other. It was the French type of syringe that worked with a piston.

He gestured to the Sicilian. "You. Go for warm water. Quickly."

"Warm? Where am I to procure warm water in this neighborhood at this hour?" the man inquired.

"You're right," said Salerno. "Fetch two pitchers of whatever you find. We'll make do."

The Sicilian made his way through the curtains, hurrying off on his errand.

The Englishman's glasses slid to the bridge of his nose and he pinched the skin between his brows as though he were getting a headache. "Gentlemen! I must insist that the danger of potential injury prohibits such an experiment. There are severe health risks, as you know."

"What risks?" asked Jordan, with increasing concern.

He eyed her anxiously. "If done improperly, an examination such as they're proposing can result in serious injuries. Torn bowels, infections, bruising, incontinence, sterility." He counted them off on his fingers.

"Nonsense. A rectal examination done with proper care by a medical practitioner carries a low risk of injury," said Salerno.

"I won't be a party to this!" said the other man, ripping off his glasses to emphasize his protest.

"Then hustle yourself off," Salerno told him diffidently. "We've determined our course. And the subject isn't protesting."

"Your subject is hardly in a position to get its way! You've obviously got some sort of hold over it."

"Your imagination runs away with you," said Salerno. "For its cooperation, La Maschera is paid in a coin you wouldn't understand." He looked her way. "Aren't you?"

Jordan averted her eyes, hating him.

Shooting them all a disgusted look, the Englishman donned his glasses, coat, and hat in that order. The door at the back of the stage let in a bluster of rain, then banged shut as he deserted them.

His colleagues scarcely noticed. But Jordan knew her only ally had gone.

Salerno dug through his bag and pulled out a stoppered bottle containing bits of black root. Selecting one at random, he extended it to Jordan. "Chew this while I prepare myself."

"What is it?" asked the bishop, intercepting and studying the root before passing it to her.

But Jordan knew the substance well and popped it in her mouth. Salerno had dosed her with it to calm her when she'd been younger and given to screaming fits during examinations.

"It's an herb that will relax the subject's muscles," said Salerno.

Jordan chewed, watching as he began filing the nails of his right hand with the rasp of a particularly evil-looking file.

"Once stuck my hand inside a woman," one of the drunkards ruminated. "In her cunt though, not her ass. Did it on a bet with my brother. Devil of a time getting my knuckles inside her as I recall. Once inside I made a fist though—in spite of her caterwauling—and won the wager."

"Was there any injury?" Jordan couldn't help asking.

"My hand was a little stiff and bruised the next day. Nothing serious."

Jordan rolled her eyes at his stupidity. "No, I meant was there any injury to the woman."

The man scratched his chin and looked perplexed. "Dunno. Never saw her again after that night. Whore, you know."

He turned to Salerno, holding out one of his hands for inspection. "My hands are smaller than yours. And I'm a man of experience. Maybe I should have a go at it."

Salerno shook his head. "You won't know what you're searching for. The shape of the organ is specific and requires a knowledge of internal anatomy."

"Well at least tell me this. What's your secret for getting the knuckles in?" the drunkard inquired with an air of seriousness.

"Adequate lubrication is the ticket to the whole endeavor. I start in with two fingers straight," said Salerno, holding up his index and second fingers to demonstrate.

"As you add more fingers," he went on, "crowd them together so the index and small fingers slide under the middle two."

"Yes, yes, but the knuckles?" the drunkard prompted.

Salerno nodded, pleased as always to have a fascinated audience. "They're the widest part of the hand, so one always encounters resistance during either vaginal or rectal insertion, though more so with the latter, naturally. As I push inside, I tuck my thumb under my fingers, forming a sort of wedge shape. Here, it's best to heed any complaint from the male patient. However, in my opinion females are more prone to hysteria so one should insist upon proceeding regardless. Once the knuckles slip past the outer ring of muscles, one must press on gradually and with utmost care."

Jordan's anxiety escalated as he proceeded to illustrate the best manner in which to infiltrate her anus. As a crack of thunder came from outside the theater, a twin bolt of anger shot through her. Suddenly, she wanted to rage at all these men. To slap their satisfied faces and punch their paunchy bellies.

She'd reached her limit of enforced obedience. She'd rather

die than return for this sort of treatment next year or even two years from now. No matter how her mother begged, this would be the last birthday she'd allow herself to be subjugated in this way. If Salerno exposed the true facts of her gender and they lost everything, so be it. She would find work. Or perhaps she could convince her mother to marry one of the many swains who doted on her.

The Sicilian returned then with two pitchers of water. Her eyelids slitted as she measured the distance to the door. He blocked it now, but she would watch for an opportunity to cut the evening short.

With a final flourish of his nail file, Salerno flexed his fingers and pronounced himself ready. After filling the syringe from the pitchers, he went to stand at the back of the stage, near the wall.

"Come over here so you don't soil the table," he told her, motioning her forward with one hand. "Cleansing with a clyster can be a nasty business."

Pretending to be woozier than she was, Jordan slowly gathered herself and half-rolled off the table. Stumbling, she made her way toward the rear of the stage where Salerno waited.

He eyed her critically as she approached. "Is that my cloak?" Aghast when he determined it was, he thrust his equipment into the bishop's hands. "Take it off before it becomes soiled beyond redemption." He yanked the garment from her. Shaking out its folds, he carefully draped it over the back of the chair the artist had left positioned by the door.

When he returned, he neglected to reclaim his device from the bishop. "On your knees now," he told her. "In a squat. That's right."

His hands pressed her shoulders downward and Jordan sank to her knees. A bucket was set on the floor, just behind her between her ankles.

"Lean forward." She didn't budge.

"The root has taken effect," he told the bishop over her head. "You'll have to wield the syringe." Salerno came and stood in front of her, holding his hands under her armpits. She had no choice but to bury her nose in his crotch.

Within his trousers, his prick dangled, soft against her cheekbone. Working with her never excited him physically. She wondered if anything ever did.

Hands fumbled behind her, spreading the cheeks of her bottom. The bishop's robes puddled over her feet as he bent closer. Cold metal prodded her anus.

Perhaps she should pretend to faint. Or to vomit. She had to do something that would offer a distraction in order to escape.

The sound of someone clearing his throat just outside the theater curtain came to her like a gift from heaven. The remaining men turned their attention away from her and toward the interruption.

"Don't do anything until I return," Salerno muttered to the bishop. Leaving her on all fours with the bishop positioned behind her, he went to the curtain.

"You think I'm stupid?" the bishop whispered to her when he'd left them. "You think I don't know?"

Jordan froze, looking back at him over a shoulder. "What the hell are you talking about?"

His eyes turned something less than lucid and his features took on a demented twist. "I saw how you made him want you. I saw. You put the idea in my head to share him between us, witch. You would take him from me if I let you."

"Who are you talking about? Never mind. Whoever he is, keep him. I don't want him," Jordan assured him.

Blood suffused the bishop's face. "You lie—"

Without warning he knelt over her and caught a hand under her midsection. His other hand worked behind her. The point of the syringe poked, then found its way into her rectum. She heard the squeak of metal and a squishing sound as he awkwardly tried to work the brass and tin piston with the use of only one hand and arm.

She tried to wriggle free of the discomfort, knowing that in seconds she would feel the cold chill of water flushing her bowels into the waiting bucket.

The voice at the curtain rose. "I bring a message for the bishop," it announced. "Regarding the matter we discussed earlier. I come to inform him that his companion has just departed in a group of others."

The clyster left her and hit the floor with a clatter. The bishop hurried off, forgetting her and his crazy threats. With a twitch of the curtain, he stepped outside it to speak with the interloper. There was a brief conversation to which Salerno and the others listened unabashedly.

This was her chance.

Jordan stumbled upright and managed to stuff her bare feet into her sturdy buckled man's shoes, which had been set by the door. Salerno's cloak, lying across the chair back, brushed her arm. She snatched it up to cover her nakedness. All this seemed to occur in slow motion, but when she glanced behind her, no one had moved and she knew only seconds had passed.

Carefully, Jordan opened the back door the disgruntled Englishman had so recently used to exit the theater. The streets here were dangerous. But remaining in the theater posed a danger as well.

Behind her, someone shouted, noticing she was poised for flight. She plunged from the room into the nearly deserted street outside, making a run for it. The door banged behind her, echoing across the piazza. She heard it open again, and then came the sound of pursuit.

The tattoo of her own clunking footsteps on the rain-washed

pavement drowned out any further sounds. Any minute she expected Salerno's hands to grab her. Her breath was strangled with the fear of imminent capture.

But it never came. The cloddish shoes were practical and carried her swiftly away from the theater, along winding brick streets. The root had dulled her reflexes and confused her mind, but the sweet smell of rain-scented air was quickly dispelling its effect.

Footsteps sounded behind her. She turned into an alley, ducked into a crevice between two buildings, and waited. The steps faltered. Nearby, she heard Salerno's voice.

"I'm searching for a young—person—wearing a crimson cloak," he told someone. "And possibly the bauta as well."

She couldn't decipher the mumbled response he was given but knew it had displeased him when his sharp curse cut the air. This was quickly followed by the sound of his footsteps veering away.

When they grew faint, Jordan slipped from the alley and ran in the direction opposite from that which he'd gone. The streets twisted and angled, but she knew her way home from here. First, she had to get over the Rialto. Once beyond the bridge, home was only thirty or so turns away by street.

Then it occurred to her that home was out of the question. Salerno would look for her there immediately, claiming she owed him more hours of her time.

Could she find harbor with one of her male friends tonight? Paulo and Gani could always be counted on to join in any escapade. But if she turned up at either of their homes wearing only a cloak, they would whisk it from her, teasing. And when they discovered her true sex—when they discovered the deceit she'd perpetrated for all the years that she'd known them as friends—she feared what their reactions might be.

She scurried onward, unable to think of anything except the need to reach the bridge, which served as the only link across the Grand Canal that divided Venice. In the distance ahead, she saw its stone arch. The smell of the sea stung her nose as she rushed toward it.

She saw no one behind her. Heard no one. But still her heart thumped in time with her steps. Her breath was tortured, her entire body tense with fear of discovery. Would Salerno jump out at her from a cross street or one of the alleys, preventing her from reaching the bridge and any chance of escape?

Only a single gondola bobbed along the quay ahead, clacking softly. She had no money for its hire. Where would she go even if she could pay?

Lanterns along the bridge flickered, casting diamonds across the murky waters of the canal. The rain had stopped, and the night was turning foggy. The Palazzos Manin and Bembo along the Riva del Ferro, where shipments of iron were unloaded by day, were barely visible across the canal. An inky blackness of sky and sea loomed like a gaping maw waiting to swallow her.

Above her, on the balconies of the houses along the Riva del Vin, courtesans with bosoms far more ample than hers discreetly offered the use of their bodies to passersby in spite of the weather. If she called to them would they take pity on her? Unlikely, unless she had coin to offer.

Most of the vendors in the shops that stood atop the Rialto had gone home for the day by now. Cries from those who dwelled in squalor under the bridge came on the wind, frightening her.

If she'd been pronounced a girl nineteen years ago, she and her mother might be there among them. They would only have received a small dowry that wouldn't have lasted long in view of her mother's capricious spending.

Whores and beggars were rife in Venice since the French had sacked the city under Napoleon. By now the two of them would be huddled under the bridges like the rest of Venice's poor. Though she might have somehow managed to find a way to survive, her mother would have withered under the strain and degradation.

Ahead, the bridge-dwellers stirred, calling to a well-dressed gentleman. "Signore! Signore! Look my way."

She heard a noise behind her. Salerno? Turning back to look, she lunged forward . . .

And crashed into a human wall.

6

The golden hammer chimed eight times in the Campanile di San Marco as Raine strode down the steps of the lecture hall. He was surrounded by a half-dozen vintners who still discussed the lecture on phylloxera, which they'd all attended.

"What do you think of the French government's increasing their 30,000 franc prize to 300,000 for anyone who can produce a cure for the phylloxera?" someone asked.

"Idiotic," said Raine.

"I agree," said one of the others. "The recitation of suggestions for a curative we were subjected to was a waste of four hours if you ask me. That blasted bug will go on its merry way sucking the sap and life from our vines with no hindrance from the French from the sounds of things."

Someone else spoke up. "Still, I think the French should be the ones to pay for a cure, if anyone does. They're the most desperate, since their grapes succumbed to the pest first."

"It's not the right way to go about things," Raine insisted. "You all heard what stupid notions the offer of a reward has put rise to."

One of his companions laughed. "And the ones the French official read aloud to us were supposedly thought to be the most viable of the lot. Considering that, I shudder to imagine what the rejects must have been!"

Just then, the bishop came running up behind the group, out of breath, causing a brief cessation of conversation. Catching Raine's eyes on him, he blushed like a schoolgirl.

Raine had forgotten him until now. Surprisingly, the loquacious bishop hadn't made his presence or his opinions known in the lecture hall.

"I believe my favorite was the suggestion that live toads should be buried beneath each grapevine to leech the phylloxera from the soil," someone joked.

"What about the idea of bringing in Venus flytraps to snap up the pests," another chortled.

"No! Are you forgetting the best of them all? That young choirboys were to be sent in to piss on our vines."

Everyone save Raine and the bishop burst into gales of laughter.

"That was my suggestion, sent in to the French a month ago," the bishop protested. "I firmly believe the acid in the urine would act as a deterrent."

"Not to mention the stench," someone else muttered.

"It's an illogical suggestion," said Raine. "They all were."

"And have you a better one?" asked the bishop.

Raine shot him a stern glance. "Hybridization, as I described in the lecture."

"Didn't you hear?" another man piped up. "He was brilliant on the subject. Convinced me that the breeding of *vitis vinifera* with resistant species is the way to go."

"I must beg your pardon," the bishop demurred. "I took myself off at times during the lecture due to momentary indigestion. What was the gist?"

"Satyr posited that creating a resistant vine is the best hope for a cure," someone explained.

"Oh?" The bishop raised his brows in a way that asked him to elaborate.

"Thus far, my experiments with cross-pollination of blossoms of different species of the same genus have resulted in a hardier vine," Raine told him. "However the taste of the grape is still not satisfactory." It was an unusually lengthy explanation for him.

"Well something must be done," someone else insisted. "Two-thirds of Europe's vines have been felled. Can you imagine? It's only a matter of time until it reaches us. We all remain under a real threat until a practical cure is found."

"Yet the Satyr vineyard has been spared," the bishop said carefully.

Quiet fell. Raine could easily discern the direction of his companions' thoughts. Everyone knew the rumors. His former wife had helped to spread them, claiming he and his brothers wielded some sort of magical force that protected their lands and them from harm. It was true.

Fortunately his ex-wife hadn't convinced many. And rarely did anyone go so far as to bring up the matter in his presence. He and his brothers were wealthy and powerful, and it was wise to keep their favor.

"We had an outbreak," Raine confessed, drawing all eyes.

"And?" someone prodded.

"The affected plants were routed and the area burned," said Raine.

It was only partially true. The Satyr vineyard had in fact escaped an attack. A relation of Nick's FaerieBlend wife, Jane, had intentionally brought in the pest. But it had been she who'd helped eradicate it before it had felled their vines. And them.

For the grapes were not simply a hobby or a means of earning a livelihood for his brothers and him. The sap that flowed through the vines was entwined with the blood that flowed in Satyr veins. Healthy vines would ensure his brothers' children's legacy. Healthy vines would allow his brothers and him to live on. Healthy vines would ensure that the secret aperture between ElseWorld and EarthWorld that was hidden on Satyr land remained secure.

The bishop hurled a proclamation. "Perhaps this plague was sent from the heavens as judgment for man's sins of overindulgence. I also suggested that processions of the pious might weave through the vineyards of God-fearing believers slinging incense. Did the French consider that?"

"Men of science must scoff at such nonsense," said Raine, uncaring that he might embarrass the bishop. "Offering a reward does no good. Better that the French turn their prize money to relieving the hardships that Napoleon caused the people of Venice. They now suffer from poverty as widespread as the phylloxera."

He gestured toward the ragged beggars and prostitutes who loitered in the shadows of an adjacent alley. Mistaking his gesture for a summons, the desperate surged forward. Since the bishop was the closest to them, he bore the brunt of exposure.

"Be gone, you poxed creatures!" he cried, batting them away. Two passing constables joined in the fray, quelling those whose only crime was that of indigence.

In the confusion, Raine slipped away from the group. They'd been talking of attending a conversazioni in the salon of an exalted acquaintance nearby. But he was tired of talk. He had no patience for idle gossip and certainly no gift for conversation.

Before he left Venice behind for the night, he had but one last piece of business to attend to. Sex. Quick. Easy. And preferably Human.

When the bishop turned his attention from the fracas, the

group of vintners had dispersed. Aghast, he glanced around for
Raine.

Spotting one of the others from the lecture, he raced to catch
up with him. "Where has Signore Satyr disappeared to?"

"I would guess he is headed off along the Canalazzo to find
himself a companion for the evening. The others in our group
departed to do the same. On my part, I'm off to my wife.
Buona sera."

But the bishop hadn't remained to hear his bid of farewell.
He was already trotting down the Riva del Vin, in search of his
tall, handsome prize.

Raine made his way along the Riva del Vin, the promenade
formed by the foundations of the buildings lining the Grand
Canal's northeastern edge. The cargo of wine he'd seen earlier
had been unloaded and whisked away to be sold to restaurants,
hotels, and individual buyers in Venice and beyond.

The Rialto Bridge lay ahead, spanning the canal. On its far
side were the Riva del Ferra and Riva del Carbon, where car-
goes of iron and coal were traditionally delivered. His gondola
already awaited him there, dockside.

But he didn't signal to the gondoliers. He'd hired them until
morning and they would wait.

Soft sirens' voices crooned to him from above. The courtesans were out on their covered balconies subtly hawking their
wares even in this weather. At the sight of him, they leaned over
the decorative iron railings, fluttering painted fans and posing
provocatively.

Unfortunately his control had slipped too dangerously to
chance taking one of them. The blood of his ancestors boiled in
his veins tonight, and he was in no mood for holding back.

Because of the hermaphrodite. It was she who'd dredged up
this sudden longing to feel the warmth of Human female flesh
against him. The sight of her had revived the fierce carnal need

he normally kept tamped down. His cock had been hard ever since he'd spied her, and it craved relief.

It was on an evening when he was in just such a state that he'd managed to frighten his former wife into leaving him. It had been Moonful then, when she'd run to the neighbors with tales of his wickedness. Of his physical strangeness. Of the way he'd Changed before her eyes with the coming of the moon. Though Nick had followed her and used a mindspell to mitigate the damage, her words had set the gossips humming about Raine and his family. Regret for his part in that still haunted him.

He hadn't found his ease with a Human female since that disastrous night. Instead, whenever the moon was full and overwhelming lust drove him to the sacred glen at the heart of Satyr lands to rut the night away, he'd taken other creatures under him. Unreal creatures the Satyr could conjure at will but who felt nothing. Shimmerskins.

A week from now when Moonful came yet again, he would do the same, here in Venice. He'd find a private, isolated residence to hire for the night where he would lock himself inside, away from discovery. It was of paramount importance that he keep himself from Humans then. He'd be vulnerable.

One of the more comely courtesans on the balconies caught his eye. Noting his interest, she trailed a hand along her voluptuous cleavage to draw his attention there. At the crest of one breast, the barest hint of an areola was visible. Her finger slipped inside the fabric, swirling lazily over the nipple it concealed. The tip of a pink tongue stroked her lower lip, wetting it. Her eyelids drooped and her cunning emerald gaze watched him. Tempting him.

And he *was* mightily tempted.

The terms of such an assignation would be tacitly understood by both parties. No words would be needed. Their coupling would be fleeting, furtive. Coins rather than endearments would be exchanged as easily as bodily fluids. He only had to knock upon this woman's door to be invited into her home. Into her body.

No. He rallied his self-control and forced himself to walk on. Courtesans moved in the same social circles as he once had here in Venice. She might recognize him and gossip. He couldn't take the chance he might tarnish the Satyr family name yet again.

Raine slipped into the shadows of the buildings that lined the canal. Willing partners lurked there below the bridge.

Were he were so inclined, he could take the lowest gutter-snipe to his bed and not fear that he might contract a venereal disease. The Satyr were immune to the syphilis and gonorrhea that were rampant in the city. Which made it all the more absurd that he'd been brought down with a simple cold.

The calls of the indigent echoed over the water. "Signore! Signore! Look my way." Enticements were offered, each more lewd than the former as the inhabitants of the nooks and crannies under the bridge vied for his custom.

His eyes roved them. They were a ragtag bunch. But he could find a woman here with whom to take his ease and be done with this terrible need. There were men. Boys. Girls. All of them desperate.

He, too, was desperate tonight. Desperate for Human warmth. But his fastidious nature recoiled from seeking his pleasure with a woman from among them.

The hermaphrodite had inspired this spurt of lust in him and she would have satisfied it best. He pulled himself up short. What was he thinking?

Once before he'd set his affections on a specific Human. The one he'd married. She'd been a colossal mistake. He'd bedded her nightly for weeks after their wedding, each time in a gentle-manly fashion. Her body had brought his to satisfaction, but he hadn't been satisfied. Lying with her had only piqued his desire, and he'd gone to Shimmerskins afterward.

Such ElseWorld beings were easily conjured from the mist by males of Satyr lineage at any time or place. They were beautiful, willing vessels whose sole reason to exist was to bring him and his brothers to orgasm as often and in whatever manner they desired.

He had but to imagine an act and impart it to such a creature with his mind. Without speaking a word he could make her understand precisely what he required, and she would endeavor to please him. She would express desire with her eyes, her lips, and her body. But it would all be false, as false as she herself was. Therein lay the problem. Tonight his body craved another sort of satisfaction. Warm. Passionate. Human. Real.

But he would make do.

He turned on his heel to head toward the dock. He would take the gondola, hie back to his hotel, and summon a Shimmerskin. Maybe two.

He took a determined step away from the alley.

Suddenly, a body came crashing against his back.

The scent of Faerie blanketed him like a quick heady puff of fresh spicy air spritzed from an expensive crystal bottle. It was there, and then gone again in an instant. It was the only scent he'd been able to detect all day. And because of that he felt its impact all the more keenly.

Instinctively, he lashed out an arm and wrapped it around the waist of the person who'd blundered into him from the alley. He felt the softness of a woman encased in yards and yards of velvet and satin.

A head lifted. Black witch's eyes gazed up into his from the twin holes of a bauta mask.

It was the creature from the theater. The hermaphrodite! The answer to his prayers. He might not have recognized her if she hadn't still worn the Carnivale mask.

A sharp elbow found his ribs. He grunted but otherwise ignored it. The scent of Fey had dissipated. Had he only imagined it?

Her dark eyes were laced with fear, her breathing was fast, and her body was heated as though she'd been running. Over her head, he surveyed the streets around them. They were dark and deserted except for the occasional straggler. The Grand Canal was quieter now in the evening hours. Where had she come from?

She punched his back and elbowed him repeatedly. "Let go of me, you dolt."

He ignored her. Since no one else stood nearby, it had to have been this creature that had brought the scent with her. He couldn't take the chance of letting her go until he knew for certain.

He clasped her arm before she could aim her weapon at a more vulnerable part of his anatomy. "Hold there. I mean you no harm."

Nimble hands groped under his coat, pinching at him and poking for his crotch with hard knuckles. He turned so she couldn't reach her goal.

"Hold, I say."

She only squirmed in response. Was she Faerie or merely a comely prostitute? Or both?

"Let go of me." Her voice was cultured. Throaty. Sexy.

His cock swelled. "Who are you?"

"Who are *you*?" she countered, trying to yank herself away.

He grabbed both of her forearms. Bacchus! Though she wasn't aware of it, the cloak shifted and he caught a fleeting glimpse of a breast. Underneath, she was naked.

She tried to knee him. He angled away, causing her to tumble forward and grab at his hips for balance. Her hand lodged in his pocket by accident, ripping it.

Abruptly she stopped struggling against him. She was staring at the ground now, transfixed.

What the devil? Raine glanced down and saw that the ribbons he'd stuffed into his pockets earlier that day had tumbled free onto the tiled street.

The woman shook off his hold, knelt, and picked them up. She stood again, holding them cupped in her palms and studying them as though they were priceless treasures.

When he automatically reached for them, she closed her hands into fists and snatched them back. He caught the straggling ends of several ribbons. Winding the strands crossways around his palm until he had a firm grip, he used them to pull her against him.

The woman held on to her prize, refusing to let go. And for a moment they were linked, tethered by rainbow threads of satin. He stared into the black pools of her eyes and saw they were flecked with gold. Her lashes were cobwebby, casting shadows on the bronze cheeks of her mask. Her breasts were soft against him. His desire for her ratcheted higher.

"How old are you?" he demanded in a level tone.

She wriggled, trying to look around him, first to one side, then the other. She frowned, obviously not finding whatever it was she wanted. "Where's violet?"

"What?" Was she simple?

"You only have six ribbons," she explained, gazing at him with brittle patience as though he were the simple one. "You have only six colors of the rainbow here. Where's violet? It's missing."

"I don't know. Who the hell cares? I bought them for my sister-in-law and her younger sister," he explained needlessly, then felt annoyed that he'd revealed even that small bit of himself.

He gave the ribbons a jerk and repeated his earlier question. "How old are you?"

She shrugged, irritated. "Nineteen. What does it matter?"

Relief filled him, but he was careful. "Don't lie. I won't seek my pleasure with girls not yet become women."

"Pleasure?" She stilled, lifting her eyes to search his. "I'm nineteen," she said slowly.

He looked skeptical.

"I'm quite sure of it because today is my birthday. And how old are you?"

"Twenty-seven, as if it matters a whit. What's your price?"

Dark eyes studied him, weighing. They were beautiful, as deep and unfathomable as the lagoon. He could drown in such eyes, lose his head.

He let go of the ribbons and stepped back, feeling ridiculous. The only thing he wished to drown in her was his cock.

"Never mind," he told her. "I'll meet any price. Come if you're willing. Otherwise—keep the damned ribbons, and I'll find another woman."

With that, he wheeled around and stalked toward the docks, hoping she'd follow. Otherwise, he'd have to go back for her.

Jordan blinked, watching his tall, erect form move away.

He'd called her a woman! It was the first time in her life anyone had ever done so with such certainty.

In spite of her unfashionably short hair, and though he'd seen nothing of her body under Salerno's cloak, this beautiful man had assumed she was female. And he was seeking to engage her in some sort of carnal encounter for which he actually planned to pay her. A giddy thrill coursed through her.

She glanced to her left. From beneath the bridge, the hollow eyes of the beggars and whores pierced her. Some were sad, some greedy. All were desperate. Once the man departed, would they do her harm? The cloak she wore was obviously costly and could be sold. If they took it and her mask, she'd be left naked. Defenseless. Even if she escaped them, she could encounter all manner of dangers as she continued to make her way home alone at this hour.

Ahead, she watched the man hail a boatman on the gondola she'd seen earlier.

"I'm coming," she called, skipping after him. She quickly reached his side, tucking her hand in his.

He halted midstride, jerking away from her hold. His silver eyes were wary now. Why, she wasn't sure.

What sort of encounter did he envision between them if he didn't want her touching him? She toyed anxiously with the ribbons, wrapping them around her palm until their ends were caught under her folded fingers.

When she noticed him observing the action, she sheepishly tucked the ribbon-wrapped hand in the pocket of her cloak. Though they were his, she refused to part with them. They somehow made her feel safe.

"I'm sorry. I won't take such liberties again," she said.

He didn't comment, only nodded and turned to lead the way to the single elongated gondola at the quay. It was graceful and slender, with a gondolier on either end and a boxlike cabin in the center that enclosed the passenger seats.

Called a felze, the enclosure was decorated with ornately carved gilding. With their convenient doors and windows on every side, such compartments were used either to display or conceal as the occasion required.

In the spring, their doors and windows would be flung wide for happy brides seated within, fresh from their weddings, in order that they might display their finery to well-wishers along the canal. Jordan had observed many such brides with envy, noting their sparkling eyes, and splendid lacy gowns. Paulo and Gani had studied them as well, offering ribald speculations about the wedding night each bride's husband would soon enjoy.

At times, a felze proved a useful setting for those intent on crimes of kidnapping or even homicide. With its doors safely secured, appointments and meetings between members of the nobility also took place there.

But more often, as tonight, the privacy such a cabin offered was used for another sort of assignation. A carnal one. The sort this man was offering.

"Back to my lodgings," he instructed the boatmen.

They took his orders and paid her no attention, no doubt assuming he'd take his pleasure with her inside the felze during the ride. They were accustomed to the peccadilloes of the wealthy customers who rode in their conveyances, especially those wandering Venice at night.

The fact that there were two oarsmen meant they were in for the long journey across the lagoon. That meant he didn't reside in Venice proper. All the better.

He turned and offered a hand to her, to assist her onto the boat. It was a commonplace gesture any gentleman would unthinkingly offer to a lady. But no man had ever offered her his hand before. How delightful.

She smiled brilliantly at him and placed her fingers in his, softness slipping into strength.

Somewhere behind them in the piazza, she heard the tap of footsteps. Salerno? She took no time to further savor the signore's gesture.

The gondola rocked awkwardly under her weight as she hopped aboard, scurried past him, and ducked into the felze.

He followed her and the door shut behind him, cloistering them both in near darkness.

7

Back on land, a lone figure scampered to teeter on the edge of the quay. Nearly dancing with frantic anxiety, the bishop watched Raine's gondola glide under the bridge. And away. There were no other boats to be had at this hour and his quarry was escaping!

His prick tortured him with thoughts of what Satyr and the one he'd procured along the canal might do together. Had he chosen a man or a woman? He hadn't gotten close enough to see, but the manner in which Satyr had handed his acquisition into the gondola indicated she was probably female.

If it was a quick fuck Satyr wanted, he'd have been only too glad to provide his own backside for his use. More than glad. He dreamed almost daily of such an event occurring between them. Had imagined playing mate to Satyr with every fuck he administered to another less-deserving body. Until he found his chance with Satyr, he would let no one else's flesh violate his own ass with fleshly instruments. His pristine rectum—defiled only by the occasional dildo or other handy object—would one day be his gift to Raine Satyr's cock.

He spied something lying on the dock below his foot and picked it up, fingering it. A ribbon. Violet colored. It was precisely the color of his zucchetto, the bishop's cap. Earlier, he'd noticed such ribbons peeking from the pocket of Satyr's trousers.

He held the two ends of the ribbon, one in each hand. Stretching it taut, he sawed the rain-dampened satin lengthwise along his lower lip. It was an omen, a tease. It must have been left behind for him, as a sign not to give up his chase.

The gondola was lost from sight now, in the mist. No telling where Satyr was lodging tonight.

Picturing him entangled in a carnal embrace with another body was nothing short of torture. He'd give anything to be near him, to join with him, lie with him. To fuck his mouth, his ass. Lick every inch of his muscled body. To touch his lips to his. To take his cock and his jism down his throat and up his own ass until he nearly strangled on them. He would welcome all Satyr had to give and plead for more.

Frustration welled up in him, sending the sting of bile into his throat. He grabbed his prick through the robes. It was rigid and hurting. Burning as though seized by a thousand vile demons. Syphilis was his affliction, a doctor had told him several years ago when he'd examined the small painless red spots that had appeared on the bishop's rod. Those and the rash on his palms and the soles of his feet had been his only trifling symptoms back then.

What had begun as minor sores a year ago had become irritated lesions, then tumors. Now his case had advanced far beyond his cock to addle other parts of him as well. A few months ago, the doctor had said the sickness was beginning to pollute his mind as well as his body. But it seemed to the bishop it was actually elucidating a great many things. Bringing greater clarity, day by day.

Suddenly, it came to him what he must do. With Satyr lost to him for tonight, he would find another in whom he could vent his frustration.

He turned back and made his way toward the alleys, where sex of every kind was cheap, easy, and anonymous.

The hermaphrodite had made him hard, but he'd been unable to ejaculate in the theater using only his hand. His cock required another sort of stroke. But he must go carefully. No one in the Church must learn of his cravings.

The cries of the impoverished throngs who dwelled beneath the bridge reached his ears, luring him like the devil's disciples they were. The hermaphrodite undoubtedly sprang from among the ranks of such malingerers. It was its fault—their fault—he now craved relief.

He located a fellow of Satyr's general stature and build from among them, and with a jerk of his head herded him toward a deserted, twisting alley. His maniacal stare warned others away as he followed the tall man he'd selected into the darkness.

Murmurs of "Faggot!" pelted him from behind. But the insults bounced off his robes. He was no faggot. He was one of the successors of the apostles with thirty priests under his direction. A humble worker in God's vineyard. One of the most respected men in all of Tuscany.

"What's your pleasure?" the man he'd chosen asked. His voice was dead, hopeless. The bishop liked that.

The man's face was handsome enough, and intelligent, though somewhat haggard. His trousers were fine quality, but worn and dirty. He probably cheapened himself in this way to provide for a family who'd once lived in high style. Yes, the bishop likely had Napoleon to thank for this particular piece of ass. He'd left Venice in tatters. Patrician families had sold off paintings, furnishings, and jewels at a fraction of their worth to make ends meet. Now some even sold their bodies.

"My cock. Your ass," the bishop told him.

The man nodded tiredly.

The bishop found a sequestered place in the alley that would allow him to keep his eyes peeled for trouble while he took what he needed. With the man's assistance, he shoved an old wooden barrel he found there into the position he desired. Then he slipped the cincture cord from his waist.

He strung the cord through a metal ring secured in the wall on the far side of the barrel. It had been used to hold horse reins at an earlier time in history but was now rusty from disuse. The bishop snapped the ends of the cord tight, testing the sturdiness of the ring.

"Give me your wrists. I'll use this to tie you."

The man regarded him, dubious. As well he should be. But the bishop kept his expression bland and unthreatening. His easy manner combined with the dignity of the vestments he wore never failed to woo the fearful to his way of thinking.

"I seek to bind you only enough to keep you from mischief. You'll be able to get loose when I'm done with you, but I'm not taking any chances you plan to thieve in the meantime."

"I'll have your coin first," the man hedged.

The bishop held his money out. A brief flare of interest lit the man's eyes at the sight of it.

"Half now. More if you please me," the bishop lied smoothly.

The flicker of life in the man's eyes died as he took the coin, tucking it in his shoe. Unceremoniously he shoved his trousers to his ankles, bent forward over the barrel, and allowed the bishop to tie his hands to the metal ring in the wall.

When all was arranged to his satisfaction, the bishop stood back to enjoy the debasement of his victim. His cock twitched under his robes as he eyed the rump offered up to him. It was sleek and blatantly masculine, its flesh glistening dully. He ran his hands over it again and again.

Then he dipped his fingers through the man's legs to squeeze his ballocks and soft prick. The man jerked and let out an anguished moan. Here in the shadows it was easy for the bishop to pretend he caressed another man. A beautiful man with eyes of silver. One who had escaped him tonight.

Thoughts of Satyr lifted the bishop's rod ever higher. He fumbled under his robes and pulled it out. The sores that riddled it stung and burned, inflamed.

His hand found Satyr's violet ribbon, and he grinned, tying it around the root of his shaft in a lovely bow. He stood for a second, admiring his stumpy, infected cock and his own twisted sense of humor.

"I've got a nicely wrapped present for you, Satyr," he crooned. Sliding a finger up the man's crack, he located the dark crimped hole he'd purchased use of for a single coin. It screwed itself tight under the pad of his forefinger.

With the thumb side of his palms he stretched the skin on either side of the vertical cleft, forcing the ring wide. A forward flip of his hips slung his cock high to flop in the crease. He pulled back until his tip poked at the ring. The man's hands clenched on the cord that held them, and he braced his legs for what was to come.

"Beg me," the bishop murmured, squeezing a buttock cheek in each hand. "I want you to beg."

The man hesitated, then, "Fuck me," he muttered halfheartedly.

The bishop savored the man's shame. "Again. Say it again. Over and over."

"Fuck me! Fuck me!"

With an unholy curse, the bishop rammed his fat, ungreased meat between the man's buns.

Under him, his victim yelped.

The sound pleased him. "Beg me for more, my darling. Say, 'Fuck me harder.' Say 'It's good.' "

"Fuck me harder. It's good," the man gasped.

He slapped the man's rump, hard with the flat of his hand as though he were on horseback and whipping a recalcitrant mount. "Say it like you mean it. Make me believe you want it and there'll be even more coin than we bargained."

"Oh God," the man said, groaning with humiliation and pain. Injecting reluctant enthusiasm into his voice, he complied. "It's good. You're so big. Fucker."

The bishop widened his legs. For leverage he grabbed the edges of the barrel on either side of the body under him. His balls slapped and flopped between his beefy legs as he bucked harder and harder.

The man's back arched and he tried to dance away. "Give it to me hard. Si, that's it. It's good. Oh God."

"That's it, my love," the bishop soothed. "You want it, don't you, Satyr?"

"Yes!" the man cried, almost hysterical now.

"You want me. You want me fucking you. You want my cum spurting deep inside you. Say it. Beg."

"Yes, fuck me harder. Give it to me. I want you. Ram it up my ass, you godless animal. Just fucking finish for pity's sake."

"No! That's not right. You must want it!" the bishop raged. He felt the painful ball of cum struggle its way through his diseased cock. "Sss! Fuck!" His bellow of agony echoed in the alley as he deposited his poison up the man's rectum.

The pulses were staccato dribbles that scorched him like hellfire. Spilling was not the treat it had once been. The bishop's displeasure fell on the flagging substitute beneath him. His hands slid up the naked back and found the man's throat. And squeezed.

"No! I have a family!" the man protested, yanking at his bindings. But he was tethered well enough to give the bishop an advantage. The man's flailing lessened, growing fainter as plump hands squeezed tighter, wringing the life out of him.

Moments later the bishop withdrew, shocked at what he'd done. Before him the man's limp body listed to one side of the barrel, his hands still tied to the ring.

An insistent drizzle began, dampening his robes and his spirits. "No one must know," he breathed, hurriedly straightening his clothing. "No one."

He fled, frightened. A gust of wind whipped his violet-colored zucchetto from his head. But he ran on, distancing himself from what had happened. The cap tumbled into a puddle. It would lie there unnoticed until morning when rumors of a cleric murderer would begin to circulate among those unfortunates that frequented the alleys and docks.

Just blocks from his hotel, the bishop fell to his knees to beg forgiveness. The downpour began again in earnest, soaking him. Taking it to be an omen that this sin had been washed away, he staggered to his feet and scurried on.

By morning he had convinced himself that the devil had entered him through that degenerate in the alley. Yes, all his actions had been the man's fault. But he dared not linger in the city. He would take himself back to Tuscany and do penance for days or perhaps weeks.

Until the urges rose again and the cycle repeated itself.

8

The interior of the gondola's felze was dim and private. The perfect setting for intimacies.

In the confined space, the man across from Jordan loomed larger now than he had on the street. More compelling. She felt the subtle pressure of his sexual interest. What was he thinking as he sat there so silently, his arms relaxed along his thighs?

Her eyes found his hands. They were long fingered and strong, though not beefy as Salerno's were. Somehow, she knew he would not hurt her with them. Her skin tingled with the need to feel their touch.

She felt herself sway sideways to the left, then slowly sway back toward the right. The gondola was making its way out of the second curve in the backward S shape formed by the Grand Canal. Leaving behind pastel-colored Byzantine and Renaissance buildings, it slid stealthily out into the lagoon.

"Where are we going?" she asked softly, so as not to shatter the velvet darkness.

"I've taken rooms in the Arbruzzi Palazzo on the Lido," her companion murmured. His voice, too, was low.

"Where Byron stayed."

The man's brow lifted. A lantern swayed on the serrated iron point of the gondola's prow, dancing light and shadow over him. He faced the bow and she the stern, so she knew her features would be less easy to read.

"The English poet Byron. He vacationed there five years ago," she explained. "All Venice was agog at the presence of such a dashing, mysterious visitor. People lined up each morning to watch him take his daily horseback ride."

"And did you line up?"

"I saw him once," she said, omitting the information that the occasion on which she'd done so had been at the author's instigation. He'd come to view her one September in Venice when she was on display and then only fourteen. He and his entourage had requested an exlusive showing and Salerno had been only too happy to oblige.

She recalled that Byron had been writing a work called *Childe* at the time, which he'd discussed with her. Though he was charming and far too handsome, he was self-absorbed and she hadn't liked him.

The lights of the city, which splintered starbursts through the rain-spattered windows, dwindled as they made their way from shore. Behind them the San Marco piazza quickly faded from sight as they were swallowed into the night and the lagoon.

Her companion half stood and lowered the gauzy drapes, effectively shielding them from the boatmen but still allowing light to permeate. The windows to the side admitted the cool mist that drifted off the water.

It was as though they were together in their own mystical world. She didn't know him. Didn't want to know him beyond tonight—beyond the pleasure his body could provide if he proved willing.

The glow of the lighthouse on the Isola di San Giorgio Maggiore slowly came into view on the starboard side. Time was fleeting. She was missing a golden chance that might never come again.

Slowly, Jordan eased forward off the seat and sank onto her knees before him. His hands fell to the cushioned seat and he altered his position, making room for her between his legs. Encouraged, she shaped his kneecaps with tentative hands. Bravely, she slid her fingers along the hard muscles of his thighs, eventually meeting at their juncture. The bulge there was thick and hot, even through the fabric that encased it.

Her gaze found his. "You want me. As a man wants—a woman."

Molten silver flickered. He gave her the briefest of nods.

Her eyes held his as she learned the contours of him through his trousers. High between her legs, Jordan pulsed for want of him. She moved slightly so that the back of her heel pressed against her core, trying to find surreptitious relief.

The manipulation her body had received at the hands of Salerno and his cronies was rough and unkind. But it had stimulated her even as it shamed her. After such events as tonight's, she was always left angry. And longing for fulfillment at the hands of other, kinder men who surely might better know how to treat a woman.

"What service would you like me to perform?" she asked, getting to the heart of the matter.

Across the compartment their gazes met and locked. Outside, the gondolier softly called out to another boatman they passed, but other than that only the rhythmic echo of the oars and the slap of the sea sang to them.

The air was almost totally black now, and she could barely discern his features. And that meant he wouldn't be able to see her well either, she realized happily. She wasn't ashamed of her body. But she wouldn't take any chances. She didn't want this beautiful man to look upon her with disgust. She didn't want his beautiful mouth to hurl insults at her and call her a monster. Not tonight. Tonight she would be his ladylove, the woman he desired.

"What do you suggest?" the man returned, crossing his arms and slackening his thighs even wider for her. He seemed reluctantly amused by her blatant eagerness.

Her pulse thumped with erratic hope and fear.

"Are you looking for quick pleasure?" She lowered the cape and let it pool at her waist, wanting his gaze on her.

His eyes hooded and she sensed something shift in him. Something succumb. He seemed to relax into the romance of the night and into the pull of her desire for him.

9

Raine stared at her. At those dark eyes that were too large for her face and that pointed chin and slender throat. At those round, wine-tipped breasts that would scarcely fill his palms yet were perfectly shaped. The rest of her body was lost to him, obscured by the cloak bunched at her waist. But he remembered exactly what was hidden beneath its velvet folds.

Under her hand, his taut cock thickened, lengthened. Bacchus, yes, he wanted her to pleasure him.

"I want to taste you," she whispered.

His eyes went to her mouth. It was plump. Moist. The same color as the tips of her breasts. The same color as finest rosé he'd ever concocted from the sacred juice of Satyr grapes.

Without conscious volition, he felt himself nod.

What the hell was he doing? She hadn't even touched his flesh yet and he was on the verge of losing control.

Was she Faerie or whore? he wondered again. More than likely the latter. He shouldn't let her work her wiles on him, regardless. Wouldn't let her. He should tell her he only wanted her company, nothing more. He should tell her so. Now.

But he desperately wanted the warmth of a Human woman against him as he found his release tonight. So he hesitated.

He studied the top of her head as her hands searched and found the opening of his trousers. She struggled over the fastenings for long moments and then let out a huff of air.

"It appears to be stuck on your c— Um, I mean your phallus," she told him.

His lips quirked at her use of such a formal term. His hands preempted hers, finding and making quick work of the fastenings. He opened the front of his trousers wide and pulled his cock free of their stranglehold.

Her blue-black witch's hair hung in loose waves ending just short of her shoulders. It wasn't as long as most women wore theirs. Nevertheless, it was shiny, lush, and beautiful, as was she. He smoothed it back, his fingers catching on the string of the bauta.

"Take off the mask," he said.

Without hesitation, she slipped it off and flung it away on the seat behind her, then dipped her head before he had a chance to make out her features. The tips of her raven hair dusted his inner thighs as she leaned over him.

He closed his eyes, waiting. Wanting. Imagining the feel of her wet mouth sucking at him.

He felt her warm breath first. Then those luscious, pillowy lips descended on him like the kiss of heaven. The O of them slicked over his crown, firm yet soft. She enveloped him to the ridge of his head and then tugged ever so slightly. The firm point of her tongue found and pressed at his cumslit as her thumb massaged the plinth where it was notched.

Bacchus! Where the fuck had she learned to do that?

He braced his palms flat against the felze walls on either side of him to keep from touching her. To keep from holding her head and ramming himself in and out of her the embarrassingly few times it would take for him to spill.

Slowly, her mouth slid lower over him, taking more of his length. And more. And still more.

His head fell back. Bacchus, she was good at this! She knew exactly how to hold him on the flat of her tongue, curling the sides of it around him, using every inch of its moist sandpapery warmth to stroke him.

She took him deeper. He felt his tip squeeze into her throat. And tunnel deeper still. She was small—how in the hell was she taking so much of him? There was no reflexive gagging. If he didn't know better, he'd swear she truly wanted this, relished it in fact.

Ridiculous. No woman wanted this. It was an act only whores offered, in exchange for payment. She had no doubt done it in just this way for many other patrons before him and had thereby polished her performance. That was all.

"San Lazzaro Degli Armeni," the boatman's mournful voice announced. They were nearing the Armenian monastery on an island just this side of the Lido. They were getting close.

He was getting close.

Cum gathered, hardening his balls to boulders. Raine gritted his teeth. His hands fisted, straining against the side walls of the felze. He wanted this rare pleasure to last. Dammit. He would control it. Make it las—"

Milky semen surged its way up his cock, fighting its way free of him. "Gods!"

It shot from him, hurtling into her throat. She jerked back from him and a second blast hit her mouth and cheek. She put her fingers to her lips, smearing the glossy substance as though surprised to find it there. Yet another spurt of cum spattered her chin. She swirled her tongue over it and then took him back in her mouth. Her hands clenched in the fabric of the trousers bunched tight across his hips. Her throat worked as she accepted and swallowed the rest of what he pumped. His slick desire flooded her, drowning her in his solitary pleasure.

Slowly, slowly the tension in his body subsided. Her mouth began to release him. Her hands massaged him gently in the wake of her retreating lips. Attuned to his mood, her touch grew ever softer, lazier. When her tongue grazed his crown, he flinched and cupped her chin with his hand, drawing her away.

"Sensitive?" she asked, lifting her gaze to his.

His eyes sharpened but couldn't permeate the darkness well enough to make out her features. He nodded, brushing a thumb over her cheek. He wanted to tell her how good it had been. How unusually good. He wanted to tell her.

But he couldn't find the words and the moment passed. Reason returned and he straightened, glad he'd kept his feelings bottled in his throat. He didn't like to remember how much he'd wanted her just moments ago. How much he'd needed her. The loss of control seemed like a failure.

He found himself hoping she would prove to be the one he sought. That would mean he could have those lips on him again and again for all of his days. His cock reinvigorated at the thought.

Still, he reminded himself—if she proved not to be Faerie, his only duty to her would be the payment of coin at the end of the night. If she wasn't the second daughter of King Feydon, he would let her go. And forget her.

"Arbruzzi Palazzo," the gondolier announced distantly. They'd arrived at their destination, the Lido, a strip of land that protected the lagoon from the ravages of the Adriatic Sea.

She picked up her bauta from the seat behind her where she'd placed it, preparing to put it on.

Raine gathered himself and refastened his trousers.

"You'll come to my hotel?" he asked. If she refused, he'd have to take her there by force, then bespell her to wipe her memory of it later. He couldn't let her out of his sight until he'd regained his olfactory abilities and could test whether she truly was Faerie.

Her fingers stilled on the mask, then she put it on and raised her face to his. "For how long?"

"The night, possibly longer." Depending on how long this cold fouled his nose.

"You want to lie with me."

Bacchus! He'd never wanted anything more in his life. He nodded curtly.

"And you plan to pay me?"

"Name your price. It doesn't matter."

"You're wealthy then?" she asked.

"Yes."

"Very wealthy?"

"Yes."

"But not Venetian. I've not seen you before."

"No. From Tuscany."

10

Good, thought Jordan. He wasn't local. Still, did she dare accept him?

He reopened the drapes in anticipation of their arrival. She surveyed him in the increased light, feeling braver within her mask than she might have without it. His dark clothes and hair were severe in style, yet within the bounds of current fashion and fastidiously kept. His throat rose as a sculpted masculine column from his starched collar. His jaw was strong, rigid, and dusted with the blue-black shadow of his evening stubble. His lips looked soft and were well shaped. His cheekbones were high and flushed from the effects of her recent tipping. Like a sundial, the strong blade of his nose cast a shadow across his face.

But his eyes were what drew her. Heavily lashed, they were an unusual color—that of the surface of the lagoon on a stormy morning. Though whatever turbulent storms raged within him were now tightly leashed.

This handsome man believed her to be a woman. A woman who appealed to him enough that he wanted to employ her for an entire night of debauchery in his hotel chambers.

This man—this beautiful man—was offering to put that huge cock of his, which had so recently been in her mouth, between her legs as well. If she went with him now, he would lay her down on his bed and push her woman's slit wide with it. It would tunnel deep inside her, and deeper still, until it was fully seated.

What would it feel like? Deep within her secret core, she yearned, wanting to find out.

Would he stroke her to orgasm with it? Was it even possible for her strange body to achieve one? Her cock had spilled many times, always in her sleep. But she'd never yet had a woman's orgasm.

Due to the years of poking and prodding by medical men, she wondered if she had been disfigured internally in some way that made such an occurrence impossible. If Salerno caught her again, he might ruin her beyond redemption.

This man might be offering her the only chance she'd ever have to experience a pleasurable joining as a woman. And she wanted it. How she wanted it. This one night. Together with this man.

But what if, in the course of such an encounter, he discovered that her body was a blend of both man and woman. What then? Things could turn ugly.

Still, she couldn't seem to make herself refuse him. Rationalizations sprang to her mind like weeds in a garden of good sense. She could hide what she was from him, she told herself. Take what she desired. All she had to do was set some rules to ensure he did not discover the truth.

"Very well. For the night then," she agreed at last.

The gondola had slowed to a standstill. It lurched once, then twice, as both of the gondoliers leaped off, preparing to tether the boat to land. Nervousness fizzed in her.

"However I wish to set some rules for our engagement," she added belatedly.

The man nodded, not questioning what she meant. Stepping outside, he reached to assist her from the felze.

A thrill coursed through her as she put her hand in his. She stored his gesture, as she had the previous one. It fell into a chest of treasured memories she would save from the events of this evening to be pulled out, examined, and cherished in leaner times.

Together they dashed through the drizzle and entered a palazzo. Far taller and broader than she, he sheltered her from the wet as best he could. Never in her life had a man offered her the protection of his body. Another gesture to cherish, later.

A door opened and her thick shoes clunked across a fine, marble entry. The sound was masculine and hard. It sought to puncture the bubble of the happy feminine vision of herself she'd temporarily created in her mind. How she wished she could kick them off.

A deferential voice welcomed him. She lifted her gaze, wanting and yet afraid to see how she was being judged here—as a man or a woman.

But there was no confusion in the proprietor's face regarding her gender. He turned a blind eye to her; obviously assuming she was a courtesan or perhaps a whore. One the man who held her wanted in his bed tonight. A wealthy, handsome man of good family, who was so desperate to have her that he was willing to pay. Even with her short hair, awful shoes, and her voluminous cloak, she felt desirable, feminine. It was exhilarating.

Her lover-to-be kept an arm around her, and she kept her head tucked into him as they mounted a magnificent staircase. Peeking from the hood of her cloak, she viewed the passing paintings and urns of flowers. Gilding glistened on the balustrade. The impression of opulence was definite but fleeting as she was ushered upstairs.

It was humid and still inside his rooms. She craved the wildness of the storm outside to match that in her heart. Without asking his permission, she opened a latch and swung a window wide, letting the sounds and smells of the rain flood the room.

She kicked her offensive shoes into a corner and turned to see him preparing to light the candles.

"No more lights," she told him. "The torches outside are enough."

Silver found black through the semidarkness as he hesitated, then blew out the taper. "Take off that blasted mask."

She shook her head. "My rules tonight, remember?"

He came to tower over her and draw his hands along her upper arms from shoulder to elbow and back. "Keep the mask then. But take off the cloak."

She wrapped the cloak closer and stepped away. "Not yet."

He set a hand at one hip. "Perhaps you should explain exactly what these rules of yours are going to entail, so that I may better plot my course with you."

"First, give me your shirt," she instructed.

Without quibbling, Raine released his top buttons. Then he crossed his arms, grasping the front tails of his shirt from his trousers and lifting the garment over his head. One by one a flat belly, narrow waist, and wide sculpted chest appeared as the pale linen drew ever higher.

His head was briefly obscured, only to emerge from the shirt when he slipped it off, revealing broad shoulders. Lightning flashed and his well-defined muscles danced in shadow and light as he worked his arms free of the shirt and tossed it away.

He ran fingers through his rain-dampened hair, combing it into dark furrows. Jordan took his shirt from where it had landed on the bed and turned her back to him.

Beneath Salerno's cloak, she managed with some difficulty

to work his shirt over her. Her head popped from its neck and her arms slipped through the sleeves to emerge from the cuffs, which she rolled to her elbows. Tugging, she pulled the tails low, until they fell just short of her knees.

In contrast to the sodden cloak that smelled of her nemesis, the linen shirt was white, crisp, and clean. And it smelled of him—sexy-warm and masculine.

Dropping the offensive cloak to the floor, Jordan noted the stains on it where she'd used it to wipe her chin and cheek free of his spill in the gondola. She wondered if semen would irrevocably stain velvet and satin. One could only hope. She kicked it away, into the corner by her shoes.

With her back still toward him, she fumbled below the shirt, wrapping one of his ribbons around her cock several times and tying it off. Threading another ribbon through that one, she looped the second satin length around her waist and tied it fast.

"What's your name?" Raine asked.

She eyed him over her shoulder.

A corner of his mouth crept higher. "Sorry. Is that question against the rules?"

She shrugged and pushed the shirttails low again, hiding her nether regions before she turned to face him. Her body was hidden now except for her shapely legs, dainty wrists, and the line of her throat visible in the deep V dipping from the neckline where she'd left the shirt unfastened.

"Jordan. It's Jordan."

She didn't give him her sire's name and was glad when he didn't press for it. And she didn't ask his name. It didn't matter. They were only passing a night together. Once the storm abated, they would part forever as strangers.

"Will you take me from behind?" she asked him. "Not as a man takes another man. But as a man takes a woman, I mean."

"If you prefer," said Raine. She didn't want him to know how her body was formed between her legs, he realized.

Though he wanted to touch every part of her, he would let her keep her privacy for now. At least until this cold deserted him and he could determine whether she was to be a permanent fixture in his life.

Jordan nodded. "Yes. It's what I prefer. What I insist upon."

"We'll call it a rule then. For tonight."

"Yes. A rule."

Under his shirt, her cock throbbed and bucked against its restraints. Though she'd tucked it tight and high against her belly, and trussed it in the ribbons she'd taken from him earlier, it yearned to participate in their lovemaking.

"Kneel on the bed," he told her.

His silver eyes tracked her as she climbed on the mattress to stand on her knees. She gazed back at him from beneath her lashes.

He removed his boots. Then his trousers. His movements were methodical and unhurried, even under her frankly carnal stare.

As he approached, she studied the shaft between his legs with the same thoroughness as the artist had studied hers earlier that night. Since she had neither the artist's talent nor his charcoal at hand, she sought to imprint the picture of this man's body in her mind instead of on vellum.

She'd seen cocks before. Paulo, Gani, and even she had sometimes whipped theirs out to piss in the streets, when the three of them had been out raising hell after dark. But their cocks had been nothing like this man's.

Like a pendulum, it swung solid, thick, and long between his legs. It was easily twice the size of her own phallus in every dimension. Veins pulsing with fevered blood grew fat and juicy along its length like gnarled vines sprawling up a tree trunk. The crown they reached toward was bulbous, with an unusually pronounced ridge separating it from the shaft itself.

High between her legs, her slit contracted softly, wanting him more than ever.

Over her shoulder, she watched him move into position on the mattress behind her. She wanted to memorize everything about him. Everything about this night, so she could call it to mind another time in the future.

His eyes were intent now and covetous. Within moments, he would invade the aching woman's cavity of her body with that hot, impressive cock. She shivered, anticipating it, wishing this precious moment—this night—could last forever.

The mattress depressed as he knelt close behind her, between her legs. His body warmed her back, bottom, and inner thighs.

His broad hands found her hips under the fabric of the shirt and then slid upward inside it to learn the shape of her breasts. She rested her hands flat over her phallus at first, making sure no errant touch of his would make its way there. Long moments passed. His handling wooed her, lulled her.

Her arms moved behind her, dipping under his and between their bodies. If he made any sudden moves toward her belly, she could thwart him quickly enough, she reasoned. And she longed to explore.

Smoothing her palms over him, she stroked the unforgiving hardness of his thighs and felt the light, masculine down that dusted them. Her elbows bent and she grasped the velvet muscle and bone of his shaft that rode high against her buttock. Skin stretched taut and smooth over its straining proportions. At the crown she found a pearl of pre-cum and spread it with her thumb.

A foolish, ravenous craving for his seed to take root in her tonight swept her. However, it was fortunate that the chances of conception were slim to none. If she were somehow to conceive, how would she care for an infant? Her mother would pressure her to abort it when she found out lest the Cietta family learn of it and turn them both out.

Still, she silently, stupidly yearned.

Raine left her to her investigation of his body. His lips found the juncture of her neck and shoulder, tasting her there before easing higher along the vulnerable slope of her throat. Her skin was warm, soft.

Within the shirt, his hands roamed her back, surreptitiously searching her shoulder blades and the sleek muscles on either side of her spine. His survey netted nothing. There was no fragile cartilage or down to be found there. Not even vestiges. Odd. Her half sister—Nick's wife, Jane—had them. Hers could burgeon into full-fledged, hollow-boned wings during times of deep stress.

Nevertheless, Jordan's lack of them was not especially telling. Not all of the Faerie sported wings. In fact, most did not. However, the absence of them was regrettable since their presence would have simplified the task of determining whether she was of Fey blood.

Without such promising evidence, he must proceed on the assumption that their coupling would likely never be repeated after this night. He must drink his fill of her. He must take enough of her to last him through all the nights ahead when he might find it his duty to mate with another less-desirable female chosen for him simply because Faerie blood coursed through her veins.

Between them, her facile hands were roving, blindly massaging his cock, knowing just how and where to touch.

He turned his lips into the fragile skin just below her ear and inhaled. Fifty hells! For a moment, he'd forgotten his cold. Because of it, he couldn't scent her, even this close. Was she indeed a daughter of King Feydon, with the blood of ElseWorld in her veins? He wanted to know. Now. Before he joined his body with hers.

Without his highly developed sense of smell, his work at the vineyard would have been impossible. But he hadn't realized how much he'd come to rely on it in a sexual context, too. The scent of an aroused female body excited him. *She* excited him, and he wanted to know her special fragrance.

Under her handling, his cock had grown heavier and hungrier. Her fingers knew exactly when and how to apply pressure. When to go softly and when to be firm. He wanted her to stop. He wanted her to go on forever.

He was suddenly glad she'd chosen this position for their mating, so she wouldn't read his desperation for her in his face. When had she begun to set the course of their situation? It was making him uneasy. He sought the familiar comfort of taking control.

His hands slid low between their bodies. Taking one of her hands in each of his, he bent forward over her, forcing her to bend with him, then pressing her palms to the bed in front of her so she knelt on all fours.

Behind her, he rose to his knees and slid his fingers up the backs of her thighs, lifting the tails of the shirt she wore to uncover her bottom. It was neatly divided like the twin curves of a ripe peach. He took it in his grasp. Her hips were narrow, just the width of the span of his two hands.

"You have the hips of a boy," he murmured in a voice that was an octave lower than normal.

She tilted her rump to nuzzle his cock. "Is that a complaint?"

He swallowed. "No. I only meant—you're small. I'll go slowly, but the fit between us may be uncomfortable for you at first. I don't have any cream, or oil."

She shook her head. "It doesn't matter. There's cream enough. It was introduced inside my woman's passage earlier tonight."

He remembered. He'd watched it happen, in the theater. Why had she allowed it? For money? For the same reason she was allowing this to happen between them tonight?

He slipped a hand between them and the tip of a finger grazed the root of her cock. She gasped and reached to stop him, no doubt worried he'd discover it.

But his fingers merely worked back toward himself, tracing her delicate folds until he pierced her vaginal slit. His broad forefinger pressed between it, then slipped easily inside to test her channel's readiness. He plumbed deep, feeling the cream he'd seen men from the audience in the theater deposit in her.

"I'm not your first customer then?" he asked.

"I suppose you could say that," she said, arching into his touch.

Raine nodded, adding another finger so he fondled her with two. Other men had invaded this passage tonight just as he was. He'd seen them do it. But she was still tight. Perhaps too tight for fucking. Her body was made differently than that of most women. He'd have to go carefully.

She gasped and hesitated uncertainly when he eventually added yet a third finger, trying to stretch her. "Oh, that's— mmm."

"Easy," he murmured, gentling his strokes until she relaxed into his rhythm again.

How much had those men paid to touch her like this, he wondered, watching her rock on him, engulfing his fingers to the base of his knuckles and then darting away. Did she really want his touch inside her? Had she wanted the touches of those other men? Had she taken cock here, as well as hands and fingers, in the hours since he'd seen her onstage?

Her channel had turned juicier now and was sucking at his fingers like a babe at its mother's breast. He pulled his slick fingers from her and took his ruddy cock in them. His tip nuzzled her feminine slit, wetting itself in her sluice before ducking just inside. Breath expelled between the grit of his teeth at the feel of her taking him. She was warm. Human enough to soothe the beast in him that had clamored for the embrace of Earthly flesh tonight.

His hands found the bones of her hips to anchor her as he pressed steadily forward. Her unusually plush labia pillowed his length as it slowly passed into her chasm. Now and then, her trembling tissues balked at the induction of so much fullness. He prayed her body would take all of him.

She was still now, braced and quiet under him. Her entire being seemed focused on the point where his body was joining itself with hers.

He paused, retreating, then returning only as far as he'd already delved. "Are you all right?" he managed to ask.

"Mm-hmm." She flexed her knees, pushing back against him so her body gulped several more inches.

The move surprised him and his control slipped, just enough. In a single lunge, he went the rest of the way home, ploughing her deep and hard. His strangled shout mingled with her cry. Of surprise or pain?

"Are you all right?" he asked again.

"Yes, I think so."

"Then, I'll—"

"Hold a moment. I feel so full of you. Let me set the pace at first."

A muscle snarled in his jaw. He hoped he could withstand whatever she had planned.

A few seconds later she made a tentative push–pull movement. Then a few more. Pulling too far forward, she lost him. "I'm sorry. Would you—?"

He stuffed himself back inside her before she could finish the sentence.

"Thank you," she said politely. "Now hold still and let me try again." She shoved inexpertly back on him, then pulled away. Back. Away.

What new woman's torture was this?

"Mmm. I can feel the ridge of your crown moving along inside me. It's wonderful," she breathed. "More wonderful than I could have imagined. How is it for you?"

"Me?" He cleared his throat. "It's fine." Bacchus, what an understatement.

Her tissues fondled him in careful, measured drags. He stared, hypnotized by the sight of his dark reddened rod ducking in and out of her wet cave. His hands turned restless on her lower back and rump.

After a half-dozen strokes, she pulled away, almost losing him again. She looked back at him. "I'm ready for you to help now."

With white knuckled fingers, he grabbed her hips and resheathed himself.

"Um, that's so good," she told him. "What do I feel like to you?"

"Like a woman," he replied without thinking.

"What a lovely thing to say," she whispered, sounding inordinately affected.

Somehow, he'd managed to stumble upon the answer she seemed to want, though he didn't know why it had pleased her so. The nuances of conversation escaped him as always.

Taking control, he pumped himself in her hard, from need as much as from a desire to head off further discussion. His eyelids drooped and he turned quiet, determined to prolong his enjoyment of this fuck.

"Oh yes. It's—oh." She moaned and sighed, each feminine sound ratcheting his desire to hear the next.

He hunched over her, planting an arm on the mattress alongside hers, so they rode together on all fours flesh to flesh, his chest to her back. The flat discs of his nipples dragged on her skin. He turned his face into her hair, trying to catch the scent of her. It was agony to remember that he couldn't know her in that way tonight. Longing welled up in his chest. Even if she proved not to be the one he sought, he was determined to take her under him again at least once after his senses returned to him.

Beneath him, she moaned and caught her breath in those little feminine sighs and pants. He found himself moving in ways that seemed most likely to elicit such sounds from her. Without conscious thought, his hand roved lower, reaching for what he knew was hidden and bound high against her belly. She caught his questing fingers, forcing him away from what he would investigate.

Frustrated, he slapped his palm to the mattress and began to fuck in earnest. Long strokes took him from her brink to her core, measuring her depth and seeking to extend it.

Around him he felt her vaginal walls start to ripple and shiver. Was it from true enjoyment or was it a well-rehearsed whore's trick meant to lure him toward quick release? Regardless, it was effective. His balls quivered, lifted, tensed.

The padding of her bottom shuddered now as he heaved into her like some sort of brutish animal. Her arms straightened and her fists clenched in the bedlinens to brace herself. Head up, she arched her rear into each impalement, opening herself to his plunder and meeting him with a hard slap of moist flesh.

He widened her legs, moving impossibly close between them. Her inner muscles gathered, holding him in an ever-tighter shimmying grip that heralded her orgasm. At last, she gave an inarticulate cry and he felt her seize on his cock in a convulsive, almost painful rhythm as she found her woman's pleasure.

His balls jerked, preparing to shoot their contents up his shaft. His swollen cock reared inside her, tensing, straining . . . toward . . .

Like a mindless, rutting bull, he came, shooting his hot syrupy jism fathoms deep. As it gushed from him in pounding syncopation, her channel milked at him—sucking, squeezing, then releasing, in a sort of carnal peristalsis. With each of his spills, breath left her in a harsh inarticulate puff.

As the last pulse of cum left him, he sneezed suddenly, shoving himself deeper and wringing one final spurt of seed from his cock. Her shoulders slumped to the bed and she moaned.

His hand cupped her belly, prolonging their union. In the aftermath of their passion, he had no cause to worry. He'd sired no bastards in her. It was impossible on a night such as this.

Satyr such as he could fuck themselves witless all month long spreading their seed far and wide without repercussions. The danger of procreating was a concern during one and only one particular night each month—that of Moonful. Only on such a night in the hours from dusk to dawn, when the moon hung fat and round, could he impart fertile childseed in a woman. If he wished. For even on that night, which was most sacred to the Satyr, he could choose whether his seed would be potent.

He ran his hand over the resilient flesh of the woman he'd just plundered.

He would never, ever give his childseed to any woman. Not even if she became his wife. The very idea cast a pall over him. Pulling from her, he stood and left the bed. Behind him, she wilted to the coverlet as though she were a finely wrought ice sculpture slowly melting under a pale autumn sun.

He located a square of linen and cleansed himself at the basin, watching her. She curled onto her side and drew her knees high, squeezing her legs together as though to savor the sensations that still pulsed between them.

If she was indeed Faerie, this night was a momentous initiation. His mating of her signaled the beginning of the protective spells he would weave around her over the coming months. The protection was weak now. But each time they coupled it would strengthen around her. Eventually, it would prove strong enough to safeguard her against whatever forces King Feydon had suspected might harm his daughters.

She lay unmoving on the mattress, silent. Her eyes were closed and pleasure shaded her features. At least those he could see beyond the mask. One of her hands lay palm up alongside her head. The other rested high between her legs still cupping her genitals.

At length, she sighed and opened her eyes. Her gaze found him across the room.

"There's a pitcher here," he told her. "And a separate basin."

She rose and came to the washstand. He heard the clink of porcelain and the splash of water. He glanced over his shoulder. She had her back to him and was washing between her legs and higher toward her belly.

Had her cock ejaculated? His own cock, still rigid and thick even after coming, surged at the thought. But he'd give her time before he took her again. And he would take her. How many times could he do so tonight without hurting her, he wondered. Twice more? Thrice?

"Can we do it again?" she asked.

His head snapped up and his eyes met her hopeful ones. Gods, yes! He came to stand before her. His hand headed purposefully toward her abdomen, wondering if she'd let him explore this time. But she caught him, mating her palm with his and folding their fingers together to keep him at a distance.

She shook her head. "Please, in the same way as before?"

His eyes narrowed. "If you wish. But I assure you that you need not hide for no feature of your body will shock me."

She didn't believe him. It showed plainly on her face as she shook her head again and gave him her back. "The same as before."

"Very well." His hands reached from behind to shape her breasts under the shirt. He cupped their weight, one breast in each palm. They filled his hands to perfection, supple and cooler than the rest of her heated body. He ran his thumbs over the crests, pondering as something puzzling struck him. Through the fabric of the shirt, he'd seen the tips of her breasts were still their natural pale wine color. Once successfully mated to a lifemate, the breasts of a Faerie generally took on a glow of another hue.

But she hadn't faked her pleasure. He'd mated enough Shimmerskins to know how to gauge false passion generated by a woman determined only to bring him to orgasm while taking no pleasure herself.

Did the lack of color in her breasts mean she wasn't the one he sought? Or did it only mean that for such a change to occur, she'd have to unbind her shaft and let her passion break free of restraint.

"Rest your arms on the windowsill," he told her. When she complied, he quickly drove into her wet woman's slit and began to fuck. Her throat arched and she braced herself as he rode her once again, his desire as great as though it were their first time. The coolness of the storm battered them both, tangling her hair.

"Oh! Oh God, you're good at this," she told him. "It's even better this time now that your seminal fluid is inside me from before."

Seminal fluid? He could guess where she had learned such clinical terms. Salerno.

She chatted her way through their lovemaking, describing how he was making her feel, telling him how glorious it was, making him feel the hero simply for fucking her.

Whore's tricks, he told himself, as they lay on the bed much later that night. All meant to make him finish as quickly as possible. And they had worked.

"Will you summon the gondoliers?" she asked sleepily.

"In the morning." Pulling her back into his chest, he curled around her on his side. "Rest now."

"Umm. No, I have to go."

But she was exhausted and fell asleep against him. He ran a palm over her smooth back—the back that had no wings—and wondered if she would prove to be King Feydon's child.

Wondered if he could keep her come tomorrow.

11

Achoo!

Raine woke up the next morning to the realization that although his cold hadn't left him, his companion of the previous night had.

He drew a tentative breath and discovered his nose was at least marginally clearer than it had been last night. Carefully, he inhaled again . . . seeking.

"Twelve hells!"

Enough of his sense of smell had returned to tell him one thing. His bed reeked of Faerie.

Mind racing, he leaped out of bed, grabbing for his trousers. First he'd summon the hotel proprietor and determine what he and his staff knew of Jordan's departure. Then he'd go back to Venice to find that fellow from the theater last night—Salerno—and ask what he knew regarding the whereabouts of his so-called subject.

Someone pounded on his door. He glared at the doorknob, remembering he'd locked it last night with his mind. It should have prevented Jordan from leaving. How had she gotten away?

"Who do you suppose it is?" a feminine voice whispered from behind him.

His head jerked around to find Jordan huddled in the pale shadows that shrouded the far corner of the room. She was still here. He was appalled at how relieved he was.

Her damp, wrinkled cloak was draped around her, obscuring the beautiful body that had pleasured his last night. Her mask remained in place, though it had become crumpled during the night, lending her a somewhat inebriated look.

He tossed his trousers aside and went to her, surprising her by taking her in his arms and burying his face in her neck. He inhaled deeply, breathing in her scent, analyzing it.

Every Faerie's glamour was slightly different. He nuzzled her, exploring the nuances of hers. There was a sweetness tempered with potent spice—cinnamon and clove warmed by a woman's flesh. The mixture was exhilarating. Addictive. There were other fragrances as well. It would take time to discern them all.

A heady euphoria swamped him as he realized there was no doubt now. She was Faerie. King Feydon's second daughter. The one meant for him.

The knock sounded again, growing more insistent.

Jordan turned her throat to give him better access. Her fingers lazily traced the muscles of his back. "Aren't you going to answer the door?"

"No."

"Why not?"

"It's my mother," he muttered.

"Your mother!" she squeaked, shoving him away. She pulled the cloak closed at her throat with both hands as she darted a quick glance at the door. "How do you know?"

"I can smell her perfume a mile away," he informed her.

"Aren't you going to let her in?"

"No." He reached for her again, drawing her into his embrace and this time drawing her hand down to his swollen cock as well. "I don't think she'd appreciate it, considering what she might witness."

The knock came yet again, this time as a fierce rapping. "Raine!"

Jordan scuttled away from him, looking scandalized. "I can't do *that*—not with your mother just outside!" She wrapped the ridiculous cloak even tighter.

Something about her expression made him want to laugh. But he was too annoyed at the interruption. Throwing on a robe, he headed for the door.

"Wait!" Jordan hissed, springing toward the small dressing chamber that adjoined his room. "Don't you dare open that door until I'm out of sight."

"Stay where you are." Raine tied the robe and then snatched the door to the corridor open with obvious irritation.

A woman dressed in emerald bombazine stepped inside without asking for an invitation. She swept him with her severe gaze, her expression indicating that she'd expected to find him lacking and did. It was clear the woman was related to him. She had the same high cheekbones and regal bearing. Gray eyes, too, though hers were far duller than his. And where Raine came across as remote, this woman was cold.

"How lovely to see you, Mother. May I introduce you to my friend, Jordan."

His mother shot Jordan a sour look. "Has Carnivale come early this year?" she said, noting the mask. "Silly me. I thought it had been outlawed altogether."

Then she ignored her as though she were a newel post and addressed only Raine. "I would speak to you in private. And for pity's sake, put on something more suitable."

Raine responded by folding his arms. The silence in the room grew weighty.

Jordan walked to the dressing room door. "I'll just slip in

here so you two can have your privacy." Once in the other room, she put her ear to the door crack, listening.

"You look well," the woman offered.

"What do you want?" asked Raine.

There was an annoyed pause. Though it hardly seemed possible, the woman had stiffened further. "Very well. I'll be quick in my purpose. It's your father—or rather, my husband. He has disappeared."

Raine's hands fisted. "And?"

"I was hoping you'd locate him."

"Why come to me?"

"Because you have the nose of a bloodhound. If anyone can find him, you can."

"Ah! So the nose you once condemned proves useful at last. How ironic."

His mother smoothed her unwrinkled skirt. "Please don't dredge up old business, Raine. Now, I have an inkling who your father may be with."

"Who?"

She hesitated. "I can trust you to keep silent on this matter. Can't I?"

Raine shielded his eyes with his impossibly long lashes.

Silent. You must keep silent. How often had he been told that as a boy, when he'd known things he shouldn't and told of them? He'd soon discerned that not everyone knew the things he did and that his knowledge made others uncomfortable. So he'd learned to keep silent.

A scene from boyhood flashed through his mind . . .

He'd been thirteen years and three months old. He and his father had been preparing to visit the stables, when his mother had entered the room, bringing a waft of her own special scent. Without thinking, Raine had turned to her, worry creasing his brow.

"You're bleeding," he'd told her with soft concern.

"What?" She stepped back from him, perplexed. "No, I'm not."

"Between your legs," Raine insisted.

Flattening a hand high over her skirt as though to hide the place where her thighs met, his mother had stared at him. "How dare you!"

His father had been stunned into silence.

Confused, Raine had stilled, knowing he'd said something wrong again.

Then his mother's soft hand whipped out and struck him full across the face. "How did you know that, you spawn of Satan?"

Raine touched his blazing cheek, hurt in more ways than one. He'd only spoken the truth. His mother was bleeding. He was worried about her.

He turned to his father. "What I say is true. Someone should see to her."

For a long moment, his father's eyes had searched his. They'd slid over Raine's strong jaw and beak of a nose, studying the boyish face so unlike his own florid, plump one. He'd surveyed Raine's tall, muscular body as though seeing it for the first time, noting his height, which had already surpassed his own stocky stature.

He'd always claimed he was proud to have fathered such a fine physical specimen as his only son. But now suspicion crept into his eyes.

He turned to Raine's mother and read the guilt in her face.

Raine stared, knowing he was the cause of the sudden tension between them but not understanding.

"Is it your woman's time?" his father asked her, his voice low and accusing.

His mother nodded.

"How did you know?" his father asked him then.

Raine spread his hands and looked blank. "I just know."

He'd heard the question so many times over the past months. Had seen the strange, fearful glances directed his way, since he'd turned thirteen and gained this strange ability.

How did he know a visiting clergyman had eaten haddock for breakfast? How did he know the rag picker in the lane had a rotten tooth? How did he know where the blacksmith had hidden his coins? How did he know the butcher had lain with a woman other than his wife? How did he know the cat had captured a bird that morning?

The answer to all those questions had been the same: he could smell the evidence of these things of course. Couldn't everyone?

In fact, his olfactory abilities were improving and refining as each day passed. At any given moment he could analyze the air and discern a variety of smells. He scented the upstairs maid's arousal when she studied his body. Smelled the mold growing in the cellar. Smelled the seeds sprouting under the soil.

But after he'd blundered in speaking of his mother's bloodtime, he learned to keep silent about such things. Though his parents never spoke of the disturbing events of that day again, something between the three of them had shifted. Trust had been eroded.

Another month passed and Raine kept quiet regarding other physical changes that had begun to worry him. For he'd begun to waken each morning to find his penis stiff and so swollen that it ached.

One dawn, out of desperation, he comforted it with the stroke of his own fist. In seconds, it seized and shot juice from its tip, soiling his sheets. It had proven such a pleasurable relief that he'd begun milking himself into spilling thereafter as a daily event.

Ashamed and confused, he wanted to know what it all meant. But the unfortunate episode with his mother and father was fresh in his mind. So he mentioned this new pastime to no one.

Nevertheless, as the days slid one into the other, he'd felt a storm gathering within him. He found himself drawn to watch the waxing moon each night with an agitated anticipation. Its pull affected him in the same way it did the ocean, building waves of sensation in his body, day by day, night by night. All toward some unknown goal.

When the moon eventually rose full and hearty as a perfect O of light, it almost seemed to call to him. To lure him toward some preordained destiny.

He'd gone to the window to gaze upon it. When its light drenched him, he felt a hard knot form an inch or so above his penis. He'd ripped his trousers open and pressed at the bulge with his hand. Something was pushing at the skin of his abdomen, from the inside. It twitched under his fingers for hours. But by morning, the knot was gone. The storm had dissipated within him as well. Relieved, he mentioned it to no one.

As the months passed and other full moons rose, he grew desperate when the knot reappeared. It was embarrassing, painful, and frightening. Still, he bore it all in silence.

That is, until the night the knot started to force its way out of his skin. Knowing that a full moon was to rise that fateful evening, Raine had been itchy all day, unable to settle or perform his lessons.

Once twilight fell, he'd been driven to gaze into the night's inky shroud, waiting. When the full moon had eventually shown itself, the torturous knot had formed again as he'd expected. It was bigger this time, and its eagerness to emerge from his pelvis had turned fierce. Abruptly, he felt his skin begin to part for it.

Terrified, he'd gone to his parents where they sat in the salon on either side of the fireplace.

"I'm having a baby!" he'd blurted.

His father had set aside his journal with a violent rustle and his mother's needlework had dropped to her lap.

They could not have been more astonished. But then he

shoved his trousers down and the twitching knot had erupted from his pelvis.

His father stood so abruptly that his chair fell over backward. His mother covered her mouth and turned red as a fever victim. They'd been flabbergasted. Appalled. Disgusted.

Raine looked down at his belly and saw it was not a baby that had poked from him. It was a second penis, slightly smaller than the first one that always swung between his legs.

"God in heaven! This is my doing," his mother had wept.

His father's brow darkened and he turned on her, his expression vicious. "Do you have something to tell me, wife?"

She paled, her expression guilty.

"Pull up your trousers, boy," his father bellowed.

Raine had obeyed, hiding yet another part of himself that made him so different from everyone else.

"Is he mine?" his father had growled.

"Of course," said his mother, drawing herself up.

But Raine had smelled her fear. Her lie.

Somehow, his father had sensed it too. Cupping Raine's shoulders, he'd brought him to stand between himself and his wife, not as a buffer but as a wedge.

"I ask you to reconsider your answer, my dear," he'd told her. "If you lie again, it will go ill for you and *your* son."

Raine's mother's lower lip had trembled. Then a damning confession had tumbled from her. "I'm sorry. As you've guessed, h-he was fathered by another man."

"I see." His father's fingers flinched on Raine's shoulders, then he'd given him a hard shove in the direction of the door. "Go to your bedchamber until you are called, boy."

Raine went. And waited. But he wasn't summoned that night. Nor for breakfast. He wasn't called until noon the following day. And then, it had been two servants unknown to him who'd come. They'd packed his belongings and then escorted him to the waiting family carriage.

His father had explained nothing to him. He had simply ridden his mount alongside the carriage, escorting him out of Venice. In due course, they'd arrived at the Satyr Estate, at one of a trio of castellos that lorded over Tuscany like a fiefdom. Beyond it lay fertile forest, vineyards, and groves that were the envy of the entire region. But Raine hadn't known all that at the time.

When his carriage and his father had entered the courtyard, a man had joined them there as though he'd expected them. He was tall, strong, and somehow familiar.

Raine inhaled, searching for his scent. Surprised that he couldn't find it, he'd moved closer, but still found it impossible to detect. He'd gazed into the older man's eyes, curious.

Eyes much like his own had stared intently back into his. A strange sense of belonging had encompassed him.

"My whore of a wife has borne you a son, Lord Satyr," Raine's father had announced. "Raise him or turn him out, it makes no difference to me. But keep him from my house. He's tainted by the devil. No doubt you'll find him to your liking."

Then without another word, the only father Raine had ever known deposited him with strangers. He'd left all the rest to be explained by Lord Satyr, who was in fact Raine's true blood father.

"You are welcome here," the man had told him, "as my son and heir." And he had been.

Raine had met his two half brothers, Nick and Lyon, that same day. All three of them had their father's blood and the blood of a human mother flowing in their veins. Only Raine was a bastard, with a mother other than his siblings.

It had been the last time he'd seen either of the EarthWorld parents who had raised him to age thirteen.

Until today.

12

"Out with it, Mother," said Raine. "Whose bed is your husband in and what do you propose that I do about it?"

The woman's eyes spit fire, but her cultured voice remained calm. Through the crack in the doorway, Jordan studied her, fascinated. How she'd love to perfect that technique.

"Very well," said his mother. "As you've guessed, he has been keeping company with yet another strumpet. I want you to find him and bid him return home before the gossips get wind of it."

"Do you have the name and location of this so-called strumpet," Raine inquired, "or am I to go door to door asking if any trollops are in residence who might have an extra gentleman in their bed?"

"Signora Celia Cietta. That's the slut's name."

In the other room, Jordan gasped. Raine's father was keeping company with her own mother?

"Stop eavesdropping, Jordan, and come join us," Raine demanded, glancing toward the dressing room.

"All right," said Jordan, refusing to be embarrassed at being caught out. When she turned the doorknob and stepped into the room, Raine's gaze swept her before turning back to his mother.

"I doubt your husband will listen to me—after all, I am . . . what did he say the day he threw me out? Ah yes, it comes back to me now—a spawn of the devil," said Raine.

His mother fidgeted under his stare and a cold silence fell. Swathed in her cloak, Jordan observed the interplay between him and his mother with interest.

"However, I'll help you under one condition. My friend— Signorina . . ." Raine looked to Jordan in question.

"Alessandro," Jordan improvised.

"Signorina Alessandro requires some clothing," Raine went on. "Several dresses. And . . ." He floundered.

"Accessories?" Jordan supplied.

Raine nodded. "Yes. Whatever a signorina of nineteen requires in the way of garments and such. Entire outfits, head to toe."

"What has that to do with me?" asked his mother.

"In return for my help, you will take her measurements before you depart this room. You will then take those dimensions to the finest shops in Venice and see her outfitted by this afternoon."

Jordan and his mother stared at him with equal expressions of shock.

"And—" Raine's voice rose, stifling his mother's protests. "You'll not ask questions."

"But acquiring all that is needed to improve this creature by this afternoon is an impossible task," his mother insisted.

"Not for one of your social standing, surely."

The woman glowered at Jordan, appearing loath to touch any part of her for fear of contamination. "Very well," she huffed at length, tugging off her gloves. "I'm no dressmaker. However, I'll do my best to take her measure."

"No," said Jordan, stepping back from the soft lady's hands that reached for her. "You'll have to guess at my sizes."

Raine's knowing gaze sharpened on her, but he didn't insist.

"Good grief," said the woman, pulling her gloves back on with a disgusted jerk. She handed her son a note from her handbag. "Here's the address of the strumpet's home. I'll have the packages of whatever garments I can locate for your *friend* delivered here to your hotel as soon as I'm able. It will be more convenient than having you visit me to collect them."

"Yes, I'm sure it will be," said Raine sardonically. "What would the neighbors think to see me return from the dead? You did tell them I was dead after you turned me out of your home, did you not?"

His mother made a show of straightening her hat before speaking. "Let's not get into that, Raine. It does no good. You may send me a message regarding the outcome of your task once you have completed it." She moved to the door, where she turned and pierced him with her gaze. "Don't fail in this, Raine. You owe me. I've lost much because of you."

Raine turned rigid, his expression fairly dripping icicles.

Once his mother had departed, Jordan had a thousand questions. But the look on his face kept her silent on all but one. "Why in the world did you ask her to buy clothing for me?"

Before he answered her, Raine re-opened the door and spoke to a servant in the hall, ordering a bath.

When he stepped back inside, he shut the door and locked it. "I'd like you to accompany me on the errand my mother requested. You'll need more to wear than a cloak, a mask, and those ribbons if we're to return to Venice."

Jordan glanced down to discover herself stroking the ribbons she'd taken from him last night, almost as if they were worry beads. She stared at the colorful strands she'd dreamed of so often. The ones that had led her to him.

Gazing at them, she remembered what had awakened her this morning. Dreams. They were new, confusing, and expected. Once the third and final prophecy of a series of dreams came to fruition, another series always invaded her slumber to take their place. Night after night, this new set would recur until they too were realized.

As usual, last night's dreams had come to her in three parts. In the first a brilliant white dove had appeared. It had been beautiful, slumbering on its back, with its wings widespread.

Next came the four legs, each encased in blue stockings. And last of all had come the snake. She shuddered, chasing the thought of it away for now.

"And then what? After the clothes and the errand I mean," she asked.

Raine came closer, tucking a lock of hair behind her ear and making her shiver. "I enjoyed last night. If you're not otherwise engaged, I'd like you to travel with me as my companion to my home in Tuscany. You'll require clothing there as well." His eyes slipped over her. Though it was the briefest of studies, she felt it almost as a physical touch. "Most of the time."

She folded her arms and edged away from him. She'd embarked on a new path last night, one of independence that she hoped would lead her away from male domination. She would not place herself so easily under another man's thumb.

"You just assume I have nothing better to do? That I'm free to go with you to parts unknown merely to frolic in your bed at your beck and call?"

"Aren't you?"

Though she was glad he didn't question where she lived, whom she'd be leaving behind, or why she'd been naked under the cloak last night, it still annoyed her that he so cockily imagined her current existence in Venice to be worthless.

She shook her head. "Last night was a singular event. I can't go with you. I know nothing of you, nor you of me."

"I'm Raine Satyr, the middle son of the three Lords of Satyr."

Her eyes widened.

"I see you know my family by reputation."

"Not really. But the Satyr name is quite familiar."

"Ah, then only the vaguest gossip has reached your ears. Let me endeavor to fill in any gaps in your education. We're wine-makers. I'm wealthy enough to keep you in good style. My family home is secluded, in the country where no one will bother us."

She waved a hand to encompass him from head to toe. "So you're affluent. Handsome. Intelligent enough to know you could hire twenty escorts more suitable than I. What do you want with me?"

"Companionship."

"And sex?"

He nodded. "On occasion."

He was asking her to be his whore for as long as he required her to be. She had to admit the idea was tempting. He still assumed her to be female. If she went with him, she could live as a woman. Wear a woman's clothing. Be addressed as signorina. She longed to agree to his proposal, if only for a few weeks. Just until Salerno gave up searching for her.

No. Such thinking skirted the edge of self-destruction. If her identity were ever discovered and revealed, her mother's house of cards would tumble. And what if he discovered the truth of the body he'd been bedding, as he eventually would? He might be angry. Very angry.

"Now it's your turn," he said. "Who is your family?"

At last the questions came, but she was ready. "I'm alone," she lied smoothly.

"How did you come to live on the streets?"

"My father died before my mother gave birth to me," she began, sticking close to the truth so as to make it less likely she'd be caught out. "When I was born a girl instead of the male heir my mother hoped for, she was rendered destitute. The family wealth was entailed away, and she considered me a great disappointment as you may imagine. Then . . . she married a . . . tailor. I grew up in their home, of course, but then . . . she and her husband left Venice recently and I wasn't invited along with them. I found my own way of surviving."

"So you're new to the streets," Raine said.

She nodded.

"You won't last long there, you know. You'll succumb to disease or mayhem. My offer will extend your life."

She shrugged. He was likely right, though he didn't know the whole of it. Both the streets and her home seemed unsafe at the moment.

Even now, Salerno might be sitting in her mother's salon upon the delicate French chaise Celia recently had re-covered with a satin fabric depicting winged faeries and frolicking nymphs. His complaints about Jordan's premature departure from the theater last night would fall on sympathetic ears. Her mother would never see her side, never listen to the litany of indecencies and invasions Salerno had exposed her to over the years. Even if she managed to convince her mother not to send her back into his clutches today, he would come for her again, a year from now on her next birthday. And her mother would send her off with him, after yet another lecture on obedience.

Perhaps escape with this man was her best hope of avoiding such an ongoing fate. He would take her far from Venice, where she could make a new beginning. But she couldn't leave her mother without a word. It would be cruel. For all her faults, her mother loved her in her own way, and she would worry.

A knock sounded on the door and a bath was brought in.

"Delay your decision," Raine suggested. "We'll bathe, breakfast, and await the arrival of your clothing."

While she bathed, he went downstairs to confer with the

hotelier on some matter or another. In his absence, Jordan availed herself of the chamber pot, then retrussed her cock and borrowed another shirt and some trousers from his baggage. He smiled when he returned and saw her ridiculous getup, but said nothing.

Fortunately, it turned out that his mother was as good as her word. Within hours, boxes filled with dresses, hats, gloves, and the like arrived.

Jordan oohed and ahhed over everything. Pulling out each of the three dresses that had come, she held them against her, one by one. Two were muslin and the third was made of chintz with two rows of flounces around its hem.

"Oh! They're lovely. Look at this lace and this stitching."

Raine eyed her face rather than the pile of feminine gewgaws. "My mother has impeccable taste."

Jordan threw the gowns onto the bed to rip into yet another package. "And just look at these adorable hats—straw with velvet ribbon and a silk one trimmed with ruches and ostrich feathers. And the slippers. Two pair, one high and one low. Oh! And they fit!"

Raine relaxed into a chair, his booted feet up on an ottoman. Though he held a book in one hand, he didn't open it. Instead he observed her frenzied enjoyment of the gifts his mother had procured, a slight smile playing on his lips.

She dug through the remainder of the garments like a pirate surveying newly acquired booty. In due course, she pulled a final item from the pile of tissue and held it up.

"A corset," she whispered in reverent awe. Though it looked like a device of torture, with its threaded back and boned sides, she instantly adored it. For the short time she would assume the guise of a female while under his protection, she wanted to experience everything other women took for granted.

She dashed into the dressing closet, where she divested herself of his clothing, and shimmied into a chemise and a muslin petticoat edged with embroidery. Then she returned to him, holding the corset.

"Help me with this," she told him, pulling it over her head and giving him her back.

Raine frowned. "You're slender. A corset hardly seems necessary."

"I want it," she insisted. "Please?"

He set his book aside and came to stand behind her. His hands methodically worked at the corset until it was fully strung.

"It's too loose," Jordan complained, looking down at herself when he was done. "It should push my breasts up. Like this," she said demonstrating with cupped hands.

He sighed. "Very well."

Laboriously he restrung it, cinching it tighter this time. "How is that?"

She took a few tentative, shallow breaths. "It's like having a great vise around my lungs."

His lips curved. "Sounds delightful."

She grinned back at him and then went before the mirror, studying the effect the corset had on her figure with approval. "It brings to mind the time I was swimming in the lagoon and dove so deep my lungs were gasping for air."

"I don't believe I've ever met a woman who has been swimming out of doors," he commented.

"Or at least not one who would admit to it," she said, not noticing when his lips widened further.

She slipped one of the muslin dresses over her head and had him fasten it up the back. Then she swished back and forth, watching the skirts sway around her. Cool air brushed her ankles and wafted higher along her legs.

It occurred to her that in trousers, the privates between one's legs were neatly tucked away and hidden from sight. But under their skirts, most women wore no trousers. No underwear of any sort.

She knew this of course. What was or was not under a woman's skirts had been a source of ongoing interest to Paulo and Gani, and she'd joined in their speculations on such things as a matter of course. But she'd never considered what it must truly be like to dress as a woman until now.

How easy it would be for a male hand to slip under one's skirts, to slide up an ankle, a calf, a knee, a thigh. And higher still. All in a flash. Such clothing made a woman vulnerable.

She picked up the pins that had come wrapped in another package and began pinning up her hair as she'd seen her mother do to her longer tresses many times. In the privacy of her room, she'd often played at arranging her own curls, imagining herself to be getting ready for a ball of some sort.

Tucking her hair under the more sedate hat of the two, she studied her reflection. "I look damned good."

Her companion's bark of laughter drew her eyes to his image in the mirror behind her.

"Spoken like a true lady," he said.

She stared in surprise. His eyes were twinkling and one side of his mouth had lifted to form the slightest of dimples in his cheek. It was the first true amusement she'd seen on his face. It transformed him from merely handsome to gloriously, magnificently handsome.

"Damned right," she told him. She was surprised at how easily a flirtatious grin settled on her lips. Perhaps feminine wiles would not be so difficult to affect, now that she looked the part of a woman.

At her lengthy stare, he seemed to come back to himself. The dimple disappeared and the taciturn man of early last night returned.

"However, the mask detracts from the overall look," he told her pointedly. "And it could bring trouble when we venture back to Venice since the Austrians have outlawed Carnivale and anything associated with it."

Jordan touched her bauta with uncertain fingers. She hadn't yet decided if she'd go with him to Tuscany. But she would go with him to Venice at least. And there, she could not wear the mask by day without attracting unwanted attention.

Watching his reflection, she slowly untied it and then let it drop to the floor.

"Well?" she asked, fidgeting when he said nothing.

He shrugged. "Well what? You're beautiful, but I'm sure you're aware of that fact."

Beautiful. He'd called her beautiful. Another precious treasure to store in that mental trove that she'd begun since meeting him.

"Naturally," she told him, lifting her chin. "But I never tire of hearing it." Smoothing the sides of the gown over her cinched waist, Jordan surveyed her reflection. She could only imagine her mother's shock when they met later this morning. *If* they met.

When he went downstairs to make arrangements for their transport to Venice, she scribbled a note.

> *Dearest Mother,*
> *Do not search for me, nor worry. I am safe and will return home when the time is right.*
> *J*

She would let fate decide whether she'd remain in Venice. Once Raine departed the gondola upon their arrival there, she would go on her own to the rear entrance of her home off the alley and assess the climate within the household.

If Salerno was in residence, she would anonymously deliver the note to a servant and depart Venice with her companion, never having made her presence known to her mother.

If it turned out that Salerno wasn't there, she would simply remove her hat, cover her gown as best she could with the crumpled cloak, and sneak up to her bedchamber. The servants were used to her wild ways and her comings and goings at all hours and would likely think little of this new escapade.

Raine would no doubt have gone to ring at the front entrance of her home. Once upstairs, she'd change into trousers and await his departure. Not knowing where to find her when he returned to his gondola, he would have no choice but to quit Venice without her.

Her lover returned, and in the mirror his lips moved, forming words. What had he said? Hastily folding the note, she turned and raised her brows in question.

"What have you decided?" he repeated. "Will you accompany me on my errand?"

She nodded. "I'll go with you. And I'll take the clothes as payment for last night. But that's all I promise for now."

He inclined his head in acceptance of her terms and held out his arm. "Come then."

13

The morning was bright and sunny and the trip across the lagoon too quick. Nervous, Jordan filled the cabin with conversation, drawing her companion out with her teasing. She later couldn't recall what subjects they'd discussed, but the time had slipped by and the trip had rarely been so swift.

They both grew quiet as they approached the city, each hardly noticing or wondering at the other's reasons for introspection.

When the boatmen took a wrong turn along the canal, Jordan wanted to tell them there was a quicker way to the Cietta home. But of course she didn't. The boat ultimately found its way and docked alongside the piazza that led to her residence.

"I'll wait in the gondola," she told Raine, "while you tend to your business."

"Come with me," he countered, holding out his arm. "I'm dismissing the gondola. We'll travel on from Venice by carriage."

She hadn't considered this eventuality. Having no other choice, she took his arm, fully intending to give him the slip at some point.

Side by side they walked across the piazza. With each sway of her skirt, chilly morning air wafted under it, forming goose-bumps on her legs. The ribbons of her bonnet chafed under her chin. The lace at her bosom scratched. She relished every single annoyance. For this uniform was the outward evidence that announced to passersby that she was female.

She gazed boldly at a group of gentlemen who passed and read the surprise in their eyes. A woman's gaze should be more timid, she realized. Used to the freedoms allotted to men, would she find such new restrictions too constraining? Would she be a woman long enough to find out?

Her home and twenty others stood like pastel pillars encircling the piazza. In front of her door, there was no sign of Salerno's carriage. Instead, a horse had been reined there. When they drew closer, she saw its saddle bore a constable's insignia.

All thoughts of her plan flew from her mind. Alarmed, she darted up the front steps, ignored the knocker, and opened the front door.

Raine followed her up the steps. Eyeing the doors' handles, which were shaped like some metalworker's idea of what a faerie looked like, he said, "Haven't you ever heard of knocking?"

Jordan caught herself up and sent him a guilty look. "I didn't think. The constable. Aren't you curious to know what's going on?"

She dashed ahead, her slippers tapping across the polished wooden floor.

However Raine came to a halt the moment he stepped into the house. Everywhere his glance fell, it found faeries, nymphs, flying cupids, elves, pixies, and sprites. They frolicked, flew, and flitted, gracing every swag, every drape, every candelabra, every chandelier, every everything. Stunned into silence by the plethora of winged decorations, he could only stare.

His nostrils flared, catching the scent of other living presences in the house. The closest one was male.

And swift upon the heels of these warm, living scents came another, colder odor. That of death. Of a Human woman dead only a few hours. He lifted his eyes to the top of the stairs.

"Damndest thing, isn't it?" a nasal voice inquired.

Raine's attention snapped from his thoughts to see a constable not ten feet away studying the room's décor. The man rubbed the bronzed breast of a winged nymph, shaking his bald head. "Someone in this house loves the wee folk, wouldn't you say? They're even molded into the brass of the chamber pots. It's bizarre."

Jordan could have told them why. Her mother had had a dream on the night her only child had been conceived. A dream that she'd been visited by the king of the Faeries. She'd told Jordan the story from the time she was a baby.

On a special night when her father had been far from home and her mother had slumbered alone in her bed, this Faerie king had delivered a very special gift—Jordan. Or so the tale went. The dream had been a vivid one, and Jordan had loved to hear it. But it had become her mother's obsession, and the decoration of their house had suffered as a result.

"Lord Raine Satyr with business for Signora Celia Cietta," Raine announced in a clipped voice. "And you are?"

Recognition of the Satyr name and all it entailed straightened the constable's spine. "Constable Maci. May I inquire as to what sort of business?" His tone had become deferential, telling Jordan that her companion wielded more power than she'd realized.

"The private sort," Raine replied.

"I see. And this is . . . ?" the constable asked, nodding toward Jordan. He slid a pen and a notebook from his pocket.

"A relative," Raine told him. It was true in a sense. They both had ElseWorld blood.

"Yes, of course." Constable Maci eyed Jordan slyly, quickly discerning their true relationship. "Your name?" He dipped his pen into her mother's crystal inkwell as he directed the sharp question to Jordan, then waited with his writing instrument poised above his book.

"Signor . . . Signorina Alessandro," Jordan fibbed. "May I ask why you're here?"

He scribbled the information before answering obliquely. "An investigation."

"Of what kind?" Jordan persisted.

The constable glanced between the two of them. "I'll get to that in a moment. First, were either of you acquainted with the Cietta family?"

"Not at all," said Raine.

"Yet you just entered this home without knocking?"

"That was my fault," said Jordan. "I saw your horse outside and I was curious. Has there been some sort of crime here?"

"Patience, patience. For now, it is important that you answer my questions. Now, precisely how do you know the Cietta family?"

"As I've already explained, we don't," Raine said irritably.

The constable sighed, then tapped his quill pen on his upper lip, considering him. "Very well. Come with me."

Jordan turned to follow him to the second floor.

Raine grasped her wrist. "Wait down here."

She shook her head, causing her inexpertly arranged hairdo to slip a bit sideways. "No, I'm coming."

"Stay behind me then. Something is off here," he warned.

Her eyes searched his, growing worried. As she had the night before on the dock, she slipped a hand in his, too trusting. This time he didn't rebuff her, but only folded his fingers around hers.

The stench of death grew more powerful in Raine's nostrils as the constable led them upstairs, then along a hallway. Suddenly, he flung a door open and extended an arm, beckoning them inside. Raine stepped into the bedchamber, but Jordan's hand slipped from his and she hung back in the corridor.

The faeries, nymphs, and putti were more prolific here, their gaiety contrasting ghoulishly with the pale woman on the bed. The others would see that the body lying atop the feather mattress was that of a Human woman. But only Raine could scent the coagulating blood that pooled in her cavities now that her heart no longer pumped it through the canals within her. Only he detected the sickly sweet tang of death that mingled with the feminine smells of soap, perfume, and powder to hang over the room like a shroud. The odors clotted his lungs, overwhelming him.

But nowhere in this house, nor in this room, did he scent the man who'd raised him to age thirteen. If his EarthWorld father had ever had an amorous relationship with this woman, he had not visited her here in this house. Ever.

Having become somewhat inured to death because of his occupation, the constable gazed about the room, seeming more perplexed by its frivolous décor than by the dead woman within it. "This is her son's room. Can you imagine?"

Behind them, Jordan gasped.

Time stilled, as frozen as the breath in Jordan's chest, as she took in the scene in her own bedroom. Her mother looked abnormally peaceful lying there with her blond hair curling about her fragile features.

It struck her like a scene from Perrault's faerie tale of Sleeping Beauty. Only Celia wasn't sleeping.

Any minute, Jordan expected her mother's blue eyes to open, bright and flirtatious. Her mobile lips would trill with frivolous, gay chatter.

Instead, her eyes stayed closed and her lips remained pale and still as she languished on her back atop the coverlet.

Ethereally beautiful, she was dressed in one of her favorite costumes, a long filmy gown made with many layers of white tulle. It was the dress of Titania, the Faerie Queen of Shakespeare's play. White wings constructed from feathers of the rare albino peacocks of Isola Bella arched high from her shoulders. They spanned the entire width of the mattress on either side of her, swooping down past her hips to end in points on either side of her knees.

A gilt-edged copy of *A Midsummer Night's Dream* lay in the crook of one of her folded arms. Its binding was ribbed and costly, and Jordan had always loved the creak and smell of its leather. Her mother had read to her from it every night until she'd grown too old for such things.

Jordan stepped closer to the bed. Her hand reached out to her mother, wanting to shake her awake. "Mm—?"

"That's right. Murder," said the constable, rocking on his heels, then his toes, and down again. "I believe Celia Cietta was murdered last night."

Jordan froze. She'd forgotten he and Raine were in the room. Both men were staring at her. She snatched her hand back, her panicked thoughts flying helter-skelter.

"M-murder?" Someone had killed her mother? While she'd been fornicating the night away, her mother had been here in her bedchamber? Dying?

Before her eyes, her surroundings began to shimmer. She clutched her midsection and felt only the stiff corset underlying her gown. She couldn't breathe. Her entire body was choking.

She turned and rushed into the hallway, then down the steps, desperate to get outside. To air. She stumbled, gripping the stair rail.

Her mother's chambermaid hovered anxiously on the landing halfway down. "Are you all right, signorina?" Several other servants lurked below in the rotunda. Why were they calling her signorina? Didn't they recognize her?

"Air," Jordan gasped, pushing past them. "I need air."

Finally, she was in the entryway, heading for a door that seemed a mile away. The servants stared with expressions varying between curiosity and alarm, but none seemed to know her. It didn't matter. Nothing mattered.

Her mother—her beautiful, delightful, conniving mother— was upstairs. Dead. Dead. *Dead.*

"Are you ill?" The sound of Raine's voice came to her as though from the depths of a well.

She wheeled on him, her eyes huge in her face. "My corset," she gasped, scrabbling her fingers at her waist. "It's too—"

And then, for the first time in her life, she fainted.

14

Jordan came awake in an instant. Her eyes flew open, alert. The man from last night was seated across from her, staring.

She was slumped in the corner of an expensive leather rocking chair. No. From the creaky lurching of the button-tufted seat, she deduced she was in some sort of conveyance. A carriage. For the moment, she couldn't manage to rouse any interest in inquiring as to where they were going.

Raine opened a silver flask engraved with his initials and handed it to her. "Here. Drink."

When she reached for it, her bodice slipped and fell forward. She clutched it to her bosom with one hand, barely keeping herself decent.

"I loosened it," Raine informed her without apology.

"Fortunately for you, I'm too tired to care." With her free hand, Jordan took the flask from him and drank. It held liquor. Wine. She swallowed several long draughts of it, then wiped her mouth with the back of her wrist. She didn't cough or sputter as a lady unaccustomed to spirits might have done.

Her companion noticed. But he was more concerned with other matters at the moment. While the woman seated across from him had slept he'd sensed magic accumulate around her. ElseWorld magic. It had wafted into the carriage, startling him with its strength. Apparently he wasn't the only one who'd located this second Faerie daughter. Feydon's relatives had ferreted her out as well.

Jordan pushed damp wisps of hair from her forehead with a shaking hand. Her temples throbbed. She felt dreadful. She took another swig from the flask and felt her bodice gap away from her.

"Tighten this damn thing," she told him, presenting him with her back. "Your free peep show is at an end. I'm chilly."

"Then take my coat," he said, removing it and settling it around her shoulders.

Without thanking him, she clutched it together at the front, snuggling into his residual warmth. Heaving a great sigh, she let her worries swamp her.

The dove from her dream—it had represented her mother. Celia Cietta was dead. It seemed impossible. She'd been so vivacious in life.

She drew another long draft from the flask.

Wordlessly, Raine retrieved it from her and handed her a handkerchief in its stead. She took it and touched it to her cheek, only then realizing she was crying.

The four blue stockings would come next, she knew, and then finally the snake. A shiny coal-black viper, it would hypnotize her, not with its eyes but with its voice. Even as she fell under its spell, she knew she would try to avoid it. For once it had lulled her, it would strike.

She didn't bother trying to puzzle these dreams out now. It was impossible to do so, as she knew from past experience. Their meanings would reveal themselves as time passed, as always. There was no way to stop them from coming to fruition. She could only wait, at their mercy.

She glanced at Raine and saw he was still studying her. Her eyes ducked away to the handkerchief her fingers were busily crumpling and re-ironing. "Stop looking at me as though I were a bug on a pin."

His eyes didn't waver.

She rolled her shoulders, trying to shake off her mood. "I'm sorry. I'm always grumpy when I awaken to find myself in a strange carriage with a gentleman I've known less than a day. How long was I—?"

"Almost four hours."

Four hours!

"You were dreaming," he said.

She stilled. "Oh?"

"You talk in your sleep."

"Oh." This was unwelcome news. "What did I say precisely?"

"Don't you remember?" He posed the question in the Else-World tongue—the language she had mumbled off and on during her restless slumber.

She cocked her head, trying to place a fleeting memory his words evoked. But the recollection was slippery and she couldn't hold on to it long enough to analyze it.

"Whatever foreign gibberish you're speaking, I don't understand it," she told him.

"That's interesting since it's the language you spoke in your dreams. Don't you recall anything of it?"

Yes, she recalled her dreams all too well, though not the language he referred to. She'd seen the snowy white bird again. Only the bird hadn't been a bird. It had been her mother. Her chest constricted and her breath grew labored. She pressed a hand to the arch of her rib cage just below her breasts.

"That corset comes off once and for all. Now," he said, reaching for her.

She slapped at his hands. "No, it's already so loose it's falling off. I'm fine."

He sat back, frowning. "Have it your way. But if you faint again, expect to wake up with it missing and tossed from the carriage into the muddy lane."

"How ferocious of you," she said snidely. She sniffled into the fine lawn handkerchief, forcing her breath to regulate itself.

"That woman back there in that house," she said, breaking the silence after a few moments. "Was she truly d-dead?"

He nodded.

Jordan's cheeks singed. "Well, don't make me pull every detail from you with tweezers. What did the constable say happened to her?"

"Since you ask so nicely . . . He informed me that suicide hasn't been ruled out. According to the servants, the signora was driven to melancholy at times."

Yes, her mother had been high strung, her moods rising and dipping without rhyme or reason, Jordan knew.

"But I thought he said she'd been murdered."

Raine inclined his head. "That's the constable's theory. There was a son, as he mentioned. It was in his bedchamber that Signora Cietta lay. The servants have reported that the son and mother fought the day before her death and now he can't be located. Thus the foundation for the constable's suspicions in his direction."

She was the prime suspect in her mother's murder!? Jordan straightened and glanced out the small curtained window, feeling a sudden urge to flee the confines of the carriage. To escape his probing eyes and the suspicions of others. To hide.

"Where are we?" she suddenly thought to inquire.

"On the outskirts of Padua. I'm taking you to my home in Tuscany."

A feeling of entrapment welled in her, turning her feisty. "You made that decision without consulting me?"

He spread his hands. "After you fainted, my options seemed limited. It was time I returned home. Yet you showed no signs of recovering. What was I to do? Leave you to the constable? Drive you back to the quay where we met last night and deposit you there instead, unconscious and at the mercy of desperate and criminal elements?"

She glared at him, annoyed that she was unable to find a hole in his argument.

"What's the harm in coming with me for a while?" he asked. "If you find my company dismal, I assure you there are others dwelling on the Satyr Estate who are less so. My two brothers live nearby. One is married, with an infant son, a wife, and her nearly grown sister. You'll have their companionship as well as every comfort a lady could want."

"I haven't lived the life of a lady, as I told you. You don't know me. And I'm not certain I want you to. Living in close quarters will necessitate constant contact."

"I'm a private person myself. We don't have to share all of ourselves with one another. Only the parts we wish to."

She rubbed her forehead. "I can't simply disappear."

"Why not? Who in Venice would miss you?"

Who indeed. She no longer had her mother to consider. If she went missing, only Salerno would care.

But if she never returned to Venice, her mother's death might go unsolved. Unavenged. And she would forfeit the right to the Cietta fortune. Her cousin, another son of the Cietta family she'd never met, would inherit.

She sighed wearily. "Do you think your father could have done it? Murdered that woman. If it turns out she was murdered, I mean."

Raine considered the suggestion. "Doubtful. He wasn't particularly driven to the sort of passions that might lead one to commit murder."

"Apparently he had some passionate impulses if he was driven to Signora Cietta's bed as your mother suspects."

"He goes from bed to bed only in an attempt to prove his virility to the world," Raine told her without inflection. "He cannot accept that he is unable to sire children."

Her brows rose in surprise. "But—"

"He wasn't my father," Raine said, anticipating her question. "Though he is my mother's husband, Roberto Altore is no relation of mine. I'm Lord Satyr's bastard. The very day my mother confessed that she had lain with Satyr to sire a son, Altore sent me to Tuscany and left my mother's bed forever."

"I see." Jordan studied the stark line of his profile as he twitched the drape at the window aside to gaze outside.

"Did you tell your mother what happened back there?" She waved a hand indicating the entirety of Venice, which dwindled in the distance behind them, having just recalled the mission the man across from her had been on at her mother's house.

Raine let the curtain drop. "I dispatched a message to her informing her of what transpired this morning. I assured her she has nothing to fear from the lovely Signora Cietta any longer."

Her thoughts spun in a thousand directions, all of them upsetting. Her temples pounded more violently and she pressed at them.

"Are you all right?" Raine asked.

No she wasn't all right. Her mother was dead. It was possible she'd been murdered. And Jordan was the prime suspect. There was no one to stand between her and Salerno now. God, had *he* killed her mother?

What would happen if she were to go back and tell the constable to direct his suspicions toward the surgeon? Would he listen? No. Better to send an anonymous letter to him containing her suspicions instead.

Her eyes flicked to Raine, noting again how handsome he was. She could go with him. Live as his consort until he tired of her. The world outside need never know that she and Jordan Cietta—son of the late Signore Cosimo Cietta and heir to a vast fortune—were one in the same. Only she, her mother, and Salerno were privy to that damning secret. And now only she and Salerno. Would he search for her? If she continued on to Tuscany, the chances of his finding her would diminish.

This man was offering to take her to his home, days away from Venice. To the country, where no one knew her or would think to look for her. Where she could live as a woman. His woman. Where she could lie with him among fresh sheets as she had last night. It would be sweet.

Of course it wouldn't last. He would tire of her at some point and choose someone else to warm his bed, just as the parade of gentlemen over the years had always eventually tired of her mother. Celia's suitors never supplied a reason for their defections. Men simply seemed to always to be in search of a female body that was new to them.

It was likely Raine would turn her out when he discovered the truth of her body's construction. Even so, she would manage. She might even find another man, who would disregard her strangeness and come to care for her just as she was. Her mother had once said that the contadini—farmers and other country-dwellers—were less fastidious regarding what was under their lover's skirts than citidini—gentlemen of pomp and status who dwelled in the cities.

Continuing on in this carriage would mean she could continue to wear dresses, petticoats, corsets, and silly hats. She could live every aspect of her life as a female as she'd once only dreamed of doing. At least until life—or death—caught up to her.

She took a calming breath. "All right," she agreed at last.

"I'll go with you to Tuscany. But only on the understanding I'm free to leave at any time."

"But of course," her companion agreed easily.

Why was it she had the feeling he wasn't being altogether genuine?

15

Satyr Estate, Tuscany, Italy
September 1823

Raine's home was like him, Jordan decided upon seeing it in the distance ahead from the carriage window. From the exterior, it appeared as a collection of severe but stately gothic towers with sharply pointed spires, all carved of brooding, gray stone. Relieved only by the occasional window or cluster of columns, it stood strong, rigid, and remote from the land surrounding it.

A great spiked fence built of tightly spaced vertical rails enclosed it within the grounds, lending it a prickly and unwelcoming air. Past a pair of iron gates that bore the insignia "SV" in ornate gold lettering, a curving path led her conveyance toward it through manicured lawns, clipped hedges, and cloistered gardens so prim and restrained they would have suited a monastery. Even the poplars and elms marched in neat columns, each one properly pruned. Here, all of nature was confined and controlled as though its master feared were one leaf to wander or one weed to rear its head, all hell might break loose. She longed to throw wildflower seeds to the wind, just to see Raine's reaction when they bloomed willy-nilly come spring. But would she be here to see it?

The carriage drew up in a circular courtyard carpeted with smooth cobblestones that spoked outward from a central fountain. The bumpy expanse met the base of the front wall of the house at right angles, with nary a shrub to relieve their meeting. The stones were bounded on two other sides by high walls unrelieved by the crawl of ivy and by wrought iron gates on the more distant fourth side through which she'd just entered.

She opened the door of her conveyance just as Raine drew up alongside. He'd passed most of the journey on horseback, so she'd been largely left alone with her thoughts. She was eager to be free of them and the carriage, and to be engaged by new sights and sounds.

Almost immediately, Raine was at the door to assist her in alighting. He offered his hand in a courtly gesture that never failed to delight her.

Stepping down, she nearly tripped on her skirts. Unaccustomed to them, she forgot she no longer moved within the freedom of trousers as she once had. Fortunately, Raine was there to catch her.

"Good Lord!" she said, peering over his shoulder. "What is that?"

He let her go once she found her footing, but she'd felt him cringe from her question. Apparently, he'd expected it.

She headed toward the object of her dismay—a fantastic fountain at the edge of the courtyard. At its center rose a larger-than-life statue she recognized as Bacchus, the mythological god of wine.

His wild hair was wreathed with a crown of grapevines and his expression was carnal, almost demonic, as he gazed down at her. A bevy of lithe female attendants carved from fine-veined

Carrera marble fawned on him, offering food, wine, and their bodies. Three of them proffered goblets from which sparkling water sprayed and splashed, cascading to bathe their feet in a shallow pool.

In one bold hand Bacchus held the weight of the nearest nymph's naked breast, the tip of his thumb brushing her nipple. With the other hand he carelessly fondled the rump of another such attendant, who in turn coyly cupped his plump scrotum. Just above her hand, the wine god's enormous cock rose at a lusty angle, startling in its size and splendor.

"Goodness," Jordan said. All in all, it was a shocking departure from the austerity she'd encountered so far.

"It was here when I inherited the home," Raine told her stiffly. Heat singed the ridges of his high cheekbones. She smiled at how defensive he sounded but sensed now wasn't the time to tease.

"This isn't a home. It's a castle," she informed him in return.

Along the six-day trip, which had included the difficult pass through Bologna, they'd been forced to quarter overnight at numerous inns. In each, Raine had purchased separate rooms for her, as well as books and needlework to keep her occupied. It was considerate of him. And she'd adored each of these tokens, simply because they reinforced the fact that he considered her female.

He had visited her room each night after the evening meal and had taken her there in her assigned bed in a quick encounter. She'd greeted him each time with her phallus already beribboned, trussed, and safely out of sight within her chemise. He'd stuck to the rules she'd set back in Venice, taking her woman's passage from behind, and had left her after they'd both achieved satisfaction only once.

By day he'd ridden alongside the carriage through sun and rain and had kept himself from her, not even so much as kissing her. But she'd seen the bulge in his trousers from time to time and known he wanted her. Why he hadn't acted on his desire more frequently, she wasn't sure. She'd made it obvious she was amenable to anything—within certain constraints. However he'd found a dozen ways to evade her attentions. Now that they had arrived at his estate, she had him.

Without awaiting an invitation, she started up the wide set of stairs leading to the two-story gabled entrance to his home. A starched servant opened the high, arched door for her and she crossed the threshold.

Inside, a spectacular marble and gilt staircase greeted her, spiraling up the first two stories of the main tower. The vestibule and front salon were studies of the austere and the opulent, though she scarcely had time to register the elegant frescoes, coffered ceilings, sweeping Persian carpets, or rich tapestries, for he ushered her upstairs with a haste that widened his servants' eyes.

At last, she thought. He would take her into his rooms and make long, leisurely love to her. He was obviously anxious. So was she.

As she'd anticipated, he quickly saw her to a bedchamber. It had been aired and made ready for her use, for he'd sent word ahead. "Will it do?" he asked once they were inside.

She spun in a circle that swirled her skirts. The room was done in muted tones of fern and peach with a simple leafy garland design painted along its borders. A swath of gauzy netting swooped from a central ring above the bed in four directions to wind around each tall mahogany bedpost until its ends dusted the floor. A writing desk, dressing table, trunk, couch, two armoires, chairs, and several flower-filled urns rounded out the room's contents.

"Will it do?" she echoed in amazement. After having spent nineteen years living amid the throngs of sculpted nymphs and sprites her mother had so adored, she was delighted with the room's tasteful restraint. "Have you lost your wits? Of course it will. This is easily twice the size of my—" She'd been going to say—the bedchamber she'd had in her mother's home in Venice. But she stopped herself and stopped her swirling.

"I'm glad it meets with your approval," said Raine. "Dinner is at seven. Please amuse yourself as you wish until then." With that, he exited into an adjoining room, shutting the door between them with a whoosh of finality.

It was obvious he wanted to be alone. But Jordan was tired of being left to her melancholy introspection. She didn't want to dwell on her mother's death tonight. She needed company. Needed his body against her, making her forget.

Testing his limits, she wandered to the door and opened it just a bit. Peering inside, her eyes found him.

His gaze shot to her, and he halted in the process of removing his shirt, with his arms crossed at his waist and the tails of the fabric bunched in each hand.

"That door was closed for a reason," he told her.

Ignoring his pointed lack of invitation, she wandered inside, sat on his bed, and made herself comfortable among his pillows. "Don't mind me. Please continue."

His hands dropped to his sides and he scowled. "Did you require something?"

"I require the sight of more skin. Pray, do continue disrobing."

"I'm not a carnival act performing for your amusement," he told her.

"No." She eased from the bed and went to him. "No. You're a beautiful man. And I want to see more of you." She kissed the skin visible at the open V of his shirt's partially unfastened neckline. "To taste more of you."

"To touch you." Her arms slid under the fabric of his shirt to encircle his waist.

"To engage in sexual congress with you in that big, lovely bed of yours."

Between them, she found the strangled knot his cock had become under the fabric of his trousers. "To feel this part of you come inside me as you did last night. And all the nights before." Her gentle palm shaped him and her voice lowered, turning sultry. "Remember?"

Oh, he remembered all right. Raine, who was notorious for fending off unwelcome advances and conversation, was struck dumb with the rabid desire to grab her to him and fuck her senseless. His hands went to her waist. He could flip up her skirts so easily. Lower his trousers just enough. Lift her just so. And be inside her in seconds.

Though he'd taken separate lodgings for them each night of their travels, he hadn't been able to stop himself from going to her room after supper. Night after night, he'd taken her under him in the same way they'd mated in Venice. But he prided himself that he'd always managed to leave her afterward and had done so if only to prove to himself that he could.

Yet after he'd left her bed the last night of their journey, he'd still been so needy that he'd gone back to his own room and conjured Shimmerskins. He'd fucked them until he was exhausted to keep himself from returning to her again.

Moonful would arrive tonight, and tension was coiling tighter in his gut as dusk approached. As the orb's light increased so would his desperation to join his body to hers.

He smoothed a hand over her hair, brooding. He didn't know how to stop his cock from responding to her. To keep from needing her. Wanting her was one thing. Needing her was unacceptable. He'd promised himself he'd ration his time with her when they arrived here. That he'd continue to mate her only once a night.

Her thumb found the notch in the underside of his crown.

Well, maybe twice, he thought. No—once, damn it all. What was wrong with him? When had he grown so weak?

Normally he could restrain himself from fucking even

Shimmerskins for days. Weeks. It was only this damned approach of Moonful. He would gladly bespell her and take her to the glen with him tonight to experience the Calling if only he could be certain he could trust himself to rein in his childseed. It galled him to admit that he couldn't. Once he'd buried his cock in her, he feared his fertile seed would gush forth unchecked like a swollen river bursting through a dam. Yes, taking her to the glen tonight would be a mistake. But he was tempted.

Ignoring his glower, Jordan sank to the floor before him in a pool of frothy petticoats and skirts. Delving into the front of his trousers she took the hard textured column of him between her seductive hands. Her breath came as a puff of air on his shaft. Then came her tongue, an exquisite lick of torture.

His hand fisted in her hair, intending to push her away. Instead, his palm moved with a will of its own, curving to cup the back of her skull and hold her. Coal black lashes shadowed the silver of his eyes, watching those gorgeous lips of hers work their wiles on him. Oh, sweet relief!

"Ah, Jordan," he murmured. "This has got to stop. I didn't bring you here for this. Or at least, not yet. Not today. Not so often."

She pulled back from his cock, her lips wet and puffy from sucking at him. Her fist still stroked him, slicking the moisture she'd left behind and mimicking the motion of a mouth. Her eyes flirted, teased. "No? You want me to stop? You'd rather join me on the bed perhaps?"

She stood, draping herself against him, but not so tightly that he might discern her body's secrets. Putting her arms around his neck she lifted her lips to kiss him.

His broad hands rose to her waist, holding her. It occurred to him that she felt surprisingly right against him. His body felt more alive, his mind clearer, and his spirit happier when she was near. The realization struck a strange sort of fear in him.

Before he'd married so disastrously he'd fucked hundreds of

Human women. Whores, courtesans, peasants. It seemed there were legions of them, all eager to bed his brothers and him so that they might boast of it to their friends. But no one had ever felt so right in his arms. Not even his former wife.

He clenched his jaw and turned away from her to fold his trousers shut. "Yes, I want you to stop. No, I don't want to join you on the bed. Not now. I have work to do."

She angled her head, intrigued. "What work?"

He ran a hand through his hair, ruffling it into disarray, and then smoothed it into its customary design. Any other woman would have thrown a tantrum at his rebuff. But not her, apparently. No one spoke to him as she did. No one teased him or pushed him into doing things he'd rather not. Others found him unapproachable, and he appreciated them keeping their distance. Why didn't she act like everyone else around him?

"I've been away for two weeks," he told her in a flat voice. "I have duties in the family vineyard. The grapes are ripening. The vines must be inspected and decisions made regarding the order in which the various plots will be harvested. The list goes on."

Her face lit up. "It sounds fascinating. I'll come along."

16

Raine led her through his house, along complicated walkways and moody passages. There were lovely, quiet rooms for contemplation and larger more lavish salons meant for entertaining. Their sparse decoration and refined elegance held great appeal for Jordan after having suffered the decorating schemes of her mother's fantasies all of her life.

When they delved deeply enough beneath the living quarters, they came to a cavernous labyrinth, which he informed her was the wine cellar. He spent some time checking various aspects of the barrels and the slowly fermenting grape juice they contained before leading her up another set of stairs more rustic than the others he'd shown her. The steps ended at an exterior door through which they passed and which led them outside into the garden at the rear of his home.

Horses were summoned, and Jordan was somewhat dismayed when hers arrived bearing a sidesaddle. The central lands of the triangular-shaped estate rose upward from his castello, so the trail would take them higher. But she was a good rider and had faith she would manage the distance to his vineyard without mishap.

She loosened her collar, fanning herself as they rode. "The day is warm for September."

His eyes drifted over the slight cleavage she'd exposed, and his hands tightened on his reins. "You'll find the climate within our compound is temperate year-round compared to that outside its walls."

"Why is that?"

He only shrugged and urged his mount ahead. "It requires a lengthy explanation."

"I'm willing to hear it," said Jordan, catching up.

"Suffice it to say that the precise combination of vegetation and terrain here bring about a fairly constant climate. It's neither too hot in summer nor too cold in winter. My ancestors located the estate on this hillside and walled the grounds for defense reasons. You'll have them to thank when winter sets in and you've no need for a coat."

"Amazing! There's that much moderation in temperature here?" she asked.

He nodded.

They rounded a rise, and she caught a glimpse of the gleaming towers of a second estate in one direction and the dark towers of a third one in the other.

"From this approach you can see the homes of my brothers," he informed her.

She shaded her eyes, surveying one, then the other. "Which is which?"

"That's Lyon's, my youngest brother's," Raine told her, pointing at the former. "And the darker one belongs to Nick, my eldest brother."

"How distant are they? It's difficult to measure by sight in a forested area as vast as this."

"Each is a half hour's journey along the exterior wall on horseback."

"And are they like yours?"

"Similar I suppose, though they differ in architectural style as you can see even at this distance. At the center of each estate is a main home with extensive gardens and grounds, which meet and mingle with the trees of the old growth forest. The forest in turn rings the base of the sloping hills of the vineyards, which forms the central core of our lands."

He didn't tell her the rest. That this ancient ground had been chosen by their ancestors for a special purpose—to serve as a sacred joining place for ElseWorld and EarthWorld. That a gate between those worlds was secreted on the grounds. Or that in centuries past, many Satyr had dwelled here, protecting the portal that led between worlds. Now there were but three.

"So you say you make wine?" Jordan prompted as they drew close to the vineyard itself.

"Mm-hmm."

"How does one make wine exactly?" she asked, waving away a buzzing bee.

He shot her such a confounded look that she laughed and leaped to defend herself. "I'm from the city. I know nothing of this business."

"You'll learn soon enough. The business of the grapes is inseparable from our lives here."

They dismounted at a pergola formed by a network of gnarled wisteria vines, which sheltered a stone walkway leading into the vineyard. Raine pointed to the various workers they encountered there and explained the tasks in which each was engaged as the two of them explored on foot.

When they paused at the crest of a slope, she shielded her eyes to take in the endless stretch of patchworked rows of vines below.

"The outer wall of our estate encircles two thousand acres of forest as well as fruit and olive groves. We have eight hundred tilled acres, though less than four hundred are currently under cultivation," Raine offered. "Of those, only three hundred are planted in grapes. The rest are in olives and fruit."

"Can I sample a grape or two?" she asked. Already taking his assent for granted, she left him to wander halfway down a row of vines.

"I think we can spare them." Raine's voice was absent as he gazed toward the adjacent hillside, having scented the approach of his younger brother. Lyon was coming up the path on horseback accompanied by animals from his menagerie. Two of his prized panthers from the smell of them.

Soon his brother came into view and reined in to scowl down at him. "Why are you not still searching in Venice? Blast it, Raine. You know I cannot go to Paris for mine until you have found—"

"I've found her," said Raine.

"What?" Lyon's head snapped back in surprise. "You've found her? Then where is she?"

"Use your nose for once," Raine said in exasperation. "Can you not scent her?"

From his superior height on horseback, Lyon located Jordan's approaching figure. His golden eyes swept her, turning appreciative. "Very nice, brother."

Raine gritted his teeth.

Oblivious, Lyon dismounted and tethered his horse by means of a sotto voce instruction to the animal. "Jane will be dying to visit you when she hears of your bride's arrival," he told his brother.

"Who's Jane?" Jordan asked, reaching them.

"We're not married," Raine said at the same time.

"Not married?" Lyon's brows rammed together.

"Stay out of it, brother," Raine said, a warning in his tone. "Now, I'll be on my way. I've only just returned and am anxious to check on the progress of the other vines."

"*We'll* be on our way," Jordan revised, meaningfully.

Confident she'd fall in with his plans as had every other woman he'd ever met, Lyon shot her an engaging grin and took her arm. "I'll come along with you on your first tour of our vineyards then, shall I, and we'll make each other's acquaintance?"

"Very well," Jordan agreed, twitching her skirts away from the nuzzling noses of his oversized felines. "Then you can explain who Jane is. And which brother you are as well. And whether or not these animals of yours plan to have me for a snack."

"Don't you have another obligation that requires your attention, baby brother?" Raine inquired pointedly. "In Paris?"

"There's time enough for that," said Lyon, blithely fluttering his hand in a complete reversal of his earlier urgency.

Disgruntled, Raine followed them down the wide steps that led toward another field of vines, listening to Lyon charm Jordan. He hadn't realized how much he'd been enjoying introducing her to the estate himself until his brother had usurped the job.

"Your four-footed locusts are enjoying the fruit again," Raine groused when Lyon's cats began to munch clusters of grapes. "Point them to their own yard, will you?"

"Liber! Ceres! These are not for you," Lyon scolded, pushing his sleek animals' black noses away from the vines. "You have your own. Now scoot." With that, he ushered his panthers into an expansive, enclosed pen filled with fig trees and wild vines weighted and drooping with ripened grapes.

Petless now, the three of them wandered through a new plot of vines, then another, and still others beyond those. Along the way, Raine lifted, inspected, and tasted a myriad of grapes. He occasionally offered one to Lyon and they discussed its qualities at length, using terms such as astringent or smoky. He offered samples to Jordan as well and she tasted them, but the nuances of their flavors were too slight for her to comprehend.

Both brothers conferred with pruners, pickers, and other black-clad employees now and then as well. These were no gentlemen farmers, she realized. The workers obviously looked to them for direction.

At times, Raine became so involved in his work that he seemed to forget that she and Lyon still trailed him. It was obvious he was in his element and that he reveled in this contact with the land.

And she had to agree it was lovely here. Peaceful, fresh, and far from the noise and filth that was Venice.

"Picking has just begun. The crush will follow and continue for several weeks," Lyon explained when he saw her gaze had fallen on a group of workers in the process of filling baskets with grapes.

"Which grapes ripen first? Or do they all ripen simultaneously?" she asked.

"The start of autumn often coincides with the maturity of the French Merlot in our earliest-ripening plots," Lyon explained patiently. "The fruit is tasted at least once a day before deciding when to pick. The order in which sectors are harvested is updated daily as we continue to test."

"Fascinating," said Jordan, hardly noticing when Lyon handed her another grape to devour. Raine had just bent low to check the dry, volcanic soil at the base of a cane, and she was intent on admiring the breadth of his muscular back where it strained at his shirt. Her eyes followed the shallow groove down his spine to his narrow waist and the taut rear below. She bit into the juicy fruit. "Umm. Delicious."

"The quintessential Tuscan grape we are known for is the Sangiovese, grown here since the time of the Etruscans," Lyon went on. "But those are not ripe as of yet."

A spurt of jealousy sprouted and flourished within Raine as he listened to his brother conversing so easily with Jordan. Lyon's facile tongue and easy manner had always appealed to women. The fact that the female element swarmed to their younger brother like bees to honey was normally a source of amusement to Nick and him. But now, suddenly, it grated. Knowing he likely owed his uncharacteristic envy to the approach of Moonful did little to curb it.

"Let's move on," he said, abruptly standing and heading down another path.

Jordan saw the turbulent flash of silver come and go in Raine's eyes. His face might be stern and haughty, even taciturn at times. But his eyes gave him away. If one searched them closely enough, it was easy to discern that they sizzled with suppressed emotion. That cloak of remoteness hid deep passions that he chose to keep leashed even as they fought for freedom. She made a promise to herself that before she left Tuscany, she would attempt to loose him from the suffocation of his self-imposed restraints.

"Careful sorting during the picking is essential for quality," Lyon was explaining. He touched her arm to draw her attention to some workers on a hillside. Raine glared at his hand, wanting to knock it off her sleeve.

"You see the pickers there," Lyon continued, oblivious to any undercurrents. "Their crates are small to avoid bruising. Our grapes will arrive in perfect condition in the vat rooms where they'll be sorted on a special table. Only the best fruit goes into the vats for crushing."

"I've never seen vines staked in such neat rows," said Jordan, watching the workers nip clusters of fat grapes with sharp hand-shears. "Normally, they mix with other vegetation and grow up trees and fences across the countryside willy-nilly."

"Raine likes things orderly, don't you, brother?" Lyon teased.

Raine shrugged.

"When he was only seventeen," Lyon went on, "he began organizing the vines on Satyr land as you see them now, into rows on stakes. Vintners in other areas of Tuscany have taken note, wondering if it is part of the recipe for the phenomenal success of our wine. But old customs are slow to change, and for now, they only watch and await the outcome of our experiment."

"Why did you do that, Raine?" Jordan asked, trying to draw him into the conversation.

"If things are orderly, the nutrients the vines receive and their health can be more easily monitored. And the organization helps ensure the grapes in each section express the sort of character we intend."

Suddenly his gaze narrowed on the empty path beyond her. "Yet another brother descends on us," he muttered.

"Where?" asked Jordan, looking around but seeing no one approaching.

"I neglected to remark on Raine's other formidable skill— that of anticipating new arrivals," Lyon told her.

A moment later the sound of hoofbeats heralded the brother Raine had spoken of. Seeing them, he turned his mount their way.

"Jordan, meet Nick, our eldest brother," said Lyon, as they watched him rein in. As Nick dismounted, his eyes were on Jordan, and hers on him.

All three brothers were tall, well muscled, and handsome beyond belief. And yet there were differences. Whereas the silver-eyed Raine was remote and stiffly polite, and his younger brother a gold-eyed, affable flirt, this eldest Satyr brother was almost too imposing with his blue-eyed, raven-haired good looks.

"Nick, this is Jordan," Lyon informed him, with a gesture in her direction. "A new *acquaintance* of Raine's, just brought here from *Venice*."

She sensed some silent communication pass between the trio of massive males. His emphasis on the words *acquaintance* and *Venice* made her wonder at their significance.

Eyes sparkling, Nick took her hand in his and pressed a quick kiss to it. "Any new *acquaintance* of Raine's from *Venice* is most welcome on Satyr land," he teased. "I hope you plan to tarry with us for a lengthy stay?"

She blushed, tugging her hand back. "My plans are fluid."

Raine's brothers stared at him as though expecting him to refute her statement. When he didn't speak, Nick stepped into the breach.

"Then we must endeavor to entertain you so well that you'll decide to tarry with us for a very long time. A local festival to celebrate the beginning of the harvest occurs only two days from now on the hillside just outside our estates; did my brothers tell you?"

She shook her head no.

"It's the first of many *festa della vendemmias* held during the season," Lyon explained.

As they returned to their horses, Jordan felt something humming in the air between the three brothers. Questions unasked because she was present. Questions that would fly once the three brothers were sequestered. They chose other matters to discuss while she listened in.

"What of the lecture?" asked Nick. Though he addressed Raine, his eyes remained on Jordan, still assessing her.

"A waste of time. No progress was made," said Raine.

"What lecture?" Jordan asked, unwilling to be shut out.

Something shifted in Raine's eyes as he helped her onto her mount. "I had just come from a lecture along the Riva del Vin in Venice the night we met," he answered once they were all headed home. "It involved the winery business."

"Do tell," she said, her eyes narrowing with suspicion. It hadn't occurred to her to wonder what he'd been doing in Venice the night they met. The theater where she'd been on display had been on the same side of the bridge as his lecture. "What was the topic?" she asked, observing him closely.

"A disease that has been infiltrating vineyards across Europe," Nick replied.

"What kind of disease?"

"Phylloxera," Lyon supplied.

Talk of it occupied them for the rest of the journey home and much of the dinner they shared there. It was a typical Tuscan repast of bread, olive oil, roasted meat, funghi, vegetables, cheeses, and wine all enjoyed with typical Tuscan leisure. But once dinner was complete, the men seemed anxious to be rid of her company.

"Lyon leaves tomorrow for Paris," Nick informed her. "You will forgive us if we borrow Raine for a business discussion for the rest of the evening?"

She had no choice but to agree.

As she made to withdraw, Lyon glanced toward the window, critically eyeing the sky. "Rain is threatening. Perhaps I should postpone my journey."

Though it was barely dusk, Jordan could already see the first stars twinkling in the clear evening sky. His demur was obviously because of his reluctance to make the trip.

"Have you forgotten the pressing nature of your obligation there? I believe the message we received some months ago indicated that time was of the essence."

Lyon heaved a dramatic sigh. "Very well. I'll take myself off to Paris tomorrow morning. I will miss the harvest festival if I must."

Raine lifted a brow. "A dozen hearts will be broken, I'm sure."

"You flatter me," said Lyon, grinning.

He took Jordan's hands in his to kiss her cheek. "Welcome to the family. I'll look forward to furthering our acquaintance when I return from Paris."

The brothers were all standing now and obviously ready to see her gone, so she took her leave of them. They holed up in the salon immersed in discussion about the various workings of the vines, she assumed, leaving her to seek her bed alone.

In her chamber, she read for some time, listening for Raine all the while. Hearing a disturbance outside, she went to her window. Among the trees below, she thought she saw two-legged shadows move. But a moment later, all was still and she decided she'd only imagined it.

She waited for Raine until well beyond nightfall, then sneaked back downstairs to listen at the door of the salon where she'd left the brothers in conference. Hearing nothing, she cracked the door open. The room was empty. Only a trio of empty wine goblets remained to indicate that the brothers had recently occupied it.

The house was dark and quiet, for Raine had told her the servants were dismissed each night at dusk and returned to their homes. Only night servants, as he had termed them, were left. They would watch over things, and he'd said she had only to ring a bellpull to summon them.

Back upstairs, she tried the door to his bedchamber again. He was still absent, but she ventured into his room and into his bed to await him. When he never came, she drifted into an uneasy slumber.

17

As Jordan bided her time in futility, the Lords of Satyr slipped from the castello keeping to shadows as they silently treaded the path to the forest, just as they had treaded it every Moonful of their adult lives. It took them to a sacred gathering place at the heart of the family's ancient vineyard, where a great ring of statues awaited.

The most imposing of them, Bacchus, reigned over the murky glen, forever imprisoned in stone. Though his pose was different, his avid, carnal features were twin to the effigy of him in Raine's courtyard fountain. Grapevines tangled themselves into the shape of a wreath to crown the wild curls of his head. In one outstretched hand, he held an ornate wine goblet, offering a toast in celebration of the ritual the three brothers were about to perform. It was a rite their ancestors had enacted under the veil of moonlight over all the centuries past.

Solemnly, the lords sipped an elixir poured into goblets from ancient amphorae hidden among the altars that dotted the glen. They divested themselves of their Human clothing, oblivious to the chill of autumn. The pelts of hair on their haunches and legs thickened into fur, and their cocks swelled long and heavy—well beyond their customary dimensions.

Suddenly, the full moon emerged from behind the clouds to observe them with its brilliant unblinking eye. With the coming of its light, cramps seized the brothers, ruthlessly undulating over their rigid bellies. Bent low by pleasurable anguish, they grimaced, their features turning savage as the last physical change of the Calling night occurred.

At length, the lords rose again almost as one. They were freakish beings now, as much animal as man, for the last Change of Moonful had endowed each with a new shaft of bone-like sinew—a second cock torn from the flesh of his own pelvis.

Raine averted his eyes from the twin cocks that now sprang high and hard from him. Very nearly the size of the enormous rod already rooted just below in his thatch, his new second phallus strained and twitched for the scent of a woman.

They'd taken care that no one would see them like this or observe what they would do here tonight. The force of their combined Will kept prying eyes from ever discovering this most secret part of their estate.

At the lords' silent commands, an iridescent vapor began to stir in the stillness of the air between them. Glimmering forms solidified from it, shapeshifting into Shimmerskins—the insentient females who had attended the Satyr since ancient times.

The mist stilled and a dozen of them stepped from it, going to the brothers. Their soft hands and lips and lush bodies worshipped them, stroking over chests, flanks, and shafts.

A woman that was half-Human and half-Faerie stepped from the shadows then, moving among the Shimmerskins to take Nick's outstretched hand. As prearranged, his wife Jane had been waiting for this moment to make her appearance. She, too, was naked.

The Shimmerskins included her in their ministrations, running their hands over her and Nick as the couple embraced. Raine and Lyon watched, envious, then they moved apart to pursue their individual pleasures with the conjured creatures.

A golden Shimmerskin favored Raine with an alluring, vacant smile. He followed her, letting her lead him to one of the altars. Bending forward, she spread her feet, planting them wide as she prepared to fulfill the role for which she'd been specifically designed. Her belly met the cold stone slab of the altar, and she placidly awaited his pleasure as enumerable beings of her kind had awaited that of his forebears over the centuries.

Raine moved close behind her. His cocks bobbed for her like divining rods sensing water. He would avail himself of both of her nether openings for this first fuck. But after one ejaculation his newly awakened second phallus would recede from her anus and back inside him. There it would remain, satiated until next month's Moonful when it would return, ravenous for womanly flesh once more.

The light overhead strengthened. He lifted his face to it, letting it bathe him in its creamy caress. His cocks jerked under the impact of a sudden bolt of vicarious pleasure. Lyon. He glanced toward his younger brother and saw he'd just plunged himself into the Shimmerskin bent on the altar before him.

Somewhere nearby, he heard Jane cry out as Nick mated her. Another bolt of desire shot through his pricks. As always he experienced his brothers' pleasure almost as though it were his own.

He stared down at the plump, glimmering ass before him. Raw, greedy lust twisted. His instincts had turned more bestial than Human now and his mind was riveted on one goal. He gripped her hips.

With a harsh growl, he plunged both cocks fathoms deep, losing himself in the welcome of the body before him, in his salacious enjoyment of the night. Her spine arched and she moaned, giving every appearance of libidinous relish. But he knew the truth of things. Shimmerskins didn't experience pleasure. They only excelled at imitating it.

Raine desperately ploughed the woman under him, repeatedly ramming himself inside her with rough, staccato slams. His flesh heated and his rapture spiraled out of control, building on that his brothers were experiencing.

The savage slap of flesh echoed through the hushed glen, punctuated only by masculine grunts and feminine sighs. From his perch above them, Bacchus smiled down on the scene, gratified by the sight and sounds of their debauchery.

Raine fisted his hands on the altar on either side of the body prostrated before him. He heard Nick's triumphant shout of release. It was quickly followed by Lyon's.

A strangled groan escaped him. Lured by his brothers' ejaculations, hot, wet seed blasted from his twin cocks to flood the Shimmerskin's orifices. The pace of his coming was fierce and fast. A welcome relief. When it eventually slackened, his breath sawed in his lungs.

It was over. For the moment.

The glow of the Shimmerskin beneath him dulled as if it were waning candlelight. Her body slowly faded back into the nothingness of the mist from which she'd first issued. Another would take her place shortly he knew, and his fucking would continue until dawn. But for a moment he was left with only his tortured thoughts.

And the knowledge that he'd pretended the body under him had been that of Jordan.

18

At that very moment, three very different brothers lurked nearby in the Satyr forest as well, growing ever more impatient. In contrast to Raine and his brothers, their words were soundless amid the poppies that grew thick around them, their breath as still and cold as death.

He's here, in the glen, the youngest of them whispered. *She's alone, available. Close. We must act.*

But he wants her. Has other plans for her, the second brother worried. *He'll not make it easy for us.*

He's weakened by his wanting, scoffed the eldest. *Distracted by his worry over the pox we've brought to the vines of Earth-World. Once we have her mind, she will do our work in bringing the pox to Satyr land. Our crossing of the gate will quickly follow.*

What will tempt her closer? What will bring her to us? the two younger ones wondered.

Desire for her mate—the second Satyr son, the eldest replied. *We will be him to her. And lure her with his call.*

Yes!

With that, the brothers' intentions intertwined and strengthened, becoming one Will. Like separate musical notes combining to form a single chord, it reached out as a tangible force, riding on the air and creeping stealthily toward the lone female it sought. Coming upon the glen ringed with statues, it paused, sensing heat. Males. Satyr. Three of them. They were engaged with females, one of whom had ElseWorld blood in her veins. But an aura of protection surrounded her. It had been woven by many months of mating with the eldest Satyr male, they knew. Though invisible, it was as strong a deterrent as chain mail armor.

The Will of the others turned away and continued on through old growth forest where moss and lichen grew, where leaves and pine needles decayed sweetly on the woodsy path. Still it crept on, reaching land whose wildness had been tamed. Onward through gardens of thyme, mint, and mums. Over the brick of paths and around hedges and fountains and beyond wrought iron fencing.

And then, it met with a sheer wall of gray stone and butted against it, finding no break that would allow it entrance. Undefeated, it moved upward along the vertical face until it found a window. Locating the thinnest of cracks between mullion and glass, it slipped through like a trail of devilish smoke.

It slid along tiles of Italian marble, past ankles clad in black cotton stockings that rushed here and there doing mundane Human chores. It whooshed up the stairs. Along a hall. Beneath a door. Into a bedchamber.

It slid across the carpet there, up along a claw-footed bedpost, and higher. Amid the pale bedcovers, it sought the warmth it sensed there. A woman's warmth. Floating softly, it hovered just a moment over Jordan's sleeping body. Then it slipped under the bedcovers and found her.

And finding her, it entered her dreams.

19

Jordan had been dreaming. Again she'd seen the dove, only now it bore her mother's features. Her mind turned away from the crushing pain and she again saw the blue stockings, and then the snake.

Then something new entered her dreams. Something unexpected and evil. It called to her in a hypnotic voice. A voice that was three male voices blended into one.

Come, it called. *Come to us.*

Its Will was strong.

Bewitched by its power, she rose from Raine's bed, slipped from the room, and fairly floated downstairs. To her left, she heard servants. But she padded past them and from the house, wandering she knew not where.

Come. We await you. The voice that was three voices beguiled her, drew her onward.

By and by she found herself passing a circle of statues. But she didn't notice those who were engaged in concupiscent pastimes there under the fullness of the moon. And they didn't see her.

She followed the triad of voices farther, beyond the glen.

Then she abruptly jerked to a halt, somehow sensing that she was being led to the last of her three-part dream—the snake.

"No," she breathed.

Come. Do not fear us. Come.

But she opened her palm and looked down at it. Saw she held one of the precious ribbons Raine had given her—the red one. Abruptly, the voice's hold was broken. She slumped to the ground.

When she awoke she found herself in the garden behind Raine's home, alone and still in her nightgown. Her feet and the hem of her gown were dirty.

Her hands were bruised and tired. She glanced down at them and was startled to see she held a pair of garden shears. She'd used them to cut the red ribbon into many short lengths.

Even stranger, it appeared she'd collected dozens of sticks as well. Each bit of red ribbon had been tied around a pair of them to form them into an X. The bizarre objects now lay spread around her on the mosaic tile of the courtyard floor like ridiculous, gaily wrapped gifts that no one in their right mind would want.

That no one in their right mind would create.

She jumped to her feet, preparing to run inside the castello and find her bed before anyone caught her at this bizarre occupation. But after a few steps, something stopped her. Some instinct made her kneel again and spread the lap of her gown in front of her on the stone floor. With fingers that trembled, she raked the odd little packages into her skirt. Then she gathered the fabric around them and clutched it to her belly. That done, she leaped up and ran back into the house via the wine cellar door.

In the cool dimness within, she stumbled and fell. Her packages scattered. Frantic, she scrabbled to gather them. Why? Why couldn't she just leave them? She wanted to.

Suddenly there was candlelight. Hands joined hers, searching and finding the wooden Xs. Gently each was placed back in the lap of her gown.

Two strange creatures had knelt beside her. Both were Humanlike and wore necklaces of tree bark and twigs. Circlets of leaves crowned their unbound hair.

"Let us help," they crooned.

She'd seen such creatures in her dreams before, long ago when she'd first changed from girl to woman at age thirteen.

"Who are you?" she asked, eager to solve this small puzzle of her childhood.

"We serve the master and all who dwell under his protection," they said in unison. Their dronelike voices held little inflection, and there was an unearthly calm about them.

"The master? Raine, you mean?"

"Master Satyr," they crooned.

Just then Jordan heard the lilting notes of a panpipe. She lifted her head, listening. The two women stood and turned to go, moving in the direction of the music.

She grabbed one of their hands and found it soft and cool. "I understood all the staff departed at dusk."

"We are the night servants," the girl replied in a monotone.

"Do you live on the premises? Or away from the estate in the servants' quarters?"

The girl raised her hand and touched Jordan's forehead. "Sleep," she whispered.

"Jordan?" a familiar voice asked. A hand warmed her cheek.

She opened her eyes to see a somewhat disheveled-looking Raine and Lyon bending over her.

She yawned, stretching, then sat up. "What time is it?"

"Dawn," Lyon supplied.

"What are you doing here?" Raine demanded softly.

She touched his face, reassuring herself he wasn't a dream. "I had trouble sleeping and wandered here. I'm afraid I'm occasionally subject to nocturnal phantasmata."

"Good grief, what the devil is that?" Lyon inquired.

"Nightmares," she said, yawning again behind her hand. "A physician once suggested I should not slumber on my back since he believed it heats the cerebellum. But heeding his advice had no impact on my complaint."

"I once had a dream I was imprisoned within a big cheese," Lyon ruminated. "I had to eat my way out. What do you suppose your physician might say regarding that?"

"That you are a rat?" Raine suggested with good humor.

Lyon gave his arm a lazy punch. Then bidding them farewell, he took himself off, whistling.

Raine lifted her and she wrapped her arms around him. Her lips found his throat, nibbling.

She felt his subtle withdrawal and hesitated. She'd rejected someone's affections herself in just such a way several months ago. Back in Venice, Paulo's younger sister Jeanette had developed a regrettable attachment toward Jordan, whom she'd understandably believed from all visible evidence to be a young man. Once his sister fixed her affections, she'd flirted, teased, and shadowed her.

One afternoon, Jeanette had cornered her as she awaited Paulo in a downstairs salon of their home. She'd shyly begged for a kiss. Not wanting to offend her, Jordan had complied.

Her cock had stirred pleasantly under the other girl's embrace and she'd wondered what would happen if she were to marry Paulo's sister one day. She could rule a wife such as this, she'd realized, and play husband to her in darkness. She could school such a wife that she was never allowed to let her hands wander over her husband's body.

Jeanette would probably accept such a situation and never know the difference. But their marriage would not make the girl truly happy. And it would not have satisfied Jordan either.

She'd yearned to play the woman herself and to experience the lovemaking of a man. She'd wanted to feel the strength of a male body against her. Inside her.

Unfortunately, with that single kiss, Jordan had managed to convince the inexperienced Jeanette that she was a masterful lover. As the girl's stalking had grown more intense, Jordan had begun to cringe whenever she spotted her.

Did Raine now cringe from her show of desire as she once had from Jeanette's?

"Would you prefer that I not touch you?" she asked him bluntly.

"I—" Raine began, halting as though it were a difficult question. "I enjoy your affections. I'm just not accustomed to being the object of them."

Relieved to read the truth of that in his eyes, she planted another kiss on his jaw. "Could you not get used to it?"

Yes, he could get very used to it, thought Raine. He feared he already had.

20

_____

Two mornings later, the entire hillside outside the gates of the Satyr Estate stirred with the day's impending festivities. It was the weekend of the local harvest festival.

Raine had explained to Jordan that buyers would congregate here for a first taste of wines blended from Tuscan vintner's grapes, all grown in prior years and aged over time. Tradesmen involved in various aspects of winemaking would vie for custom at booths they'd set up. There would be demonstrations of the various processes involved in wine production as well as frivolous entertainments.

But Jordan was most excited about the prospect of meeting Nick's wife.

"So tell me about Jane," she begged him. "What does she look like? Is she intelligent? Amusing? She must be to have been chosen by your brother."

Raine shrugged. "You'll meet her in less than an hour. Then you may judge for yourself."

"Oh, you! You're such a—man." Suddenly recalling that

less than a week ago she'd been a man herself, she giggled at her preposterous statement.

Raine smiled down at her. His lips felt odd and stretched. He hadn't smiled so often in past years as he had since meeting her.

His eyes traveled over her. She was garbed as befitted a lady of her station today. Her short hair had been swept up under the beribboned straw bonnet she'd brought from Venice. A bevy of dark curls peeked out at her temples.

From his superior height he had a pleasing view of the curves of her bosom. The golden autumn sunlight dusted the swells where they'd been forced upward by the constriction of a corset.

Other men noticed her as well, attracted first by her giggles and chatter and then by her face and figure.

He wrapped an arm around her, laying claim, and she leaned into him. The faint perfume of Fey filled his nostrils. The thrill of being near her bubbled through his veins, and a cautious joy seeped into his bones.

A few moments of silence passed and he waited for her to break it, as she no doubt would.

"Female clothing is indecent, is it not?" she eventually offered by way of conversation.

His brow quirked. "I see you are even worse than I at social gambits."

She ignored his teasing and waved a hand at a group of revelers they'd just passed. "Those men were staring at me. At my bosom actually. Did you notice?" She lay a hand over the area of her body under discussion.

Strangled laughter escaped him. "Yes, I noticed, but you aren't supposed to."

"So I am to display my bosom, yet pretend to be unaware of the fact that men are ogling it?" She sighed. "I suppose it's all in an effort to snare a husband. But since I don't wish to snare one, it seems unfair to advertise my charms so blatantly. I think perhaps that women should wear garments reflecting their level of interest in flirtation. For instance, the more bosom a woman's gown reveals, the more available she is."

"Remind me never to set you up in business as a dressmaker," Raine responded dryly.

"But—"

"Ah!" he announced, cutting her off. "You are about to get your wish. My eldest brother has arrived. With his wife."

"Where?" Jordan looked around. "I don't see them."

"I assure you they are nearly upon us," said Raine.

Sure enough Nick appeared at the end of the path with an attractive, blond woman at his side.

"How do you do that?" she marveled. "Know when people are coming before you even see them."

" 'Tis a gift," he said, smiling.

"It's rare to see Raine enjoy himself in a woman's company," Jane murmured to Nick as they approached the other couple.

Nick covered her hand, which lay in the crook of his elbow, with his, studying his brother. "Yes, it bodes well for the future."

When the foursome met and all had been introduced, Nick caught his brother's eye. Raine knew the question that was uppermost on Nick's mind. To satisfy him, Raine turned to Jordan. "Will you marry me?"

"What?!" Embarrassed, she glanced at Nick and Jane then back at him. "What nonsense. You are only stirred by the sight of my exposed bosom this morning. The feeling will pass and you will regret having asked such a question."

Nick and Jane burst into laughter.

"There, you see, big brother?" Raine said with feigned chagrin. "I have officially asked her to wed me. She refuses."

Jordan frowned at him, wondering if she was currently the butt of some sort of jest.

"It's best to ignore their teasing," Jane confided, leaning close. "Now, let me say how delighted I am to make your acquaintance. It will be wonderful to have another woman on the estates."

Jordan gazed into her eyes and found them warm and friendly. An odd feeling of recognition swept over her. But it seemed unlikely they'd met before.

"My wife has been beside herself to meet you," Nick announced as the four of them turned to stroll among the booths. "She has been up since dawn, giddy with excitement."

As they walked, Jordan noticed she was outpacing Jane, who took smaller steps. She slowed, thinking that perhaps she could learn something of being a lady from Nick's wife. She decided to observe the other woman throughout the day and mimic her.

Raine and Nick selected wineglasses for them all from a display on a nearby table. Wine would be poured into them at various vintners' booths, to be sipped and sampled as they wandered among the exhibits.

The air around them was redolent with the fragrance of ripening grapes and wine. The sound of conversation and laughter was overlaid with eager descriptions as the winemakers tried to sell others on the superiority of their vintage.

"... flavors are supported by vanilla oak characters ... shows a nose of ripe cherries and rich black plums ... the undertones are derived from a lengthy maturation ... with a backbone of tart gooseberries ..."

"Look there. He's 'raising a barrel,' " Raine told Jordan, pointing toward one of the coopers. "It's one of the first steps in constructing a wine cask. First, the three metal hoops are forced into place, so they grip the staves."

He indicated a second cooper, this one working at an open fire. "He's toasting the inside of a barrel. The amount of charring will have an effect on the aging of the wine it will hold. A winemaker can choose from light, medium, or heavy toast, based on the variety of grape and style of wine he plans to age in a given barrel."

A neighboring vintner came over to pour an offering from a bottle of his wine. The foursome tossed the dregs of the last sample they'd been given into the grass and allowed him to refill them. Jordan giggled and raised her glass to her companions. "A toast!"

Raine smiled at her, wondering if she weren't becoming a bit tipsy.

Nick caught Jane's eye and silently indicated that he wished to speak to his brother privately.

Signaling her understanding, Jane linked her arm with Jordan's. "Have you seen the vats yet?" she inquired.

Jordan shook her head.

Jane waved to Nick and Raine. "I'm going to show Jordan around," she called, tugging her in another direction.

Nick nodded and then watched Raine watch Jordan depart, seeing the longing in his brother's expression. The signs of Raine's interest were subtle, but after all these years he could read him better than most.

"You can't continue to keep her in your home without marriage," Nick said when the two women were out of earshot. "What of her EarthWorld family? Won't they object?"

"She claims to have none that are living."

"Still, Feydon's letter required the protection of marriage," said Nick. "Have you sensed anything of the danger to her that he mentioned?"

Raine shook his head and they set off along the path, nodding now and then to acknowledge acquaintances. "I don't know its source yet. But I'm keeping her close and watching over her."

"And mating her."

Raine stiffened.

"I felt your enjoyment of her when you first came together in Venice, even over so great a distance," said Nick. "But I also know you're not joining with her as often as you'd like. Why hold back?"

"Mind your own business, brother."

"This *is* my business. Family business. You didn't take her in the Calling two nights ago. Will you in the next?"

"No."

"Why the hell not?"

"May I remind you that you didn't take Jane for several Moonfuls after you first brought her here?"

"And as it turns out, I put her at unnecessary risk because I delayed. Only a Calling night with Jordan will offer her the level of protection necessary to keep her—and therefore the gate between ElseWorld and this world—safe. Feydon's offspring cannot be allowed to get a foothold here through her. No matter what her opinion on the matter, you must bring her to the glen next Moonful and get the deed done."

"I'll not sire children on her."

"Your choice," said Nick, shrugging. "Though I think you're making a mistake."

Two young women from the village came up to them then, offering celebratory wreaths of leafy vines they'd woven. They each crowned one of the brothers, then lingered to flirt.

Nick pulled away, thanking them with good humor but subtly spurning any advances.

Raine stared at them coldly, removing the crown and handing it back. Eyes wide, the young woman who'd given it to him retrieved it and backed away. Both women moved off, whispering and shooting uneasy glances back at him. They'd no doubt heard the rumors his former wife had spread about him. It was a timely reminder of all the reasons he should continue to maintain his control around Jordan.

"You perpetuate their mistrust of you by keeping your distance," Nick observed.

Raine rolled his shoulders, burdened by the weight of his brother's concern. "I've had enough of your advice for one afternoon. Why don't you go locate your wife and offer some to her?"

"Excellent idea. I believe we'll find her with your Jordan in the vat rooms."

Following the sounds of laughter they made their way to one of the smaller vat rooms. Three women were inside, crushing grapes in three enormous wooden tubs. Eight feet across and made of thick oak staves, the vats stood waist high, and the liquid within them rose several inches above their knees.

Having abandoned their bonnets, shawls, and shoes on a nearby table, Jordan and Jane were being tutored in the job of treading. As they slipped and slid, they attempted to emulate the easy, rolling rhythm of their teacher, the saucy and seasoned Signora Tutti. She urged them on with equal parts instruction and vociferous encouragement.

Jane was carefully following the woman's instructions, intent on doing things just right.

But Jordan's stomping was more enthusiasm than skill. Her short hair had escaped its pins and straggled to fringe her nape. Her cheeks were flushed and her eyes sparkling. Her skirts were tucked into the waistband of her dress, but they'd fallen loose here and there to soak in the grapes. Raine knew she would later notice their bedraggled state and lament the stains.

"Jane!" came Nick's sharp command. He stepped to the rim of the vat where his wife worked.

Raine turned his head and saw the lust that had darkened his brother's eyes. Jane stilled, reading it too. Her eyes darted to Raine as if to determine whether he too had intercepted his brother's avid gaze, then she blushed when she saw he had.

How she could still blush after living with his earthy, salacious brother for these many months and already bearing him one child, Raine would never understand. But she was good for Nico. It was easy to see how happy she made him.

Gracefully, Jane rested her hands on Nick's shoulders and allowed him to lift her by the waist from the vat. After assisting her into her shoes and grabbing up her hat and wrap, he quickly spirited her away.

Raine considered the two of them until they were out of sight, knowing that within minutes Jane would be out of her dress and under his brother. There were many hidden places nearby to engage a woman in coitus, and he and his brothers knew them all by now.

He couldn't help but envy his brother's satisfaction in his choice of bride. But though Nick had found bliss with his FaerieBlend wife, it didn't lead him to expect the same.

His eyes returned to Jordan. Above the wine vats, ropes had been hung that treaders could grasp to maintain their balance. She had availed herself of their use, as had Signora Tutti. With her arms raised, Jordan's softly rounded breasts plumped at the neckline of her gown, shifting in time with her movements.

Her knees rose and fell from the mush, splashing juice in an uncertain rhythm. It dripped and sluiced down her naked thighs. Bits of pulp clung to her skin, then slid away or plopped into the vat, splattering.

Raine cursed under his breath. The sight of her like this affected him. Beneath his trousers, his cock rose and grew thick and heavy.

Suddenly his head lifted, as he caught a new scent. The air around him had turned pungent with male interest. A half-dozen men stood nearby, observing the treaders for the sheer pleasure of it. Every eye watched Jordan, he realized. Leered at her, in fact.

He studied her, seeing what those men saw. She wore no underclothes beneath that skirt. Women rarely did. But usually their skirts brushed the ground, offering little chance that a man might glimpse the treasures they concealed.

However, with every boisterous stomp of her foot, Jordan offered the tantalizing possibility that her hiked skirt might accidentally reveal more than it should. Why, it flirted at the edge of indecency!

Jordan chose that moment to lick grape juice from her fingers. Signora Tutti tossed a teasing instruction at her. She threw back her head and laughed, displaying the smooth line of her throat.

The other men shifted, wanting her. Wanting not just her body but also the inner joy she brought with her. As he did.

"Jordan," he barked, motioning her to climb out of the vat. "Come. You'll attract fruit flies before long if you keep at that."

She pouted at him. "Not yet. I'm getting good at this. You're only worried that you'll soon find yourself having to pay me a true treader's wages. Isn't that right, Signore Lutz?"

When the foreman didn't reply, she glanced over at him with a question in her eyes. He only blinked at her with a besotted smile on his face.

"Signore Lutz!" Raine growled.

The foreman straightened abruptly and cleared his throat. Noting Raine's scowl, he wiped his expression clean of any interest in his employer's woman. He tipped his hat distantly to her. "Yes, signorina, I'm sure you're right about that."

Raine picked up her shawl and stepped to the edge of the vat, holding the garment out toward her. Wordlessly he gave it a jerk, indicating that she should join him and let him wrap her in it.

She grinned saucily. "No. You come in. With your big feet, you'd surely stomp the grapes twice as efficiently as I can."

Signora Tutti giggled, eyeing their byplay from the adjacent vat. "You think I won't?" he said.

"And splatter that snowy white shirt?" teased Jordan. "Crumple the line of your trousers? I *know* you won't."

Raine turned to the foreman. "Dismiss your workers, Signore Lutz. I wish to have a private word with the signorina."

The foreman clapped his hands sharply, urging the workers from the room. "You heard Signore Satyr. Go! All of you."

With a knowing wink at Jordan, Signora Tutti slipped from the vat and made herself scarce as well.

When they were alone, Raine used his mind to lock the doors. Then he began removing his clothing.

"What are you—? But you haven't bathed," Jordan protested, holding her hands out as though to stop him. "Signora Tutti scrubbed Jane's and my legs and feet until they were pink before we were allowed in."

He ignored her, removing first his boots, then his shirt, then his trousers.

Grasping one of the ropes overhead in one hand, he swung his legs over the side of the vat. Once inside, he dunked himself until he was submerged to the waist. When he rose to stand again, rivulets of deep blue dripped from him, cascading down his flanks, his hips, his thighs, his balls, and his cock.

All the while, his hungry gaze devoured her. From across the pool, Jordan stared at him, her eyes dilating as she realized what he intended.

Juice sloshed in waves, slopping over the edges of the vat as he advanced toward her. Under his feet, the sodden mush squeezed between his toes.

Her voice rose in dismay as he drew nearer. "What are you doing?!"

He stalked her until she was against the far wall of the vat. There, her hands came out to seize the points of his hip bones, keeping him mere inches away.

He let her stay him and stood before her, not yet touching.

"Raise your skirts," he told her.

Her breath caught. "Yes. All right. But not like this. Let me turn."

"Not this time." In a flash, he slicked his hands upward along the outsides of her thighs, lifting her dampened skirts high and flipping their weight over the rim of the vat so the bulk of them hung outside of it.

That part of her that she'd endeavored so hard to keep hidden from him was abruptly exposed.

Completely flustered, she struggled to tug the fabric back down around her. But his hands pinned it on either side of her against the inner rim of the vat, pulling it taut across her abdomen.

He nudged her slippery thighs apart with his own and pressed his juicy groin to hers. For a split second, their thatches nuzzled. Phallus pressed phallus.

"No!" Frantic, she wriggled, sliding in the slush, finding her footing again and trying to shimmy away.

His lips brushed her hair. "It doesn't matter to me what you grow between your legs," he murmured.

Instantly, she froze. A terrible quiet fell between them, like the aftermath of a bomb blast.

Her dark eyes crept upward to lock with the silver of his. "You know."

"Did you really think you could keep it from me?"

"How? How did you know?"

"We've lain together," he hedged.

"Did you know back in Venice?"

He nodded.

"You didn't say anything. So I thought—" She gave an anguished moan. "I thought—Oh God." She covered her eyes with her fingers, pushing at him with her other hand. "Move. I want to get out."

"No." His voice was low, commanding.

She shook her head, struggling to escape him. To escape her humiliation. "Please, I don't want you to be—disgusted."

His heart caught. At that moment, more than anything he wished he knew how to reassure her. To tell her how much he wanted her. To tell her how desirable she was to him. But he didn't have the gift of expressing his feelings. "I won't be."

"So you say."

His chin nuzzled the top of her head. "Are you ashamed of what you are?"

She straightened, her skull bumping the underside of his jaw. "I'm most certainly *not* ashamed, though others have tried to shame me and make me uncertain of what I am."

How often in his life had he, too, been given cause to wonder what he was—Satyr or Human? He struggled to comfort her now. Though he had no flowery words, he could give her the truth of what he felt.

His lips found the side of her throat, where the warm scent of her was at its most beguiling. "The fact that you're made with both male and female parts pleases me," he told her. "I find you more interesting than any other woman I've ever met. More attractive. I assure you I desire you just as you are."

Jordan stilled for a long moment and he felt her weighing his words. Then she sighed against his chest, a sound of something broken beginning to mend. "Oh, Raine," she whispered, her voice tight with emotion. Raising a palm to cup his cheek, she kissed him.

His hands tightened on her waist, drawing her inexorably closer. His breath became hers and hers became his. Their tongues met, tangled, and mated with slick desperation. Their cocks thickened, prodding each other's bellies.

His hand wandered lower between them. Hers caught it.

"Let me touch you," he urged against her lips. "Let me."

Her grasp convulsed on him, her nails leaving half moons on his skin. But then reluctantly, one by one, her fingers let go.

His hands fell to drag through the slush that surrounded them both. Then his dripping, wine-sluiced fingers rose to work their way between her legs, opening the slit between her testes.

She stood waiting, her heart frozen in her chest.

"Relax," he whispered at her ear. But she couldn't.

He fondled her with knowing strokes, pressing between the thickened sacs to find and saw in her inner slickness. The heel of his palm pressed at the base of her phallus with each thrust until her pulse quickened and she began to move on him. With his other hand he scooped more of the rich viscous velvet from the pool and basted the length of her shaft.

And then—for the first time ever—a hand other than her own took her cock in its grasp.

A choked sigh escaped her.

Ever so gently, he began to masturbate her. The fingers of his other hand still worked high between her thighs, shafting her slit to the same rhythm.

Her thighs quivered along his and she shuddered, swaying dizzily.

"Breathe," he instructed. She took a great gulp of air and opened her eyes to see the rosy head of her prick peeking out from his fist, then disappearing, only to appear again. It was juicy-wet and fatter than she'd ever seen it.

His cock stood at attention, sliding against the inside of his wrist each time his hand pumped her. Without conscious intent she reached and took him in her palm, quickly finding the pace his fist had set on her flesh. Together they worked each other's rods, slicking them together, then apart. Hands shaped and groped, each learning the terrain of the other's body.

Passion rose in Raine, hot as a flashfire. He wanted to take her like this, to fuck her here in the sacred nectar of grapes he'd planted, tended, and chosen. Wanted to grind himself into her while they were immersed in the fruits of his labor that were so important to his survival and to that of the two worlds that met on Satyr land.

He lifted her, and her hands rose to grip the hard muscles of his shoulders. His cock, marinated with the pulpy juice that was his lifeblood, found her feminine slit. His big hands cupped the cheeks of her bottom and his splayed thighs took her weight as she wrapped her legs around him. Together, they watched as he pushed into her, in one . . . Easy. Fluid. Glide.

Emotions roiled in his chest as he sank home. This—their first frontal joining on his land—was a momentous occurrence. She linked her hands behind his neck and arched her throat, moaning her pleasure. She felt so good against him.

Their bodies began to move, swaying together in an ancient carnal dance. The air around them turned humid and sweet with passion.

Her cock bobbed, firm against his belly. Adjusting one hand to take more of her weight, he wrapped her shaft in his fist again, milking it in time with his harsh thrusts inside her.

Jordan drew close and whimpered against his throat, uncertain what to do with the sensations rushing at her. She brushed her lips over his jaw and whispered words of desperate encouragement.

Abruptly, Raine surged inside her with newly fevered need. Somewhere, Nick and Jane were coming together. He felt their ecstasy and it fueled his own. Grape pulp and juice sloshed in high rhythmic waves splashing over the sides of the vat as he rutted her ever more fiercely.

Her cock jerked in his fist. She gave a soft inarticulate cry as it creamed over his fingers.

With a strangled shout, he wrapped both hands around her ass, drove himself impossibly deep, and erupted.

She came as a woman then, too, arching into her second release and clasping her knees tight to his sides. He bucked her hard with each ejaculation, wringing spurts of scalding lava from his cock. Her inner walls sucked at him, beguiling his cum. They kissed, their breath rough and gasping.

Later, when his heart had slowed, Raine rested his chin on the top of her head and gazed across the room with unseeing eyes. Her inner walls still spasmed around him and her own cock's jism was slick between their bellies. He stroked her hair, enjoying its softness.

The pool turned calmer, until it only lapped at them. Outside the vat room, voices rose and fell. Until this moment he hadn't noticed them.

Jordan was truly his now, whether she realized it or not. Having mated her on Satyr land, he'd initiated the bespelling that would keep her from harm in all the years to come. With each successive coupling, the bond between them would strengthen. Ancient forces that protected his land and all who dwelled within would weave more securely around her.

She slumped against him, her forehead on his chest. "Signora Tutti and Signore Lutz will be quite annoyed. I'm afraid we've definitely ruined their vat."

"I don't care," he murmured. "My brothers and I have grapes enough to fill hundreds more like it."

"I don't care either," she whispered, finding his mouth with hers. She caressed the sides of his face, his throat, and his nape with her hands. "That was good, Raine. I've never come with my male and female parts at the same time. In fact, it was better than good. Like bathing in honey, eating chocolate, and kissing all at the same time."

He laughed and loosened his hold on her until she slowly slid to stand on her feet again. At last her nipples pulsed the telltale hue of the Faerie in the presence of her mate. The color reminded him of a soft wine-dipped rose, and it was so pale she didn't seem to notice it.

She splashed her fingers in the juice. "What do you do with all these grapes next, after they're crushed?"

"This particular vat will be unusable in the future, its juice thrown out."

"But normally."

"They'll be fermented for eight to ten days. We make sure to taste all vats regularly to broaden our understanding of the long-term characteristics of each plot." His warm, wet hands lifted to cup her breasts and his thumbs brushed over her nipples. "You'll have to marry me, you know."

Her heart lurched, wishing. But she knew it couldn't be. She rose on tiptoe and kissed him lightly on the chin. "No, I don't know."

He frowned. "Those workers are all aware of why I dismissed them from this room earlier. Your reputation will be in tatters after today, if nuptials are not announced."

"Now you're really ruining the vat. In fact you're ruining the whole vat experience." She gave him a little push, which didn't budge him.

"Jordan . . ."

"No!" she said, her frustration turning to anger. "Leave it. You don't truly know me. If you did, you wouldn't want to wed me. I'm happy to warm your bed without marriage. But a husband has too strong a hold over a wife. I don't want another man—I mean, any man—to ever gain such a hold over me."

Hoping to forestall further argument, she grasped his shoulders and lifted herself, wrapping her legs around his waist again.

His hands rose to support her thighs. His prick was still hard and long, still wet with a mingling of their desire and juices from the pool.

"You know of course that if we wish to continue with this sort of activity, society requires a wedding," he told her.

She rested one hand on the vat's rim for leverage, took his

cock in her other fist, and then backed her hips away long enough to lead him to her slit. Their eyes caught.

"Society seems quite distant at the moment." She pushed forward and his crown widened her.

"Jordan—" he warned, his voice rough.

"Yes?" she asked innocently.

Sensation welled up in him, and he pushed inside her, deep, content to shelve his arguments for the moment.

Then he began to fuck her. Not with the heat of carnal hellfire as he had moments ago, but with the slow sensual rhythm of a lazy autumn afternoon. And he felt something gentle stir inside him. Something born of the heady scent of Faerie, the distant sound of revelry, and a strange sort of wanting for this woman. This woman with both Human and ElseWorld blood in her veins, who it was preordained would become his wife.

21

Outside the vat rooms, Raine left Jordan's side, having a business appointment with another vintner he'd only just remembered in time. She smiled to herself, wondering if the other man would dare question Raine regarding the strange color of his hands. Thanks to their time in the vats, they were now a bluish tinge below his crisp white cuffs.

As were his feet. She'd wanted to giggle when he'd come out of the vat and she'd seen them. He'd pointed out that her feet looked the same. And they did. Dyed by the juice, they both looked almost as if they wore—stockings. *Blue stockings.* Precisely as the second part of her dream had foretold. A chill washed over her as she realized the significance of the dyeing, and she tucked her own similarly dyed hands under her wrap.

Now that the second phase of her dream had been fulfilled, the third would come. The snake. If Raine knew of her peculiar foresight, would he fear it? How foolishly he'd claimed he wanted to take her to wife, heedless of her warnings that he knew nothing of the real her.

She wouldn't wed him, but she wanted to keep what she had

here with him as long as she could. To do so, she must bury her past so thoroughly that it never again came to light. Raine thought he was the only man to ever discover what her skirts held. He assumed she'd grown up in such skirts and that she'd lived her life first as a girl and then as a woman.

What would he think if he knew she'd once run wild in the streets of Venice flaunting the Austrians edict that Carnivale was to be disbanded? What would he think if he knew she'd formerly ridden astride, kissed another woman, and spent her nights drinking and gambling among loutish male companions?

What would he think if he learned his newest lover had once been a man?

Peeking from the vat rooms, she glanced one way and then the other, hoping to slip out and make her way up the hillside to the estate without being intercepted.

Seeing no one about, she dashed out. But her luck didn't hold. A woman stood in her path, just ahead. She was a stranger. A beautiful one, wearing a refined gown of gored mauve silk that perfectly matched the feathers in her hat. Jordan wondered if she could pretend not to see her and simply pass by without speaking. She ducked her head.

"Signorina Alessandro?" the woman inquired in a hesitant voice. Her expression betrayed doubt that Jordan could possibly be the person she sought.

Having grown accustomed to the false surname she'd supplied to Raine back in Venice, Jordan reluctantly paused. "Yes?"

Up close, the woman was even more beautiful than she'd seemed at first. Her skin was pure and creamy, her dark auburn tresses artfully arranged, her gown pristine and unwrinkled. Beside her, Jordan felt disastrously unkempt. She patted her hair and the hat she'd replaced on it without the use of a mirror, wondering precisely how bedraggled she appeared.

The woman drew nearer. "You're Raine's fiancée?" she inquired in modulated tones.

"What? No! We're only friends. Acquaintances really."

"Friends," the woman echoed. A confused frown creased her perfect brow. "But you're staying with him at his home, are you not?"

Jordan stiffened. "I'm not sure that's any of your concern. Now, if you'll excuse me." She lifted her stained skirts and went to sweep by the other woman, attempting to affect a haughty disdain.

But the woman stepped to block her path, gripping her forearm with urgent fingers. Her face drew nearer. "He's a handsome man. Wealthy. Virile. I was fooled once, too."

At close range, Jordan observed a rather unnerving wildness in the depths of the woman's eyes. "What do you mean?"

Manicured fingernails marred Jordan's skin. "I married him," the woman hissed. "But I regretted it. Don't make the same mistake."

This beautiful creature had been Raine's wife? Jordan felt dowdier than ever.

"Ah! I see you two have met," said a tart voice. From out of nowhere, Jane had come upon them. Jordan had rarely been so glad to see another person arrive.

The other woman took no notice of Jane, but only tucked Jordan's bluish hand between her own scratchy lace-encased ones. "Heed what I say. Don't marry him. He's a spawn of the devil, I tell you."

Jordan snatched her hand away. "Raine's no such thing. I shall wed him if I please and I shall tell him to sue you for libel, or slander, or whatever, if you continue to spread such gossip."

"Take your wicked lies elsewhere, Natalia," said Jane, giving the other woman a gentle push. "Or better yet, swallow them forever."

Raine's former wife fled Jane's touch. "Don't come near me!" she shrieked. "I know what you do with them when the moon comes. How can you stay with the one who's their leader?"

She clasped the golden cross at her throat. "Repent before it is too late! Repent!"

Jane sighed in disgust. "Take yourself off or I shall tell my husband of your lies. I assure you he will not be pleased to hear of them."

The other woman's eyes widened in fear and she fell back a few steps. Continuing her diatribe, she scurried down the hill and away from Jane's threat. "Don't take him to husband, Signorina Alessandro. You'll regret it, I tell you!"

Jane turned her back on the fleeing woman and took Jordan's arm. "Let's go, shall we?"

Jordan considered Raine's ex-wife's disappearing figure a moment more, then allowed Jane to lead her away. They headed uphill, along the winding, sun-dappled lane that would take them to their homes inside the gates of the Satyr domain.

In the aftermath of the other woman's accusations, the ensuing silence between them seemed uncomfortably loud. "How long ago were they married?" Jordan asked, breaking it.

"Two years. But for a very short time. I hope you don't take her advice to heart. Believe me when I say Raine is a good man."

"But what happened between them?"

"I'm not the best one to tell it, since it all happened before I came here. But as I understand the situation, Natalia was incapable of passion. She spurned Raine's lovemaking, as she likely would have spurned that of any man she'd wed. When she left him one night, she spread gossip that damaged his reputation. It has given him an abhorrence of being the subject of wagging tongues. He feels he brought shame to the Satyr name and subjected his brothers to dangerous rumors."

"Dangerous?"

Jane's eyes dodged hers. "There are secrets in this family that aren't mine to tell you. Raine will share them in his own good time if you stay. He's a wonderful, loving man. I hope you'll give him the chance he deserves."

The true question was, did she dare give herself a chance with him? His reputation had already suffered because of one wife. If he only knew how it could suffer if society found out *she* had once lived as a *he,* he'd quickly cease his pleas for a marriage between them.

"I'm only here for a while," Jordan told her. "I intend nothing permanent."

Jane hesitated, then squeezed her hand and said in a companionable voice, "Well, we shall endeavor to enjoy our time together, however long it is. My younger sister Emma is quite anxious to make your acquaintance as well. We shall both be pleased to welcome you at our house for a visit, and very soon. We're involved in the most interesting botanical experiments!"

Together, the two women chatted their way to the gates, unaware they were being watched.

Having finished his business appointment, Raine made to depart the festival when he found himself standing before a splendid exhibit—by far the finest at the small harvest celebration. Every attention had been paid to detail—from the carpet, which had been set on the ground to delineate the bounds of the exhibit, to the swags of velvet overhead, which shaded it from the pale sun.

A display of wine had been set on a linen-draped table to serve as an offering for those who wished to partake. He was considering whether to bother sampling it, when someone bumped into him, quite literally.

"Oh, pardone! Pardone!" The bishop dusted his hands over Raine's thighs and crotch as though to brush away any damage. He'd orchestrated his timing well, making certain to fall against his quarry in such a way that his fingers would fondle his genitals in a move that would appear quite unintentional.

"Unhand me, man!" Raine told him, pushing him away.

The bishop backed off, well satisfied to have gotten a feel of

The One He Desired, as he'd begun to privately call this man. Why, he wouldn't wash his hands for the next month!

"Lord Satyr! Welcome to the exhibit of the Church of Santa Maria Del Gorla. Such another amazing coincidence finding you again!" he effused, clapping his very happy hands.

Raine stared blankly at him, but the bishop's spirits refused to be crushed by his lack of recognition.

"We met in Venice at the recent conference on phylloxera," he said by way of a reminder. "Fascinating, was it not? We should meet again one evening to further discuss our efforts at combating that insidious pest."

Raine shifted from one foot to the other.

Sensing he was losing his audience, the bishop rushed on. "Earlier I sampled a vintage at the Satyr Vineyard exhibit. Such perfection! On the palate the flavors explode in a fusion of rich passionate fruit and well-integrated flavors. Such a fine texture! And the aromas!" He kissed his fingers.

Raine shifted again.

The bishop's conversational pace increased. "Now, in exchange, you must try some of my grape." Popping a cork on one of his best, he handed Raine the entire bottle.

"Sorry, I seemed to have dropped my glass during our recent encounter," Raine told him.

The bishop waved his hands. "No need for a glass. Take it from the bottle and tell me your opinion."

As Raine took the offering and lifted it to his lips, the bishop's pudgy fingers anxiously steepled under his plump chin. He had imagined this very moment countless times over the past year. Had imagined the praise The One He Desired would soon heap upon his efforts. Had fantasized that after tasting this wine, Raine would recognize his superlative expertise and that he would sling an arm around him and offer to escort him throughout the festival so that they might test the other less worthy offerings and discuss them.

Liquid trickled from the bottle's throat and Raine swished it in his mouth. Something caught his attention and he halted mid-swish. Transfixed, he stared into the distance over the bishop's head. Then he spit the wine into the grass and wordlessly returned the bottle.

The bishop clasped it to his chest and rose on tiptoe, awaiting his glowing conclusion.

"I have decided to wed," Raine announced without preamble.

To the bishop, his statement was as shocking and unwelcome as a heart attack. The wine bottle slipped from his fingers, thunking to the carpet. Where had this horrible notion come from? He followed Raine's gaze and found it lay upon two women walking together in the lane leading upward toward the gate to his estate. One was the wife of the eldest Satyr. And the other he didn't know. But whomever she was, the bishop didn't like the hungry expression on his companion's face when he gazed her way.

At the bishop's feet, the contents of his bottle bled away as did his hopes in Raine's direction. He knelt to mop it up with his handkerchief. Normally he'd leave this menial work to servants. But in his despair, he hardly knew what he did.

Raine bent and set the bottle upright, stemming the tide.

"Well?" he asked. "Will you see to the bans?"

The bishop gathered his wits and the bottle and stood, pursing his lips in disapproval. "You're divorced. The Church will not recognize a second marriage."

Raine flicked his fingers in an innately Italian gesture. "A hefty donation will persuade them to think differently. It always does. Now will you post the bans or shall I seek out another official?"

The bishop's expression tightened. "Very well. You may bring your fiancée in to speak with me. Unfortunately my schedule is rather full. Perhaps next month?"

"You may not speak with her at all," Raine instructed. "I don't wish her to know bans are being posted. Not yet."

"But this is highly irregular—" the bishop protested.

Raine's eyes narrowed. "If you're unwilling, I will make alternate arrangements."

"No! No! I'll do it. Of course I will. You only took me by surprise with your request."

Another vintner arrived, capturing Raine's attention. "Keep me apprised," he told the bishop. With that, he abandoned the church's exhibit entirely.

The bishop glowered at the woman on the hill, his heart as eaten with jealously as his cock was eaten with disease. He had to get a look at her. Now. Without delay.

Taking only the bottle from which The One He Desired had so recently drunk, he abandoned his booth. Then he huffed and puffed his way up the lane after Raine's sister-in-law and the other one.

Darting off the path into the woods, he sought to gain ground. The women were in no hurry and he quickly passed them without them being aware. He hid behind an outcropping of rocks and waited ahead of them.

When they came into view, he very nearly gasped. Why, the one that The One He Desired had chosen to wed was as ragged as a quayside whore! Her features were comely enough. But her dress and manner were appalling! What in God's name had attracted him to her? What was so special about her?

What was so *familiar*?

Frowning, he chewed the flesh of his inner cheek between his molars, searching his memory for where he'd seen her before. The two women disappeared inside the gates. But still he sat, pondering. The sun dipped lower, pinkening the landscape. Below him, the festivities continued, becoming raucous as more revelers arrived and more wine flowed.

He swirled his tongue over the lip of the bottle from which

The One He Desired had so recently drunk. Had he enjoyed the brew? He'd never said. The bishop's talent was highly regarded, though he knew he was thought to be something of a copycat. It was true that he had no ideas of his own, but he was a brilliant mimic. With each particular brew, he'd tried to copy the Satyr lords' offering of the previous year. But always, something was missing. Some indefinable ingredient.

He suspected the Satyr practiced some sort of magic on that land of theirs. They were so secretive. So handsome. The lips of The One He Desired were as sensuous and shapely as a woman's, but his cock . . . oh . . . there had been nothing womanly about that when the bishop had cupped him earlier . . .

And then, in a sudden flash of memory, he had it! That person with Jane Satyr was La Maschera—the one who was both female and male. The one that had escaped Signore Salerno that night at the theater. The abomination with a cock swinging between its legs. Raine must have stumbled upon it somehow and brought it here all the way from Venice!

Hmm. He stuck his tongue deep into the throat of the bottle and suctioned it out again with a little *pop!*

Salerno no doubt missed his creature. Did he know where it had fled when it departed the theater that rainy night? Oh delicious news.

Leaping to his feet, he abandoned the woods and the festival, leaving the bottles and decorations at his exhibit for whomever might decide to steal them.

When he arrived home, he announced that his bag was to be packed and a carriage readied. He was traveling to Venice.

Then, still clutching the bottle The One He Desired had touched with his beautiful lips, he went to find someone willing to fuck him with it.

22

Jordan and her attendant started in surprise as Raine strode into her bedchamber dressed only in a dark brocade night robe.

It was no wonder she was shocked to see him. He'd intentionally made himself scarce of late. She'd probably seen more of Jane and young Emma than she'd seen of him in the weeks since the harvest festival. Enamored of all things botanical, they'd engaged her in their ongoing efforts to affect a cure for the phylloxera. The growing closeness between the sisters pleased him, and he hoped it would soon be time to apprise Jordan of her blood relation to them. However, he had other matters on his mind tonight.

"Leave us," he instructed the maid. His grim curtness sent the normally placid night servant scurrying. Her vacant eyes widened with a confused sort of concern for her charge as she curtseyed and departed. She'd taken Jordan's hair down but hadn't yet managed to get her undressed.

"You scared her," scolded Jordan. "You know how skittish the night servants are. Why are you acting like this?"

Since last Moonful when they'd assisted her in the wine cellar, Jordan seemed to have taken the existence of the dryad night servants in stride. She'd taken his word for it that all was not right with them and that she mustn't speak of them to others who'd find them strange.

He pressed the door to the hall closed and turned the lock behind the fleeing maid. Then his silver eyes found Jordan. She stepped back at the raw hunger he couldn't conceal. The control that was so much a part of him had slipped dangerously.

He stalked her, his tread and words both careful and measured. "I have avoided your bed more often than I'd like since you came here. It was a foolish decision."

"Yes. I agree wholeheartedly." She retreated from him, leading him toward her bed.

"One that I'm afraid will prove to your detriment this night."

Her back hit a tall bedpost and she cocked her head to study him. "I didn't ask you to avoid me. Or my bed."

Raine loomed over her. She had a good point. He had only himself to blame for his pent-up need. His large hands grasped her shoulders as though he feared she'd try to escape.

"I was determined not to come to your bed until you agreed to a wedding between us. However, tonight I—can't—seem—"

Suddenly, his fingers bit into her flesh, bruising it. His eyes dilated, round black moons eclipsing his silver irises to mere halos. Pain contorted his expression. As he convulsed forward into a crouch, one white-knuckled hand clutched at his abdomen while the other groped for support.

She knelt on the carpet. Holding and soothing him, she smoothed his hair back in an effort to see his face. "Raine? What is it? What's wrong?"

Her eyes held concern and curiosity. He avoided them. It embarrassed him to be brought down in front of her. To have it made so plain to this woman that he was out of control and at the mercy of ancient forces she would find incomprehensible if she knew of them.

Frenzied words escaped his lips, each syllable bitten off. "The Calling," he gasped. "I promised myself . . . but I am weak tonight. Knowing you are near, I must have you or be driven mad. I didn't know it would be so . . . my only excuse."

"What are you talking about?" she asked in obvious confusion. "What Calling?"

He shook his head, grimacing. After long moments, he straightened and staggered to his feet. "The pain lessens." When he stood, his robe parted naturally in a line along his front. In the shadows of the breach, there were two cocks now. Both were hot, sanguine, and roped with thick, blood-rich veins.

Catching the scent of her woman's slit, his man-cock strained at attention from its nest. A second cock rose above it, this one more suited to breech another tighter sort of entrance in a woman's body. Beyond the window curtains, the moon waxed full now, urging him toward rut.

Carefully, he folded the fabric closed again and retied the sash so the stiff folds of his robe helped disguise what he was not yet ready to reveal.

"I must take my ease within your body tonight," he announced grimly. "Do you understand?"

Jordan nodded. "You wish to have concupiscent relations with me," she said like a schoolgirl reciting a lesson.

He raised a brow at her calm attitude. "You're willing then?"

Her smile blazed and she threw her arms around his waist. "Thank God. You've been so distant lately. I thought you no longer wanted me, now that you've considered the truth of what my skirts contain."

Raine laughed hollowly, his arms automatically encircling her. Between them his pricks twitched, yearning to taste her. He rubbed a hand over her back, searching her dress for the most expedient way to exit her from it. He needed to touch skin. But he was too needy and she wasn't ready. Better to let her keep her clothes for the moment.

"Bacchus, I should have taken you before this night . . . this is not the way . . . but I must. I only hope you will forgive me when it is done."

She drew back and her black eyes twinkled at him. "You sound quite desperate to have me. I like that."

He only grunted. She had no idea what was to come.

Taking her arm, he tugged her into his chamber. He felt himself growing frantic. Attempting to regain some semblance of self-control, he sat on the edge of his bed. He withdrew a slim metallic cylinder from his pocket and placed it in her palm, hoping she didn't notice how his hand shook.

"Take this key. Go to the lacquered cabinet in the corner and open it while I can still let you. Take the elixir you find there and pour yourself a glass of it. Then come back to me."

She twirled the shaft of the ornate pewter key between a finger and thumb, her eyes brimming with questions.

"Make haste!" he added, waving her away when she hesitated.

Jordan hurried to the cabinet to do his bidding. Ramming the key into the lock, she fiddled a moment to align pewter teeth with pins, darting concerned glances at him all the while. After a bit, the lock gave a *snick* and the door creaked open. Inside there was a single shelf upon which sat a dark decanter and a jeweled goblet.

She removed the bottle and squinted at the markings on its throat, finding the ancient language indecipherable. She unstoppered it, sniffing. "Is it a medicine of some sort?"

He laughed darkly. "Yes, medicine."

"Then surely you must be the one to take it." Removing the goblet, she splashed the decanter's ruby-colored contents into it and brought it to him.

Perched on the edge of the bed, he watched her with a predatory expression.

She sat beside him and put the glass to his lips, wanting to soothe whatever was the cause of his suffering. "Here, take some," she coaxed.

He turned his jaw from her. "No, Jordan. I partook of a similar brew earlier this evening with Nick. If you truly wish to help me, you must be the one to drink it."

"But—"

"Now. Quickly. 'Tis Moonful."

Glancing toward the window, Jordan glimpsed the harvest moon. Perfectly round, it clung to the breast of night's velvet cloak like a shining orange pendant.

She looked back at him, unsure. "Can you promise me you aren't ill?"

The moon chose that precise moment to slant a veil of light across his cheek. His fingers gripped the mattress, nearly ripping it.

"Just do as I ask. Drink. Please." He exhaled the last word on a hiss.

"I'm drinking, I'm drinking." She put the goblet to her lips and tilted it. Over the rim, she studied him in confusion.

His loss of control was so unlike him that it was likely frightening her. But she'd seen nothing yet.

Her expression pursed. The elixir was as smooth as silk, but it tasted different to every individual. She obviously didn't like it. A moment later, she set it aside half-finished.

"More," he urged.

"Ugh!" But she lifted the drink again and managed to get most of it down.

They sat there then, side by side on the edge of his bed, silent for the moment. She sent him a sidelong glance and took his hand in hers, toying with it where it rested on her thigh.

"What are we waiting for?" she asked softly.

"Just wait," he breathed.

Slowly, he sensed the Change come over her. The elixir was designed to bring it about in both of them. The brew he'd taken earlier had sharpened his need. Its spirits were zinging through her system now, warming her and calling her toward lust.

Beside him, she shifted and pressed her knees together as though trying to capture some sensation high between them. He scented her burgeoning arousal. It was almost time.

His gaze slid sideways to graze her. "How do you feel?"

"Good. I feel good. Does it seem overly warm in here to you?" She fanned herself with one hand. With the other, she plucked at the neckline of her gown, offering him tantalizing glimpses of the breasts that swelled beneath.

He groaned helplessly and pulled her to stand. "Remove your gown."

Her hands dutifully slid to the clasps at her bodice. The lethargy stealing over her made her slow and clumsy. She slipped two of them from their hooks, then a third. Then, appearing to tire of their purpose, her hands fell away.

"Undress," he pleaded with the last of his good intentions.

"Help me," she teased, shooting him a coquettish glance from beneath the fringe of her lashes.

Raine snarled low in his throat. He turned her around and ripped at the fastenings, tearing the dress off her in his haste. Spying a letter opener on her writing desk, he grabbed it and sliced the strings of her corset.

In dazed surprise she looked down at the lovely gown and corset that now lay in rags at her feet.

"I'll buy you another gown. And another corset," Raine promised, hoping to head off any rebuke that might require a time-consuming discussion he could ill afford. "A dozen more. Just make haste onto my bed. I beg you."

Jordan's eyes widened, but she did as he asked, climbing onto his mattress wearing only her chemise.

Raine devoured the sight of the delectable creature awaiting him on his bed. Her golden skin contrasted with the darkness of his bedcovering, the darkness of his soul. She'd sat with her knees together and folded tight, with her feet tucked beneath her rear. She'd turned her back to him, still reluctant to showcase those parts of her that made her so unusual. But her choice of position suited his purposes just now.

His robe hit the ground. Naked, he joined her on the bed, kneeling behind her. Lifting the chemise high over her head, he tossed it away. The fur of his thighs bristled against her softness as he forked his legs around hers. He moved close until his cocks prodded her lower back.

Low between them he lightly kissed her puckered anus with the pad of a forefinger. "I'm going to come inside you here," he whispered at her ear. "With my cock."

She looked at him over her shoulder. He read the worry that pushed its way through the effects of the ancient elixir. "Will it hurt?"

"It may prove uncomfortable, at least at first. But I'm told that the presence of an object in the rear ring often intensifies the pleasurable sensation of contractions during a woman's orgasm."

She smiled at his clinical description. "Then by all means."

The Calling was usually a serious, carnal business, so he was surprised to find himself returning her smile. He lifted her hips, so she stood on her knees, then aligned the crowns of his shafts to her openings, preparing to link with her.

Abruptly, he checked. "Cream. Damn. What am I thinking? Don't move."

Leaping from his bed, he dashed to her room and located a squat jar of cream on her dressing table. Unscrewing the lid, he gazed at the thick, milky substance within. At the bottles and boxes on the table. At the varied feminine things Jordan had accumulated since coming to his home.

The smell of Faerie glamour wafted to him. The scent was sweetness tempered with spice, the smell of fresh autumn and pale sunlight. It surrounded him, permeating her room and belongings.

He lifted his silver gaze to the mirror that hung on the wall. And saw himself.

Saw how horribly changed he was physically. Saw the soft down of sepia fur that now covered his legs from thigh to ankle. The fur not of a man, but of an animal. Having sprouted with the onset of the Calling, it would not disappear until the coming of dawn.

Though he wanted to turn away, he forced himself to look. To see himself for the half-beast, half-Human he was. To see the huge vein-roped man-penis jutting from his dark thatch, its blood-purpled head straining in search of quim. And to see its twin, a second ruddy penis angling high from his pelvis only three finger spans above it.

It was the nature of the Satyr and he had experienced such changes before—at least a dozen times each year. But he'd always avoided looking at himself when he was this way. This was how his first wife had seen him. As Jordan would.

His eyes wandered over the jars and vials on her dressing table, the cushion she'd sewn for the chair, the embroidery project she'd tossed in a basket nearby. Like her, everything here was feminine and delicate. Fragile.

Tonight he might hurt her. At a certain point, he might not be able to stop himself from taking her again and again, whether she was willing or not. It was a horrifying thought.

Had it been some last shred of decency in him that had made him come in here, he wondered. After all, he had salve of his own, in his room. At times, he resorted to using it to masturbate himself the multiple times necessary to assuage his nightly need. It was makeshift, but at least he hurt no one. Disgusted no one. Used no one, save himself. Maybe fate was offering him a second chance to regain his self-control before he made a terrific mistake.

If he could bring himself to climax a half-dozen times or so here in her room, perhaps he could take the edge off. It was not too late to summon Shimmerskins to relieve him if that didn't work. What was one more such night spent with only his hand and conjured women for comfort? After a modicum of satiation, he might even be able to make his way to the glen to continue his fucking. The farther he got from Jordan, the better.

He scooped cream from her jar. Half sitting on the dressing table, he gripped his fevered cocks, one in each hand. His brothers' pricks were slipping inside their women even now. Nick would be with Jane in the sacred glen under the full moon. Lyon would be secreted somewhere in Paris more than likely taking Shimmerskins under him, unless he'd already found Feydon's third daughter. The rise in his brothers' desire sent a new, sharp hunger churning in his gut. All too soon his brothers would be in full-blown rut. Gods help him then.

With unsteady hands, he began massaging himself, praying he had the willpower to keep himself from the woman who waited in his bed. Earnestly, he milked the engorged shafts in his strong hands from root to crown and back. The rhythmic pumping elongated and thickened him to the point of pain. But the feel of a fist wasn't what he craved. His desperation mounted.

A sudden noise alerted him that he was not alone. Turning his head, he saw that Jordan had followed him and was now standing in the doorway between their rooms. She lounged against the doorjamb watching him from below half-lowered eyelids.

Why had she left his bed?

He stood and turned his back to her, continuing the stroking all the while, only to realize she would see his reflection in the mirror. Still, he kept up the motions with his hands, needing the stimulation.

"Shut the door," he muttered, his tone dangerously even. "Use my bed. Sleep."

She pouted. "I missed you."

Frustration welled up in him. Perhaps it was best she see him for the half-beast he truly was and learn to fear him whenever the moon waxed full. He turned to face her again, letting her view him in all his salacious glory. The slurp of his creamy fists was loud now, lascivious. His dual penises jutted from his body like great sausages grown too long and fat for their casings.

But she didn't run. She only watched, her eyes locked on the movement of his hands.

Watching her in turn, Raine noted the subtle signs of arousal. The more visible venous patterns across her breasts. Her lips had a taken on a sensual curve and her cheeks were flushed and heated. Her unique Faerie scent reached out, intoxicating him.

Why wasn't she repulsed? Did she think all men changed in this freakish fashion under a full moon, sprouting fur and a second shaft?

Her hand lifted. Oh so gently, she brushed her fingers over a wine-tipped nipple and sighed as softly as a whisper. She toyed with the small tender point of flesh, twisting and plucking. Her other hand drifted downward, finding her own small penis. It angled high, tumescent. She took it between her thumb and fingers and stroked it in imitation of him.

Since she'd first entered her bedchamber, he'd been treading a razor edge between reason and cold-eyed need. At the sight of her touching herself, he toppled completely over the edge into the mind-numbing insanity of crazed lust.

All thoughts of avoiding her tonight deserted him. She was his. He would take her as he was meant to. Damn it all.

He straightened, grabbing the cream jar.

With sultry eyes, she watched the heavy sway of his cocks as he advanced on her.

"I need you," he told her, his voice rough. "I apologize if it causes you any—distress."

She only nodded. "Hurry."

"Bacchus! A lamb to the slaughter," he gritted. Grasping her shoulders, he turned her and pressed her against the nearest wall. Flattening her palms on it, she brushed her nipples across the wallcovering—an embossed velveteen pattern that he recalled his former wife had painstakingly chosen for this room.

Even as he went to knee her legs apart, she was already spreading them for him. He delved a hand deep into the cream jar, dredging out the remainder of it in one scoop. Then he let the jar fall to the floor where what was left of its contents slowly oozed out over the expensive carpet. The resulting stain would forever be a reminder of this night.

From behind her, the trough of his cream-filled hand dipped through her thighs. Sloppily, he palmed a sufficient quantity of the ointment through her pubic hair and along the plump folds of her labia, then drew it high toward himself to moisten the crevice between her buttocks.

His thumb pressed at the ring he found there. "When I begin to delve inward here, push outward with your muscles," he instructed. She didn't answer. "Jordan—!"

"Yes, yes, I hear you," she said. "I'll try, but it's hard to remember."

Cursing himself for a lecherous bastard, he moved close, gripping a creamy cock in each hand. There would be time enough for regrets later. He worked the broad crown of his lower man-penis just inside her slickened vaginal opening, then nudged the cheeks of her rear apart with the head of his pelvic penis, quickly finding the aperture along the vertical divide.

He glanced down at the play of sacred moonlight across her smooth back and the swells of her buttocks. Gods, she was beautiful.

He planted a hand on the wall by her head. His other hand

angled low across her belly, holding her as he flexed his hips, introducing himself. The muscle guarding the opening in her ass defied him, but his crown prodded on and punctured it. Heeding her gasp, he held a moment, gentling her.

Long seconds later she turned her head, whispering. "Please, I'm dying. Come inside me."

Her words had scarcely evaporated from the air before he was thrusting, lodging himself ever deeper in both rectum and vagina. Though his Satyr blood urged him on, he forced himself to be careful with her, giving her body time to grow accustomed to him. When she whimpered, he soothed. When she begged, he slogged onward. Grudgingly, her slits took more of him, and more and more, until . . .

. . . at last, both cocks—that of Satyr and that of man—were buried to the hilt in her.

"You're tight," he said against her ear.

"Is that bad?" Her words were thready, and he knew her body was still adjusting to him.

"No, it's—" He searched for words to describe the sensation of having both of his cocks lodged inside her and found none that were adequate. "Good. It's good, Jordan."

"I'm glad." Her hand reached back to caress his cheek and he turned his lips to kiss her palm.

Enfolding her hand in his, he pressed it to the wall as he began to saw his cocks in a measured lunge and retreat. Their fingers twined, mating as their bodies did. He tried to maintain an easy pace, deluding himself he remained in command of his wits.

But the Calling soon made a mockery of his control, swamping him with cruel need. When she started to move with him, animal instinct overtook him and his very existence was reduced to one desperate goal—to fuck his mate.

He gave himself up to the barbaric rapture of rutting her under the fullness of a sacred moon. Air rasped from her lungs each time he slammed into her, and she caught tiny, fluttering breaths each time he pulled back. He tasted her neck, whispering. The dark words of the old Satyr language fell from his lips unbidden, tying her to him in the ancient ways.

His words soon degenerated to mindless grunts associated with the rhythm of his fucking. Long moments passed with only their toneless gasps and the humid slap of flesh and bone to relieve the silence. He had no idea whether the feminine body before him was experiencing pleasure or pain. His own body had grown selfish, devoted solely to its own rabid hunger, as it hurtled toward climax.

Savagely he fornicated, unable in the heat of the Calling to withhold anything of himself. Unable to take care with her as he should. The beast in him humped her, ramming with a strength that shuddered and reddened the cheeks of her buttocks.

Climax welled in him. He growled—a low, feral sound that vibrated with carnal intent.

He kneed her legs wider, until her smooth thighs lay over his furred ones and he supported her weight. Her feet dangled as his thrusts nailed her to the wall.

Abruptly, his entire body tautened. A primal roar tore from his throat as he . . . fell . . . over . . . the . . . edge.

Twin streams of molten cum blasted from his balls to his cocks, spewing his sticky-wet seed deep inside her. Distantly, he heard her gasp at the unexpected sensation. His coming urged her body over its own precipice and he felt the walls of her channels wrench on him as she found her own woman's orgasm.

What he fed, her body swallowed in hungry, rhythmic gulps. Together, they rose on each wave, gasping as it crashed over them, relaxing against each other during its ebb, only to rise again.

When the surge of their coming eventually turned lazy, she slumped her forehead against the forearm she'd braced high against the wall, trying to catch her breath. "That was—"

"—Amazing." His chest pressed against the warmth of her back and he surrounded her middle with his arms, in a brief grateful hug. He kissed her temple, the flush of her cheekbone, the damp tendrils of her hair that clung to the back of her neck.

His gaze found the window. The moon hadn't wandered far across the sky. The Calling would be upon him until dawn. Could she withstand his attentions till then?

Though he'd reached satisfaction, the heat of his passion still roiled. He would die if he could not have her again. And again.

She jerked in alarm as his pelvic cock twitched, then retracted from her. "What's ha-happening?"

"My second cock is done for the night," he told her. Satiated, it recoiled inside him where it would stay leashed until the next Calling. But his man-penis remained well rooted in her, still throbbing with enthusiasm.

His lust would swell dangerously again within moments. But he would have time to move her before he took her again. Lifting her off his remaining shaft, he carried her to his room and lay her on her back upon his bed. Lazily, she watched him move over her.

The sight of the small, shy rod that lay stiff and unsatisfied on her belly sent saliva bursting over his tongue. Without thinking, he lowered his head, licking the pearl of pre-cum he found in its cockslit.

She came to life, digging her heels into the mattress and shoving herself away and higher along the bed until she half sat upon his pillows. "What do you think you're doing?"

He gazed at her in disbelief. "You made no demur at my sprouting fur and a second cock, yet now you are astounded by my desire to do this?" He gestured toward her phallus.

She hid it under the cup of her hand and shook her head. "It's just that this is a part of myself I never considered sharing in *that* way."

He slipped his palms under her knees, taking one of her legs in each hand and forking them wide on either side of him. Slowly he pulled until her inner thighs met his bent knees and she reclined under him again. His eyes held hers as he bent and kissed the back of the hand she'd lain over her prick. His tongue lapped between her fingers, licking at the shaft she tried to shield.

"I've never tasted another cock," he told her between kisses. "Never taken one between my lips. Never even considered doing such a thing. But this particular cock is part of you. If we're to be lovers, we can't let it come between us. Well, I suppose it may *come* between us at times."

She glared at him. "Are you actually daring to make a joke?"

"I'm trying to put you at ease."

"Ease?" She gave her prick a quick squeeze, feeling how swollen it was. "It's not working."

"Then move your hand and let me apply something other than words."

She raked her teeth over her lower lip. "I'm not sure."

He tried another tack. Gently, he rubbed a middle finger between her labia, feeling the slight roundness where testes had puffed it into unusual fullness. With both thumbs, he separated the folds protecting her vagina.

Gods, her pussy was the most beautiful thing he'd ever seen. Like a velvet heart with rose petals swirled around its center. He licked it, tasting himself. Some of the semen he had given seeped from her, trickling onto the bedcovers. His seed. But not his childseed. He'd been careful.

She moaned and her head fell back.

His forefinger replaced his tongue and he felt her inner muscles contract and grip him. His mouth went higher, until it again nudged at the feminine hand that clutched her cock. Her fingers inched away, just a bit. Just enough.

Angling his head, he took the base of her root in his mouth, sliding silkily along it. Below, his finger continued to play, ducking lazily inside her channel and back out.

Her fingers tensed, then relaxed and inched a bit higher, toward her belly button. Then higher still. He took advantage of each retreat, moving his wet, open mouth up her as she slowly yielded ground. Until finally, her hand retreated to her waist and he had her.

His tongue swirled over the smooth velvet plum that capped her shaft. Then he claimed the entire prize, engulfing her fully into the slippery heat of his mouth.

She drew in a sharp breath and then exhaled on another moan as he worked the firm O of his lips over her crown, sucking, tonguing, and lipping its plinth. From time to time he stroked from crown to root, then back again. In this, there was little guesswork for him. Having a cock—sometimes two—himself, he knew exactly what would feel best to her.

Goosebumps formed on her skin and her thighs quivered. Her knees drew up.

She touched his hair, halfheartedly pushing at him. "It's feeling a little too good. Maybe you should move away," she whispered. "What if it, you know, spends?"

"I'll drink it."

Her eyes widened, fascinated. "Oh God." Her head fell back again, exposing her throat. Seconds later, her clawed fingers crimped the bedsheets as her prick convulsed, spurting its offering into his throat. Just a few drops came with each spasm, but he savored the salty, tangy-sweet taste of her cum. Gently, he suckled, taking it until she had no more to give.

Then he rose over her.

"Jordan," he murmured. It took everything within him, but he somehow summoned up the humanity to ask. "I need you.

Can you take me inside you again here?" He touched a finger between her labia.

Jordan's lashes fluttered and her dazed eyes stared up at him. Licking her lips, she managed to nod.

Joy burst within him when he saw his own lust mirrored in her eyes. She wouldn't fight him, nor would she turn him away. Later, when she was sore from his attentions, he'd introduce her to yet another feature of the Calling—the Seeker. Its ropy length would unfurl from his tailbone. Scenting her slits, it would seek them out and secrete a healing balm there that would ease any chafing his taking of her had caused, thus allowing him to continue his rut with her until dawn.

Leaning closer, he kissed her lips. She draped her wrists on his shoulders and gave him a sweet smile. Her cock was soft between them now. He could still taste it in his mouth.

Returning her smile, he allowed the dark enjoyment of Moonful to fully overtake him again. To drag him into a carnal vortex where he could see to his needs and focus only on his pleasure and hers. The plump knob that tipped his engorged penis slid home, deep into the welcoming wetness of her.

23

The next morning, for the first time in all his twenty-seven years, Raine awoke with a woman in his bed. A woman who, for the good of this world, was destined to be his wife whether she wished to be or not.

Fortunately for him, this soon-to-be wife seemed comfortable right where she was at the moment—tucked against him. His hand was between her legs now, idly toying in her slickness. A copious slickness for which his cock was responsible.

The Calling had tethered them last night, more thoroughly than a hundred matings on nights when the moon was only a sliver could have. The bond between them would grow stronger over time, with future matings under future full moons.

Next to him Jordan slept on, as women always did after a Calling. There was a pale bruise on her neck. He raised the cover and found several more on her breasts. Last night his control had slipped its leash. He'd been unable to stop himself from taking her time after time. It had been good. Sweet, pure pleasure. Now that his body had tasted hers during Moonful, he would not be able to stay away.

Frustration at himself—at his lack of control—rose up in him.

A soft hand curved his hip.

"I love you," Jordan murmured. Her eyes were dreamy, her skin warm and flushed from sleep.

He stiffened and rolled from his bed.

"No," he informed her, jerking on a shirt. "You don't."

"I don't?" she asked. Raising on one elbow, she patted his pillow and tried to tease him into a better humor. "Why don't you come back to bed and let me persuade you otherwise."

He'd like nothing better. Her slit wasn't chafed or ill used, he knew. The Seeker had intermittently seen to her comfort. Even after last night's sequential debauchery, he could still have her again now without hurting her. His cock hardened at the thought.

But his jaw hardened as well. "I have work to do. The vines need—"

"They can wait a bit, can't they?" She leaned forward so her nipples peeked above the coverlet.

He yanked his trousers on. "Sleep. You must be tired."

She lay back, yawned, and stretched her arms high above her head. "Yes. Aren't you?"

"The Satyr are invigorated after a Calling night. Our female victims have the opposite reaction."

That implacable cloak of control was back. However, now Jordan knew more of what lay beneath it. Raine's passions had completely overwhelmed his self-imposed restraint last night. And she'd loved it. Loved him. But she sensed he would only withdraw further if she persisted in trying to hold him here this morning.

She yawned again, gazing at him with black, knowing eyes. "No matter what you believe, I was not your victim last night. And I do love you, you know."

"You learned more of what I am last night," he said, ramming his shirttails into the waist of his trousers. "But you don't know me. You don't even know yourself."

"What is so terrible that it would change my feelings about you?"

Muscles bunched in his chest where his shirt hung open and a tendon flexed along the side of his neck. He took a shuddering breath as he surveyed her, seeming on the verge of shattering into a thousand pieces.

She pushed herself up into a sitting position. "Raine, what's wrong?"

Spying the dress he'd removed from her last night lying on the floor, he snatched it up as though to offer it to her. His expression turned appalled as he obviously only then recalled how he'd ruined it last night. Throwing it to the floor, he stalked into her room. She heard him open her armoire. When he returned, he tossed a fresh dress, shoes, and a wrap to her.

"Get dressed and come with me," he said. "I'll show you what it is you think you love."

After putting on his boots, he stood over her, more impatient than she'd ever seen him. Once she complied with his instruction, he hustled her through the house, out into the rear garden, and beyond.

The light of dawn was a hazy pink, filtered through the canopy of hawthorns. Ahead, a cool breeze swept the pale morning sun across a grassy meadow turned amber by morning's frost.

Raine held her wrist, pulling her along as though expecting she would try to escape. But she followed willingly, wanting to know what it was that he would reveal of himself.

He drew her onward, through the crunch of autumn and under the forest's skirts where purple phlox and red clover grew wild. Small hillocks of flowering faerie thyme clung here and there. The air smelled of dew and damp morning.

Now and then, he lifted her over a lichened stone wall, or a trickling brook, or held olive branches aside for her to pass. She still savored these small courtesies from him and was almost glad when they encountered such obstacles along their way.

In moments, they passed through a series of acanthus-wreathed Corinthian columns and entered a large, circular clearing. Raine pulled her to the center of it, where he abruptly halted. He stood behind her, fingers biting into her upper arms. "Here. Look around you."

In brittle silence, he waited for her to take in her surroundings. She did as he asked, gazing slowly from left to right, absorbing everything. Why had he brought her here? What was it he wished her to see?

Altars dotted the glen like gleaming white tables at a wedding feast, waiting for guests to arrive. Around the outer edge of the clearing, pale statues rose larger than life, forming a ring. There were dozens of them, each fine in detail and craft. They were beautiful. Salacious. And strangely familiar.

Sudden recognition shivered over her spine.

She stepped from him and spun in a slow circle, her gaze moving over one statue, then the next and the next and the next. Those at the far end of the clearing were less easy to make out.

Nervously, she hugged herself, surveying the ground around her feet. "Are there snakes here?"

"Snakes?" He looked at her as though she were speaking in a foreign tongue. "No. Why in the world do you ask?"

She shrugged, embarrassed.

As though sleepwalking, she went to stand before one of the statues. It was a particularly appealing one, of a nymph. Scantily clad in only the barest veil, the creature smiled from her perch, beckoning all who came to join her in sensual revelry.

Jordan stepped closer. Her hand slid over the sparkling granite of a pristine foot clad in a delicate sandal.

"What is this place?" she breathed in awed tones.

"A place for rutting." Raine's voice was cold, clipped. "A

place where the pagan rituals of my ancestors have been reenacted time and time again, throughout the centuries. A place where my brothers and I gather once a month at Moonful. Where our bodies change in ways that make us as much beast as man. Where I am driven to fuck myself senseless from dusk to dawn."

Just as he had last night. With her.

She glanced at him. "You must hate that. Losing control."

He waved toward the statues, his expression tortured. "Look upon them. The drunken Silenus, Pan with his pipes, the half-naked maenads. Drunken revelry, deviant behavior. This is what I come from. What I am."

He wanted to shock her, she realized.

"If you are to turn away from me," he told her, "away from your own beginnings, then do so now. Do not prolong this pretence of love."

"My own beginnings?"

"We—you and I—come from a place called ElseWorld." He threw the words at her like stones, hoping to bruise her. To test her. "Magic is thick there like fog and commonplace. Every sort of fantastic creature dwells there."

She read the truth of what he said in his face. "Are there more there, made like me?

He nodded.

"And are they accepted there?"

"They're revered, kept in harems of the richest and most powerful of men and beast."

"So they're not free."

"No, not free." He turned away.

He'd shared his secrets with her—these secrets that made him what he was. Her what she was. She would confide in him as well.

"I've been here before," she told him.

He swung around, shocked. "What did you say?"

She was silent, loath to tell him more.

He made a gesture that encompassed the entire glen. "My brothers and I have erected a forcewall around this area. No one can enter without our expressly allowing it."

"I tell you I've been here before. I'll prove it." She closed her eyes. Without looking, she began to name the statues in order, even the ones whose features were too distant to discern. "There's Bacchus, the wine god. There are four nymphs at his feet. Next there are the bearded fornicators—four of them with their phalluses embedded in females. And then there are the two maenads, both fawning over one of the Satyr. And Priapus is there—"

Raine took her elbows, and she opened her eyes to find him staring intently down at her. "How did you see them?"

"In my dreams, years ago when I turned thirteen. Back then I thought they were ice sculptures. But I see now that they're stone. It was exactly like this in my dream." She pointed toward the distant edge of the glen. "Except Nick and Jane were standing over there, at the far end, though of course I didn't know who they were then."

She drew up, her expression turning to one of surprise. "Look. There they are now."

Sure enough, Nick and Jane had appeared at the far end of the glen, holding hands. Seeing Raine and Jordan, they came to join them. Jordan couldn't help but notice how rumpled both of them were. Jane's hair was askew and her dress was grass stained. Had they passed the night together, here in the glen as Raine had earlier described?

Jane shot her an embarrassed look, then spoke softly to Nick. "I'll continue to the house and tidy up."

But Nick sensed the tension in the air and kept her hand in his. "No, stay for the moment." He put an arm around her, tucking her to him so he supported her weight.

Nodding, she snuggled against him and covered a yawn with her hand.

Seeing it, Jordan couldn't help but yawn, too.

The two women grinned at one another in private amusement, each accurately gauging the reason the other was so weary.

"What is it?" Nick demanded of his brother.

"Jordan tells me she's been dreaming. Having nightmares," Raine told him baldly.

Nick shrugged. "And?"

"The dreams began at age *thirteen*," Raine added pointedly.

Nick's interest keened.

"So?" asked Jordan. "What's the significance of that?"

"It's the age of change," said Nick. He looked down at his dozing wife, gently petting her hair as he held her to his side. "Jane came into her ElseWorld powers at thirteen as well."

ElseWorld powers? Jordan hugged herself, suddenly wishing Raine would hold her close, too. But in his concern, he was all business.

"Tell us," he instructed.

Jordan squared her shoulders, preparing to reveal more of her deepest secrets. "Well, the first nightmare I can really remember came on the eve of my thirteenth birthday. But that's not unusual. Birthdays have never been pleasant occasions for me. The dreams I have then are rarely good ones."

Jane forced her eyes open. So she hadn't been truly asleep after all. "What happened in that first dream? Can you remember?" she asked kindly.

Jordan spread her hands, looking around the glen. "I saw this place. The statues frightened me then. They seemed so prurient. I've dreamed of them now and then over the last six years."

"And what of your other dreams?" asked Nick.

"Most dreams come to me as a series of three unrelated events.

They're often too puzzling to interpret at first. But they hint at things that actually do occur at a later time. For instance, when I met Raine, I was drawn to him because of the ribbons he carried. I'd dreamed of them. Dreamed that they offered—" Since Raine had repudiated her love, she was wary of reiterating it in front of his brother. "—something good," she finished lamely.

"Just before I came here, another such series of dreams began," she went on, the words tumbling out. "The first of them was fulfilled in Venice." She broke off, then rushed on, trying to avoid the memory of the dove and the shocking sight of her dead mother. "The second was about blue stockings, and then I wound up in a vat of grapes at the harvest festival, resulting in blue feet. Which is somewhat the same as blue stockings if you think about it. Now, only the third vision of the dream sequence remains unfulfilled. Once it occurs, I'll no doubt dream up an entirely new trio."

"Describe this third vision," Raine prompted.

She glanced around and her voice grew hushed, full of memories. "I'm drawn to a park—this very one. It's darker though. Night. There are white pillars, statues, and altars like the ones here."

"Go on," said Nick.

"There's also a snake here somewhere. I don't want to go to it. It wants to give me something. A gift. Whatever it is, I don't want it. Still, the snake keeps pulling me closer. If I accept its gift, I'll have to open a gate of some sort and let them inside. Don't ask me who 'them' are because I don't know."

"How does the snake in your dream appear to you? What does it look like?" asked Raine.

Jordan raised and dropped her shoulders in a shrugging gesture. "Like a snake. Writhing, flicking tongue. Beady eyes. Snakey."

"Are there any particular markings on its scales?" asked Nick.

"It doesn't have scales, now that you mention it. It's smooth," she said. "Black. What do you suppose it all means?"

"You're obviously a receptor," said Jane, blinking sleepily. "Few possess such an ElseWorld talent."

Jordan rolled her eyes. "Curse, more like. And what's a receptor?"

Over her head Raine and Nick exchanged a potent glance.

"She'd be highly prized by Feydon's offspring," said Nick. "And not just so that they can gain a foothold in EarthWorld."

"Will someone tell me what you're talking about?"

Raine considered her a moment. "Do you resemble your father?" he asked.

Jordan tugged at one of her shoulder-length black curls, wondering warily where this might be leading. "Not especially. I never met him, but I've seen his portrait. I favor my mother."

"That's because the man you believe fathered you was in fact not the father of your blood," Raine told her bluntly. "You mother gave you Human blood. But you also have the blood of Faerie in your veins, lent to you by your true-blood father, a king from a world that adjoins this one."

"Are you serious?" Jordan squeaked.

Raine, Nick, and Jane nodded as one.

Jane patted her hand, offering comfort. "Understanding will come with time. After due consideration, you'll find that many occurrences in your life up to now will begin to make sense to you in light of this newer context."

So her mother's dream of the circumstances of Jordan's conception nineteen years ago hadn't been a dream at all. It had been real. She stood there, reeling.

Nick gazed fondly at his wife. "Jane is your sister, born of the same father but a different mother."

Sister? This news was such a shock Jordan hardly knew what to say. To learn that she wasn't alone in the world and that this gentle female creature was a relative seemed more preposterous than all she'd heard before. She gazed at Jane with new interest.

Jane smiled at her. "I'm glad that news is finally out. It was our ElseWorld father who sent a letter directing Nick and Raine to find us. The letter claimed we and a third sister who has yet to be found were each endangered in some way."

Jordan stared at the three of them in turn, then she directed her gaze at Raine. "So our meeting wasn't accidental? You brought me here because of instruction you received in a letter from an adjoining world?" she asked coolly.

"I brought you here to offer you my protection," said Raine, planting his hands at his hips.

"Part of that protection requires a wedding," Nick added.

Raine glared at his brother.

Jane cupped Nick's shadowed jaw. "That's a private matter to be discussed between these two, don't you think, darling? Now, I'm exhausted. Will you see me to the house?"

Tugging on his arm, she coaxed him from the glen. And Jordan and Raine were left alone, surrounded by silent stone creatures.

Raine tossed a gauntlet. "I've asked a clergyman to post bans."

"What? Why?"

"So I can take you to wife, of course."

The idea of actually acquiring a husband was a strange and almost forbidden notion. Jordan allowed herself to imagine it as possible for the barest moment and then shook her head.

"I'm sorry, but my answer must remain no," she said.

His tone turned soft, belligerent. "Less than an hour ago, you said that you loved me."

She nodded.

"Then wed me."

"No," she said. "Because you don't love me."

He was silent, lending a tacit agreement to her statement that wounded her.

"And for other reasons," she added quickly, when it seemed he was about to argue further. "I don't plan to marry. Ever."

"Why the devil not?" Raine was surprised at how much it mattered to him. He'd thought it was only King Feydon's edict that was forcing his hand in this matter.

"By marrying, my very existence would be suspended. By law, I'd become a satellite to your planet."

"And be protected under my wing."

"Or suffocated there." Jordan shook her head automatically. "I won't take a husband—you or anyone else."

"Jordan—" he began, obviously planning to argue her to the ground.

"Do you truly wish to wed a woman who is not completely female?" she demanded, her voice rising. "One you found on the streets in Venice, naked save for a mask and a cloak?"

His voice turned surly. "How exactly did that circumstance come to pass? You never said."

She wandered away from him to brush away a golden leaf that had tumbled onto the surface of one of the altars. "My clothes were stolen from me that night." It was true. Salerno had taken them. "You saved me from what was likely a horrible fate and I'm grateful. But I believe any debt I've incurred has already been repaid in your bed."

Raine's jaw stubborned. "If you wish to continue to warm my bed, we must wed. Otherwise, you're in danger. ElseWorld is disturbed. Chaotic. Warring. The gate that your third dream hinted at is real. Many in that other world would like to snatch you through it. A prize like you would give one of the factions an advantage."

"Is it so bad there? In ElseWorld?"

"It was once a paradise," he informed her. "But I haven't been there for years. Only Nick has gone to that world in recent times as our envoy. He claims some sectors of it are unsavory now, not fit for civilized living."

"You say there are others like me there, made with both male and female parts. Perhaps it's where I belong."

Raine shook his head. "Your going there would put Earth-World in peril. There are those in ElseWorld who would leech your Human blood. The tiniest drop of it would enable a hundred of them to pass through the gates into this world. To bring their battles here. Once on our soil, they would seek to subjugate all those unlike them."

"Why have they not taken Jane for their purposes?" asked Jordan.

"She is married and mated, with offspring. All lend her protection against them." He stuck his hands in his pockets, glancing around. "Some in ElseWorld are watching us. Nick and I have felt it. They won't leave you alone until you're thoroughly mated and bound to me."

"How much more thoroughly can we mate beyond last night's many joinings?" she asked in disbelief.

He went to her. "I only mean to imply a continued, regular joining between us, over time. Over a course of months. Six at a minimum. Which in this world of course requires a wedding."

She made a disgusted noise and kicked the base of the altar with her slippered foot. "Very well, I shall give you the plain truth. You will no doubt desire children of your wife. But it's doubtful I can give them to you, nor to any man. I am infertile."

Infertile. The word reverberated in his head like thunder. No woman was infertile for a man of Satyr blood. During the Calling if he chose to give of his childseed, it would take root and grow in any woman he mated from the age of 15 to 115 with no difficulty.

That she believed herself unable to conceive might be a devastating matter to her, but he couldn't help but consider it convenient.

"Did you hear what I said? You've seen what's under my petticoats." She placed a hand over her skirt where it covered her genitals. "Because of that, it's likely I am made wrong for childbearing. I'm incapable of giving you heirs."

"It's not important."

"Every man wants children." Her mother had told her that often enough.

"I don't."

She shot him a skeptical look.

He found himself prodded into further speech, an unusual occurrence. He had been known to remain silent under the fiercest or most beguiling of stares.

"I'm not suitable father material," he admitted.

She waved a hand as though swatting an insect away. "Nonsense. You were born to be a father."

He stared at her, astounded. "And you're an expert on my strengths and faults, after so short an acquaintance?"

"I am." She counted his assets on her fingers. "You're hard working, loyal to your family, a patient teacher, wealthy, intelligent, handsome, amusing—at times. Now not being one of those."

He shook his head, bemused. "Suffice it to say I do not want children. I will be content with a companion if the situation I offer is agreeable."

"A sexual companion?"

He gave her an exasperated look. "Yes, by the Gods. Do you object?"

She batted her eyelashes in the way she'd once seen an opera actress do in the Piazza San Marco. "Not in the least."

Clasping her fingers behind his neck, she leaned against him and gave him a quick kiss. "I will lie with you."

His hands came to rest at her waist as she kissed his throat. "Live with you."

She slid from his hold and went lower, kissing his chest. "And love you."

She knelt. Unfastened his trousers. "But I have vowed that no man—not even you—will ever have control over me again."

Her lips delved into the shadowy gape of his open trousers to take him in her mouth.

Raine's fingers threaded her hair and he threw his head back. "This . . . discussion . . . isn't . . . over . . . ahhh!"

24

Salerno's beady eye peeked out from the vertical gap between his front door and its frame. When he saw the bishop on his step, he muttered, "Go away," and slammed the door.

But the bishop hadn't journeyed the distance from Tuscany to Venice in order to be turned away from his mission. He put his pudgy face close to the place the crack had been. "I know where La Maschera is to be found," he shouted.

The door was jerked open. Salerno stood there in the gap, hands on hips, eyeing him suspiciously. "Tell me."

"By and by." The bishop pushed past him and entered his home. "But first I will have some medical treatment from you. A cure in fact."

"For what ailment?" Salerno inquired, shutting the door and following him.

"A private one." The bishop's eyes shifted around the room, checking for eavesdroppers, then he lowered his voice. "And I'll have your assurance that all confidences I share this day will remain safely guarded."

"Yes, yes. Why should I gossip about one such as you? What

is it that ails you for God's sake so that we may move on to the more interesting subject of the information you possess?"

The bishop leaned close to him and whispered. "It's the French Disease."

Salerno took a hasty step backward. Nodding, he rubbed his clean-shaven chin with one hand as he surveyed his visitor head to toe. "Syphilis? I might've guessed. You have the look about you."

"And you have the look of a quack about you. Do you have a cure?"

"Doesn't every doctor? Who knows if any work? What are your symptoms?"

"Tumors, fever, aching bones, dizziness. A strong desire to kill the whore that gave this pox to me."

"I guess I needn't ask if you've become subject to angry outbursts," Salerno said snidely. "Any loss of feeling in your legs?"

The bishop shook his head.

"Follow me then." With that, he led the way from the room. As they passed deeper into the passageways of his home toward his pharmacy located in the rear, Salerno treated him to a discussion of various authoritative speculations on the causes of his malady.

". . . In his work *Contagion*, the poet and physician Fracastor adhered to an age-old belief that the planets play a role in outbreaks. When they line up a certain way, some think conditions are ripest for the emergence of the disease."

Only half-listening, the bishop ogled the strange items set on every shelf, countertop, and table they passed. Dried bat wings, shrunken insect carcasses—a weird lot. Finally they arrived at the back of the establishment. A doorway led outside to a small enclosed area filled with various bizarre mechanisms.

"Do you wish to examine me now?" the bishop asked, making to hitch himself onto the examining table.

Salerno shrugged, digging through some vials he'd located inside a glass-front cabinet. "No use. If you've got the pox, you've got the pox. What cures have you tried?"

"Mercury salve, caustic, the avoidance of exercise, purges."

"The gamut. Well, I have a new method. A device. You'll see." He selected a vial at last, measured some of its contents out, and stepped outside.

An hour later, the bishop found himself sweating the morning away, sitting in a fumigation tub in the garden behind Salerno's apartments. Only his flushed, florid face was visible where it protruded from a hole atop the great square-shaped iron compartment.

A fire below the enclosure heated and vaporized the mercury Salerno had taken from the vial and set at the bishop's feet. Its pollution swirled around his flesh and its fumes swamped his nose. Periodically, a comely young Sicilian woman replenished the blaze, scalding him and raising a fog of his curses.

"Your so-called cure is worse than my disease!" the bishop shrieked.

"You may depart at any time," Salerno suggested. "But I wouldn't advise it. Your case is advanced."

"And you're telling me this as though it was something I didn't know?" the bishop railed.

"There are limited number of treatments for the French Disease. Though interestingly enough, in France they call it the Italian Disease. No one wishes to take credit for such an infamous malady," Salerno told him. "Isabella! More wood!" he called. At Salerno's instruction, the servant came into the room and stirred the fire higher.

The steam hissed, causing the bishop to gasp. "I'm boiling, you fool. Let me out of this sweatbox before I expire."

Salerno waved the young woman away, saying, "Leave us a moment."

When she obeyed, he tapped the latch on the tub and studied the bishop. "You came bearing news. Let's have it and I'll let you out. Where is La Maschera to be found?"

"In Tuscany! In Tuscany, damn you!"

Salerno's thin lips tightened. "A big place. Precisely where in Tuscany?"

"The Satyr vineyards. The middle brother of the three is fucking your little prodigy. He even wishes to marry it, can you imagine?"

The claws of Salerno's hand grabbed the bishop by the throat. "Is that the truth?"

"Yes, I swear it on my mother's name!"

"Very well." Salerno released the latch. The bishop crawled his way out of the cruel containment just as the Sicilian girl returned. Seeing his flushed, dripping nakedness, she let out an outraged cry, flipped her apron over her eyes, and rushed back out.

The bishop's eyes followed her. "Was that truly a cure or did you just mean to torture me?" he gasped.

"It's touted as a cure. You'll have to let me know."

Seeing the direction of his gaze, Salerno added, "It has been suggested that the raping of a virgin may cure some of the ravages of syphilis. You might try it for good measure. I could arrange such a thing. For a fee."

The bishop's eyes flew to the doorway through which the girl had just disappeared, contemplating. He felt his prick stir. His eyes went back to find Salerno's knowing ones. "How much?"

25

Frustration was Jordan's sole companion as she waited a full hour after dinner one night, pacing, reading, pacing, working at her embroidery, pacing again. Then, at the stroke of nine and wearing only her nightgown and robe, she made for the stairs carrying a small, carefully packed bag. Stealthily, she crept down the circular staircase that led to the wine cellar.

Taking the last of the steps, she sited down the perfectly aligned rows of barrels that seemed to go on forever. At the far end of the cellar, there was a hazy light.

Once again, Raine was working late here among the casks. His experiments with hybridization along with his testing of the vats, racking of prior years' wine, blending, and seeing to a share of Lyon's duties while he was in Paris were taking all Raine's waking hours and then some.

He'd still found time to do his duty with her each night, continually refortifying the protective veil he claimed his love-making helped weave around her. But he'd recently been bedding her with a perfunctory efficiency, which told her he was miffed at her refusal to fall in with his marriage plans. She'd tried to cajole him in a variety of ways, but his mind and heart remained distant and by now she'd grown needy for his full attention.

So she'd plotted and planned. And tonight she was determined she would have all of him to herself.

Earlier, she'd measured out pinches of an herb Jane had supplied when Jordan admitted she sometimes had difficulty sleeping. It was the truth. Her dreams often deprived her of sleep. But she hadn't taken the herb herself. Instead, she'd dropped it into Raine's wine at dinner this evening.

Silently, she moved along the corridor now under the brick-vaulted ceiling and between the barrels stacked three high. She'd learned a great deal about winemaking over the weeks here. These barrels would last only five years at most. After that, their oak turned neutral and would add little beneficial flavor to the contents inside.

She swiped a finger along one of the metal hoops binding the staves of a barrel together. No dust. She rolled her eyes. Raine kept his cellar as meticulously as he did the rest of his home and estate. In a way it was fortunate, since she had no housekeeping skills to offer him.

This was the first-year cellar, Raine had told her. At the end of fermentation, about a month after the harvest, wine was racked—set in racks—here in these barrels where it would remain for about a year and a half. She felt a moment's sadness, knowing it was unlikely she would be here long enough to see this vintage bottled.

She found Raine in the cozy warmth of the small steward's room. He'd taken to napping here each night in this narrow bed. He was asleep on his back now, one broad hand alongside his head and another on his chest.

Stealthily she crept forward and touched his cheek. He didn't awaken. The herbs had done their job.

She set her bag on his worktable. Its surface was littered

with the tools of his blending efforts. A scale. Spoons of various sizes. Measuring cups. A half-dozen crystal glasses. A spittoon in which to expel wine he sampled and analyzed.

A corklike cylinder caught her eye. She picked up the glass bung. Each barrel stored here had one, forced into a hole on its upward side. It was cold, smooth, interesting.

She set it aside for the moment, opened the bag she'd brought, and spread its contents over the tabletop.

Raine awoke, instantly aware that something was amiss. He was lying on his back, in the wine steward's bed. But when he tried to rise, he found the action thwarted.

His head whipped aside to discover one of his wrists tied to the headboard with a leather strap. His head whipped to the opposite side where he observed his other wrist to be similarly lashed. A hard tug revealed his legs were encumbered as well, loosely anchored to the two bedposts at the foot of the bed. He was naked, splayed upon the feather mattress in an irate X.

He scented another presence nearby and his cock tightened with recognition. Jordan.

His eyes searched the dimness outside the circle of light given off by the candelabra on the small table beside his bed and found her.

She stepped nearer, her figure an indistinct blur in the area between light and shadow. She wore a long robe that completely swathed her petite figure.

"Untie me," he growled.

She took a fortifying breath. "Not yet."

He stared at her, clearly shocked by her defiance. "I don't find this amusing, Jordan. If I have to summon a servant to release me, you won't enjoy the consequences."

"The day servants have gone for the evening, and I've locked the doors against other interlopers," Jordan informed him. "I have you all to myself until morning."

Fierce anger blasted at her, but his voice was calm, controlled, and all the more intimidating because of it. "I'll ask you once more to untie me."

She shook her head slowly, refusing to quail.

He strained against the bonds, testing their strength.

"Stop! You'll only injure yourself." She sat beside him and tucked a hand high along his inner thigh, nudging his ballocks gently with her knuckles. "Do you think the world will end if you relax your control for a single night?"

"Quite possibly. I've told you about ElseWorld. About the gate. I must be on constant guard. Whatever you're planning, I advise against it," he warned.

With her other hand she caressed his masculine jaw darkened by evening stubble. "Forget that for tonight. Just for tonight."

His muscles turned rigid under her palm. In rejection or anticipation?

"I've allowed you liberties when I wasn't sure I'd enjoy them," she reasoned. "Yet I did enjoy them in the end. How does one know if a new experience will be fulfilling unless one tries it?"

His lips curved cruelly. "I hate to destroy the little fantasy you've created here, but this situation is nothing new to me."

Jordan gasped, uncertain. "Other women have restrained you?"

He raised an arrogant eyebrow, obviously pleased by her dismay. "Shall I tell you what delicious and perverse sexual acts they performed on me while I was incapacitated and at their disposal?"

He was baiting her, she realized, hoping to get his way.

Instead of releasing him, she leaned closer, gently combing the hair at his temples with her fingers. "Yes. Tell me everything they did," she suggested. "Then I won't repeat their performance and bore you. I wouldn't want you to nod off before you have sufficiently pleased me. Not after the trouble I've gone to. I had to cut your clothes off, you know. And arranging your limbs was a sore trial."

Raine snarled in frustration and yanked even more violently at his bindings.

Stepping away from the lurching bed, she forced herself to watch his struggles with outward calm.

"Where in the name of Bacchus did you learn to tie knots like this?" he demanded.

Along the docks of Venice when I was a boy, roaming the streets with other boys, she thought. But he didn't know about that part of her life. And she didn't want him to.

"I've lived on the streets, as I told you. I was taught all manner of useful things true ladies are not."

He fisted both hands and gave the bindings a final yank, but they held. Sensing the futility of fighting her, he turned his face to the wall, shutting her out.

"Shall I tell you how I undressed you?" She sat alongside him again and massaged a hand over his hip bone.

He pretended to ignore her, but she heard his reaction to her suggestion in his altered breathing. Felt it in the coiled bunch of muscles and the tension of his flesh. Saw it in the thickening of his phallus at the apex of his thighs.

Long, silent moments passed, testing her will to continue. This unbending control of his was strangling him, though he couldn't seem to understand that. She would leave him one day soon. But before she did, she would give him this gift—the knowledge that he could surrender his control now and then. And that the world would not come crashing down around his ears as a result.

She stiffened her resolve. "Pouting?" she inquired.

When he didn't respond, she felt momentarily defeated. If he'd experienced restraint before at the hands of others without overcoming his fear of appearing weak, what could she possibly hope to prove? Her shoulders drooped and she considered unbinding him. But then a new thought struck her.

"During those other encounters," she mused aloud, "I imagine you made sure you were bound only as long as you wished to be. Your paid companions wouldn't have defied you if you had asked to be untied. So all the while you were restrained, you must have known you were ultimately in control."

His head rolled toward her, stormy silver glinting at her from twin slits.

"Therefore this will be a new experience for you after all!" she said, with burgeoning confidence. "Restraint against your will."

"By Bacchus, untie me, woman."

"No. At least, not yet," she said.

"Damn you!" he fumed. "Get on with it then. Do whatever you plan to do and be done with this game."

"Very well." She gathered herself and her resolve and rose on her knees to straddle him. Holding his gaze, she began to undress. The robe slid from her arms and flowed gently down her body to drape over his thighs.

The gown it uncovered was golden silk with French lace insets that cupped her breasts affording tantalizing glimpses of her nipples. The lacy bodice had slim straps and was fastened in front by means of seven ribbons tied from chest to hip. Below them the lace gave way to a skirt of translucent silk, which alternately revealed and concealed with her movements.

A delicate finger toyed with the first ribbon tied between her breasts. He watched intently as she pulled at it and then another below it, loosening them one by one.

"You won't entice me to your cause, no matter how you may behave like a common strumpet," he growled.

Her hand paused and then continued its work. "The night is young, and I thought your tastes ran to strumpets."

"Huh," he grunted. The heat of his eyes burned every inch

of skin revealed as she opened her gown with exquisite care, slowing unveiling what lay beneath.

"Do you like my gown?" she inquired when the silk gaped from breast to waist. Only one tie still held fast at her midsection.

"I'm in no mood to offer compliments to you," he replied. But his eyes were riveted to the single tie that remained.

She ran the fingers of one hand idly along his erection where it angled high from him, hard alongside hers. The pad of her thumb smeared the creamy drop that had seeped from his tip and spread it over her own. His eyes heated.

"Still, I see it has tempted you."

"I'm sure you chose it knowing the effect it would have," he replied grudgingly. "I suppose Jane supplied it."

She nodded. "It's such a delightfully wicked gown, don't you think?" she whispered in falsely scandalized tones.

His laughter was tinged with sarcasm. "Exactly. Why do you imagine I find it so appealing?"

"I'm glad. But I believe I should seek to quell this streak of wantonness in you," she said gently.

He smirked. "Good luck. I have had no success in doing so myself lo these many years."

"Perhaps if I remove temptation from your sight." From the table beside the bed, she gathered the silk scarf she'd brought. Holding it stretched taut between her hands, she attempted to place it over his eyes.

"Don't you dare," he warned. He thrashed violently, refusing to cooperate. After struggling with him for several moments, she desisted and giving him a perplexed look, tossed the silken square away to land on the bedcovers somewhere above his head.

"If you won't untie me, why don't you untie that last ribbon there instead?" he suggested, glancing pointedly at the solitary bow still secured at her waist.

She smiled down at him, pretending to consider his suggestion. "All right," she agreed at length.

Leaning forward so the curves of her breasts were inches from his gaze, she fumbled for the end of the last remaining ribbon tethering the fabric of her gown. She gave it a yank.

At precisely the same moment, and before he could realize her intent, she reached over his head and folded the silk scarf over his face.

"There, now I have released the ribbon as you requested," she told him, sitting back.

He jerked in sudden awareness that she'd managed to blindfold him after all. "That's not exactly what I had in mind," he said ruefully.

"I'm truly sorry, but I simply couldn't allow you to see me like this." The flat of her hands caressed his chest in slow circles. "My gown is quite indecent and I fear it might put scandalous ideas into your head."

He chuckled in spite of himself. "Too late."

She stretched fully atop him and rested her chin upon her fist at his breastbone. Now that his eyes were hidden, she was free to gaze at him with all the love she felt for him. The pads of her fingers circled one of his taut, brown nipples. "I touched you here with my mouth. While you were asleep. Did you know?"

He grunted, his attention caught.

"Like this." She bent her head and lightly suckled him.

He gasped at the unexpected caress. "Take this vile rag off my eyes. I want to see you."

She pulled herself higher and kissed his throat. "No."

He swore. "Just remember I *will* eventually get loose. Then we shall see how brave you are, my pretty tormenter."

"Let me have my way with you," she coaxed, nibbling her way along his neck. "Bend to my will. Just for tonight. Please."

A moment later, she felt him angle his head to the side to

allow her lips better access. The movement was infinitesimal. But joy soared within her. He was accepting and even enjoying her attentions. It was a chink in the armor of that rigid control. She proceeded to taste him as she'd longed to—his throat, shoulders, chest, belly, and lower—as though she had all the time in the world.

When she met his cock she sucked at the head, lightly, lovingly. Her fingers threaded through his thatch to find and fondle his sacs.

He groaned deep in his throat.

"I enjoyed undressing you before you woke," she went on as she tasted him. "Having you in my power. I could have done anything to you. To your body. Did you feel me take your phallus in my mouth as you slumbered? It stiffened under my lips, so I wondered."

He didn't answer, but she felt his interest, and his cock quicken at her words.

"It became quite erect. Thick and ready for my passage, as it is now. I thought of taking it inside me as you slept. But I decided to wait until you awakened after all. Still, it pleased me, knowing the decision was mine. Knowing the control I had over you."

His hands convulsed on their bindings.

She took him deep in her mouth then, until his crown crossed into her throat and her lips met his groin. Then slowly she released him again. "Tell me before you climax. I will be annoyed if you come without my permission."

He laughed in disbelief. "What?"

She fisted his wet crown and stroked the notch in its underside with her thumb. "I must have your agreement on this matter or I won't continue."

Long seconds passed.

"Do I have it?" she asked.

"Do I have a choice?" he muttered.

"Yes. You may agree. Or you may misbehave. In which case I'll dress you in my nightgown and leave you here to be discovered by your steward in the morning."

He snorted. "Then I suppose I agree."

"Excellent." With that, she began to suck and tug at his cock as if it were a favorite treat.

"Ye gods, Jordan, of course I'm going to come if you keep that up."

"No. Tell me if it becomes too much for you, and I'll stop. Remember, you have given me your word."

Her moist lips sheathed him again.

His head fell back and he groaned. "Bacchus, I've created a monster."

Over the next half hour, she brought him to the precipice of orgasm a dozen times, but each time he forewarned her and she desisted before he climaxed.

He accepted her game stoically at first, but soon was urging her to relent. "If I get any stiffer I'll only be fit to pose on a pedestal among the statues in the glen. Now take me into your passage," he snarled.

"Very well," she agreed. "But once you're inside me, you must give me your seed immediately. Or I'll leave you again."

"Yes, yes. Gods. Just hurry." His voice turned greedy at the promise of impending release.

She moved over him and did as he asked. As soon as he was fully embedded in her, she felt him erupt. His body arched like a bowstring. Leather strained, creaking oak bedposts as he silently spurted into her. She removed the scarf from his eyes, wanting to watch his beautiful face caught in ecstasy's grip.

The next time he came, she came as well, spilling her semen on his belly. This time, silver glinted through the darkness, watching her as she undulated her hips, massaging the unguent between them.

Much later, when she remembered, she reached toward the

table. His eyes followed the movement and narrowed on the small glass plug she'd found there. She sucked it into her mouth, wetting it, then slipped it low between the cheeks of his rear, touching it to his pruney ring.

He tightened the muscles of his buttocks effectively sealing off the divide between them and gave her a fierce look. "No."

Sensing she'd pushed his control as far as she dared for tonight, she relented. Perhaps he'd never give up that part of his body to her.

For now she was content with what he offered. But could she be truly and completely fulfilled engaging in coitus solely as a woman to his man? On occasion, her cock would long to be buried deep inside *him* when it came. What then?

She would suppress those masculine desires, as she'd suppressed her feminine ones all these many years. It would be worth it to be with this man, to sleep in his arms and explore his body. Yes, it would be worth it.

For now.

26

"Will you lie with me again?" Jordan asked Raine the following night. She'd found him in his bedchamber standing in front of the corner cabinet.

She watched him insert the strange pewter key in the cabinet's lock and withdraw the decanter. The same one from which he'd bade her pour herself a draught exactly a month ago.

Raine took a long drink of the elixir. He dabbed a pristine handkerchief across his lips before answering her. "No."

"Are you punishing me for last night's tricks in the cellar?" she asked.

"No, I enjoyed them. As you well know." He flicked a glance toward the night sky beyond the windowpane. "However, it's soon to be Moonful."

"I know that," she informed him. "I want to spend it with you engaging in the same activity as we enjoyed last Moonful."

Though Raine could have her—would have her many times on all other nights—the ultimate bliss of a Moonful with her was never to be his again. He'd vowed to avoid taking her in another Calling, and it was a vow he planned to keep. Though it galled him to admit it, he simply couldn't trust himself not to impart childseed on a night such as this. And bringing another child into this world who would be troubled by the duality of EarthWorld and ElseWorld blood was an undertaking he'd leave to his brothers. He would not become a father.

"No," he told her. "I can give you all my nights save those of the full moon. Be content with that."

"If you're worried I'll conceive, don't be. I've told you I can't."

He let out a bark of arrogant laughter. "During a Calling there's not a woman I can't impregnate if I don't regulate my childseed."

"Even a woman without a uterus?"

"It's not a certainty that you don't possess such an organ." He eyed her. "Do you want children?"

"I would gladly bear your children, Raine, if only I could. I love you."

"No. You love fornicating."

"True." She grinned, trying to tease him into granting her wish. "Fornicating with you."

"You've never had relations with another man for comparison." He replaced the bottle. The lock snicked shut.

"Shall I?" she teased. "Then you could no longer taunt me with that obstacle to my claim of wanting only you between my legs."

"Let's put an end to this discussion. It's time I made my way to the glen. I've bolstered the forcewall around the castello. None will enter to disturb your rest." He kissed her forehead and went to leave her. She clutched at him.

"Jordan," he warned. Firmly, he removed her hand from his arm. "I must go. Now. Alone."

She folded her arms at her waist, gripping an elbow in each

hand to stop herself from reaching for him again. She wanted to beg him not to banish her from his side, even for one night.

Because she loved him.

Because she wanted him to love her.

Because she needed him to keep the dreams at bay.

But she said nothing more and watched him walk away.

27

That night the dreams came to Jordan again as she'd feared they would. Though Raine had strengthened the protective forcewall around his home, it was no match for intangibles.

She had sought her bed early and shut the drapes, not wanting to know when Moonful arrived. Raine had been adamant that he would not visit her. He would spend this Calling away from her as he had vowed to do every other such night forever.

Every month when the moon rose full and lush, the silver of his eyes would glaze with lust and his Satyr blood would send him to the sacred glen. There he would summon those Else-World women—Shimmerskins. The sight and smell of them would swell his cock. He would run his broad hands over their smooth skin. Grip their hips. Rut with them. Spill his seed in them.

It was a cruel betrayal, and it hurt.

Were she to wed him, she would be sentenced to bide every Moonful for the rest of her life in her solitary bed.

But tonight, though she slept with no one, she was not alone. A dreamlover sought her out. He took the form, the scent, and the sound of the one she truly loved. His words slipped into her mind and captured her. Held her more surely than real tethers ever could.

He beckoned, wooing with false, honeyed words that drew her like a hummingbird seeking his nectar.

Come to me. I await you, here in the glen.

Her head turned feverishly on the pillow, mussing her hair. "No, you spurned me tonight. Told me to stay away."

I was wrong. Forgive me. Come to me tonight and I will treasure you. Give you children.

"Children." She echoed the word on a sigh as a kernel of hope blossomed in her heart.

Like one of the undead, Jordan rose.

"Raine?" she breathed. "Where are you?" The words were pulled from her against her will, tasting foreign on her tongue. A strange language spilled from her as easily as a trickling waterfall though she'd never spoken it before to her knowledge, nor been taught it.

I'm close. So close. I'll guide you. Come to me.

In a slumberous trance, she slid from her bed and found her way down the stairs. The massive front door of the castello opened soundlessly, letting the night into Raine's home. A breeze blew her gown against her, outlining her breasts, slender thighs, and the short taut phallus that hung between them.

Leaving the door swung wide behind her, she stepped outside into the front courtyard. The tiles were cold under her bare feet, and the fountain was a muted splash. Wandering beneath Bacchus's lascivious gaze, she glided around the side of the castello into the peace of the back garden. There, all of nature seemed lulled by the magic riding the air.

The moon had not yet risen and the night was a black void. But she found her way effortlessly, pulled by a force beyond her ken. A force, which though she had no way of knowing, was determined to pull her into another world forever.

Her nightgown was thin, but she didn't notice the crisp chill in the air that lifted her witch-black hair. Didn't recognize it as a harbinger of the winter that was to come. The sweet smell of grapes grew stronger as she trod the well-manicured lawns. Diamonds of dew on the grass bathed her bare feet and slicked her ankles.

Something drew her deeper, toward the densest part of the wood. She rounded oak, elder, and hawthorn trees grown thick with ivy, then picked her way through ferns, and finally stepped over a brook.

The velvet voice of her dreams turned more urgent.

Come. I await you, need you. Want you with all my being and soul.

"I'm coming, Raine. I'm coming. Where are you?"

This way, my lovely. This way.

Her footsteps quickened, taking her farther into the forest.

Nearby there were others who'd come to the glen as well. Two male and one female. Their bodies were strong, beautiful, and naked in the blue-black twilight.

They'd paused together beneath a large statue—the most imposing of those that ringed the isolated glen. Above them Bacchus stood on a pedestal, grapevines wreathing his hair and a chalice extended in one hand as he reigned over yet another sacred Calling night on Satyr land.

They'd been taking wine in preparation for the ritual that preceded Moonful. But when they heard her light step, their three handsome faces turned her way.

Nick's grip on his wife tightened. "Who the devil is that?"

"My houseguest," Raine gritted. He swirled the ancient goblet he held, and then slung its contents down his throat.

"How was she able to approach without being turned back by the forest?" Jane wondered.

"The forces that protect it may have sensed her Faerie blood and become confused," said Nick.

Both looked to Raine, waiting.

His jaw had turned to granite and there was a dangerous glint in his eyes. He'd told Jordan he planned to keep himself from her tonight. Yet she'd defied him and sought him out. In moments it would be Moonful. His cock was aching to plunder female flesh. He'd been moments away from conjuring Shimmerskins with whom to take his ease. But now that he knew Jordan was near and within his grasp, there could no longer be any question of taking Shimmerskins tonight. Only she would do.

At the sight of her, his cock had risen tight and hard. Needing her. Not just any woman. Her. Bacchus help him, he wanted her with a desperation he'd never known.

"We're here!" Raine called, thinking she must have lost her way.

But Jordan didn't seem to hear. She moved on past them, obeying some other summons more powerful than his own.

"Jordan!" he called, the first stirrings of worry prickling his spine. "Something's wrong," he muttered.

"I'll go after her," Jane whispered, pushing from Nick's arms.

Nick held her fast. "The hell you will. Did you see her face? She's under some sort of spell. I'll not take the chance you'll be drawn into the clutches of whatever pied piper calls her."

"But—" Jane protested.

"I'll go," said Raine, cutting her off. Dropping his goblet to the moss, he stepped away from the stone altars.

"I bid you both good night," he told them, letting them know he would stay with Jordan once he found her. By then he would be completely in the Calling's vise. No matter how he tried, it would be useless to try to keep himself from her. He would be in no state to make his way back to them.

In the pitch darkness that preceded Moonful, he lost sight of her. Still, he tracked her easily by scent alone. She smelled of dew and warm skin and Faerie perfume. And of the humid warmth of arousal. She was sexually excited.

His cock—already impossibly hard—swelled. It swung like a pendulum, thick and long, as his steps quickened.

Now and then he could see flashes of her pale figure between the trees that separated them. He outpaced her, drawing closer.

Where was she going? She'd known he would be in the sacred glen. Had her sense of direction misguided her? Or was it something else?

"Jordan!"

A faint aroma reached him. Papaver somniferum—the sleep-bringing poppy. She'd entered a vast field of them.

His heart quickened as he perceived her destination. In the midst of the poppy field a pedestal of rock rose some nine feet in all dimensions—height, width, length. Upon its surface reposed three life-sized statues all carved from ebony marble. They were gods—brothers—who held themselves distant from all the other gods and creatures immortalized in stone within the glen.

Under their influence, the tissuelike poppies bloomed in the surrounding field night and day year-round, bringing sleep but never sleeping themselves. The bright splashes of pink, mauve, and red were almost garish by daylight, but their colors were leached now under the gloom of the unlit forest.

In the center of the trio on the pedestal Morpheus reigned in sensual abandon, lying on his back. He was flanked by his two brothers Phantasos and Phoebetor. The stone of his body and that of his siblings was untarnished, strangely immune to the ravages of weather or the infiltration of flora.

One arm was folded to pillow his head of tousled dark hair and his jaw was cocked at a rakish angle. His smile was one of sexy beguilement, and his eyelids drooped as though he himself were half-asleep.

Why had Jordan come here? Unless—she'd been *called*.

Phantasos ruled the objects found in dreams, and Phoebetor

had the ability to assume animal characteristics. But in the world of dreams, Morpheus held the most power, for he could assume the shape of any living creature.

Raine broke into a run, surefooted even in the pitch of night. He was no more than fifty yards behind Jordan now.

She was whispering. He heard her speak his name but couldn't understand her words at first. Then he realized she spoke in the language of ElseWorld, which she didn't know at all. A chill washed over him. Someone was putting words in her mouth.

He drew closer, within thirty yards. The moon chose that importunate moment to show its face with shocking suddenness.

Like a giant oak, Raine was felled to his knees by its light. A second cock burst from his pelvis. Gripping the emerging appendage, he staggered to his feet and limped on in agony. But again, he stumbled and fell.

In minutes the Change would be complete. In minutes the pain would subside. In minutes Jordan could be lost to him forever.

Mesmerized by the spell of her dream, Jordan stood amid the poppies that reached to her knees and stared unblinking at the massive statue before her.

Here, all was dim under the cool umbrella of the conifers. The surrounding forest had fallen unnaturally quiet.

Yet all around her hundreds of unreal, translucent beings watched, as motionless as trees. Some had twigs sprouting from their scalps instead of hair, others sported hirsute thighs and hooves, and still others had beautiful white wings that reached from their shoulders to points that dusted the ground. A curious sort of tension surrounded them, like a giant, sticky cobweb. They were waiting for her to do something.

Above her on the pedestal, she didn't see Morpheus and his brothers. Instead, it appeared to her that Raine and his brothers reclined there.

"Raine?" she whispered. Eyes that were not Raine's and a smile that was not his smile seemed to beckon her closer.

At last you've come to me. My brothers and I have worked hard to bring you here.

"Why are you and your brothers lying here? Where's Jane? I don't understand."

All will be clear to you soon. Come closer, my darling, and let us gaze upon you.

A labyrinth of vines as thick as her arms forked up the side of the statue's foundation. Unseeing, but guided by some strange force she couldn't comprehend, she found her footing on one of the thick vines. Gripping another, then another, she scaled higher, then higher still.

Soon she was atop the platform, standing among the prone males. To her eyes, they weren't Phoebetor, Morpheus, and Phantasos. But rather it was Nick who lay to her left, Raine beside her, and Lyon beyond him to her right.

A frown creased her brow as she surveyed Nick and Lyon. There was something wrong with the way they were staring so fixedly at her. But the reasons why their presence should disturb her seemed fuzzy and distant.

Touch me, so that I may touch you, my darling Jordan. Lay your hands upon me.

She smiled at Raine, pleased by his soft words. Putting her hands on his cheeks, she caressed their smoothness.

At the contact, Morpheus's hold on her intensified.

So beautiful. Draw closer that I may gaze into your eyes.

As Phoebetor and Phantasos watched, she knelt beside their brother.

Put your lips to mine.

Embracing him, she touched her lips to his in a long, lingering kiss.

The strangely still audience of hundreds broke into hushed whispers like the rattling of dry corn husks.

She pulled away. "You're cold," she murmured.

Then warm me. Ready me.

She ran her hands over his chest. Felt his granite muscles. She glanced lower, to the cock that speared eternally skyward, then back at his face.

Take me with your mouth.

Unable to deny the hypnotic voice, she leaned over his hips and took the ebony snake of her nightmares between her lips. Willingly, she slicked it in her mouth, slowly taking its unforgiving length to the root.

Yesss. Again. And again. Ah. That's it. That's good. Now— it's time. Come over me.

She wiped the back of a hand across her lips and stood, ready to obey.

"Jordan!"

She paused, cocking her head to listen. The masculine voice was faraway and familiar.

But the strange crowd of onlookers urged her on with their whispers, drowning out the distracting voice.

Love me, my darling, Morpheus crooned.

Unconsciously feminine in her movements now, she lifted the hem of her gown. Placing one knee alongside his hip, she swung her other leg over him until she straddled him, poised high on her bent knees. Her skirts floated down to obscure her genitals and his. The stone on either side of the altar was hard beneath the bones of her knees, but she didn't notice.

Hurry, my darling. I ache for you.

Though she didn't see his brothers move, suddenly they were beside her, touching her, kissing her. Yet when she turned her head to the left toward Nick or to the right toward Lyon, their handling of her desisted and she saw that they still reclined in the same oddly frozen positions as before.

Look at me, my love. See the wanting in my eyes. The loving. Accept me. Accept the loving touches of my brothers.

She dragged her eyes back to her dreamlover. Immediately, the caresses of his brothers came again. Lyon's broad hand clenched on her buttock and his other held her breast for his hungry mouth. Nick brushed her hair back and put his hot lips on her throat.

She swayed. "Yes . . ." Suddenly, it somehow seemed right that Raine's brothers were here, gazing upon her like this, petting and wanting her.

"Jordan!" The distracting call came again. But her dreamlover's voice obscured it.

Take me into your body. I can give you the child you want. Tonight. And once I've had you, my brothers will give you children as well. You'll bear three as you were meant to. You'll finally know your true heritage, that of goddess.

The hypnotic voice made the impossible seem possible, made her want . . .

"Three children. Yes. Yes, I want your child, my darling, and those of your brothers as well. I'll love them, love you. All of you."

She reached beneath her skirts and took his slick reptilian cock in one hand. She shifted her hips, finding its tip with her slit.

"Jordan!" Raine called, frantic with pain and fear.

But she was caught in Morpheus's hypnotic web and no longer heard Raine's tortured summons, or any sounds of EarthWorld. The dream was her only reality now.

She shimmied her shoulders and her bodice slid to catch at her elbows, baring her breasts to the moonlight. She gazed down at her lover.

Now, my sweet. Take me. Fuck me.

"Yes." Tensing her thighs, she sank until the ebony snake pricked her. It was cold, smooth. She sank farther and the glossy tip of unyielding marble speared deeper. Gradually, oh so gradually, its dark hurting length filled her.

Ahhh! Yes, that's it. So good.

When the bulbous tip finally jabbed her womb she gasped and threw back her head.

No, don't close your eyes. Look into mine.

Jordan managed to raise her heavy eyelids and do as he asked.

That's right. Now move on me. Grease my pole, like a good little cunt.

Bracing her hands on his shoulders, Jordan rose and sank on him over and over in a sensuous dance as old as time.

Once he's had enough of you, come to me, Nick's voice rasped at her ear. *My rod will stretch your well-buttered bun to its limits.*

And then to me, said Lyon's voice. *Once I fuck where my brothers have had you, the circle will close and the gate will open.*

You'll spawn a dynasty, three fiendish voices whispered in unison. *Children.*

"Children."

You'll be a mother to gods.

"A mother."

Nearly delirious now, she worked herself over her sinister lover, arching, thrusting. Euphoria swelled in her, rising ever higher, pulling her toward fulfillment . . .

The gauzy sweep of Jordan's nightgown shrouded her genitals. But from her gasp, Raine knew the exact moment Morpheus's cock first punctured her. As she slid lower, he knew it would be slipping ever deeper inside her. Taking possession.

No! She was his! The possibility that he might lose her to another frightened him more than anything in his life ever had.

If Jordan achieved orgasm under the stroke of her dreamlover's cock, Morpheus could rightly consider it an invitation to bear his offspring. Such an invitation would be deemed valid in ElseWorld. Raine's claim to her would lessen and that of his rival would grow. Morpheus would try to take her through the gate. To make her his. Forever.

Unless Raine stopped him. He stumbled toward her, hunched like an animal, his teeth bared with an agony not yet passed.

Above him, Jordan checked and Raine saw her chest expanding and contracting with her breath as she fought the pleasure–pain of full impalement. She'd taken all of Morpheus's stone pole inside her now.

Flattening her hands on the supine statue's belly, she leaned her weight forward and pushed her hips up using her knees for leverage. Her hips began to buck, working steadily on him. She was moaning now, murmuring love words in the Fey language.

He'd reached the base of the statue. Vines grew up the sides of it, thick and forbidding. They fought Raine, scratching his forearms, his hands, ribs, cheek.

Jordan's breasts rose and fell with each passionate slide of her hips.

Raine climbed higher, nearer. Almost—

She was making sharp, staccato moaning sounds now. She threw her head back, and her throat was a long, smooth column. A subdued shriek left her and she stilled, teetering on the razor edge of orgasm.

In seconds, she could be lost to him forever.

"Jordan!" he shouted.

28

Raine's hand came around Jordan's waist, lifting her off Morpheus's ebony horn. But the pull of her dream was strong, and she fought him, anxious to return to her former position. Her movements were as calm and mechanical as though she were in a trance.

Fear clutched him, finding an outlet in anger. He pulled her back against him. "Did that bastard Morpheus make you come?" He shook her. "Did he?"

Jordan's head lolled on his shoulder, rolling side to side. She moaned, cursing him in the language of the Fey.

This was his fault. She'd said she'd been having dreams. He should've considered that something like this could happen. How long had Morpheus been working on her?

"Let go of her mind, you bastard!" he shouted at the statue. But only a smirking silence answered him.

If he couldn't break the dreamspell her erstwhile lover had woven, she might never wake from it. Morpheus would gladly take her mind and leave her body to die, just to spite him. Raine would give her over to him at the gates of ElseWorld before he'd allow that to happen. Yet if Morpheus achieved such a victory as taking a Satyr's woman from him, his prestige would skyrocket among his peers.

But he was getting ahead of himself. All hinged on whether Morpheus had brought her to release. It was impossible to know for certain. But even if he had, if Raine brought her to release as well and gave her his childseed, it might prove strong enough to overcome whatever hold the dark god had garnered over her.

By now, Raine's need to fornicate was almost a living thing. It tortured him, ratcheting his anger higher. Near the statues' heads, there was a flattened rim where vases of poppies rested. Jordan still wrestled with him, knocking one of them to the ground in her efforts to return to Morpheus.

"If it's cock you want, I've plenty for you," he told her. Bending her forward over her dreamlover's muscular chest he shoved her gown high to reveal the ripe peach of her rump.

Imprisoned in stone, Morpheus could only watch.

"Yes, I'm going to fuck her, you bastard," he snarled. "She's mine. She'll reach her pleasure with me dozens of times before dawn."

The statue gazed at him with smug, knowing eyes. *Take her. But remember that tonight I had her first,* he seemed to say.

Jordan reared up, fighting him. Morpheus and his brothers still polluted her mind. He would have to find the words to lure her back to him.

"Jordan, it's me. Raine."

He planted a widespread hand at the small of her back to anchor her. She bowed up under him, but he pushed her legs wide and pinned them with his knees. His twin cocks found her nether openings.

At his touch, she paused in her struggles, uncertain.

"Jordan, it's Raine," he told her again. He prodded inward, ignoring the fact that another lover was responsible for the slickness he'd found in her female slit.

"I'm coming into you now, Jordan. Can you feel me? My crowns are inside you now. You're so small and tight. Gods!"

He pulled her up to lean against him and murmured into her hair as he pushed both pricks into her. "I'm going deeper now. Do you feel me?"

As the pleasure of spearing her swamped him, he concentrated on trying to keep his own mind from being taken by the Calling. On trying to pull her away from her dreams and back to the living.

"It's me who's fucking you. Do you hear me?" His thatch met her rear as his cocks slid home. "Feel me? I'm inside you now, as deep as it's possible to be."

She didn't reply.

He withdrew. And penetrated. Withdrew and penetrated. The dusting of hair on his powerful haunches rasped her inner thighs as he retreated, only to return for another taste of her. And another, and another.

One hand held her waist and his other cupped her breast as he fucked with harsh shallow lunges. Then he drove fathoms deep.

"My cockslit is touching your womb," he whispered passionately. "Do you feel it?"

She mumbled something garbled—a mixture of English and ElseWorld tongue.

Raine felt the inevitable reaction to being inside her begin to swell within him. "I'm going to give you my childseed," he told her. "Try to relax and welcome it. Do you hear me, Jordan? This is important."

Nothing.

He fucked her hard then, rutting with desperate pummeling strokes. Concentrating, he summoned from his innermost core the most potent childseed possible. It welled like a mythical force within him, wrenching his balls tight and high.

"Umm," she murmured, beginning to tilt her hips in time with his rhythm.

"Bacchus, it's good." He gripped her now as if Elseworld raiders were threatening and he must stake his claim.

His cockslits gapped, readying. His throat worked and a rough shout escaped him as his hot shafts wrenched, hard, in unison. Abruptly the dam broke and they convulsed. His mancock fountained its gift into the void that was her yearning womb. For the first time in his life, he gave his childseed to a woman, planting it deep. An unexpectedly sweet, pure joy washed over him at the sharing of this most sacred, fertile semen. With her.

The heaving cavern of his chest sheltered her as he gave of it, again and again and again. In the aftermath of his taking, he sensed his seed taking root in her, and he hugged her tight to him. He'd done his best with her and prayed it would prove to be enough.

The cream in the divide of her buttocks slicked his pelvic cock as it retreated inside him, well satisfied for the night. Her nipples had engorged as he mated her, he noticed, pulsing with a light of pale rose. Something they hadn't done with Morpheus. He took heart from that. But she remained distant, her mind still stuck in another place. Did she even know who had been mating her just now?

He took her phallus in his hand, finding it stiff and eager. Perhaps he could reach her another way—by stirring her anger. "You want to be a man?" he taunted. "Then by hell you can fuck like one."

Lifting her over his shoulder, he climbed from the statue and headed for that place on the estate where his powers would be strongest. Minutes later, he slipped through a natural arch formed by three trees of the Faerie triad and entered the gaping maw of a cave.

Once inside, Raine lost no time. Focusing on a spot of nothingness he watched a sudden shimmer of amber-colored light appear there as if by magic. As he set Jordan on her feet, the light enlarged, solidified, and took female shape.

With fluid grace, the glistening female assisted him in leading Jordan toward the large stone altar in the center of the cave. Just beyond this lay the gate that joined EarthWorld to ElseWorld. Tendrils of magic curled from it, forever dividing the two worlds.

The Shimmerskin sat on the altar and pushed itself backward. Knees high and feet braced wide along the edge, it reclined backward, resting its weight on its forearms and bent elbows. It was beautiful, submissive, and ready to perform the task for which Raine had brought it here.

He drew Jordan to stand between its legs and angled her jaw toward the amber female. "Look at her."

Jordan stared with unseeing eyes as emotionless as those of the iridescent creature before her.

"She awaits you," he whispered. "Go ahead. Mount her."

Did she even hear him? Raine ushered her closer to the Shimmerskin. Reaching across her belly, he took her tumescent cock in his big hand. He dragged the tip through the Shimmerskin's moist folds, back and forth, back and forth.

Jordan's head lolled against his shoulder, as though it had suddenly grown too heavy to support. Her lids drifted closed.

He pushed her head forward with a shift of his shoulder. "Open your eyes."

Her eyes opened to slits. The Shimmerskin smiled at her, showing even, white teeth. Sitting higher, it reached for her phallus. Taking over Raine's movements, it sluiced Jordan's plum along its own glowing slit.

"Fuck me," the creature whispered to her, soft as a sigh.

* * *

Desire shot through Jordan, stiffening her prick to the point of pain. The cobwebs began to fall away, but the return to wakefulness was frightening and difficult.

She shuddered. "Raine?"

"Thank Bacchus," she thought she heard him murmur. A masculine hand brushed her hair aside and Raine's lips kissed the angle of her neck. "I'm here," he told her.

She reached toward the glistening female's hand where it rested on her cock. Its fingers turned to link with hers.

"Come inside me. I'm wet. Ready for you," the Shimmerskin urged.

"I'm not sure . . ." Jordan mumbled, still teetering from dream toward reality.

"Your cock is sure. It wants her." From behind, Raine slid a hand between her legs and shoved a thick finger into her. "Your quim is sure. It wants me. But you can't have me until you take her."

He took her hand and fisted it around the root of her phallus, then guided her tip farther inside the creature's slit. The Shimmerskin groaned and lay back, tilting its hips. Its cunt sucked delicately at her.

"Fuck her and I'll fuck you," Raine's dark velvet voice promised.

Jordan's shaft bobbed its enthusiasm for the proposed venture. Still struggling toward full awareness, she watched her crown spread the Shimmerskin's pussy lips as though watching someone else's disembodied rod doing the deed.

Her hands reached out to grip the womanly thighs that diverged around her own. They were warm, soft. Between them, its slit was a wet, welcoming cave. Blood rushed to fill her cock, and it hardened to new dimensions.

"Fuck me," the Shimmerskin urged.

Jordan shifted her weight, pressed forward . . . and slid into heaven.

Her soft bush met the smooth, hairless pubic bone of the body before her. A pair of glowing eyes smiled into hers.

With a will of their own, Jordan's hips began to move. She withdrew, shoved, withdrew, shoved, controlling the pace of their copulation. The Shimmerskin arched with each thrust and its channel took her in long, slow gulps that were like fiery licks.

A hand pressed at Jordan's back and she leaned down, breast to breast with the creature. It reached up and threaded fingers in her hair, pulling her closer. It kissed her and she kissed it back.

From behind her, she felt a huge cock push into her feminine channel. Raine.

She moaned against the lips locked with hers.

The trio moved together, awkwardly at first until they found a more rhythmic dance. Each time Raine bucked into Jordan from behind she was forced deeper into the Shimmerskin. When he pulled away, she mimicked his movement and retreated from the Shimmerskin's passage.

Kisses, caresses, and groans entangled until male and female were indistinguishable. Together, they fornicated, hurtling toward release. From the walls of the sacred cave, fauns, nymphs, and faeries sculpted in high relief by artists who were long dead gazed down on the scene with lusty approval.

In abrupt unison, Jordan's cock and vagina seized. For long seconds she hung on the edge, hardly able to bear the fullness of her emotions, the fullness of her feminine channel and the tightness of the channel squeezing her cock. At last, she gave an inarticulate cry and convulsed in hard ecstatic pulses. Starbursts exploded in the darkness of her mind, a near-blindness wrought by pleasure as she came as both man and woman in the same moment.

Her coming drew Raine's, and he gripped her hips hard as his cock surged and spilled. As each spurt of his seed pumped into her, so hers pumped into the female under her, over and over until neither had anything left to give.

Gasping, Jordan slumped forward and for brief seconds lay against the Shimmerskin. Its pale eyes smiled into hers. Then it faded into the ether from which it had come, and her breast lay upon the smooth stone of the altar.

Jordan blinked, fully aware now. "Raine?"

"Yes, I'm here, my love." The endearment slipped out so easily he didn't notice it.

His lips touched her nape, hot and moist, and she sighed. Still lodged inside her, he pulled her to stand back against him and crossed his hands over hers on her belly. From this night, she would grow his child. He knew it as certainly as he knew he had once promised himself such a thing would never come to pass.

Tonight his hand had been forced. He hadn't even been able to wait nine months so the early birth wouldn't look strange to Humans. He'd thought Nick remiss in impregnating Jane after only five months of marriage. Yet here he'd given Jordan a child before he'd even wed her.

In the way of the Satyr children, his and Jordan's issue would come into this World one month from now during the next Calling. Which meant it would be necessary to take her again next Moonful to facilitate that.

It was done. He was a father, something he'd sworn never to be. Or was the child in her belly that of Morpheus? Time would tell.

But either way, he would never let her or her child go.

29

"Do you remember what happened last night?"

Jordan jolted in surprise at the sound of Raine's voice. Surreptitiously, she swept the project she'd been assembling out of sight, beneath her skirts. It consisted of two small branches denuded of leaves, hastily scarred and then bound and tied together with a bit of ribbon. Every morning she was driven to create another of these strange little talismans. It was embarrassing. Crazy.

Trying to conceal her agitation, she stood and went to her armoire, tossing the creation in with all the others like it. There were so many. Soon she would run out of the ribbon she'd taken from Raine the night they met. What then? She shut the mirrored door on them and saw he'd come close. Had he seen?

Hoping to distract him, she flirted, sliding her arms around his waist. "Of course I remember. We made love. Out in the glen," she said. "Though I'm not sure how we got there."

"You were sleepwalking. I found you. You'd been called to the sacred glen by Morpheus, a creature of ElseWorld who wishes to take you from me."

She paled, straightening. "I thought that was a dream."

"No. You were impregnated last night." By Morpheus or himself, he didn't know. Did she?

She lay a hand over her belly. "That's not possible. I'm almost certainly barren!"

"No woman is barren for a man of Satyr blood. As I've explained, I could impregnate a woman five times your age if I desired."

"But I probably don't even have a uterus," Jordan quibbled, still unable to believe him. "Even if I do have one, I've been told it's likely my male organs would supercede my female ones so that I could never bear a child."

"You must take me at my word. You are breeding. I estimate you will give birth in four weeks."

Jordan smirked. "Someone needs to instruct you on human biology."

"I'm attempting to instruct you on Satyr biology," he replied. "Satyr children gestate in four weeks as do all children born of ElseWorld."

Stunned, Jordan roved her hand over her abdomen, testing it shape. It was already hard and slightly distended. "How efficient."

A fleeting fragment of memory came to her. "Were Nick and Lyon in the glen with us last night as well? Or was that part of my dream?"

Raine's eyes sharpened on her, attempting to weigh what she knew. "Nick was there, with Jane. But we spent the Calling apart from them."

"And Lyon?'

Raine gave her a quizzical look. "He's in Paris. Remember?"

"Don't act as though my suggestion is particularly bizarre. On Satyr land, many impossible things occur. Such as four-week gestations within the wombs of those without wombs."

"You have a womb. Trust me on that. My cock has greeted it

more than once. In view of your condition, I trust you finally comprehend the necessity of marriage between us?"

She looked worried. Marrying her would bring trouble to him, but he'd never forgive her if she insisted their child be born a bastard.

He mistook the reason for her concern. "It is not unusual for first children to come early."

She followed his line of thought. "Eight months early? Everyone will assume we anticipated any wedding vows we might undertake."

"Does that bother you?"

"Not in the least. I assumed it would bother you."

He shrugged. "Gossip can be dealt with."

This from a man who abhorred wagging tongues?

"I only wish for healthy Satyr children," he said.

"Will the birth be normal?" she asked.

"Fairly."

"*Fairly?*"

"Yes, fairly normal for a Satyr birth." Though in truth he couldn't promise her it would be a Satyr child or another sort of child she would birth.

"You'll have to do better than that by way of explanation."

"Come, I have matters to discuss with Nick. We will visit his household and you can ask Jane your woman's questions."

30

When they arrived at Castello di Blackstone, the courtyard and gardens were a profusion of flowers. Even in autumn, there was a disconcerting abundance of greenery and color everywhere Jordan looked. She'd been struck by it each time she'd visited, but still she shook her head in amazement.

"Your sister has quite the green thumb," Raine murmured.

"An understatement to be sure," said Jordan.

When they called in, they were told that Nick was out in his office, which was located nearby on his property. Only Jane greeted them in the salon, appearing somewhat groggy.

"I apologize for keeping you waiting. I overslept." She glanced at Raine, blushed, and then sheepishly looked away.

It was left unspoken between them all that she'd been up all night engaging in Calling sex in the glen. As had her sister.

"I would like you to explain the way of things regarding the birthing of Satyr children to my soon-to-be wife," Raine announced. "She is breeding."

Jane's eyes widened, moving from Raine to Jordan and back again. "I see. Congratulations."

"Thank you. But he can't know such things, can he?" Jordan scoffed.

Jane ushered Raine to the doorway and nudged him out into the corridor. "You may return in one hour," she said before shutting the door on him.

"He's wrong, isn't he?" Jordan demanded after he'd gone. "It's next to impossible for me to have children."

"A Satyr can choose whether his seed is fruitful." Jane informed her, ringing the bell for tea.

"But I'm probably barren. It's possible I don't even have a uterus."

Jane's brow wrinkled. "Does Raine know?"

Jordan nodded. "Though he refutes it."

"You joined with him last night, didn't you? I was there in the glen. I saw you."

"Oh." Jordan's cheeks pinkened. "I don't remember that. I wasn't—myself."

"Don't be embarrassed. It's the same with Nick and me during Moonful." She sighed. "At least Raine has forewarned you about what's to come. When my birthing time came, Nick said nothing and I was horribly worried, thinking myself grown so big that I might bear quadruplets!"

The tea tray arrived, and once they were seated Jane began serving. "One other thing I should warn you about," she said as she poured. "He won't touch you in a carnal way for the next month."

Jordan's gazed at her in horror. "Why ever not?"

"It's the way of the Satyr." Jane rolled her eyes, smiling. "I can't believe I just said that. Nick uses that expression to explain away anything he wishes me to accept without question."

"Men!" Jordan said in disgust.

Both women giggled, then yawned.

*   *   *

Raine found Nick in his office poring over a collection of Egyptian scarabs he'd recently acquired. He looked vital, well rested. Just as Raine always felt after a Calling night.

"Fascinating, aren't they?" Nick enthused, holding up a particularly large specimen. "Mementos of Napoleon's failed Egyptian campaign."

Raine's orderly nature shuddered at the expensive clutter filling Nick's salon. He lifted a priceless pair of silk-and-gold-threaded medieval gauntlets from a chair and sat. "Scarabs eat their own dung, don't they?"

"Yes! Efficient little devils." Noting Raine's serious expression, Nick abruptly tore his attention from his collection. "What happened last night with Jordan?"

"Morpheus happened."

"Fuck," Nick breathed. "Were his brothers in on it?"

"I'm not sure. But Morpheus was the one trying to mate her."

"And did he?"

"He met with a degree of success. I'm not certain of the extent of the damage."

Nick rubbed a hand over his face. "Is she breeding?"

Raine nodded.

"And you don't know if it's yours or Morpheus's?"

"That's correct," said Raine.

"Bacchus. If it's his—"

Raine's eyes narrowed. "I won't let him have her regardless."

"Even if you can keep him from taking her, he'll want the child. And he'll have a legal claim on it if it's his."

"Screw his claim."

Nick's chair creaked under his massive frame as he sat back, folding his hands over his chest. "If she bears his issue, will she let it go?"

Raine looked away. If she were forced to choose between him and a child, he shuddered to think which way she'd lean. "I'm not sure. She has made it clear motherhood is something she desires."

"If you challenge Morpheus's right to it—"

"Which I will," said Raine.

"Just be aware the ElseWorld Council will at the very least allow him Seeing rights," said Nick. "And quite possibly Visitation. It will give him a foothold in our world. We cannot allow that to happen."

"That's all assuming he succeeded with her. I did my best to ensure that any child she bears is Satyr, not Morpheus's offspring. In the coming weeks prior to the Birthing I will endeavor to teach her to control her dreams so that he cannot reach her through them again."

Nick nodded. "The repercussions of her being drawn farther into Morpheus's web will adversely affect more than our family. If he's allowed into EarthWorld, others from ElseWorld will soon follow."

Raine stood and went to the window. Running a hand through his hair he stared out at the vineyard at the center of their lands. For the first time since he'd come here as a boy, he almost wished he could leave all this behind, taking Jordan with him. Somewhere safe. Somewhere these unnatural dangers didn't threaten her. But there was no such place.

31

"So, I understand from Jane that you and I are not to have concupiscent relations for the next month," Jordan grumped as she and Raine strolled through the forest. Nick and Jane had entertained them with luncheon. Once they'd returned home Raine had disappeared for several hours and by now it was late afternoon.

Raine lifted her over a low stone wall and then stepped over it himself. "That's right."

Her eyes turned mischievous. "Where exactly is the line drawn?"

"What do you mean?"

She moved close. "For instance, can I touch you here? Or do this?"

Raine pushed her lips away from his neck and pulled her hand from his crotch. "Though it pains me to say it—no, to both."

She sighed. "It's going to be a long month." Looking ahead, she saw the path would soon turn rocky, slowing their progress. "Where are we going?"

"We've arrived," he informed her, pausing beside a rocky pool. "Here, I have something for you." He pulled a small jewel-encrusted vial set on a gold chain from his pocket and draped it around her neck.

She lifted it from her chest to stare down at it. "It's lovely."

"I'm glad you like it because you will wear it from this day forward. That vial contains a potion of rare oils I blended together that will act as a dreamcatcher. It's a sort of net that will enable you to separate the real from the unreal during your sleeping hours."

She wrapped the vial in her hand. "It's that easy?"

"Almost. To function properly, it must first be activated." He turned away, causing the air around him to undulate. In moments, two Shimmerskins appeared, both beautiful and with iridescent skin.

"Why are they here?" she asked, frowning.

"To take part in the ritual."

"What ritual?"

He shot her an exasperated look. "The ritual of the oils—the activation ritual I just mentioned to you. During the process, you'll be especially vulnerable to nightmares. But once it's finished, you'll have more control over them. As long as you continue to wear the amulet."

Jordan threw up her hands. "That statement opens so many questions, I scarcely know where to begin."

"This pool is an incubation chamber built of rock from the temple of Aeslepius, the god of healing," he explained patiently, indicating the rocky pond. "You'll spend this night here with the Shimmerskins and by morning the ritual will be complete."

The glimmering females came toward her. She eyed them suspiciously, moving behind him. "You mean I'm to stay here with them? Without you?"

"Yes, though I'll be on guard nearby."

The Shimmerskins found her where she hid, caressing her with their delicate hands.

"Stop that!" she told them. But they kept on. "Are either of these the same creature from last night in the glen?"

"They're never the same. When they come to us, they are newly born. When they go, they cease to exist."

"Then they're not like the dryads," she said.

He shook his head. "Dryads are living creatures. The Shimmerskins are needed tonight to facilitate the ritual, aiding you in learning to control your dreams rather than having them control you."

She searched his eyes, scarcely daring to hope what he said was true. "What do I have to do?"

"To begin with, choose a code word. One you'll remember easily but won't accidentally say."

She felt cool air on her back. The Shimmerskins were undressing her! She shrugged them away. "What exactly does this ritual entail?" she demanded.

Raine took her shoulders, holding her for the touch of the glimmering hands. "Let them minister to you as they will. Reach for the edge of pleasure. But you mustn't let its wave crash. Use your code word. It will tell them when to cease stimulation."

Jordan glared at him. "Stimulation? So as I understand it, I'm to spend a night here, being brought to the edge of pleasure over and over by these creatures but not succumbing?"

He nodded. "Have you chosen a word?"

"Yes."

"What is it?"

"Asshole."

Raine scowled at her. "This is important. Choose a damn word. One you'll remember but won't accidentally say."

"All right," she said, hands on her hips. " 'Birthday.' "

"Fine."

"Fine."

"Whenever the temptation to orgasm grows too strong, say, 'birthday' and the Shimmerskins will wait until you have calmed enough for them to continue."

The Shimmerskins were massaging her breasts now, having lowered her bodice to her waist. She batted the creatures' hands away. "Tell them to stop for a moment so I can think!"

Though he neither spoke nor moved, the Shimmerskins abruptly desisted and stood serene and still.

"How did you do that?" she asked.

He shrugged off the question. "You must see reason, Jordan."

She pressed a hand over her abdomen. "I want this child, Raine. Jane said that carnal pleasure could endanger it."

"That's essentially true. But as long as you don't let the wave crash . . ."

"Can't this ritual wait," begged Jordan. "The dreams have been with me for six years now. What's another month?"

Raine looked doubtful. "It's imperative that we act quickly. Your dreams could be used to snatch you from reality again at any time. Through them you could be taken ElseWorld where you would be lost to me, as would your unborn child."

"How? I'll refuse to go."

"You can be driven insane by your dreams if you refuse."

She eyed the Shimmerskins balefully. "But what if I can't resist temptation during this ritual? You say my succumbing to it could harm our child. I'd rather suffer harm myself than take that chance."

Something shifted in his face as he struggled to determine the best course. "Very well," he said finally. "We'll let the ritual wait."

He took her hand and they turned back to the castello. Behind them, the Shimmerskins wavered, then slowly faded from existence.

"Why did you choose 'birthday' as your code word?" he asked.

She shrugged. "Because my birthdays have always been an awful trial. Just like I suspect this ritual of yours will be."

He planted a kiss on the top of her head and silently vowed her next birthday would be a celebration rather than the horror all her previous birthdays must have been.

32

Late that night, Jordan's sleep turned restless. She was writhing, her skin clammy. She stood and made for the door, her mind caught up in chaos.

Strong hands clasped her and led her back to the bed. Raine. She wanted to tell him she was all right, but she couldn't organize her thoughts or elude the grip of her nightmares to do so.

In her dream, she was fully dressed in a muslin gown and wearing a hat decorated with posies. She was in the rear garden on her way to Raine's stable when her mother suddenly materialized beside her in much the same way as a Shimmerskin arrived. From nowhere.

When she saw that Jordan was dressed as a woman, Celia Cietta put a hand over her own impressive bosom. "God in heaven. Look at you!"

Jordan forced her lungs to resume working properly. "Buon giorno, Mother," she replied, just as if it were a common occurrence to encounter someone who was no longer living.

"I've come to take you home," her mother said, taking her arm. Her fingers were cold.

Gently, Jordan pulled away. "I already *am* home."

"No! You must come with me. If you don't return to Venice, your father's family will take away my fortune," her mother wheedled.

"I'm not coming back, Mother. I plan to wed soon."

Her mother paled. "Wed? To a man or a woman?"

"A man. A good man. The one who seeks to awaken me even as we speak."

Her mother surveyed Raine, who had his arm around Jordan and was trying to cajole her into wakefulness.

"He's handsome enough. Does he know? About you?" Her mother fluttered a dainty hand in the general direction of Jordan's genitals.

"We share a bed. How could he not?"

Revulsion filled her mother's face. "You should be ashamed."

Jordan slowly shook her head. "No. You've always been the one too ashamed to speak of my differences. I've never been ashamed of my body."

Her mother's tone turned venomous. "Then you should be. Now more than ever. You look ridiculous in that getup. No female was ever so lacking in feminine grace. Your hair is askew. Your gown and hat display an appalling lack of care and refinement. Your ensemble is indifferent and negligently arranged."

"I'm happy here. Can't you leave me alone?"

"You're living a lie."

Jordan's lips trembled. "No. The lie ended when I came here. I wish to live as a woman. I plan to be a wife to Raine. He knows what I am and he will have me."

"No man will keep you as wife for long," her mother scoffed. "He'll want children."

Jordan patted her abdomen. "That doesn't seem to be a problem. I'm already with child."

Celia gasped and glared at her in horror. A moment passed, then her face turned sly. "That can be undone."

Beside her mother, Salerno abruptly materialized. Wordlessly, he took Jordan's wrists and held them crossed tight together at her chest. Another man with a sinister look appeared as well. It was the bishop from the theater in Venice. He came behind her, lifting her skirt. He raised a clenched fist.

Jordan looked to her mother for help, but Celia had already disappeared into the vapor from which she'd sprung.

Grabbing her belly with the flat of one hand, the bishop rummaged his oily fist between her legs. Without warning, he rammed it high inside her vaginal throat. And higher still, fisting her impossibly deep. Deep inside her womb his hand unfolded to grab and strangle those who grew there. Those who were as yet unborn.

She sobbed, begging him to stop. Fearing it was too late.

And then, just as suddenly as they'd appeared, the two men were gone.

She crumpled, doubling over as a tremendous cramp hit her, wreathing her belly and twisting her gut.

"Raine," she'd whispered feebly.

"I'm here," he answered. But he still seemed far away and she took no comfort from his soothing words. She was alone and in pain. She pushed up on all fours. Within her womb, opposing forces raged. Blood clotted. Tissue tore from its moorings. It poured from her, smearing her inner thighs and soaking the bedsheets beneath her.

Hours later she finally made her way back to consciousness. But even before Raine told her, she knew. In the dank darkness of her dream, she'd given birth.

They'd been boys. Twins. ElseWorld children who were already far advanced in development after only one day of gestation.

One was olive skinned. Raine's child.

And the other had skin the color of ebony stone.

Both were stillborn.

33

The twins were buried in the Satyr crypt in a private ceremony attended only by family. For days afterward, Jordan ate little and refused all conversation. Raine was frantic with the need to comfort her, but when she turned him away he sought solace in his work.

On the afternoon of the fifth day, she approached him, having found him in the garden at the rear of the house. She carried a basket on one arm. Her parting gift.

Seeing her, Raine leaped to his feet. She wanted to weep at the pain she read in his face. Pain she'd brought to him.

"I'm leaving," she said baldly.

He took her shoulders in his hands, his expression urgent. "It wasn't your fault. Postponing the ritual didn't cause the miscarriage. Is that what you think?"

Yes, that was exactly what she thought. "It doesn't matter." She shook her head wearily and stepped back from him. "I'm leaving. Returning to my former life in Venice."

She'd seen Salerno in her dream the night she miscarried. And that meant something. He was still looking for her. If he came here, he would bring devastating scandal and shame. She couldn't let her sordid past touch Raine and his family. They didn't deserve that.

Storm clouds gathered in Raine's eyes. His reaction was subtle, but she knew how to read the signs now.

"What life?" he sneered. "The streets?"

"Raine—"

"You do understand that you're in danger if you leave? That Morpheus will keep after you? That even if he stops, other ElseWorld creatures will continue to hound you?"

"I'm willing to take that chance."

"You're that unhappy here? At the side of a man you supposedly love?"

Biting her lip, she shook her head. She had to take her leave before she broke down. "I have something to give you before I go."

She handed her basket to him.

He glared at her offering, confused by it.

As well he should be. The basket was full of sticks, tied in pairs with bits of ribbon—the ribbon she'd taken from him back in Venice. Every morning for weeks, she'd been driven to create the strange objects. She'd tried many different kinds of branch and twig and had tied the ribbons in various ways—braids, bows, and knots of various sorts. None had ever pleased her exactly, never seeming quite right. However, once she'd tied just two sticks together each morning, something within her had calmed and she'd been able to go about her day. Ashamed, she'd kept the stockpile hidden. Until now.

When he failed to take the basket, she jiggled it at him. "I don't know what it means. It's something to do with you. Some message for you."

Raine was too angry to listen. He knocked the basket from her hand, scattering its contents into the leaf-strewn path. "If you truly wish to leave me, then go. And take your witchcraft with you. But only travel as far as the confines of this estate allow. Find a home with your sister or I'll build one for you. You can't leave Satyr land. You're too important. There's more to consider than your personal preferences."

Turning away he intentionally ground her gift under the heel of his boot. Twigs snapped and pressed deep into the soil as he left her.

She stared at her scattered offering, knowing she'd hurt him. "I'm sorry," she said to no one in particular, for he'd already departed. In spite of his arguments, she knew what she must do. She couldn't let the scandal that was her life besmirch his. Couldn't let him learn the truth of what she had once been.

In her pocket, she touched the only ribbon left whole now, the indigo. Then she stared down the long road that wound downhill, toward Florence.

At some point that afternoon, Raine looked up from his vials, mortars, and the other equipment he used in blending the wines.

Nick glanced at him and saw the tension in his face. "What?"

"Something's wrong." Alarmed, Raine stood, rattling everything on the table askew, searching the air for Jordan's scent. It was gone. *She* was gone.

He rushed from Nick's office and raced toward home, moving through the forest faster than he ever had in his life. Reaching his castello, he took the stairs three at a time, sprinted down the hall, and threw open the door to her bedchamber.

He reeled back a step at the disgusting smell that assailed him. Her room reeked. Not of Faerie now, but of a hideous concoction of chemicals. French perfumes.

She knew he abhorred perfume. Where had she gotten it? Filched from Jane, no doubt.

Holding his nose, he ventured inside. A half-dozen or more bottles sat on her dressing table, empty. She'd doused herself with it to literally throw him off the scent. Well, her ploy wouldn't work.

He unfettered his nose and forced himself to dissect the scents, separating acrid from sweet and spicy from tart. Lifting one bottle after another, he quickly analyzed their odors, committing them to memory. But doing so was futile, he realized. If he were to follow the trail of any one such scent, it could as easily lead him to a stranger who wore the perfume as it might to Jordan.

Frustrated, he slammed the bottle he held to the surface of the table. Then he swept the entire collection of them to the floor with an outstretched arm.

Nick entered the room and surveyed the haphazard pile of bottles decorating the floor. "She's gone?"

Raine shoved his shaking hands into his pockets, unwilling to let his brother see how her departure had affected him. "Apparently."

"Will you go after her?"

Raine gestured in the general direction that Venice lay and shook his head. "You know I can't. There's work to do. The casks are ready and the wine must be blended. And with Lyon gone, your Will alone isn't sufficient to keep the forcewall bolstered well enough to keep interfering Humans out of our estates and our business."

Nick put a hand on his shoulder. "Continue your work then and I'll summon Lyon home from Paris. He'll be here within the week if he has good weather for traveling. Once the forcewall is strengthened by his coming, you can depart to search for her."

Raine nodded, then went to stand at the window. A moment later he heard his brother take his leave. He gazed beyond the forest to the fields, distant towns and slopes, edged with misty purple mountains and the spears of cypress trees.

Where was she?

34

"How lovely you look, Signore Cietta," a sarcastic voice murmured.

Jordan had scarcely stepped beyond the bounds of Satyr land when she heard it. A familiar hand took hold of her arm. Signore Salerno.

Stunned for a moment, she could only gaze mutely into his cold eyes. Then, gathering her wits, she yanked at her arm making to dash away. But he held her too well.

"Lord! What's that stink about you?" he said, ducking his head as far from her as he could. "Perfume?"

"If you don't like it, then release me," she replied, kicking at him with slippers that did little damage.

"You'd best not offend me. I'm sure you would prefer that news of your recent sojourn here with Lord Satyr not become common knowledge in Venice," he threatened, giving her a shake. "There are those who would be quite enthralled to learn that he has engaged in carnal acts—possibly even committed the crime of sodomy—with the infamous La Maschera. Ah! I see from your expression that he has committed such a crime. Tut, tut!"

"What do you want? In exchange for your silence."

"For now, only a little information."

"What information?" She spat the words.

"Did you kill your mother?" he asked.

Her eyes widened and she shook her head, "No! I suspected you."

"I'm no murderer."

"Nor am I!" She tugged against his hold again. "How did you find me?"

"An informant. I've been lurking here for days and had begun to wonder if you would ever leave the estate. Then today you made things easy by falling into my lap."

She continued to fight him as he dragged her toward his horse, but he easily defeated her efforts.

"He haunted me for a time after she died, you know," Salerno offered.

"Who?"

"The constable. He knew I'd visited the house the morning of your mother's death and that I'd taken you with me. I think he suspected some sort of conspiracy between us. But he couldn't pin her murder on me. And in truth I had no hand in it. If you aren't the culprit, the constable's case remains unsolved. But no matter."

Jordan knew why the constable had looked in Salerno's direction. She'd penned an anonymous note to him implicating the physician.

He fumbled in his saddlebag searching for something, then drew out a cloth, which he clenched tight to her mouth and nose. It had been soaked in some foul-smelling vapor that made it difficult for her to breathe.

"Where are you taking me?" she gasped.

"Why, back to Venice, La Maschera. Now that your mother is gone, every day can be your birthday."

Jordan's eyes rolled back in her head as she lost consciousness.

35

Raine dreaded the passing of days. Worry threaded the minutes, the hours. Where was she? Was she safe? He withdrew into his work, as he'd done before she'd come. The crush was over now and he sampled the vats regularly.

He filled the rest of his empty hours pacing the estate and watching the vines gradually change color, going from gold to a flamboyant red.

Autumn would end with earthing up. Ploughs would work between the rows to create a mound of fertile soil around the trunks of the canes, which would protect them from winter's cold. Before long, the vines would lose their leaves and enter the dormant stage from mid-November to mid-March when the Bacchanalia would take place. He wanted Jordan here then. He couldn't imagine participating in the celebration without her.

If Lyon didn't return soon, he would quite possibly go insane.

One afternoon, he came across bits of ribbon scattered in the path of his back garden. He knelt to examine them. It was the bundle of sticks Jordan had left behind. A gift, she'd called it. Over the days since she'd gone it had rained once or twice and they'd been soiled. The mud had dried, leaving the ribbons dull and stiff.

He picked up one of the bundles that was still largely intact and examined it, wondering why she'd chosen to create such odd items. One of the branches was from an American species of tree and the other from a native plant of Italy. Pulling the two twigs apart, he noticed that the bark had been scraped away between them at the exact point where the sticks met. He picked up another bundle and saw the same design—American and Italian species joined. It was as though she'd meant them to be . . . grafted together.

The meaning behind these bizarre crafts struck him like a thunderbolt. Her dreams had caused her to make them, she'd told him. It was some sort of message for him, but she hadn't understood its meaning.

However, he did. It was quite possibly the very solution he'd been after for these many months. The solution they'd all been after. Could the cure for the phylloxera be grafting the rootstock of an American vine onto an Italian one? Bacchus! If she was right, she'd saved an entire wine industry.

Yet he'd thrown her efforts away. Called it witchcraft. And he'd seen something die in her eyes when he had.

36

The bishop sat in Salerno's establishment in Venice once again, studying the sores and scabs on his cock below his raised robes. Though his disease had been dormant for years, it now seemed intent on eating away at him in earnest. He was growing fat and forgetful, and on several embarrassing occasions he'd found he could not control his bowels.

"I've come for another treatment," he told Salerno.

"More of the fumigation?" asked the physician.

"No, something new is needed," said the bishop.

"Very well," said Salerno. He began to measure and pour ingredients into a jar. Then he stirred them together and plunked the drink he'd concocted on the table.

"What is it?" the bishop asked, gazing warily at the brew.

"Eggs, froth of snail, a pinch of this and that. Ginseng, ginger, salt."

"Why have you agreed to help me so easily?" the bishop demanded, still suspicious.

"Don't worry. It's not poison. To be honest, I'm grateful to you for the information you passed on to me during our last visit. Because of you, La Maschera has returned to Venice."

The bishop brightened. "Does Satyr know?"

Salerno shrugged. "Probably, by now."

The bishop leaned forward. "Has she given you any trouble?"

"So you've decided La Maschera is female, have you?"

"Naturally," said the bishop. "I heard there were children."

"Really? I kept to myself so as to avoid discovery, so I learned nothing of it."

The bishop had begun to take the brew, and Salerno waited impatiently for him to draw a breath between gulps. "This rot is disgusting," the bishop complained, once he'd drunk half of it.

"Yes, yes, but what of these children?"

"There were two," the bishop supplied. "Stillborn though. Not surprising I suppose, given her innards. Wouldn't it be fascinating to open her up and study them?"

"Yes, well . . ."

"You know, if she gives you too much trouble, you might arrange an accident."

"Accident?" Salerno echoed, not comprehending. "What sort of accident?"

"If, during the course of scientific investigation, some serious damage were to befall her, it would be beyond your fault. In fact, I could serve as a witness to attest to the accidental nature of her demise. Wouldn't her inner workings be easier to fathom if an autopsy could be performed on her? That's all I'm saying."

"Ah! I take your meaning and you are correct," Salerno said, tapping a finger on his chin. "And nothing substantial would be lost, for a good taxidermist could preserve La Maschera's body and organs for ongoing display. Well, perhaps one day such an accident will be warranted. But I'll not take you up on the suggestion for now."

Locked in the adjoining room, Jordan heard the speculation in Salerno's voice. With growing disquiet, she listened to him ponder the unthinkable. When she'd decided she'd rather die than remain in Salerno's hands, some evil force of nature must have been listening in on her thoughts.

"The children are interesting news indeed," said Salerno, eyes alight with excitement. "It verifies that La Maschera has functioning female organs. Now only the male organs need be tested for reproductive capabilities. If La Maschera can wield its puny prick well enough to produce issue in another woman's belly in addition to having grown a child in its own, it will become notorious. And I will be its discoverer."

"How *did* you discover your prodigy anyway?" The bishop screwed up his face and started glugging the gloppy mixture down again.

Salerno hooked his thumbs in the waist of his trousers. "I suppose there's no harm in telling of it to you, for you have an interest in keeping La Maschera's identity safe. I discovered the creature through a fortuitous event that occurred some nineteen years ago when I was called to the Cietta home here in Venice to assist at a difficult birth. Though I was but a young physician then, I was shrewd enough to make the most of the opportunity that issued from between Celia Cietta's legs that night," he boasted.

The bishop stilled mid-sip, but Salerno was in a loquacious mood and didn't notice his companion's increased interest.

"As you may have guessed, the babe was La Maschera," he went on. "The mother was greedy and naturally wanted a boy child in order to inherit her dead husband's fortune. Her child's gender turned out to be ambiguous, of course. I saw the potential for my future in such a creature and struck a bargain with the mother so that I might display it from time to time. But the mother is dead now, and Jordan Cietta is completely in my hands thanks to you."

Salerno flicked his fingers toward the liquid remaining in the glass in front of the bishop. "Drink up, man. It's not poisoned, as I've assured you."

But the bishop set the glass down unfinished. "Am I to understand that Jordan Cietta and La Maschera are one in the same? And that you pronounced her status as male upon her birth, even though that wasn't strictly true?" His mind was slow these days and he wanted to be certain he'd gotten the odious facts right.

"Yes, what of it? I assume you will keep this information to yourself as you have no wish for Lord Satyr to track down the creature here."

The bishop stared into his drink. "I have no love for the church. Did you know? I was forced there due to a lack of resources and I've done the best I could."

"Such is the case with many an impoverished gentleman," Salerno sympthatized.

"Yes. May I have a bit of that wine there beyond you to wash the taste of this vile brew away?" the bishop asked mildly.

"Certainly." Salerno turned to pluck a bottle of wine from the rack that stood along a wall. "I'll even give you some of the Satyr Vineyard brew. Nothing's too good for the man who had a hand in bringing La Maschera back to me. Now what is it you plan to do after—?"

Something hit Salerno from behind and he slumped to the floor, unconscious.

The cold-eyed bishop stood over him, a poker in his hand. "What do I plan to do? I plan to fuck you exactly as you fucked me nineteen years ago. I'm Jordan Cietta's closest male cousin, damn it all. If it weren't for you, I'd have inherited the Cietta fortune. I'd be wealthy and respected. My cock would likely not be rotting away because I'd have had clean women in my bed."

Energized by a terrible anger, the bishop lifted Salerno and bent him, chest down, over a wooden trunk. Locating a knife, he cut the seat of his victim's trousers away so only the cheeks of his rump were exposed. With his hand, he smacked the other man's ass a half-dozen times, then stood back to admire the imprint of his fingers on the reddened flesh.

He fell to his knees behind the physician in a position of prayer. He raised the front of his robes and lay their weight on Salerno's back. Spitting in his hand, he fumbled under his robe, using the spittle to slick his cock. His malingering shaft rarely rose on command anymore. But rage had lent it strength.

He wrenched Salerno's cheeks apart with fingers and thumb. Locating his bunghole, he stuffed himself inside it with a low hiss. Cursing all the while, he sawed and bucked, allowing the other man's rectum to scratch the itch of his disease.

Salerno awoke to terrific pain. His ass burned like the fires of hell. He was being sodomized. He, a virgin who had avoided any sort of sexual relations his entire life for fear of contracting disease.

"Fuck me over, will you?" his rapist ranted. "I'll give you a fucking you'll not soon forget, you conspiring shit-spirited bastard."

With a great roar Salerno bucked off his rider. Blindly sweeping his arm behind him, he struck the assailant down.

Blinking stupidly, the bishop lay on his back on the floor with his robes hiked to his waist. His cock was hideous—half-wilted and rotten with syphilis. And it had just been in *his* ass. The bishop had administered more than just a fucking. He'd served up a death sentence. A slow, cruel death sentence.

The bishop stirred, coming awake. Hands shaking with fury, Salerno went to deal with him.

Raine arrived in Venice hours later, having left his estate days ago the very moment he sensed Lyon was within easy range of returning home. While still in Tuscany, he'd made long-distance inquiries to learn the whereabouts of the physician who was his only link to Jordan. Now he quickly made his way to Salerno's establishment.

Once Salerno knew of his interest in La Maschera, he would undoubtedly try to keep Jordan by any means he could. So he'd come prepared to bargain. To threaten. He planned to wed her. But if Salerno exposed her for a hermaphrodite, there would be scandal. Such a scandal could not be allowed to besmirch the Satyr name. Raine could take Jordan and leave Tuscany, but that would endanger EarthWorld. Three were needed on the estate to guard the gate.

It all boiled down to one thing. If Salerno refused to cooperate, he would have to die.

Such was the state of Raine's thoughts when he arrived at the physician's door. Finding it unlatched, he pushed it open and went inside. He found the man he sought seated calmly in his laboratory. The bishop lay beyond him on the floor, robes hiked to his waist, blood pooling from a great gash at his temple.

"Ah! Yet another guest comes calling. Lord Satyr, is it not?"

Raine nodded toward the bishop. "You killed him?"

Salerno patted the iron poker lying on the table next to him. "He had it coming, believe me."

"I trust you don't have the same fate planned for all your guests."

"Be grateful I took him down. He was cousin to Jordan Cietta."

"Who?"

"La Maschera. The one I assume you seek—the hermaphrodite. Surely you knew that your lover and the heir to the Cietta fortune were one in the same."

Raine's jaw hardened.

"So you didn't." Salerno shrugged a hand at the bishop. "He was in line to inherit. If I'd allowed him to expose her ambiguous gender, then my part in her mother's deception would have been exposed as well. And I couldn't have that."

"What the devil are you talking about?"

"I was the physician attending Celia Cietta when she gave birth. I pronounced her issue—Jordan—to be fully male. Only half a deception, as you have good cause to know. It was my proclamation that tilted the Cietta fortune toward Jordan and her mother and away from the bishop. Hence the reason for his wrath. It serves us all that he dies."

"And do the secrets of La Maschera die with him?"

Salerno spread his hands. "As I told the good bishop, I have no desire to expose La Maschera's connection with the Ciettas. My only interest is in studying the one you seek, but now that's likely impossible unless I bribe the courts."

Raine took a step forward. "What does that mean? Speak plainly, man, or suffer the consequences."

"Jordan Cietta was arrested in this establishment not half an hour ago. Fortunately, the good constable was too stupid to visit this room or he'd have discovered another body to burden his caseload."

Raine swore. He turned to go, then paused. "When I leave here do I have your assurance that these secrets you've shared will remain secrets?"

Salerno nudged the bishop's body with his foot. "He sodomized me while I was out. Bastard."

"What has that to do with anything?"

"Look at his cock. He was infected with syphilis, an advanced case." Salerno slung back a long draught of Satyr wine.

"By sodomizing me he's killed me as well. Though my death will be slower than his was. More agonizing."

"I see."

"Only Jordan's mother, the dear bishop, and I were privy to the mysteries of your lover's body."

"Then if word of Jordan's connection with La Maschera circulates, I'll know from where it issued," Raine said pointedly.

"It won't," Salerno hastened to assure him. "There's no benefit to me in speaking of it or in rousing your ire. I'm well aware of the power the Satyr family wields. However, you'd better hope it serves you well. The constable has taken it into his head that Jordan Cietta is a murderer."

37

Munching some cod set on a plate, the jailor eyed Jordan's expensive waistcoat and trousers. Once he'd gotten her in his clutches, Salerno had seen to it that she was dressed as a gentleman again.

"Non poveri?" the jailor inquired of the constable who'd taken her from Salerno's quarters and delivered her here. The constable in turn looked to her for an answer.

Non poveri. Not poor. If she went to that section of the jail her treatment would be better, but she had no money. And her family would be expected to pay for food and linens, even a mattress and bedding. She had no family to turn to.

"Poveri," her jailor decided, correctly reading her hesitation.

"For what reason am I being arrested?" Jordan demanded for what must have been the hundredth time since she'd been yanked from Salerno's clutches only an hour ago.

"For the crime of murder," the constable finally informed her.

"And whom did I murder?" she asked, already knowing what his answer would be.

"Why, your mother of course." Then, to the jailor, he warned, "Keep this one separate from the riffraff. He's not to be harmed in your cells. I want him whole for his trial."

The jailor only grunted. Carrying his plate, he continued eating as he led her away by the chains that hobbled her hands. Downstairs where sunlight never went, they passed the section for the vecchi—the elderly. The stench of it nearly felled her. Eventually, she was delivered to the roughest sort of dank cell to await the whims of the courts. But at least she was housed alone.

"I'm hungry," she declared after her jailor shoved her inside and turned to go.

In answer, he unfastened his fly and set his cock on his plate alongside the unfinished cod. "This is all you'll get to eat from me tonight, signore!" he said, shoving the plate toward her.

She turned her back.

He only laughed. "You'll be willing soon enough, when the hunger gnaws at your insides."

She turned to eye him. "Don't count on it."

He looked closer. "Hmm. Nice piece of jewelry there." Quickly, he reached an arm through the bars. Snapping the chain holding the amulet Raine had given her, he took it from her neck.

Her pleas for its return went unanswered. Even though the amulet hadn't been activated, it had seemed to lend some protection from her dreams. Without it, her first night in the cell was filled with nightmares fiercer than any she'd had before she'd gone to his estate. It was as though all the demons of her dreams has stored themselves up over the days since Raine had given the bauble to her, and now they'd broken loose in her mind.

Her clothing was suitable for the young man she'd once pretended to be. But it wasn't sufficient against the cold. When dawn eventually came, she bathed in the tepid basin of water that had been left for her and gnawed moldy bread and cheese.

Around noon, her jailor came for her and delivered her to the constable, who took her up several flights of stairs into a courtroom where an initial hearing was to be held.

Head held high, Jordan entered the courtroom, now flanked by the constable. She was exhausted, but her entire body was tensed in preparation for what was to come.

Her mother was dead, and she the primary suspect. There would be no one here to speak on her behalf, and she could respond only when addressed. Despite her innocence, it seemed a foregone conclusion that her accusers would prevail.

Both the curious and the cultured were in attendance in the audience, she saw. Many of the lowborn as well, for they came regularly to the courts to gawk at the prisoners for entertainment. And then, as her eyes continued to survey the onlookers, she encountered someone she hadn't expected. Raine.

She cringed as his silver eyes swept her. Confusion filled them at the way she was dressed—as a man. Today he would learn the truth of her upbringing and how she'd spent her days before she'd met him that night here in Venice.

She only prayed he would not discover her connection to La Maschera. When Salerno had abducted her, he had sworn to display the nude drawings of her to Raine if she didn't cooperate. Would he make good on the threat if he were brought in to testify?

Shame singed her cheekbones. She couldn't bear it if Raine saw those horrid drawings. Would he think differently of her if he saw her stooped, the cheeks of her buttocks spread so her anus gapped? Or if he saw her seated upon a chair, fingers spreading her own labia to expose her vaginal tissue for the artist?

She averted her gaze from his, determined not to glance his way again. It would be too painful to watch his dismay harden to disgust as the proceedings wore on.

38

Raine stalked her in her cell.

She'd never been so happy to see anyone in her life. "Go away," she told him.

"Am I to understand you have been masquerading as a boy for the past nineteen years?"

Jordan folded her arms, gripping her elbows. "No. You heard my accusers. I'm male. The only masquerading I've done has been since the night I met you."

Only inches away, he looked her up and down. "You want to be a man? Is that what you want?"

She remained silent.

He crowded her against the wall with his body. She turned her nose into the hollow of his throat and inhaled deeply. She'd missed him.

A hand planted on each side of her, he whispered, "Is that why you begged me to stick my cock in your woman's slit so often? Is that why you came with me to Tuscany? Why you reveled in the role of my woman?"

She shrugged. "I'm tired, Raine."

He leaned closer. "Admit it. You are a female, are you not?"

Was she? "That's an unanswerable question. I have two sets of contradictory genitals. They both lead me in different directions."

"Yet they led you to me, to my bed. And you seemed content enough there. Eager, in fact."

"You were a diversion," she lied. Belying her disinterest, she caressed his face, knowing she might never have another chance. "I always planned to return to Venice and take my position in society. As a man."

"Because you wanted to?"

She shook her head, suddenly done with lying. "It's my preference to face the world as female. But at times, I find that . . . I prefer to play the man."

Her words fell into a void.

Then his voice came to her, low and loving. "You could do that. In Tuscany. With me."

Her throat tightened. "You'd lie with me as a man lies with a man?"

His head nodded against her hair. "I don't care about your gender. I want you." Through the fabric of their trousers, his cock nudged hers. Both were thick with desire. "And you want me."

Though her heart was breaking, she slipped under his arm and away from him, determined to remain firm. "It doesn't matter what we want. If the court finds out what I am, it will touch your family. I'll bring the taint of my past to your good name."

His tone turned brisk. "There are ways of mitigating that. My family wields a certain power within the courts. Now, let me be certain I understand the facts." He began counting them off on his fingers. "The Cietta estate was to go to a male cousin unless your mother managed to produce a male child. And your mother bore you, a child that was not entirely male, passing you off as your father's male heir in order to inherit. Is that correct?"

"How did you know?" she asked in dull surprise.

"Answer me."

She shrugged a shoulder. "Yes, then. You can understand the reason for her ruse. The rules of society are unfair. She simply tried to tilt them in her favor."

"With Salerno's endorsement."

"My mother said that on the morning of my birth, the entire Cietta clan gathered to await the arrival of the only child of my recently deceased father. They held their breath, hoping for a girl child. Upon seeing I had a phallus, my aunt wept. She looked no further, never suspecting that a vagina lurked between my thighs. Salerno and my mother claimed I was a perfectly shaped boy child, and the world believed. My mother and I inherited the fortune, and my aunt's son got nothing."

"Your mother lied about your gender all these years to retain an estate that was not rightfully hers?"

"I see you do not sympathize. Perhaps you must be female to understand the position she was in."

"What I don't understand is how she could have in good conscience sent you to Salerno on each of your birthdays."

Jordan paled. Her eyes darted around the cell searching for a place to hide from the knowledge that he knew all of her shameful secrets now. But there was no place to run from the truth. "How did you know about that?" she asked tonelessly.

"I had it from Salerno himself."

"I see." Had Salerno shown him the drawings? She wouldn't ask. Didn't want to know. "Do you think I murdered her?"

Raine swatted the air with the back of his hand. "You didn't murder anyone. You were with me the night your mother died. All night. The hotelier on Lido will attest to it."

"He never saw my face. I wore a mask that night, remember? Besides, I might have done the deed earlier, before we met."

"Did you?" He knew exactly how long her mother had been dead and how long Jordan had been in Salerno's possession, then his own, that day.

She shrugged. "Maybe."

"Liar," he said softly. "You couldn't have done it. I saw you earlier that night in Salerno's theater, onstage. Where you'd passed the entire day."

Pressing her palms to her flaming cheeks, Jordan bowed her head and swung away. "You know?" she gasped. "You've known all this time?"

"Yes."

"And said nothing."

He came behind her. "Look at me."

He waited until her eyes found his and then took her in his arms. "What happened to you under Salerno's watch wasn't your fault. You were a pawn."

"I hated it," she mumbled into his chest.

"I know." His broad hand stroked her back.

"But I didn't kill my mother. For all her faults, I loved her."

"I know."

It was stuffy in the cell and her breath felt strangled. She pushed away from him to stand on her own. "You should go. And don't come back. Forget me."

He pulled her back to him and kissed her forehead. "Not likely. You're coming to Tuscany with me as soon as I can arrange it. And, Jordan—"

She looked up at him.

"We'll have more children."

She shook her head, afraid to believe.

After that, she'd told him dozens of times to go. Finally he did. And she wished him back with all her heart and soul.

39

Jordan's conditions improved greatly once Raine departed, and she determined that he must have greased some palms. She was moved into the non poveri section, where fresh bedding and linen were supplied. Her jailors there were far more deferential, and food rather than genitals was served to her at mealtimes.

Toward evening the following night a new jailor brought a cloaked figure whom he let inside. It was the only guest she'd had save Raine. She regarded the stranger, wary.

After the guard had locked the door and gone, the visitor lowered the hood of the cape. Within was a woman about Jordan's height and weight, but perhaps a decade older.

Dark haired and plain of feature, the woman stared back at her, awed. "La Maschera," she breathed.

Jordan's brow knitted as she tried to place the face. After a moment, recognition dawned. "You're part of that society that always came to the theaters. One of the LAMAS, are you not?"

The woman drew in a gasp and crossed her palms over her

heart, appearing delighted Jordan had recognized her. "Yes! I'm the one who sent the poem."

"Poem?"

"Yes! But I do beg your pardon. You must receive hundreds of devotions. Please do excuse my conceit in assuming my humble offering might stand out in your memory. But perhaps you do recall it? It was titled 'O Ambiguous Love.' " She blushed, causing the sprinkling of freckles over her cheeks to darken. "Shall I recite it for you?"

"Um, well . . ."

The visitor went down on one knee.

O to gaze upon your breast, my love
O to gaze beneath your mask
O to twine my eyes with yours, my love
O t'would be a favored task
O to touch . . .

"Thank you," said Jordan, urging the woman to her feet. "That's quite enough. I do recall it after all, and I truly appreciate your efforts. But tell me—why exactly have you come here to this jail?"

"Signore Salerno informed LAMAS of your invitation only yesterday. I came to him as soon as I heard of it, and he dispatched me only moments ago here to you. However . . ." She paused, a confused frown forming between her brows as she glanced around the inhospitable cell. "I'm not quite sure where he intends that we are to—"

Jordan rubbed her temples to soothe the throbbing another sleepless night had caused her. "What invitation?"

Her guest giggled coquettishly. "The, um, personal one."

Jordan stared at her. "Can you be more specific?"

"Oh! Poetic words always escape me when I most need them,"

the woman wailed in response. "If only I'd brought my pen and paper. But I shall do my best to improvise." She whirled away, deep in thought. Moments later, she turned back. Clutching her breast, she began . . .

> O tonight I have come to you with an amorous fervor in my bosom
> Hoping you choose me for the task you have set
> O I vow I will gladly lend myself
> And twill be a night we'll not soon forget
> O signore, let my softness yield to your—

Jordan took a backward step, shaking her head in disbelief as she realized the drift of the amorous poem. "No. NoNoNo."

The woman straightened, refusing to be deflected so easily. "I know I'm neither young nor pretty. But I have two sisters—both married—and they've borne a dozen healthy children between them. So it's likely I am fertile, though untried."

For each step back that Jordan took, her visitor took a step forward.

"I'm sorry, but Signore Salerno has misled you and your society," said Jordan. "I made no invitation asking for a female partner to bear my offspring."

The woman stopped in her tracks. "You don't want me?" Hurt filled her face

Jordan spread her hands, exasperated. "It's not that. You're quite attractive. It's just that I'm in love with someone else."

"Oh. Another woman?"

"Well, no."

"A man then! But he could never bear your child." A new determination filled the woman's face. She rushed to kneel at her feet, and the skirt of her dress rustled and pooled around her on the floor, drawing Jordan's eyes.

"Give me a chance. Let me tempt you," she said. Her fingers worked at the fastenings at her throat, ripping them wide to reveal the fleshy rounds of her bosom. "Oh, La Maschera, let me be the answer to your concupiscent dreams."

"Dreams?" Jordan echoed. An idea came to her as she watched the woman commence to divest herself of clothing. "An interesting choice of words, signorina. Perhaps you *are* the answer to my dreams after all."

She pulled the woman to stand. "Here, let me help you off with those garments. But let me also suggest another direction you might put your efforts to, which would lend even greater assistance to me."

When the guard returned an hour later, he found the cloaked visitor waiting by the door. Her hair was in disarray and her clothing crumpled and askew. She ducked her head, avoiding his knowing leer.

"I'm ready to depart," she told him.

Beyond her, La Maschera stood at the small window, staring aimlessly into the street.

The jailor made a disparaging gesture toward him. "Tiny little prick like that one has. Doubt it made much of an impression on a signorina such as you. I'd offer my services, but I've got orders to take you to Signore Salerno."

The cloaked figure only shrugged.

He peered closely at her. "Not much of a talker, eh? I like that in a woman. Come on, then."

He opened the door and let her out, then relocked it behind them.

Jordan felt the jailor's eyes on the sway of the cloak as he unknowingly escorted her upward into the sunlight and escape. The woman who remained alone in the cell had given her the location of the other members of LAMAS. They would come for her when Jordan made them aware of her situation. The woman and she had concocted a false tale she would tell the jailors, of being overpowered and left to rot by Signore Jordan Cietta.

Outside the jail, Jordan simply walked away from the unsuspecting guard and found her way to freedom.

40

Raine lifted the latch and slipped through an unlocked window into the Cietta house. Once inside, he was struck anew by the proliferation of winged creatures that adorned its rooms. But he viewed the interior with fresh eyes today, knowing now that this was the house where Jordan had once lived. First as a boy, then as a man.

Pretending to be entirely male must have been difficult for her. She'd done it out of loyalty to her mother, he was certain. Loyalty to a mother who'd blithely loaned her out once a year to be displayed naked on a stage for the purposes of scientific study. What must it have been like for Jordan to be poked, prodded, and questioned by grown men when she was only a child? She must have been terrified. He ached to think of it.

Better informed now, he noted that her mother's likeness was to be found in many of the Faerie depictions, cavorting among other creatures of fact and myth. It was obvious she'd retained some memories of King Feydon's surreptitious visit to her bed those many years ago, and that they'd haunted her life.

Though he saw Celia Cietta's face everywhere he gazed,

nowhere did he find a single likeness of Jordan. Jordan—her only child—who'd loved her mother more than she'd been loved in return.

He slipped upstairs into the bedchamber where they'd viewed Signora Cietta's body that day. Studying the room, he realized the décor was somewhat more masculine here in this room than in the rest of the house. Less cluttered. The constable had said that this was Jordan's room. Why had her mother died in Jordan's bed rather than her own?

He lifted the book lying on the bedside table. It was the same book Celia had been clutching in her death grip—a leather-bound copy of *A Midsummer's Night's Dream*—Shakespeare's quintessential faerie story.

When he thumbed through the pages, an illustration plate fell from between two of them. He bent and picked it up. Titled *Titania's Awakening*, it depicted Oberon and Titania, Shakespeare's king and queen of the Faerie, bathed in a pool of golden light. A multitude of characters from the play surrounded them. Dancing Faeries cavorted, carefree and joyful. But others such as witches and demons were sinister and more erotic.

On the back, a note had been written in a spidery feminine hand. It was a mixture of garbled quotes from two of Shakespeare's more famous plays, *A Midsummer Night's Dream* and *Romeo and Juliet*.

> *What visions I have seen, My Dearest Oberon! Queen Mab gallops by night through my brain and then I dream of love. Of you, my Dearest Oberon. How I have missed your attentions these years and been enamored of asses too long . . .*

There was more but he skimmed it, his eyes falling to the end . . .

Tonight I leave this world and come to you. Await me,
my Dearest Oberon. For in moments, I shall come to you
in death's final sleep.
   Yours, Titania

The imprint of a woman's rouged lips had been pressed upon
the page, there beside the signature.

A suicide note. Celia Cietta had not been murdered after all!
She had killed herself. And he held the proof.

Suddenly his nostrils flared. His head lifted. Jordan. She was
here. He strode into the corridor to find her standing below-
stairs in the vestibule. He peered beyond her as though expecting to see jailors shadowing her.

"I escaped," she told him without further explanation. "What
are you doing here?" She motioned toward the folded illustration in his hands. "And what's that?"

He went to her and held her as he explained his news. There
would be time enough to take Celia's last letter to the authori-
ties after he saw Jordan safely home to Tuscany.

Together they left the house by the front door, locking it.
Locking Jordan's past behind them for good.

EPILOGUE

Jordan woke slowly. Her cock was stiff and her pussy was wet. She'd had a new dream during the night as she lay in bed beside her husband of only three days. A wonderful dream. It was the kind that was so rich in color and detail that it was difficult to believe it hadn't actually occurred.

But she knew it would one day.

It was the sort of dream that she had now. No longer were her dreams full of obscure hints of doom. Now they foretold of joyful fates and destinies. Of her future.

Under Raine's continued tutelage, she'd learned to filter the visions that came to her in the hours of darkness. Nightmares were kept leashed and at bay.

The dream that had visited her this night had come in three parts. The first had begun on the morning of her next birthday—her twentieth, only eight months from now . . .

In the dream, she'd awakened, sitting up in bed with a gasp. It was morning. Her birthday. Her heart pounded in her ears and dread prickled over her body. Salerno would be here soon. She pulled the bedcovers aside, preparing to run. She wouldn't go with him this time, she swore to herself. She wouldn't subject herself to the degradation of another birthday spent pinned by a thousand eyes and lashed by the curious tongues of strangers.

Then Raine's arms had come around her waist, pulling her back into the haven of his muscled chest. She'd slapped and clawed him at first, still caught in the grip of old fears. Then she recalled where she was and who held her. The tattoo of her heart had slowly calmed and she'd relaxed into his strength.

He'd stroked her hair and kissed her, murmuring sweet love words. With his touch, he'd soothed and softened the horror and humiliation of all the other birthdays that had come before.

Then, in the way of dreams, she'd unexpectedly found herself in the midst of a different scene—the second in the dream sequence.

It had been a celebration that same day, held outside on the lawn of Raine's home. Hers and Raine's home now.

And the whole Satyr clan had been there. Jane and Nick had their son Vincent in tow as well as Jane's sister Emma, who had grown half a foot taller and was looking quite the lady.

It had been a festive occasion marking Jordan's twentieth birthday. And Jane's, as well. And that of yet a third sister. All had been born within a year of one another and of the same father—an ElseWorld king. With each birthday, revelry commenced for all three daughters regardless of whose factual birth was being marked, so it was almost as though each had three birthdays a year.

Lyon had been in attendance, along with his new bride—the third FaerieBlend sister. She was feminine and petite with polished manners and a lustrous mane of hair the color of almonds. Her vocabulary had been sprinkled with French, and her easy laughter and temperament seemed well matched to Lyon's. It pleased Jordan to note that he stayed by her side, unconsciously touching her now and then as though to reassure himself this confection of womanhood was real and his.

In turn, his wife had seemed equally smitten, feeding him bits of cake as though he were a favored, overgrown pet. She'd been affectionate toward Jordan and Jane as well.

There had been mountains of gifts for all three sisters, all expensive and innovative as each brother vied to top the other with his extravagance. Wine and laughter had flowed freely. There had been no room for sorrow on this birthday.

Then the dream had shifted again to yet a third and final scene.

It had been that same night, in the sacred glen. Raine had taken her there for a more private sort of celebration. She wore a frothy nightgown of Florentine design, one of his many gifts to her that day. He was already naked, his clothing scattered on the moss around them. Overhead, the moon was a three-quarter slice and diamond stars glittered and winked.

His cock was thick and ruddy with desire, and it pressed urgently against her belly as he drew her close. Moonful would come just days later, and his passions were building in preparation.

In one hand, he held a precious silver box carved with ancient designs and words that told her it had originated in Else-World.

"Another gift?" she'd asked when he offered it to her.

He'd only nodded, but his eyes told her this gift would be the most important of all those he'd given her that day. Solemnly, she'd opened the hinged silk-lined box and lifted out a single strand of satin coiled within. A gold ribbon.

When she'd looked at him in question, Raine had held his hands out to her, with the insides of his wrists pressed together.

In the pitch velvet of night, he whispered to her. "Happy birthday, my love."

And then she'd understood that he hadn't just gifted her with a single ribbon. It was more. Much more. For this one night, he was giving her the gift of sexual control. A chance to exercise her male side.

"Oh, Raine," she said, her voice trembling with emotion. Silver and black met and held.

He watched as she took the yard-long ribbon, wrapped it around his wrists several times, and then tied it off, leaving the long ends to dangle. She brushed a hand over the bond, enjoying the sight of the fragile satin tethering his masculine strength.

Glancing around the ring of statues and altars, she searched for a place to begin. "Where?" she asked him, anxious now.

"You choose," he told her. His voice was low, his passions stirred.

A thrill slipped up her spine.

She led him by the arm to a circular altar with three statues standing at its far side and an unencumbered slab of granite occupying the front half of its circumference. It had been her favorite of those in the glen ever since she'd first seen it. All three figures were nymphs, dressed in frothy veils. But unlike many of the other female statues here, these nymphs worshipped no one. They were hermaphrodites, their bodies shaped like hers.

Raine knelt before her, his face turned up to hers. She parted the front of her gown for him and his eyes found her cock. His head jutted forward and his tongue lashed out, licking upward from its root with one long, slick stroke until he had her plum. How easily it slipped inside the juicy, hot cavern of his mouth.

She cradled his jaw gently in her palms, feeling the muscles and tendons at work as he suckled her. Her head fell back and her hands curved around his neck, brushing under the fringed length of his hair. If he kept this up, she was going to . . .

He stood and presented her with his back. Hands outstretched, he bent at the waist to lie chest-down over the altar with arms loosely extended overhead. With shaking fingers, she tied the ends of the ribbons that bound him around a slender stone ankle of one of the hermaphrodites. She glanced up into its knowing eyes, sensing that it would enjoy what was to come almost as much as she would.

Jordan tested his bonds. They were delicate against his strength and something he could easily elude if he chose to. But he wouldn't try, she knew. That was part of his gift to her. For this special night—to celebrate her birthday and her freedom from domination—he was hers to command.

She found a position behind him and smoothed her palms over the taut muscles of his buttocks. She parted the front of the lacy, feminine nightgown and her cock peeked out, intrigued.

A fierce need to take him in this way swelled her shaft thicker than it had ever been. She slicked a finger with her mouth, then rouged it over the crinkled brown aperture within the crease of his rear. She tucked the finger inside, testing the firm grip of him. The muscles of his buttocks clenched and he shuddered. Her rod twitched with anticipation.

"Relax," she told him, in much the same way he'd once instructed her.

She braced a hand atop the altar alongside his rib and pressed her groin high between his legs, coddling his balls with her own. She drew back slightly and with her hand directed her cock to his threshold.

Holding his hip bone with her other hand, she parted his inner thighs with her knees. Then slowly, slowly, she pressed forward. Inward. Deeper. Deeper still. Until her mound met his ass.

Raine exhaled on a hoarse groan and his hands clenched on his golden bonds. Muscles flexed and rippled over his back.

She withdrew and pierced him again. "You're tight," she told him. "Good."

"Bacchus. Yesss," he agreed. His voice was choked, fevered.

She reached under his belly and found his hard, throbbing

cock. She stroked it from root to crown in time with each thrust she administered.

Their breathing turned harsh, synchronized. She let go of his shaft and gripped his hips, losing herself in the ecstasy of the moment . . .

There, she lost the dream as well.

Blinking awake, she stared at Raine's handsome face asleep on the pillow next to hers. Whisper soft, she caressed his stubbled cheek, careful not to rouse him. When she looked at him on the morrow, her eyes would hold a precious, sweet, thrilling secret—the knowledge of what was to occur between them on the night she reached the age of twenty.

This would be one birthday that could not come soon enough.

She looked forward to it.

Author's Note

Grape phylloxera is a tiny aphidlike insect that feeds on the roots of grapevines, stunting their growth or killing them. The pest was accidentally imported to England and France on American vines around 1862. It reproduced with devastating speed, and by the end of the 19th century, phylloxera had destroyed two-thirds of Europe's vineyards.

The destruction was eventually halted by the discovery that this nearly microscopic insect does not attack the roots of American grapevines. By grafting the rootstock of European vines onto American ones and replanting vineyards with the new grafted stocks, Europe's wine grape industry was saved.

For the purposes of this story, the date of the infestation is set at approximately thirty-nine years prior to the actual date. In addition, the account of how the phylloxera problem was solved has been fictionalized in the series, and all characters involved in that process herein are products of the author's imagination.

This book is a work of fiction. Dialogue and events are the product of the author's imagination, and any resemblance to actual events, groups, or individual persons, living or dead, is entirely coincidental.

Turn the page for
a sizzling excerpt from
ANIMAL LUST!
On sale now!

1

Cumberland, England, 1800

Sweet mother! What a blunder she'd made! Jane's hand shot to her mouth, and she bit the skin of her palm.

Jonathan had never loved her. He lied.

Tears blurred her vision and streamed down her cheeks. She tripped and stumbled, barely seeing the wooded trail before her. The flesh of her sex burned, and her legs ached. How she needed a nice long soak in a tub and time to sort this out. Dash it!

When had she misunderstood his intentions? They had been secretly touching and kissing behind his tavern for months. The whole town thought they would marry. Then, today at the fair, they'd snuck into the woods.

"Lovely, lovely Jane, ye give me a tickle, won't ye, love?" The smell of the ale from his breath wafted about her.

She shouldn't, but how she fancied him. What could it matter?

"You will marry me?" she breathed into his hair, her head spinning in aroused bliss.

He grunted as her touch ran down his muscled back.

He'd grunted! Her teeth ground together as she ran without seeing the trail before her. Sweet mother! He had never said he would wed her. She had craved his touch and the feelings he created in her so madly she'd mistook the grunt as an affirmation of his designs.

She'd given her innocence to a man who had no intentions of wedding her. Her fingers clutched her stomach. She could be with child, and she had no way to take care of a babe nor herself. Daft, truly daft.

Her head spun. She gasped for air as her legs tangled in her skirts, and she tripped, landing, limbs spread wide on the hard, damp earth. Oh. She lay, lungs burning, unable to breathe, and closed her eyes. Her entire life had changed in one act of wanton misdeed. She would pull herself together. She would find a way if she carried a child, but for now . . . she would grieve while no one could see her.

"*Lovely Jane.*" *He buttoned up his trousers as he inhaled a deep breath, the crisp air clouding as he exhaled.* "*Not bad for a green tickle, and no worries about the clap.*"

The clap. He'd rutted with her like she was no better than a tavern wench. He loved her. He said he loved her. Her eyes closed as tears welled.

" '*Twas a lovely, Jane. Ye have a sweet little honeypot. Take good care of it and we'll come out here again sometime.*" *He turned and headed off into the trees.*

By God. What had she done?

With her face down in the dirt, tears silently ran down her face. Her limbs trembled, and her head spun. She hadn't cried in an age. The act depleted and exhausted her. *Pull yourself together, Jane.* With a sob, she straightened and got to her feet on shaking legs. She was a wealthy merchant's daughter. He was friends with her pa. How dare he treat her ill?

Panic grabbed at her heart.

This act ruined her prospects of a normal life and brought

shame on her family name. Her father's business would suffer. How could she be so selfish? Her family, she held dear.

Frantic, her gaze darted around the forest. Nothing but trees. *Think, think, you fool. . . .*

Her fingers pinched the bridge of her nose. She would go to Jonathan and beg him not to say a word. Dash it all. Her eyes squeezed shut.

If she could only figure a way out of the woods. She held her breath, listening for any sounds from the fair. Nothing. What is the rule? Follow the sun and it will lead you to the north. . . . No. . . . Sweet mother, she should have listened to her father when he talked about directions.

She stepped toward the setting sun; pain spread through her ankle and up her leg, and her temples throbbed. Ouch! She put weight on her leg and swayed. She could limp but not far.

The forest grew darker. Where was she? She hobbled up the path. Dash it all. Lost, that's where. She picked up her pace. Frost eased up around her heart, and she pushed aching dreams down. Just ahead, a road loomed, and the sun dipped below the horizon. The lane, rutted and ill used, surely led somewhere. . . .

Thunder cracked in the distance as she stared up at the large wooden door. Darkness brewed, and she passed not a soul on the road to this place. The house stood four stories tall, with huge spires that reached to the sky. She had resided in Cumberland for five years, and not once had she heard of an estate such as this. Lifting her hand, she knocked as rain plummeted to the earth in large wet thunks behind her.

She knocked again; shivers raced over her skin. The door creaked open.

"May I help you, ma'am?"

"Oh, indeed." She practically jumped at the man sticking his head out of the small crack. "I'm lost and injured." She pointed to her ankle. "And, well, you see, it is beginning to rain. Would it be possible for me to stay here this night? I could sleep in the kitchen or . . . or . . . the barn. I shan't be any trouble."

The man's eyes went wide behind his round spectacles, and his face twisted in what looked like horror.

"I . . . I . . . know this is highly irregular, but please?"

He schooled his features back to a serious line. "I'm sorry, ma'am. There is no safe way for you to stay here."

Safe? "Pardon?" *Oh, please just let me in.*

The wind whipped up and blew down the last of her pinned-up hair. A shiver racked her body, and her teeth chattered.

"Oh . . . Oh . . ." He glanced into the house. "Very well, ma'am. You will do as I say, do my bidding exclusively. Without fail. Women should not be in this house."

He was concerned about propriety? What a jest! She was ruined. Tears touched her eyes in shame, and she shook them away. What silliness! This man possessed no way of knowing that.

"I will do as you wish, sir." She had no choice. Either she stepped into this house and escaped drowning in one of Cumberland's deluges, or she would try to find her way back in the dark and probably die. She cringed. That was a bit too pessimistic, but she just couldn't go another step this night.

He hesitated and then opened the door just enough to admit her. She slid into the darkened hall and glanced around. A grand staircase stood twisting up to the roof. Dim light shone through a window above the door and illuminated the entry and the paintings that covered the walls. Where did the stair lead? An eerie chill raced up her spine, and she stepped forward, eager to see what lay at their end.

"This way, miss."

Startled, she spun around and followed the servant down a hall that went off to the left of the entry.

"I will put you in the east wing. You will lock your door.

Every bolt. I will bring you warm water to wash. After, admit no one to your room."

A bit protective for a servant, but then again, maybe his master was a real curmudgeon. The last thing she wanted was to end up back out in the rain now. "Very well, sir. I have no wish for you to lose your post. I can surely sleep in the kitchen."

"No!" His voice was a sharp shrill.

Her brows drew together as her eyes adjusted to the dim light in the hall they trod down. Why was he so nervous?

"Until I tell Lord Tremarctos you are staying with us, you will stay out of sight." The man swallowed hard. His hand moved upward as though to tweak his collar and then stopped midair as he glanced at her from the corner of his eye.

Odd! Surely she had nothing to fear. Besides, tiredness ruled her, and the events from the day shook her so terribly it would be no problem to stay locked behind a door in this house.

This house. . . . Her gaze darted around the hall, and she almost stopped and spun on the spot. What a beautiful house! The floors shone of a dark, polished marble. The doors stood floor to ceiling with massive iron hinges bigger than anything she had ever seen.

In the dim light she could tell that the house shone with delights she would never see again. Truly a pity. She wished she could see every detail. They turned a corner, and she followed the man up three flights of narrow servants' stairs. At the top of the hall another male servant approached, and the man who let her in waved his hand, calling him to them.

"Bring me hot water, a pitcher, and have Jack send up tea with cheese and biscuits."

"Sir." The man inclined his head and stared at her as she passed.

Her attire was a mess! Nevertheless, politeness dictated that he shouldn't stare. Her fingers picked at the mud that covered her dress, and her gaze settled on her dirt-splattered hands. She rolled her eyes. Just her luck! Finally she saw the inside of a fancy house, and she looked as if she'd spent the day gathering greens from the garden.

Halfway down the hall, they stopped and he pushed open a door. She stepped across the threshold and stopped. Her eyes widened, settling on the well-appointed room. "Oh, sir, a servant's room will suffice."

"No, ma'am. None of the servants' rooms have doors. And . . . well, you promised to lock yourself in."

She turned as he bent to light the fire in the grate. The sputtering flame cast more light into the dark room. Oh, how she wanted to get warm, wash the filth from her body, and curl up in that huge, heavenly bed. Her mouth dropped open. My goodness, the mattress was enormous; the posters were carved but with such dim light she couldn't see the design.

The linens looked a scrumptious deep shade, too dark to discern in the glow from the fire. The image of her lying on deep scarlet silk, naked, flashed before her. Her hair spread across the pillows as a lover caressed her thighs, his head between her legs, licking the entrance to her womb. Her knees wobbled as tingles scorched through her sex. Oh, my! Her hand shot to her mouth in shock, and she shook herself, trying to erase the image from her mind.

Never in her life had such thoughts entered her head. When she imagined the act with Jonathan, loving never involved a bed, and never with his mouth there. Her hand smoothed down the front of her dress to the apex of her thighs. Would kissing there be pleasurable? Her cheeks flushed warm, and she snatched her hand away. Thank goodness no one could see her thoughts!

She was tired; that was all. The man who had passed them brought up water and filled a tub for her to wash in; he was followed by a gentleman with a tea tray. She waited until they left, bolted the door as requested, and then sat down on the chair by the fire. Tears trickled down her face; they were the last she would allow because of Jonathan. Tomorrow would be a new day, and she would find a way out of this mess. But tonight . . . she let herself cry once more.

A noise pierced her slumber. What was that?

The sound increased as her eyes fluttered open to darkness. The fire in the fireplace burned no more, and the rain outside fell in a deafening pour.

Crack.

Lightning lit the edges of the curtain as a scratching from the other side of the door grew louder. Her heart increased to a fast beat. What was that? A dog?

She pushed back the covers, scrambled to her feet, and crossed the icy room to the door.

She shivered as she stood before the white painted wood. Her gaze scanned the line of eight locks the servant had requested she bolt. She had felt silly when she listened to him, but his nervousness about letting a woman stay here made her wonder what lay beyond that door. Leaning toward the door she placed her ear to the crack.

Sniff, sniff. A low rumble of a growl came from the opposite side. "I can smell you." *Sniff.* "The virgin's blood, the semen, dripping from you."

She jumped and scrambled back, an arm's reach from the door in outrage. How . . . how could anyone know what she did today? She had washed . . . thoroughly. There was no possible way anyone could smell her folly. Was this a dream?

"Who . . . who is there?" Her voice wavered as she reached out and touched the bolts she had thrown that night.

"Let me in." The growl, so low and throaty, made the hairs on her neck stand. "Let me taste what you have so freely given to another."

She continued to stare at the door; shame and panic boiled

through her body until her body shook. The scratching increased. The sniffs echoed as if the person outside her door stood beside her. "Let me in. . . . Let me in. . . ." the raspy growl rang, and sweat slid down her back.

It would not give up. Somehow she sensed it.

The sound of something dragging widened her eyes, and with a bang, the door shook on its hinges. "Let me in, damn you!" It howled in outrage. "I will have you. There will be no denying me."

"No. . . . go. Leave me be!" She yelled into the blackness and stepped back from the door as the wood once again shook and creaked with the weight of the pounding.

This surely was a dream. Nothing like this could be real.

Her body shook, her gaze stuck on the door. *Please let the locks hold firm.*

A sharp cry of pain came from the other side of the door, and a breath tickled her neck. Her hand shot to that spot as she spun, expecting to see someone there. Nothing. The curtains blew, and the window snapped open with a crack.

Dash it all! She jumped and hurried for the window. The wind howled, blowing her hair back from her face in a gust. She grasped the sodden wood in her hands and tugged; She stared out at the night. Rain came down in sheets, and as the wood frame clicked shut, lightning lit up the gardens below.

A figure clung to the wall at the base of the building. Crimson eyes stared up at her. She gasped, bolted the window, and pushed away from the glass, the curtain falling back as—she swore—the eyes emerged above the edge of the sill.

The cry rang in her head once more. Her heart pounding, she spun and stared at the door.

Nothing. Not a sound except the pounding in her heart. Her body shook uncontrollably as every shadow in the room moved, alive and coming for her.

This is just a dream.

Close your eyes and things will all get better.

She jumped, nerves taut as she stumbled back to the bed and crawled up on the mattress. Her eyes darted back and forth between the window and the door, searching for anything she could make out in the black, but all stayed still.

Just close your eyes and things will be well. In the morning you can leave this place for home.

As she forced her lids shut, quiet met her.